GRYPHON RIDER ACADEMY

CHOSEN

Copyright © 2022 by Elise Hennessy

All rights reserved.

No part of this book may be reproduced in any form or by any electronic or mechanical means, including information storage and retrieval systems, without written permission from the author, except for the use of brief quotations in a book review. This book may not be redistributed to others for commercial or noncommercial purposes.

This novel is entirely a work of fiction. The names, characters and incidents portrayed in it are the work of the author's imagination. Any resemblance to actual persons, living or dead, events or localities is entirely coincidental.

Flutterbye Trail Press
797 Sam Bass Road #2541
Round Rock, TX 78681

First edition

Editing by Red Loop Editing
Cover Design by Black Bird Book Covers
Chapter Art by Etheric Tales
Map by Reva Design
Printed Interior Design by Enchanting Covers
Published by Flutterbye Trail Press

ISBN: 978-1-954582-10-1 (E-book)
ISBN: 978-1-954582-37-8 (Paperback)
ISBN: 978-1-954582-33-0 (Hardback)

Feedback: Encounter a problem with this book? Let us know at elisehennessyauthor@gmail.com

BOOKS BY ELISE HENNESSY

Books in the Altare World

GRYPHON RIDER ACADEMY
Second Chance
Chosen
Storm Front
Wild Flight
Gryphon Rider Academy Omnibus 1: Books 1-4

ROYAL SPY INSTITUTE
The Crown Heist
Five & Chance

Also by Elise Hennessy

BLOOD LEGACY SERIES
Dream Walker
The Winter Key
Queen's Return
Court of Illusions

Shadow Dance
Rule the Night
Dhampir's Wish
Blood Curse
Blood Legacy: The Complete Series

MAP

You can find a full-sized version of this map at: www.elisehennessy.com/maps

GRYPHON RIDER ACADEMY 2

CHOSEN

ELISE HENNESSY

CHAPTER 1
THE BALL

HOW TIMES CHANGED. A year ago, I was seated before the bathroom mirror, letting my sister wrestle my ornery scraggle of red hair into an attractive style. I spoke well of a young man who'd invited me to the annual ball held for the gryphon knight corps. He was an up-and-coming gryphon rider with a charming smile and eyes only for me. Rissa had patiently straightened and combed my hair, working her magic to make me beautiful for the night while she hummed along as I chattered about Victor Callan and hoped for a kiss before the evening was done.

I cringed inwardly as I remembered just how highly I'd thought of him as Rissa and I lined up together behind a different girl. My sister had spread out her makeup, equipped with enough cosmetics to dress the faces of an entire flock of women for the upcoming ball. I took the combs and brushes. A year ago, my job was to groom gryphons. This couldn't be that much different.

Ellie Kobarn squinted between us, as her glasses were buried somewhere under Rissa's makeup. "Relax," my sister said, flexing her fingers eagerly.

"I'm totally relaxed," Ellie reported. The two of them had

only met a couple days ago when I'd flown back to the capital with my academy friend, so Rissa didn't know yet that Ellie never went completely still. She fidgeted. She twitched and startled easily. But most notably, her mind was not stationary. I saw it most in her honey-toned eyes, which glimmered and darted with the spinning of a brain primed and ready for the most difficult problems.

This year, as I bent to the task of making Ellie flawless, I nearly tripped over the curious gryphon edging closer to watch. Two of them crowded the bathroom. For Ellie and me, it was an ordinary occurrence to have two massive beasts relaxing in our living spaces, but Rissa kept darting nervous looks their way, especially as the smaller of the two nosed at the makeup brushes and clasped one carefully in her beak, retreating with it.

I kept a laugh securely locked behind my lips as Rissa's expression said it all: she was willing to give up that brush forever.

"Puzzlebox," I cajoled. "That's important. We need it back."

The white gryphon had nicked a blush brush and was rubbing its puffy bristles over her companion's beak and pushing it into the soft feathered ridge of his brow, dusting his tawny plumage with pink specks. She turned big eyes on me when I came over to pluck it away from her.

She lifted her beak as I took hold of the brush's handle. Quickly, I replaced it with a more slender brush with a fine U-shaped fan of hairs. I didn't know what it was for, so maybe Rissa wouldn't miss it. For a moment, Puzzlebox squeaked at me, looking confused as to how I had her brush when there was still a handle in her beak.

Then she went back to rubbing her new toy over Ari's face. My gryphon yawned and shook his head, scattering a cloud of blush residue. *What's she doing?* he asked me over our Link. He and I were a bonded pair, sharing emotions and thoughts in a steady stream through the unique magic that Linked a gryphon to his rider.

"She's making you pretty," I shared to him privately, just a thought in the back of my mind. A smile threatened to split my face in half as I watched her antics before I went back to tending to Ellie's hair.

"Well, one of us should be pretty for the ball," he quipped.

"We're not going to the ball."

At the same time, Rissa asked, "Are you sure you're not going to the ball, Sivana?"

"Very sure," I answered.

My sister was kneeling in front of Ellie now, hard at work with her brushes. Her lips pinched into a disapproving rosebud, the kind of expression I'd seen countless times on our mother's face. Rissa was Mother's thirteen-year-old double, down to the platinum hair she kept in a perfect bun, not a hair out of place.

"Because I could've sworn a nice young man came by yesterday, asking for you," she said.

I rolled my eyes. "Yes, and I told him no."

"The son of a *duke*." She circled one of her tiny brushes in an exaggerated gesture of frustration. Poor Weslecker. He'd gotten quite the grilling when my little sister had answered the door and heard he was calling on me.

"I'm not going to that ball," I sighed. "Even if Prince Mateo himself comes to the door."

For a moment, she paused, leaf-green eyes widening to exaggerated circles. "What, is he going to?" she asked.

Rissa made sure I knew Prince Mateo Cortes was, in her words, "the most handsome Cortes." She was still rooting for me to fly off into the sunset with him, which was ridiculous. He hated me.

"When he does, you'll introduce me, right?" she added with a girlish giggle.

"I really doubt he's coming," Ellie said for me.

Rissa made a *tisk* sound with her lips. I knew my parents hadn't told her everything that'd happened to me while I was at Gryphon Rider Academy, but she had to know it wasn't sunshine and rainbows. The last time I'd seen her had been Yule time, with my right arm in a sling after a near-deadly "training accident."

I had two months off this summer before Ari and I had to report for our second year at the Academy, and I intended to use that time to refocus on what was important. Like how earlier today, Ellie had burst into my room waving an ancient, leather-bound tome.

"You have to read this!" she'd exclaimed.

The book now rested next to my bedside lamp, waiting for the bustle of pre-ball preparation to fade so I could settle in for an evening of reading. A book titled *Lord Orion's Blessed Beasts* couldn't hurt me, while a ballroom full of my fellow cadets certainly could with yet another barrage of barbed and hurtful words.

That was what truly had changed from last year: everyone at that ball now knew exactly who I was. I wouldn't be going as the girl Victor was seeing during the rare times he was in Kaiamear. No, I'm something new, something unheard of: *Cadet* Sivana Walker, the first female gryphon rider.

When I entertained the idea of going, I asked myself: dress or uniform? There was no right answer to that question.

If I wore a uniform, I would stand out. The only female wearing cadet black amidst a sea of colorful dresses, serious and professional next to the giggling gaggles of women that tended to form at events like this.

And if I wore a dress, fellow cadets and guests alike would wonder why I'd set aside my cadet identity for a night. Didn't I want to be seen as a gryphon rider?

Worse, if I came in on the arm of any of the young men I attended classes with, the whispers of fraternization would spread instantly.

Sad for Acton Weslecker, who seemed to genuinely want me to go with him and have a good time, but I had an image to uphold and a gryphon to protect. I couldn't let him know how flattered I was that he'd gone out of his way to invite me.

"There. Look how beautiful you are," Rissa said, stepping aside as I swept Ellie's brown locks over her shoulder. She was transformed for the evening, her thin frame perfectly wrapped by a soft blue gown she'd borrowed from Rissa when my clothes fit like bags on my petite friend.

Mother had offered to hem the voluminous skirts, but we'd insisted they were perfect where they skimmed the ground. They concealed the flat shoes Ellie wore, as she'd wobbled and fallen like a newborn fawn in every pair of heels she'd tried.

"Uh, ladies? I can't see." She stood and tried rooting through the mess on the countertop. It took a minute, but I found her glasses and blew off a residue of powder that'd gotten on one lens.

Ellie fixed the round frames on her pug nose, magnifying her intelligent eyes and the blue shadow that lined her lids. She fidgeted with her fingers as she saw her reflection. "Wow. Do you think Noah will like it?" she asked.

"You're going to knock him dead," I said.

"But do *you* like it?" Rissa countered.

"Yes!" she exclaimed.

My sister tapped her chin thoughtfully. "Try doing this. Beautiful and poised." She laced her fingers together and rested them over her middle. Ellie did the same, muting her twitchy energy for the moment.

Puzzlebox sat up and released an eager squeak before dashing out of the bathroom. "Sharde's here," I murmured.

A moment later, there was a knock at the door. Rissa and I shooed Ellie through our family's apartment, and I held Puzzlebox's scruff so we could open the door without her knocking over her rider on the other side.

Rissa and I stood back, sharing an eager glance from how Noah Sharde's face lit up the moment he saw Ellie. The resident slacker of Gryphon Rider Academy cleaned up well; he'd put in an effort this evening. His blond hair was cropped military short, and his dress uniform was properly pressed with no errant wrinkles from being tossed on a floor for too long.

Like all the others in my year group attending the ball tonight, he had a new feature: a cadet rank on his shoulders. We'd graduated to being second years by the grace of the gods, but as the bottom two, Sharde and I were both Cadet-Lieutenants, the lowest rung in the hierarchy we'd be competing to climb once the Academy was in session again.

"Hi, Ellie," he said, his mouth hanging open as he looked her over. "You look, um, different."

"Oh, like a good different?" she asked shyly.

"Yeah! Definitely a good different. I, um, I like it."

I covered my mouth to keep from snickering. "You look nice too," she said. "I don't think I've seen you like this before?"

Yelling sergeants couldn't keep Sharde in regulation, but it seemed Ellie could inspire him. I knew under the layer of makeup, she was blushing heavily. She had the hugest crush on him. I was just glad he was starting to clue in on it.

I released Puzzlebox, and she leaned on his free side, looking over at him adoringly. She was still yearling size despite approaching two years of age, coming a little under the line of his shoulders when she should be taller than him at this point, even if he was a lanky teenager whose body had grown straight up before it only just started filling out.

"It's not a trouble to look after her for the night?" he asked me.

"Not at all! She's been having a great time," I said with a smile. "Go have fun, you two."

We waved goodbye, and Puzzlebox returned to my side

with a soft twitter, watching them go before looking up at me with a question in her eyes. I ruffled her soft neck feathers. "C'mon, Box, we've got a date with a book," I said.

Rissa and I returned to the bathroom. "Last chance," she said, already starting to put her makeup away.

"Maybe next year." Though I doubted much would change in that time. I knelt in front of Ari and rubbed his wing to show him I was there. He lifted his head and stretched out his front legs, careful not to scratch the floor with his wicked, eagle-like talons.

Rissa went back to the room we shared while I carefully inspected the marbles Ari wore in his eye sockets, making sure Puzzlebox hadn't gotten any makeup on them. "Feeling pretty?" I teased. I wetted my fingertips and cleaned off some lingering spots of loose blush on his feathers.

"The prettiest."

The Link was a bit of a miracle. While I spoke in words, Ari and his kind communicated with images and feelings. We were only able to communicate clearly with the Link, though as a caretaker, I'd prided myself on *nearly* understanding what my gryphon charges were saying when they projected various images into my mind.

"Ellie's gone, so it's time to relax," I told him, coaxing him to his paws to walk him to the front room, where there was more space for him, Puzzlebox, and me to sprawl out.

"I was already relaxing," he grumbled but came along with me and waited for me to loop back to my room and retrieve the worn copy of *Lord Orion's Blessed Beasts*. I settled on the ground and used him as a backrest, and Puzzlebox draped herself over my legs and snuggled in for a rest.

It was getting late for the gryphons, who rested from sunset to sunrise. One of the only perks of Ari's blindness was he'd lost his sensitivity to the day-night cycles that ruled the rest of his kind. He was wide awake if I was, and vice versa. The waning light reminded me of our first flight together.

It's happened after what I'd thought would be his last sunset, the night before his scheduled execution. He'd failed to thrive after losing his first rider, my father's best friend, Alamid Maros, in the same attack that had blinded him. But the gods hadn't been done with him yet, as a rogue attack from a lone rozash had spurred him into demanding I get on his back for one last service to our country.

That decision had turned me into the first female gryphon rider, and together, we'd braved a year at Gryphon Rider Academy to show that he deserved a second chance despite his disability. I had yet to prove a woman deserved to stand by a gryphon's side in the otherwise all-male military school, but I'd survived to attend the coming year.

I knew Ellie was conducting research in the palace's extensive library, but she'd returned with this book, saying it would help Ari. No force of magic or miracle would return his eyes, so I wasn't sure what, exactly, she expected me to take from it. My thumb traced the fading motif of a rearing gryphon on the cover before I cracked it open.

Anything that might help us succeed into the next year at the Academy was worth my time.

CHAPTER 2

GLORIUM

I was about five when I became aware of a problem with how I formed my words. They would get stuck in my throat, stuttering out painfully, half-formed. I was blissfully unaware I was different until my mother tried to fix it.

"Take your time, Sivana."

"Just take a deep breath and try again."

Or sometimes, too frustrated with me, she would just snap the word I was trying to say. With her belly rounded with Rissa, her patience waned quickly due to exhaustion. I retreated from her, not understanding why the rage monster made my kind, goddess-fearing mother angry at me so often.

Why couldn't I just talk as easily as everyone else?

I would follow my father to the gryphon stables to get a rest from her and baby Nate, inevitably ending up in the same stall as his gryphon on slow days when they weren't needed in the air. It was Valtora who seemed to understand the kind of mothering I needed. She'd already patiently taught me how gryphons communicated, to the point where I *almost* understood her as if we had a little Link all our own.

When I started bringing my brightly colored books and

labored over reading them to her, she would sit still and listen.

Read it again, she would urge when I had trouble with a particular page.

We celebrated my triumphs together, too. *Such a smart hatchling*, she'd coo, her ultra-sharp beak mere millimeters from my baby-soft skin as she groomed the hay out of my hair.

Father would find me snuggled up to his gryphon and watch, his face squinched up at first with concern, then growing awe over time as he realized it was working and my stutter was becoming more manageable. I gained confidence resting up against the gryphon's chest, her massive talons curled around me in an embrace.

Reading *Lord Orion's Blessed Beasts* took me back to lazy days in a puddle of sunshine with Valtora. Back then, the books were much smaller, and so was I, dwarfed by the giant golden beast everyone else seemed so afraid of. Out of habit, I read out loud to Ari and Puzzlebox, when she woke, head tilted curiously toward the sound of my voice.

The hours passed, and I lit a lantern to keep reading despite the jaw-cracking yawns all around. If I'd known this would be a history lesson, I'd have skimmed it first. We were somewhere into King Altare's founding of the gryphon knight corps when there was a knock at the door.

I paused my reading and looked over the edge of the book warily. It was pretty well known that my father was Commander of the First Gryphon Flight and thus his family had quarters here in the palace, where the ball was always held. Weslecker had found out where I lived without a problem… What if a less friendly classmate did the same?

"Let me in. Please? I have cake," came a muffled voice.

Speak of the Gatekeeper…it was Weslecker again. I exchanged a glance with a sleepy Puzzlebox before breathing a sigh and getting to my feet. After a peek out of the peep-hole, I let in the young man at the door.

Weslecker stood straight-backed and prim, the picture of noble elegance in his pressed uniform. He was burdened by two plates stacked with more than their fair share of cake squares.

"Don't worry, no one noticed me departing the event," he said.

Despite the constant teasing from our flight-mates, he still sounded a lot like a snobbish aristocrat who'd woken up one morning and decided to become a gryphon rider. He offered me cake with a boyish smile, and I took it.

"Thanks. You didn't have to do this," I said. I felt a little flutter in my chest to know he'd left early to come see me instead.

He lifted a shoulder. "I've been to so many balls already. Mind if I stay here?"

"Um, I'm just reading a book right now."

I noticed Rissa down the hall out the corner of my eye, grinning broadly and making a playful swoon. I gestured behind my back for her to go away.

"What about?" Weslecker was asking, oblivious. "Wait, let me guess. It's about gryphons."

"How'd you know?" I stepped aside and gestured for him to come join me on the floor with the two gryphons. I rested against Ari again, while he folded his legs and immediately had Puzzlebox at his side, inspecting his cake.

"Have you met yourself?" he teased, dragging his plate away from her.

I glanced up from feeding Ari a square of strawberry cake.

"He does have a point," my gryphon said.

"Okay, fine. Ellie insisted I read it, but so far, it's the same history of gryphons I've heard hundreds of times." I flipped it up from where I had it resting on the pages I'd stopped at.

"You know, King Altare became the first gryphon rider and fought dragons and—"

I skimmed over several pages and came to a halt on a new chapter with an ink drawing that could've been straight out of Lord Orion's chapel. But I'd never seen the God of Man depicted astride a gryphon before. Scrubbing my eyes, I took another look, but that was still Lord Orion with his strong, masculine features and billowing robes of state, sitting on the back of a beast in flight.

"Weslecker, look at this." I practically shoved the book in his face.

"We're not at the Academy. Call me Acton," he insisted, taking it from me to hold out at a more manageable distance. "You know, I've seen something like this before. My tutor took me to the ruins of the First Church of Orion, and I thought it was strange even then. It was a mural with Lord Orion riding a gryphon, but from a different angle. His back looked hunched. That was the only time I've seen him depicted any way except like the perfect man."

He passed it back to me and, to my surprise, didn't complain when I started reading the chapter aloud. "Scholars have argued for centuries about the original purpose of gryphons, ignoring a key fact of their creation. While Mother Nilara made living creatures and populated the world we occupy, it was Lord Orion himself that shaped the first gryphons and had his wife breathe life into them.

"All of the gods' blessed beasts were created by their patrons for a specific reason. We see it with Lord Da..." I drifted off, staring at that name for a moment before omitting it with a cold feeling. No one spoke the Gatekeeper's true name without inviting the presence of death into their home. "With the Gatekeeper's nightblooms, he made creatures of life and death to allow his mortal Mercy access to the afterlife. Mother Nilara's dragons were formed of stone and magma to protect priceless treasures. And Lord

Anrathor's battle beasts were made to fight alongside his berserkers.

"The blessed beasts of the gods have all adapted to new roles in our age, muddying our understanding of what they used to be. Dragons are all but extinct, bred out of existence by the rozash. Mother Nilara has not interfered with the fate of her beasts, only watched from on high as their numbers dwindled from year to year. Gryphons, on the other hand, have outpopulated every other blessed beast, untouched by a greater calling besides existing.

"So, why did Lord Orion want gryphons in the first place? We argue while ignoring the greatest clue: our God of Man needed a beast to traverse the sky, unlike the rest of his deity family. I present to you Glorium, the gryphon he chose for the task."

Together, Weslecker and I peered at the next page. Drawn there was the likeness of a gryphon in stained glass, surrounded by beams of light as if it, too, were a deity. Tiny script at the bottom suggested it came from the First Church of Orion...the same location that'd been destroyed for hundreds of years at this point.

Next to the glass beast was Lord Orion, his godly hand resting on its wing. Turned to the side, he was depicted with two ragged stumps sticking out of his shoulder blades. I traced the ink with a fingertip, my brows drawn together.

The God of Man was never shown this way. He had a smooth, human back in every drawing, carving, and statue. I exchanged a glance with Weslecker. "Did you see this in the ruins, too?" I asked.

"No. Does it say when this book was written?" He took it from me to inspect while Ari stirred, projecting confusion over our Link.

"It looked a lot like Lord Orion with...well, without wings. Like he had a pair growing out of his back but they were cut off," I explained, puzzled about it too.

"Did Ellie tell you where she got this?" A note of nerves wove into Weslecker's voice. "It seems old, but this image… it's blasphemy."

"Before we jump to any conclusions, why don't we read what it says about Glorium?" I suggested. It was hard to look at this version of Lord Orion, blasphemy or no. No one dared show his likeness as anything but perfect. What if the God of Man wasn't physically immaculate?

What if he needed the company and service of a gryphon, and that was why he had them made in the first place?

Weslecker started reading the next section aloud. "An age passed before Lord Orion chose a gryphon. Their population grew and spread, and occasionally, a beast would attempt to cross further to the north, where mountains pierce the sky and the snowfall never melts. The first to reach the sacred home of the gods was Glorium, a gryphon said to be coated in ice from his long journey. The God of Man laid his hands upon the beast in reward and anointed each filament of his feathers with iridescent magic.

"It was from this beast that King Altare learned that he could Link with his own gryphon, for Glorium was blessed beyond measure from Lord Orion's magic. He was the closest thing to a god for his kind, able to connect with multiple humans and speak with them. His Links were the strongest humankind has known, capable of sharing more than just communication, but the other senses as well. Because of him, many have experienced the completion of a soul-level connection with a gryphon.

"Alas, the changing of times has led to many questioning whether Glorium truly existed. With his purpose fulfilled, he serves Lord Orion alone."

I held up my hands, blurting, "I saw a couple of his feathers." Only a few days ago, in fact, pinned to an old cushion in the depths of Fortress Aerie. I could see them in my mind's eye, impossibly glossy, each filament shining with a different color of the rainbow. I'd admired them, not realizing their significance. "I know this seems crazy, but...Glorium exists. Which means the rest of this might as well."

Weslecker's brow furrowed. "Why are we learning about him in an old book, then?"

I turned the pages back to the image of Lord Orion's hacked-off wings. "That's why," I said with certainty. "I think I need to find this gryphon, Wes...Acton."

He flicked a skeptical look up at me.

"Glorium shared his senses with humans, but we know Links go both ways," I said like it was completely obvious when I knew this was a stretch based off an ancient book. "What if Ari could be blessed the same way? What if...he could see through my eyes?"

Ari made a low noise behind me. *"That's impossible."*

I smiled over my shoulder. "So is a gryphon Linking with a woman."

ARMED WITH THIS BOOK, I was up at dawn to head to the Gryphon Yard, the highest point in Kaiamear where the stables were kept. I greeted the caretakers already hauling in breakfast for the beasts, confirming my hunch: Night, the Commandant's gryphon, was still here. If anyone knew how a couple of feathers from a legendary gryphon made their way to the Fortress, it would be the Commandant.

I figured I had some time before he left the capital, so I wandered to the First's stable and peered in on Valtora, who was just starting to stir. She fixed me with one golden eye and clicked her beak, projecting a feeling of welcome.

"Good morning, skymother," I said quietly. Without fear, I came into her stall and sat with her, obediently massaging her shoulder joint when she spread one of her grand bird wings across my lap.

Valtora was a wild-born gryphon and hated most humans. Her care had been completely my responsibility when I worked here since she allowed me to groom and feed her without trying to snap off one of my limbs.

Here to read to me? she asked me without words. Before my Link to Ari, I understood her best, knowing she saw me with a book and fondly remembered when I was small enough to snuggle between her front legs.

"If you want." With a shrug, I told her what Weslecker and I had learned from the old leather-bound book I had tucked by my side. At some point, this became a back massage for her, and she shot me a look accompanied by a sharp sense of disbelief by the time I was done talking.

My knuckles stopped rolling through the tension I'd found in her flight muscles, and she snipped her beak until I started up again. *I have met the gryphon you're talking about. Glorium.*

In place of his name, she projected an image into my head: the outline of a male gryphon with iridescent feathers, nearly obscured by the viciousness of a snowstorm. My mouth dropped open. "Where was this?" I asked.

Instead of answering, she projected a clearer image of her son, demanding I go get Ari to translate for her. "Yes, ma'am," I said.

But first, finish my massage, she added with a regal lift of her beak.

CHAPTER 3
A WILD GRYPHON'S SECRET

WITHIN THE HOUR, I was snuggled between Valtora and Ari. This conversation would be a lot faster with him here to translate for us.

"She says your idea to find Glorium is very dangerous," he informed me.

Valtora eyed us with a feeling of concern. *I would rather not risk my hatchlings. Isn't what you have good enough?*

"I'm not a hatchling anymore," he complained.

She reached past me to groom his neck feathers, and while he tilted his tufted ears back with a grumbling warble, he let it happen. *"She says you've accidentally stumbled upon a wild gryphon secret."*

Between his translations and her projected images and feelings, I got the full picture. "Skymother" wasn't just something she wanted me to call her; it was a title she'd earned by succeeding in something only the strongest and most confident wild gryphons undertook.

I sat in thoughtful silence as Valtora explained how all gryphons felt it in their gut: a calling. It started as nothing but a stirring in the gizzard or a niggling thought that grew more and more persistent as a gryphon aged into adulthood. A sense of wanderlust to leave their birth flock and make something of themselves.

For most, it stopped there. But for beasts like Valtora, frigid northern breezes held the promise of purpose.

"We know what it means. Those truly called north follow the path of our ancestors, flying alone above the ancient veins of the River of Origin," Ari translated. *"It's a dangerous journey across eldrafn-infested highlands and mountains stripped of prey. Half the gryphons that set off never return, but the ones that do come back stronger and larger than before. They lead their own flocks and successfully raise the most hatchlings.*

"She believes they fly the path of Glorium, for he was there when she needed him most. If not for him, she would've died in a blizzard."

In that case, it sounded like these wild gryphons went to the home of the gods, a location as purposefully remote from human civilization as possible. "Tamed gryphons never feel this same calling?" I asked.

Ari hesitated for a few long moments. *"It's hard to say. I think...maybe I felt it once. Like a need to fly and get away from everything, but it passed after a while."*

Valtora clucked, sadness glimmering in her eyes. For a few moments, I felt her motherly sorrow like it was my own, her regret that her son hadn't gotten this opportunity. Then her attention shifted, and she projected a memory that took my breath away.

This is the destination, she told us.

It was a plateau high in the air, a grove of fruit trees and impossibly green grass growing past the teeth of a rocky overhang. Sweet-tinged air had called for Valtora to land, and so she had, crashing just inches from a riverbank and scattering a layer of accumulated ice. A shadow passed overhead, Glorium flapping hard as he cleared the cover of low-hanging clouds and disappeared.

The water ran crystal-clear under Valtora's beak, rushing

past with the constant roar of a nearby waterfall. Rocks glimmering like gemstones tumbled under the river's surface.

She cut off her memory abruptly, shaking her head with a clear wince. *"She doesn't remember everything that happened after,"* Ari translated. *"But she returned with one of the river rocks in her gizzard and founded a flock as Skymother Valtora."*

I frowned, wondering what was omitted between her landing in this mystical place at the base of the River of Origin and her return as a skymother. "Would you say the river rock is what made you stronger?" I asked her.

"She thinks so. She grew larger and had a better hold of her magic afterward," Ari told me. *"But she's never shared senses like you're hoping to do with me. She doesn't know of any gryphon that can do that, except what you read about Glorium."*

My shoulders slumped. "Well, it was an idea. Lord Orion blessed Glorium personally, so of course he'd have powers beyond a normal gryphon." No wonder Weslecker had looked at me like I was crazy when I'd immediately jumped on the possibility.

Ari nudged my arm with his beak. *"It would be nice. To see again…"* I felt his wistfulness as if it were my own.

"If I could give that to you, I would," I promised him privately.

We stayed with Valtora for a while, sharing an ebb and flow of emotion alongside companionable silence. In my years as a caretaker, I'd learned this was part of how the beasts bonded.

There was something honest and to the point about how we felt in the wake of her story. I was disappointed it wasn't quite the miracle of Glorium's legend but grateful for the rare glimpse of Valtora's former life as a wild gryphon. Ari projected affection that I'd followed this lead so quickly and lingered on what he'd lost in this quiet moment. And Valtora…she lifted our spirits with a warm undertone of motherly love for us both. But she seemed to be remembering something too, a bitter note to her otherwise sweet emotions.

By the time we bid the skymother goodbye, we all felt more or less the same: bittersweet. I wished I hadn't gotten my hopes up, but the idea was too tempting not to dig into. I guided Ari with a hand on his wing, taking him back into the palace with me. Like Sharde, I preferred to have my gryphon either with me or with people I trusted. Unless he protested, I intended to keep Ari beside me all summer.

I noticed his ears flick forward when we approached my family's apartment. I didn't think too much of it until I was inside and recognized Mother's voice lifted into shrill, angry octaves. It was muffled behind the door to the master bedroom.

My parents barely ever fought, but I heard Father responding in the low tone that suggested he was about to explode. Every muscle in my body protested being here, my heart leaping to double time. *"They're arguing over you,"* Ari said.

I hesitated at the threshold, ready to turn and bolt like I was still a kid hiding from the clash of two strong personalities. I edged the door closed silently behind me instead and tiptoed closer to the master bedroom to pick out what they were actually saying.

"…need I remind you that one of her *instructors* tried to *kill* her?" Mother snapped.

"It was handled," Father said coolly.

"That's entirely the problem! You didn't handle it. The Crown Prince did. And that's what this is about!" It sounded like she flapped a sheet of paper around sharply.

"What do you want me to do, Talase?" Now Father was shouting too. "She can't just *leave*! She's a gryphon rider now. Property of the corps and the Crown!"

"You're so good at talking to your chain of command. Why don't you bring this to them?"

I glanced toward Ari, biting my lip. I had a bad feeling about what my mother was truly demanding.

"Talk to your daughter while you're at it!" Mother shrieked. "It's not safe for her at that school! You know it. I know it. I won't stand back and wait for her to return to Kaiamear in a body bag!"

The air hung heavy in the wake of her words. I rubbed at the goosebumps forming over my arms. I hadn't realized this was such a point of contention between them, but now I wondered how often they'd had this argument. Father's sigh sounded like the peak of frustration. "I'll talk to her," he said more quietly.

"*Thank* you!" Hearing that emphasis, I scrambled to draw Ari past their door and make it to my bedroom.

Mother ended her arguments like that, which meant she might come bursting out of the master bedroom at any moment. Which she did, right as I expected. "Sivana Annaliese!" she snapped behind me as I was opening the door for Ari, and my shoulders lifted up to my ears before I turned toward her.

Mother's expression was composed, though she looked me over with a distinctly disapproving rosebud pucker of her lips. "Come with me a moment," she said more gently, gesturing toward our bathroom. I had hay in my hair still, some stubborn bits tangled behind my neck. "This came for you. We're nearly late."

She handed me a badly wrinkled piece of cardstock as she attacked the knots in my hair. I winced as I read the invitation. Crown Prince Isaac wanted me to show up for tea in his solar. "We?" I echoed.

"An invitation with this little notice is hardly more than an ambush," she said briskly. "I insist on you having a chaperone."

While she was obviously still angry, I breathed a sigh of relief. My last meeting with Prince Isaac had also been a trap, when he'd caught me alone in my dorm to tell me he'd helped me and expected repayment in the future. I wouldn't be such easy prey with my mother there as well.

She was immaculate as always, her hair drawn up into a perfect bun and her figure hugged by the white robes she wore when working in Mother Nilara's temple as a healer. Slender and elegant, she was the role model of womanly excellence I'd strived for. With my freckled and wind-chapped reflection looking back at me, I realized I had fallen even farther from the goal.

A year at the Gryphon Rider Academy had erased the softer edges of my curves, replacing them with lean muscle. My skin was unevenly tanned, and my hair was even harder to tame than ever. I hadn't cared to notice these physical flaws until now, as Mother inspected me and tisked. "You haven't been moisturizing," she said before turning my hand over and running her soft fingertips over my numerous calluses. She whipped out her lily-scented lotion and had me rub down my arms and face. My dry skin burned.

"Mother," I sighed.

"Just a little makeup, and we'll get you into something nice," she said.

I put my hands up, shielding myself from the brushes she was starting to dig up. "No. I want to go in my cadet uniform."

Her leaf-green eyes flared with the embers left over from her argument earlier. But she'd never told me directly that she disapproved of me going to the military school. I could see her weighing the decision now, a hint of the calculating noblewoman she was raised to be rising to the surface.

She gestured I go put it on instead, waiting until I donned my dress uniform and had plaited my hair into the simple braid I often wore at the Academy. She took one look at me and nodded. "Let's go."

CHAPTER 4

APPEARANCES

"Whatever Prince Isaac was expecting…it won't be this," Mother said as we walked toward the servants' stair at the back of the palace, Ari on my other side. She was practically gleeful, a sharp difference from earlier. I was nearly afraid of the complete flip of her emotions.

On the way, we discussed what to expect. Politics, I decided, was entirely not for me.

The crown prince likely expected me to show up dressed in my best for a meeting with him, all flustered at his sudden invitation. He already had the upper hand choosing the time and place for this.

"It's about power," Mother whispered. "He tells you to come, you do. It shows your respect for him to appear as he's asked, no matter how abrupt the invitation. If you're properly in disarray, you're a prime target to agree to whatever he's going to ask of you."

I wiped my damp palms on my pants. "Like what?" I whispered back.

"That depends." Her lips tilted in consideration. "If it is something outrageous, he likely won't breathe a word of it while I'm there."

I swallowed past a sudden lump in my throat. "Do you think it will be something like that?"

"Yes," she said without hesitation. We stopped in the middle of the stairwell, alone for the moment. She held my shoulders, her leaf-green gaze searching mine. "This man is very dangerous, and he thinks he holds your future in the palm of his hand. You must be pleasant while also agreeing to nothing."

"Not even that I owe him a favor?" I murmured.

"*Nothing.*" She gave me a little shake. "I'll do my best to help you. And you will be…"

"Pleasant," I parroted. "While making no promises."

I hoped she knew how difficult that sounded. She nodded in approval and picked invisible lint off my uniform before we kept walking. When we reached the second floor, we startled a pair of guards with the sudden appearance of my gryphon.

"*You've talked to this man before,*" he said, trying to ease the bundle of nerves in my gut.

"*Poorly.*"

"*While wanting your mother's help. And look, here she is.*"

The woman in question had led me to the crown prince's solar, speaking to a man in palace livery at the door. The servant's gaze flicked between the three of us before he retreated into the room. Mother's chin tipped up a notch in pure noblewoman entitlement as hushed whispers sounded from within.

He came back a few minutes later. "The crown prince will see you now," he said, gesturing for us to enter.

"No announcement? Is this an informal affair, then?" Mother's voice drifted behind me as I walked in with Ari. The solar had massive windowpanes overlooking the queen's garden. One was propped open, letting in a pollen-scented breeze. It was a relatively small room, with a thick rug underfoot and a table as its centerpiece. I saluted the man standing at the head of the table and held the pose until he waved away the respect.

Crown Prince Isaac reminded me of his royal father in that moment. His jowls quivered with restrained displeasure, but the expression was there and gone, replaced with his usual courtly smile. The first time I'd met him, I thought he was the pinnacle of royal warmth. He'd saved Ari from the execution block and secured my place at the Gryphon Rider Academy when the king told me to my face that my Link to Ari was a grievous mistake and an affront to the gods.

And now, well, I knew he wanted something from me in return. Question was whether we'd find out what it was today.

"Good afternoon, Sivana. I'm so glad you could come," he said, gesturing for me to sit at his right hand. There was a placemat set out on the next space over and a servant reaching to pour a serving of tea into the cup, while a cushion was flung behind both chairs as an afterthought.

"Thank you for the invitation, Your Highness," I said politely.

First, I helped Ari onto the cushion after resettling it a comfortable distance away from the crown prince. He nibbled on my fingertips. *"Good luck."*

I breathed out a quiet, tense sigh. *"Thanks."*

"I was not expecting the pleasure of meeting with two beautiful ladies this afternoon," he said once we all settled at the table.

Mother took up her teacup and the saucer, sitting with perfect ramrod posture. "Don't mind me, Your Highness. I merely wished to chaperone my unmarried daughter."

"I assure you, Mrs. Walker, I have no intentions toward her in that way. You may be aware that I am still looking for a bride to strengthen Altare's ties to her allies."

Mother took a measured sip of her tea. "Be that as it may, Your Highness, Sivana is quickly growing into the country's darling. What with the *Kaiamear Gazette* reporting on her so consistently."

I sat as still as possible, listening to them volley back and forth. I didn't miss some of the subtleties, like how Prince Isaac implied that a marriage to me wouldn't strengthen Altare or how Mother had quickly gotten an opening to needle him on how his underling, Miles Glimmerwick, kept printing articles about me in the local newspaper.

My belly chose that moment to growl, startling a laugh from the crown prince. "Here, young lady, have a biscuit," he said, offering me a plate of delicately glazed cookies.

I could feel Mother's gaze, her intensity trying to tell me something. She probably didn't want me to correct him, because those were definitely not biscuits. "Thank you, Your Highness," I said in my best pleasant tone, taking a few to put on the tiny plate next to my tea saucer.

I hadn't had anything to eat since Weslecker brought me cake last night, and all this sugar was bound to go straight to my head.

"So, I understand you have two months off," the crown prince said. His sausage-like fingers clasped his teacup with practiced delicacy. "What will you do with that time?"

"I was planning on spending time with my family. My brother's due back from the Tulari Academy any day now," I answered and tried not to flinch when Mother prodded the side of my calf with the tip of her shoe. Keep my replies short and sweet, right.

"I imagine it must be nice to see them after such a long time. That's how I feel about seeing Mateo. Though he's already flown off. On to the next adventure, I suppose." He tipped his cup along with a shrug.

"Oh, I didn't know he already left," I said.

"If you ask me, he's just showing off for our little sister. She doesn't get out often enough."

That was a bit of an understatement. Princess Odalis was a

rare sighting unless she had to make a state appearance alongside the rest of her family. But she and Mateo were not really my business, so I didn't ask where they went. Knowing him, he was also using this as an opportunity to strengthen his gryphon, Mireille.

"Well, I believe Glimmerwick will be happy to hear you'll be staying put…" I lost track of his words as a sudden blast of ice-cold air flowed from the open window.

Every hair on my body stood on end, and I shivered violently. Prince Isaac inspected me with a raise of his brow. "Are you quite all right?"

"I believe she just had an allergic reaction to the idea of another interview," Mother put in sardonically.

Ari clicked his beak, and I glanced over my shoulder to see his fur and feathers ruffled. *"Did you feel that?"* I asked him.

"Colder than Fortress Aerie's winter," he grumbled.

Now this was strange, because the other two people in this room still seemed confused at my sudden shudder. "I'm fine," I said quickly.

"Good. I believe he should do a full series of interviews while you're here. Gather quotes for while it's harder to reach you," the crown prince remarked. That sounded about as appealing as plucking off my fingernails, but I just gave him a tight smile. Agree to nothing, after all.

We made small talk as chilly fingers draped themselves over my neck. I did my best to contain my reaction, because Prince Isaac was sheened in a light layer of sweat, and Mother was composed as ever, neither noticing the sudden invasion of winter or how it whispered an invitation in my ear.

Not in words, though. Just a feeling that took root in my gut. Ari shifted restlessly behind me. I wondered if he understood what was going on better than I did, considering the wind seemed to talk like a gryphon, sharing a sense of urgency.

I chafed to leave. Perhaps sensing that, or just seeing that his questions were getting him nowhere, Prince Isaac cut the meeting short. In and out in what felt like an hour; that wasn't bad. Mother's eyes gleamed with a rare hint of approval until I turned and pecked her on the cheek. "I have to go," I said.

At the servant's stair, she started climbing, probably expecting us to follow, and I descended rapidly with Ari instead, dodging the bustle of a hot kitchen where the stairs ended. I guided Ari toward a back entrance despite his lifted beak at the savory scents in the air.

"I'll feed you later," I promised, walking him down a short alleyway to a more open space where goods could be offloaded into the palace kitchen. I took a deep breath of warm summer air while Ari's pelt prickled.

He turned his head in my direction, beak pointed off center from my chest. *"Climb on. I think it wants to guide us."*

A chill wind nudged me toward him.

"Pushy, aren't you," I muttered before sliding into his saddle and cinching myself down. Ari's front paws danced impatiently as I sorted out the two sets of reins, sliding them properly between my fingers before I squeezed his side with my knees. "Open road ahead. You're free to fly."

Ari took off without hesitation.

THE STRANGE SENSATION of cold vanished once Ari circled in for a landing with my help. We scattered a few civilians when he released a screech to signal our descent and touched down in an unusual spot. However, as I dismounted and lifted my head to the gilt stonework before us, I had a gut feeling that this was right.

The stairs of Lord Orion's temple were guarded on either

side by statues of rearing gryphons, their beaks frozen mid-scream. A robed and heavily tanned man swept leaf debris to one side of the temple doors, which were perpetually thrown open in welcome. Hanging to his mid-chest was the symbol of the God of Man, a leather circle etched with the same spell rune that marked the faces of Tulari mages.

His gaze fell upon Ari, and he leaned his broom to the side, making the gesture of Lord Orion, touching his finger-tips to the leather symbol before resting them on his forehead. I flinched preemptively, expecting a sudden flick toward me like Victor and his buddies had taken to doing at the Academy.

Instead, I heard a distinctive "That's her!" behind me. I glanced over my shoulder, realizing our sudden appearance had drawn attention.

Heat tickled my cheeks from the focused attention of over a dozen people, with more trickling in as an older woman waved both arms over her head and continued to announce my presence.

Two men were the typical beggars that occupied Temple Row, their muddy brown robes meant to imitate clergymen when they rustled canvas bags at passersby and proclaimed Lord Orion's favor on those who feed the poor. One of them eyed Ari, who shuffled closer to me, projecting unease as I froze.

Problem was, everyone started talking at once the moment I faced them. My name was shouted from the throats of complete strangers, and I didn't know where to look or what they were saying as their voices blended together.

"I, uh..." I put up my palms, backing up a step. Ari snipped his beak, making a sharp noise that deterred some. Most crowded in closer, yelling to be heard.

"I just want your autograph!"

"My daughter's your biggest fan!"

"Did you get my letter?"

The man watching Ari darted his hand out and took hold of one of his broad flight feathers, trying to tug it free. My gryphon's defensive feelings spiked to pure ire, and the feathers along his neck lifted as he posed to bite. *"Ari, wait!"* I shoved that grasping hand away before the stranger could lose it.

I could already see the front-page headline of the *Kaiamear Gazette*: FEMALE GRYPHON RIDER LOSES CONTROL OF HER BEAST!

"That's quite enough. We respect gryphon riders here," said another stranger close by. I realized it was the robed clergyman, now holding his broom like he'd need to beat someone away. He gestured with a jerk of his head, and I took the message, guiding Ari away from the crowd by mounting the steps toward Lord Orion's temple.

Looking back, I saw that the crowd had swelled to several dozen people, all held at bay by the clergyman, who commanded respect and disappointed muttering before the group dispersed. I related the sight to Ari, whose tail continued to lash angrily.

"To try and pluck me. The nerve," he grumbled.

"It's okay now. They're gone." I smoothed down his neck feathers, my fingers trembling. I lifted my hand with an unsteady breath, realizing I was shaking all over.

I'd felt cornered in that crowd, suffocated by the wave of demands from several people, all wanting something different from us. In my dress uniform with my gryphon by my side, I'd been unmistakably a target to swarm.

"We can't come into the city like this," I said slowly, realizing this was another change to adjust to. No more afternoons window shopping or early-morning haggling over the freshest produce.

If I was noticed in civilian clothes without my gryphon, it'd be so much worse on one of the main streets. I'd have no escape in the form of Ari or a clergyman who'd taken pity on us.

"You look lost, lady gryphon rider," our savior said, now sweeping the stairs a level below where Ari and I stood.

I felt Ari's side of the Link, realizing we both had lost the urgent drive to move forward from the moment we'd landed in front of the temple. Surely we were meant to go inside, but nothing was forcing us to.

"Have you ever felt called to come here right away?" I asked. There was no other way to describe the feeling that'd seized Ari and me.

The man looked up, his dark eyes shining in amusement. "Can't say I have. Lord Orion knows I arrive in my own time, but I will always show up and fulfill the day's task eventually." He leaned on his broom, punctuating the *eventually* as he left a pile of shriveled leaves on the step with him. "Why do you ask? Did something happen that you have no explanation for?"

"Something like that," I said.

"Are you sure this is where you were called to?" He gestured down Temple Row, where the holy places of the other three Altarian gods resided. "Perhaps your phenomenon meant to bring you to the Mother instead. The *Kaiamear Gazette* told me you are quite the devout Nilarite."

I shifted uncomfortably, unsure if I should share that Mother Nilara never spoke to me. She'd embraced my mother and anointed her a healer in the silver and white temple next to the one where we stood, and I had no doubt when it was Rissa's time, she too would become a white-robed devotee in Mother's footsteps. I'd been nudged toward that path as well, but the prayers had felt empty with no hint of a reply from the goddess.

"Ah, you hesitate. The Gatekeeper, then? Perhaps you have need to bid a visit from one of his Mercy," he suggested.

"No, I don't think so," I said quickly. Though I had best go and ask forgiveness for accidentally reading his true name in a book printed in an age when it must've been more acceptable to name the God of Death.

"Then there are two possibilities left. Either you are here for war, or peace." A serene smile crossed the clergyman's face, creasing the crow's feet etched in his face. "But if you were called by Lord Anrathor, you would be on a battlefield, not standing in the threshold of my Lord's home. So, I have a question, lady gryphon rider."

"Yes?"

"Why do you seem afraid to go inside and learn why you're here?"

I wanted to answer that I wasn't scared, but my hands still trembled where they were buried in Ari's fur. We were standing outside, in clear view of the populace coming and going from Temple Row, rather than retreating to the relative peace of the sanctuary behind us.

Ari nudged me with his beak as I realized I was stalling. *"He called both of us,"* my gryphon said. *"I'm going inside to see why."*

With all the confidence of a lord, Ari turned and walked forward without me. "Thank you for your help, sir," I said to the clergyman.

"It's Duncan," he replied, making the sign of Lord Orion and waving farewell. "Best wishes."

I waved back before hurrying after Ari to save him from walking into a wall.

CHAPTER 5

CALLED

It was a slow day in Lord Orion's temple. Most of the acolytes and clergymen were cleaning, which meant many pairs of eyes turned toward the sight of me guiding Ari to the inner sanctum. Usually, I visited the shrine alone or with my family, and during those times, I was one of many Altarians coming to pay respects to the God of Man.

But with a gryphon by my side, it seemed like every man who labored here had to pay respects. Ari was magnetic. Everyone from the youngest acolyte to the most elderly men wearing Lord Orion's gold made the sign of their god toward the gryphon.

"You're popular," I told him, relating the respect. I wondered how often these men had a gryphon inside the temple. It was unusual to see a group of civilians with no fear of the massive beast by my side.

Ari's feathers brushed out in pleasure. He walked with his head held high all the way to the inner sanctum, where a freshly polished golden statue waited with an offering bowl and a freshly lit curl from a pot of incense. I stopped Ari close to the statue and took a tour around it, inspecting the back for any sign of imperfection.

Nothing, just waves of detail in the sculpted waves of his robes of state. I knelt next to Ari and made the sign of Lord Orion, heart to mind, and bowed my head in prayer.

Certain lucky people received signs and even direct conversation with the gods at their respective shrines. Mother walked away from Lady Nilara's temple practically glowing with the mother goddess's radiance, her eyes filled to the brim with faith. I envied it most in moments like this, when I had the same reception I always do.

Silence.

Frustration started a slow boil in my belly after my prayer greeted Lord Orion in my mind and suggested that I'd arrived as he'd asked.

It was a mirror of the crown prince's invitation to his solar. As Mother said: he told me to come, and I did. I showed my respect for him to do as he'd requested, no matter how abrupt the invitation. Or unusual, in the case of the chilly wind.

Would he leave me with no answers to his true intentions, like Prince Isaac did? Each minute I waited here, knees absorbing the chill of the stone floor, I wondered if I was foolish to think Lord Orion had sent a breeze of his magic to summon me here in the first place.

Ari's beak nudged my arm. *"Would you pull the feather that almost got plucked?"* he asked, extending his wing as I glanced up. I could see the large feather hanging loose from its fellows. It must've been irritating him.

I reached over and tugged it free. The feather was nearly a foot long, shading to a dark brown at the edges of its filaments. It was a shame a stranger had tried to steal it, since it was so vital to Ari in flight. He flexed his wing before curling it tightly to his flank, sitting back on his haunches as he waited next to me.

I ran my fingertips over the side of the feather, having a thought. Perhaps it wasn't enough to simply show up. I placed the feather into the offering bowl and sucked in a surprised breath as a chilly gust blew back the flyaways from my face. Ari puffed up against the cold, a startled chirp escaping his beak. It felt like the wind swirled around us both, suspending us in a bubble of freezing air.

Bowing my head, I waited, trembling. Sensations and images filled my mind: wind through my hair as Ari carried me in flight, the bite of sharp chill on my cheeks, and the certainty that I wasn't meant to be here, sitting idle in Kaiamear. Valtora's memory of a river far from here, surrounded by an oasis of thriving greenery. A push from behind by the cold breeze.

My chin hit the ground. I startled, eyes opening, to realize I was prostrated before the statue of Lord Orion.

"Well, that was pretty clear," I commented to Ari. I dusted myself off and stood, rubbing my arms as summer air touched my goosebumps.

The gryphon was rigid, his eyelids screwed up tightly. I tentatively touched the Link between us to feel Ari seized with a strong sense of restless energy.

He stumbled backward. *"We've been called,"* he murmured while releasing a throaty croak I recognized as his signal for being lost in blind darkness. I came over to stroke his neck, and he pressed to my side. *"The wind called it the Path of Glorium. Now that we know what it is…we've been called to go."* When I felt his fear, I looped my arms around his shoulders, pressing our foreheads together.

"If Lord Orion has ordered it, we'll do it," I said, rubbing down his wing.

"This was meant for wild gryphons. I doubt a human and a gryphon have ever made the journey together."

"Maybe it won't be so bad," I suggested. *"Valtora talked about there being little food. We can carry enough for a long journey, plus blankets and clothes for extreme cold."*

He considered silently for several moments. *"Do you think he could give me my sight back?"* he asked quietly.

"There's only one way to know." Though we both shared a bubbling hope.

If we met with Lord Orion, perhaps we could do what no other gryphon-rider pair had done. The god could make him like Glorium, capable of multiple incredibly powerful Links where he could share extra senses with others. He could see through my eyes if the God of Man could not give him new eyes to see with.

In that moment, I knew the summons was for Ari, not me. I was only called because Ari could not make the journey alone, but that was okay. Even if Lord Orion did not speak with me, he could help my gryphon. That was worth however long it would take for us to fly the Path of Glorium.

"C'mon, let's get ready to go," I said. We walked out of the temple, earning another wave of respect from the men who worshipped here. But this time, I had the uncanny feeling some of their gestures were toward me.

I LEFT Ari with Valtora as the afternoon shaded to evening, to talk through what came next with a gryphon who'd already done it. As I emerged into the sunshine, my gaze swerved up toward the sky. From the position of the sun, it was northeast. The echo of Ari's calling was in my chest, suggesting I needed to go in that direction, that we had to fly hard and fast.

I touched my fingertips to my heart and forehead and headed inside. I had a problem to address before Ari and I made the flight: my family.

Valtora would undoubtedly tell Father the truth about where Ari and I were going if I didn't share it soon. And I couldn't see Mother accepting that I was flying away from Kaiamear tomorrow, especially on a dangerous journey that killed half the wild gryphons who attempted it. She desperately wanted to sit me down for lessons in politics and how to speak to the royal family, considering my perilous position with the king and crown prince.

I entered my family's apartment slowly, ears primed for any additional arguments. It was quiet, for now, but Rissa was in our shared room when I snuck in and closed the door behind me. *Gods above,* I couldn't catch a break. She'd see me packing and want to know everything.

"Guess who came by," she said with a giggle, looking up from the textbook she was studying.

From her big smile, it wasn't hard to guess. "Weslecker."

"Yes, *Acton* was here. He left you this." She slipped an envelope out from under her textbook and handed it to me.

I sat on my bed and opened it. "Why do all the invitations come when I'm not around?" I grumbled.

"Be less busy, maybe," she sing-songed.

Weslecker had left a handwritten invitation to join him and a few friends at one of his parents' summer estates. He'd included a map with a few directions and landmarks to look out for, since the location was on the west coast by the ocean. I pushed the papers back in the envelope, my lips twisting.

Very few of my academy friends were staying in Kaiamear for the summer, but I still needed to pen Ellie an apology that I was leaving abruptly. She and I were supposed to spend more time together.

First, though, I dug out my saddlebags and placed the invitation at the bottom. "Maybe he'll still be there later," I said mostly to myself.

Rissa turned in her chair. "Can we talk for a second?" she asked.

"Yeah, sure." I headed to our shared closet to see what I had to wear for cold weather.

"Like, without you moving around," she amended.

Sighing, I sat on my bed again and faced her expectantly.

"Acton likes you," she said, perching her chin on a fist. "You know that, right?"

"Yes, clearly. But we're just friends," I said.

She shook her head. "Anyone who can sit there while you read to them over a gryphon book has to *like* you. He doesn't just like you; he *likes* you." She leaned forward with each emphasis.

My smile faded. "Rissa, he can't...I can't."

"*And,*" she continued over my protest, "he's calling on you like a nobleman does. That invitation"—she pointed at my saddlebags—"means he wants to be seen with you."

Well, that meant I couldn't go, then. I shook my head slowly, flexing suddenly damp palms. "Thank you. I'll have to talk to him."

Her lips pinched. "Why does it sound like you're about to turn him down?"

"I have to. If we courted, we'd break the Academy's rules. I can't fraternize with anyone, especially not with a boy from my flight." And if it got me kicked out of the military school, that would mean Ari's head on the execution block.

"Sivana—"

"Do you know where he went? I'd better go talk to him now."

"Sivana," she said more sternly. "Do you like him?"

I threw my hands up. "Why does that matter?"

"It matters. Because if you *like* him, then you can't go charging off and telling him to leave you alone because of... frat...whatever that word was. It wouldn't be a 'we can never,' but a 'we can't right now,' and I think you have to pick between them," she reasoned.

I held her leaf-green gaze for a moment before inspecting my fingernails. With everything else going on, this was the last thing I wanted to worry about right now.

"Look, I'm always at Lady Nilara's temple. Thousands of women come and go each week, asking for relationship advice from the healers. I picked up a few things, okay?" A note of uncertainty hit her voice, sounding much like the little sister I knew.

"Well, you haven't been wrong about my relationships yet," I said, giving her a smile. I did like Acton; he was far kinder than Callan ever was.

"You need to bring Prince Mateo by. We can plot how to steal his heart." Her expression turned impish when I pretended to retch at the idea.

I stood and started pulling clothes to pack away. "What are you doing?" she asked.

"Would you believe I finally felt something from the gods?" I inspected a flight jacket lined with dark fur, remembering that it was a Yule gift from Weslecker.

Rissa gasped. "The Mother finally spoke to you?"

My lips twisted as I tossed the jacket in the pile to be packed. "Uh, no."

I told her about the chill breeze and the feeling I needed to bring Ari to the heart of the River of Origin. She was uncharacteristically silent as I packed, so when I was done with the tale, I turned to see her staring at me, pale.

"Sivana," she murmured before bursting out, "you're going to *meet the gods!*"

"Well, Lord Orion wants to see Ari—"

"He can't see him and not you! And what if you meet the Mother or Lord Anrathor or even..." Her throat bobbed as she swallowed hard. "What if they haven't spoken to you because they *knew* you'd see them in person one day?"

"Don't be ridiculous," I scoffed.

"You're ridiculous!" she exclaimed.

I stuffed the saddlebag more firmly with a scowl. "Whatever, Rissa."

She popped to her feet. "Tell me how I can help you."

I bit my lip, because there was something she'd be able to do that I couldn't anymore. I fished out my coin purse and passed it to her. "I need food that can travel. Dried meat, especially."

She gave me a jaunty salute, her hand placed crookedly from the military perfection demanded of me and my peers. "You got it. I'll get as much as this can buy me plus…" She reached into the desk and retrieved another pouch, pouring silvery coins into mine. "Whatever this gets!"

I smiled wide enough to hurt and saw her off with a hug.

CHAPTER 6

LINK THIEF

I chickened out. I didn't tell Mother I was leaving the next morning or shared where I was going with Father, either. We had a pleasant family dinner together, and by first light the next day, Ari and I set off due east with saddlebags full to bursting with food, clothes, and survival gear.

Rissa would tell Mother everything I'd told her, and Valtora would share information with Father. I sent a message to Ellie and Weslecker, thus freed to leave on a journey with my best friend. The moment the wind whipped past my ears as we flew, I shared a sense of relief with my gryphon to be moving toward where we were called.

Ari and I decided to fly to Fortress Aerie first, the last bit of human civilization where we'd find a bed and a warm meal, as a few cadets always stayed there over the breaks. It took us the entire day to fly there, made longer because it was the first time we'd made this journey without Ari being tethered and guided by another gryphon. I missed a couple key landmarks, adding several hours of flying in circles.

The sun was well below the lifted horizon of distant mountains when I guided Ari in for a landing at the top of the fortress, where the gryphon stables were located. Most of the shutters were closed for the night, but there was always one landing platform left open, just in case. The gryphons weren't prisoners here. Those with Links were allowed to free fly since they would always return to their rider eventually.

A couple startled caretakers came to check on us and tried to take hold of Ari's reins. "I'll take care of him," I promised, seeing their expressions when we came face to face. I hoped to stay for an evening quietly, but I had the feeling they were going to go tell someone about my arrival immediately.

I freed Ari from the weight of the saddlebags and rubbed down his flanks, making sure he was dry and in no discomfort from our long flight. He pushed me away when I got out the combs and brushes. *"I'm starving,"* he complained.

"Me too," I murmured. Placing the grooming tools aside, I took him down several flights of stairs, feeling a phantom sense of several boys and their gryphons pushing and jostling around me. I'd nearly fallen down several times and gotten trampled in the crush of cadets who'd push into these stairwells in a hurry not to be late to their classes.

Right now, it was just Ari and me, taking the steps at a tired pace. The only threat was tripping and falling over our own feet from a whole day of flying. I didn't share my worries with Ari out loud, but I was nervous about the prospect of a long trip together when tuckered out over a single day's worth of travel.

Of course, he sensed the direction of my thoughts anyway. The Link made it hard for us to keep thoughts and emotions to ourselves.

"I think we'll be okay. We had to be here by a certain time for dinner. Out in the wild, who cares if we're a little late?" he reasoned.

Speaking of dinner, it smelled incredible as we walked into the mess hall. The vast dining area was empty, though, and the kitchens closed for the night. "Gatekeeper take me," I muttered.

I went up and knocked on the door, hoping a cook was still sorting leftovers. Ari's tufted ears swiveled back, and I glanced over my shoulder before sucking in a nervous breath.

"*It's the Commandant, isn't it?*" he asked, a touch of humor to his tone.

It definitely was. The Commandant walked into the mess hall, unerringly spotting us and marching our way. He was a wiry, white-haired man who washed his breakfast down with coffee flavored with cadet tears. His job was maintaining discipline at Gryphon Rider Academy, and he was the one to make decisions on our ranks and futures.

By his side loped his massive beast, Night. She was still the glossiest gryphon I'd met, with black feathers reflecting a clear sheen on each filament. Considering what I knew about skymothers, I wondered if she had already completed the same journey we were about to undertake. Her yellow eyes were narrowed in censure as they stopped a few feet away. I'd learned she was just as tired of cadet mischiefs as her rider.

"Good evening, sir."

"Good evening, Cadet Walker. Why are you here?" Straight to the point, as always.

"We're hungry, sir," I said honestly, gesturing to the closed kitchen.

Night croaked, releasing a burst of sensation. I understood the simple feeling she conveyed perfectly. She was saying, *Us too.*

The Commandant reached for a keyring on his belt, the keys jingling as he thumbed through them and stepped toward the door. I drew Ari out of the way, noticing his beak lifting and turning toward the click of metal, before he nudged me to make sure I was still beside him. The keys sounded a lot like the bells I'd taken to wearing when we flew together, I realized.

"You're in luck. We just got back," he said with a sigh, letting us into the kitchen. I was somewhat familiar with the setup from multiple punishment duties, so I found the freshly preserved fish fillets first and started filling two bowls for the gryphons.

Night rested on her haunches before me, snipping her beak like I didn't give her enough. "Don't feed her extra." His instructions drifted from the other side of the kitchen. Night shot a betrayed look in that direction.

The Commandant returned with two bowls and gestured that I join him in the mess hall. He picked the closest table and put the second bowl across from where he sat while I arranged for Ari and Night to eat next to us. The dining hall had served a beef stew this evening, and the lukewarm mix in my bowl was rather thick but still delicious.

"We just arrived as well, sir. I only wanted to spend a night here," I said.

He raised one strict brow. "The fortress is not an inn, young lady."

"Yes, sir." Part of last year's training included when my superiors wanted an explanation and when they didn't. Usually…they didn't care for excuses. They wanted nodding heads and cadets following directions with a crisp "yes, sir!"

Unfortunately for me, this was one of the rare times the Commandant wanted me to explain myself. Ari and I had expected this, so I told him my cover story: I was taking Ari out for some strenuous flying across the country to prepare for next year and keep our skills sharp.

He eyed me skeptically but finally nodded once in acceptance. I figured there would be too many questions if I talked about getting called to do this by Lord Orion… Plus, the possibility was there that the Commandant would forbid us from going on such a risky journey.

"Let me remind you that Ari is an asset of the Altarian military," he said after a short, assessing pause. "Don't damage him. You were given two months off to *rest*."

"Yes, sir."

His lips thinned with displeasure.

"Night's asking what we're really doing," Ari reported.

I lifted my bowl to slurp up the last bit of gravy still in my bowl. Well, what we were about to do was a wild gryphon secret... *"You can ask her if she's a skymother. She might understand from there."*

When I looked up at the Commandant, he was frowning over at his gryphon, who'd balked. They exchanged a glance, something passing between them.

"She said yes, she is," Ari told me.

"Well, Cadet Walker. Night suggests that I should be giving you some supplies for your...flights." The Commandant still sounded suspicious, but he stopped asking questions and instead let me take some military rations from the kitchen storage and waved me off to my old dorm, where Ari and I passed out for the evening.

WE LINGERED at the fortress for breakfast, and Ari complained when I also took the opportunity to groom his fur and feathers before placing the saddlebags back onto his flank. They were as heavy as they'd be, stuffed to the brim with the provisions the Commandant had given us.

"Sun's up," I said, observing the sky from the edge of an open shutter. I turned to Ari, thinking this was really it. If we were going to do this, there was no easy way to turn back when we ventured north into the wild mountain range past Fortress Aerie.

"I'm ready. I still feel the call," he said before I could ask.

I did too. It was like someone had tied a string to my belly button, insistently tugging on it. *"Let's go,"* I said, swallowing my nerves. There was no sense in stalling.

Ari and I swooped out of the fortress, following the instinctual pull of the calling that had Ari's beak pointed north. I'd wondered what was beyond Fortress Aerie. Other cadets suggested it wasn't all that special, just rocks. We crossed a valley first, and I saw what they meant. Other than the ribbon of silver water far below, we were framed by treacherous, sheer walls of rocky ground.

To pass some of the time, we went over Valtora's advice again. *"The wild gryphons will avoid us because of you,"* Ari said. *"Gryphon riders this far north are usually a sign the trappers are out. But if we come too close to a nesting ground, we'll get attacked and chased away."*

Considering it was summer, most mated pairs would be tending to freshly hatched chicks. When I was a caretaker, it was my favorite season, as the females of the First had allowed me to bear some of the challenge of rearing baby gryphons. However, now we'd need to be careful where we tried to roost for the night.

"The eldrafn prefer the far north, where their winds are strengthened by winter storms. We can try to avoid notice by flying low to the ground," he continued.

"And if we do see one?" I asked nervously. Fighting the immense birds of lightning and wind was a third-year topic and one of the last things a cadet learned before being sent out to squire for one of the gryphon flights. Eldrafn were rare, and Rathi villages were considered prosperous if they had a single one tamed and ready for combat.

"Wild ones usually blow themselves out like real storms unless they have a stable food source and a way to regenerate their winds and electricity," Ari said. *"We probably won't meet one."*

"But if we do?"

He hesitated. *"Well, we're probably dead. Valtora said wild gryphons call eldrafn 'sky terrors' because they can and will capture and eat one of us whole."*

"Lovely," I snarked.

We spent a long time in companionable silence afterward, crossing over green highlands bisected by the thin river we were following. The distant dots of scraggly mountain goats cropped grass far below us. There were no gryphon nests yet; I figured we were still too close to Fortress Aerie. Wild gryphons were smarter than to hunt this close to the hub where the beasts were taken and tamed.

We had no trouble finding fresh water or places to rest within the dry grass humming with insects that covered most of the highlands. There were no signs of wild gryphons, and perhaps that lulled me into a false sense of security that this would be an easy trip.

After all, we were making this journey in the summer, when the far north was likely to be at its least deadly. I was starting to enjoy the time, despite the dry and bland rations every morning and evening.

Of course, I should've known the wild beasts would find us. While we traveled along another rocky valley, a shadow swooped out of the sky from a high cliff, clipping Ari's wing and sending him sideways and off balance. The sky erupted with the screeching of enraged gryphons echoing all around us.

I craned my neck, counting three winged shapes on our tail. *"Faster, Ari. We must be close to a nest,"* I said. Leaning my weight forward, I made myself as small as possible on his back as he gained speed. Our heartbeats raced in sync. He followed every minute shift of the reins pressing on the corners of his mouth and forehead as I guided him quickly through the rest of the valley, emerging into a blinding flash of sunlight sizzling down on our backs.

I caught a glimpse of movement to our right before we were rammed by a flash of silvery feathers. *"Hold steady!"* I white-knuckled the reins when Ari rolled with the momentum of the shove and labored to catch us before we pinwheeled through the sky.

The saddlebags slapped his hips as we came out of the roll. We wouldn't outpace any wild gryphon with Ari weighed down, but we *needed* the supplies.

I thought this harrying group would turn back once we were clear of their territory, but they—five strong now—lunged and snapped at our heels for what felt like an eternity. It was only when I noticed the first sprinkling of white amongst the snow pines and alpine grass below us that another winged shape swooped down, straight at us.

It was one of the pursuing gryphons, talons held out. And I panicked in the few seconds we had before impact. This beast tangled its claws in my saddle, pinching Ari tightly as it got two good holds on us. We screamed, Ari, this wild gryphon, and I, as wings tangled and we fell out of the sky and landed with a bone-jarring thud.

Ari and the other gryphon struggled, dragging down the steep incline until my side wedged against a pine trunk with enough force that I knew I'd be black and blue under my riding leathers. I winced and lifted my flight goggles, getting a good look at the wild beast who'd grounded us.

He was male, with the skinny hips and sloped belly like a prized racing hound. His white-scaled talons were badly tangled with the saddle, and he tore at the leather, trying to free himself. Sunlight dappled over his feathers, bringing out blue tones in the otherwise silver feathers with an iridescent shimmer.

I would've admired him under any other circumstance. But other gryphons were landing around us, their angry eyes fixed on me trying desperately to free this gryphon before he cut a vital strap on my saddle. I was aware all five of the beasts who'd chased us were now here, so it was a surprise when a sixth swooped down and pinned my back to the ground with its merciless talons around my throat.

I was face to face with an angry beast's yellow gaze, his hooked beak nearly pressed to my cheek. My lips parted in shock as his emotions rolled over me in a powerful burst. So strong, in fact, I could understand his meaning.

How dare you cross my territory, Link thief. His fury and scorn were a potent force to keep me pinned to the ground just as effectively as his bulk. The talons around my neck started to close in. I knew how a bug felt the moment it was uncovered hiding in someone else's home: unwelcome and soon to be dead.

"Stop!" Ari shrieked. *"Get off my rider!"*

The beast that had me pinned raised his head, chuffing. *Allow me to free you from this parasite.*

"I am Arimus, son of Valtora, a wild gryphon who used to rule these skies. I order you to release us now," Ari snapped.

In that moment, a ray of sunshine sparkled over the male's plumage, so dark it was nearly black. He froze, staring at Ari with narrowed eyes. *Arimus?* When he said the name, my mind picked up the image of an egg cushioned by soft golden down. *I sense that you speak true, but...*

"Release us," Ari repeated.

Prove that you know her. Valtora...my mate. My lost love.

In response, Ari released a floodgate of memories. Early impressions of Valtora clucking over him as a newborn. Her snarling any time someone tried to approach her and her baby. Then later, when they were both tamed. The warm affection she washed him with along with grooming his plumage.

Valtora teaching him to fly.

Stop!

I gaped, realizing who this male was. Ari's father. By the blessing of the gods, the gryphon jerking away from us was Ari's kin.

"Mother told me of him, but she'd hoped we would not cross paths. His name is Roshawk," Ari told me privately.

As soon as I was released, I noticed the other wild gryphon tangled in the saddle had ripped itself free. Hopefully we would have some time to inspect the straps and make sure everything was still in order. We literally could not make this journey without a saddle.

With fumbling fingers, I undid the riding harness keeping me tied to the saddle and got off Ari's back. He sat back on his haunches, assuming the rigid-backed pose of a proud and properly trained military gryphon. With me stepping back to give them room, Roshawk circled his son, and the other five wild beasts watched while keeping a wary eye on me.

Thoughts and images flowed between the two gryphons, a conversation I wasn't quite privy to. I waited with my heart in my throat, knowing there was still a chance we wouldn't fly away from this encounter. Roshawk growled in displeasure occasionally.

Across one of his flanks was a gnarled crimson scar, raised lines branching up into his wing, where no feathers or fur grew. It looked like the remnants of a lightning strike. One of his tufted ears was nearly gone, ripped in a jagged cut from a battle long past. As he circled Ari, he limped with the front paw closest to his lightning scar.

Roshawk stopped in front of Ari, snapping his beak inches from Ari's without my gryphon so much as flinching. The wild gryphon whipped to face me, his fury so overwhelming it nearly knocked me backward.

Why is my son blind, Link thief? he demanded with just his anger, nearly shouting it at me. *What did you do?*

"This was not her. She saved me," Ari answered for me.

"I c-could tell you what happened?" I offered.

Roshawk glanced to the other gryphons and clicked his beak. In a flurry of feathers, they took to the sky. He gestured with his beak to follow, and I looped back to Ari's side to help him walk. Pain radiated between us, my side hurting just as much as Ari's joints from that hard fall.

"I didn't expect to meet my father like this," he said over our Link. *"I didn't think we'd see him at all."*

"Better him than any other wild gryphon," I replied. We followed him to a patch of sunshine overlooking the valley below. There was no sign of the river we'd been following... I worried that meant we were woefully off course.

I had Ari pause for me to take the saddle and bags off his back so I could hang back and inspect the leather after helping him sit at his father's side. Roshawk growled and feigned a lunge while I was getting Ari settled, his fierce expression promising a painful death if I thought to come any closer.

Instead, I hung back and described Roshawk's scars for Ari to have an idea of the male who was still watching him in turn. His lightning-scarred flank was turned to the sun as he basked.

Finally, it seemed this wild gryphon was satisfied and clicked his beak at me. I recognized the same commanding way he signaled toward me as when he'd ordered the other gryphons to leave. *"He wants you to come sit on my other side. Don't go any closer to him,"* Ari translated.

I approached slowly, aware of the hostile gryphon watching my every move. I settled next to my gryphon and smoothed the feathers along his wing out of habit.

You are fond of this Link thief? I caught Roshawk asking dubiously.

I realized he was saying "Link thief" in place of "human" each time, like I was mud between his talons. Ari shifted to cover my lap with his muscular shoulder. *"She is my best friend and rider. I won't let you harm her."*

Roshawk huffed but turned away from us as two gryphons landed a few yards away with the fresh carcass of a shaggy-furred goat. Both of the newcomers were male, I noticed, eyeing me with identical expressions of trepidation. I shifted uncomfortably, unused to so much hostility and fear just by being here.

With another click, Roshawk sent them away and got to his paws. *A fresh meal for my son. And then you will tell me why you are here and how you were...damaged.*

CHAPTER 7
MOON DUST

They talked for hours. I nibbled on a ration, feeling distinctly left out and unwelcome after Roshawk and Ari had stripped the goat of its flesh. The occasional wild gryphon would land and confer quietly with Roshawk. He ordered each one around, first having them remove the goat carcass, and after that, it was beyond my human senses to comprehend.

I understood Ari just fine as he funneled memories to his father, filling in the details of his life in broad strokes of events. He spoke wistfully of his first rider, Alamid Maros, who'd died falling from the saddle. The feeling of Alamid's weight leaving his back still haunted Ari, a horror he admitted reliving in his nightmares.

Then Ari explained how I'd saved him from the darkness of his loss and gotten him back on his feet after a period of mourning. His wild father didn't seem to understand any of the politics behind a female rider, but he finally started to soften by the time Ari told him why we were here, to fly the Path of Glorium.

Roshawk fixed me with one fierce eye. *If you expect me to thank you, you will only be disappointed.*

"That's fair," I replied.

He turned back to his son, nudging his neck gently. *But you are welcome to stay in my territory if your life is in jeopardy,* he told Ari. *You may even keep the Link thief.*

"Stop calling her that. She didn't steal anything," Ari grumbled.

Roshawk growled deep in his chest. *Humans only know how to take. You have been coddled by them for so long you do not realize what has been stolen from you.*

To my surprise, Ari growled back. He was usually too mild for aggression, but Roshawk's words or tone were rubbing his feathers wrong. "*You may hate humans, but you will not disrespect my rider,*" he replied heatedly.

For a moment, they were beak to beak, rumbling like a storm on the horizon. But to my surprise, Roshawk bowed his head first. *Very well. I respect what is yours. You have explained yourselves enough. Allow me to share what was taken from me.*

My mind filled with images and memories from Roshawk. Sparkling under the sun was Valtora, a younger version of her with thicker fur and even shinier feathers. She was prancing around with a fish flapping in her beak, head held proudly that she'd caught it.

Countless memories of her swept in, tinged by bittersweet loss. At least two years' worth of moments with Valtora, ending with her roosting in a nest they'd made together, tending to a single egg.

Then came images of other gryphons, some I recognized as tamed beasts, like Snowpoint, Mireille and Ironfeather's mother.

I am tired of loss, tired of being hunted by Link thieves. So forgive me if I cannot find any sympathy for the human you've carried into my territory, Roshawk said clearly. *I am far from my nest tonight to make sure she does not see where it is. Some in my flock chose to have chicks this year, despite the danger.*

"Danger?" Ari echoed.

Every year, humans hunt us with more desperation. Separating mates, stealing eggs. Despicable.

"If you want to see Valtora again, I could try to arrange it," I offered, though the words dried up on my tongue the moment his glare flashed over at me.

Do you not get it? he snapped. *I cannot see my mate again. Your kind will steal me, too. I still feel her noble strength over our mating Link, but she is far. It is…how it should be.*

I leaned back on my hands, pondering the words "mating Link" and turning them over in my head. It was common caretaker knowledge that gryphons mated for life, but we'd witnessed some formerly wild gryphons pair in captivity. The way Roshawk spoke, something clicked into place for me.

Valtora, despite being the most motherly gryphon I knew, had never sought out a new mate. She was still connected to this male, loyal to him half a world away. I bowed my head with a humbled sigh. "I'm sorry, I just want to help," I said. But now I understood why he looked at me with hatred. Losing her was a wound that wouldn't heal, because he would rather never see her again than be captured and tamed.

Roshawk's emotions became muddled, harder for me to understand. Ari took up translating for me. *"He says he has alerted his flock that we're allowed to be here. He started a patrol to harass and chase away trappers, but we're welcome now. Well…I am,"* he added the last bit hesitantly. *"I say we fly away at first light."*

"No complaints here." Well, my side was throbbing, and fatigue pulled at my eyelids as we sat here, but the saddle behind us was miraculously intact after our encounter with the other wild gryphon. I'd need to keep inspecting it to make sure no tears took root in the leather.

When we expressed a desire to rest for the evening, Roshawk clicked his beak and turned to me. *You would not deny me one night with my son?*

I checked my Link with Ari and sighed. He wanted the moment of companionship with the father he'd never thought he'd meet, and I couldn't deny that, no matter how rude Roshawk was. He led Ari into the trees for a more comfortable spot, and I did the same, wedging my bedroll in a place where I wouldn't go rolling down an incline.

I DIDN'T SLEEP for long, too much restless energy and pain from my bruises. I opened my eyes to a clear sky dotted with thousands of stars surrounding a huge crescent moon that bathed the land in silvery shades. The hair on my arms lifted. There was some charge to the air, like the world held its breath on this dry, warm night.

I'd dressed down to light clothes to pass the night and lifted the hem of my shirt to view the skin rapidly discoloring from hip to shoulder. From how it throbbed, I worried something had fractured.

"Oh dear, did you get hurt?"

Freezing up, I wondered if I'd mistaken the question and who'd spoken it. That sounded like Mother in the deeply concerned tones she used to use when I was small and presented her with a scrape or bruise in the hope she'd kiss it better.

I peered around the prickly white branches of a snow pine to see a woman standing on the ridge where I'd sat with Ari and Roshawk. Her silhouette was undeniable. The platinum hair up into a perfect bun, the straight noblewoman posture I'd never quite been able to emulate. Her Nilarite-white robes billowing in a gentle breeze.

To see her again reminded me of how I'd left things off with her, avoiding a confrontation by omitting the fact I was leaving for who-knew-how-long. I hoped she wasn't too cross with me. I missed her terribly in that moment.

This was a dream, of course. I'd never been more aware of how surreal a situation my mind had made up for me than seeing my pristine mother out in the middle of nowhere. "Well, come here. Let me see you," she said, and I walked toward her with my heart in my throat.

My imagination whirled with a hundred possibilities of what she'd say next. Maybe she'd just be happy to see me again. Would she mention how she didn't want me to return to the Gryphon Rider Academy? Or maybe she'd just scold me for putting myself in danger again.

Instead, I realized the woman standing there wasn't Mother. I was a few paces away when I noticed she was too tall, her hair too shiny, and her posture a little too confident. Her head turned, and her eyelids lifted, silver light shimmering from her irises in a pulse of unearthly power.

My heart stopped. All breath wheezed out of my lungs.

"Hello, Sivana." Now that I realized something was off, her voice was higher, ringing with a pleasant lit. "I've waited so long to finally meet you."

My tongue stopped working too, stumbling over several sounds as I attempted to form words. Any words. My bruises jarred as I fell to my knees, ready to prostrate myself in front of her.

"None of that. Please, stand." She didn't make a move to help me up, her hands laced over her middle. If she were Lady Nilara, it would make sense. One touch from her would be full of magic.

And I was not worthy of the Mother's magic even now, I noticed. I stood and asked in a hush, "My lady, are you really…?"

A curl of amusement lifted her lips. "Yes. You see my form as your mother, the woman you associate most closely with me. My true appearance is beyond the comprehension of most. It's for your protection."

"Of course," I murmured. And it was no surprise who she'd chosen, when my mother was the most devout person I knew.

I had the oddest sense of discomfort. How I used to yearn for Lady Nilara's attention when she lavished it on Mother and even Rissa. Here in the middle of nowhere, feeling terrible after that conversation with Roshawk, I was finally in front of the goddess who'd never answered my prayers.

It was like a relationship where I'd done all the talking. I had nothing to say once the shock wore off.

Perhaps in her infinite wisdom, she understood this. She faced the sky, letting the moon wash her skin and hair in shades of silver. "I'm pleased to see you and your gryphon are traveling to my home. But I have heard the prayers of Talase Walker and am here to talk to you on her behalf."

My expression fell. Of course she wasn't really here to talk to me. Mother's fingerprints were on this meeting too, no matter how remarkable.

"Stop that," she said gently. Her hand framed my cheek, close enough for me to feel the warmth radiating off her. "I'm here to grant you the protection Talase prayed for. She demanded a boon for years of faithful service, and how was I to reply except say yes? Your family is remarkable. Talase, Clarissa, and you are all dear to me.

"But sometimes it's hard to believe at all. I've watched you turn away, while your sister plans to pledge to me in your mother's footsteps."

"Rissa believes you've spoken to her and seen her future cloaked in moonlight," I said, finding it difficult to meet her eyes. "I think even the smallest sign of your regard would be life changing."

"I agree. Which is why I have never spoken to you," she said.

It seemed she was ready to cut to the chase. I swallowed hard, not wanting to deliver any offense to the powerful woman standing there, watching me with all the patience of an immovable stone. "I-I'm not sure I understand that decision." My voice cracked, and I glanced up, holding in the sudden flood of emotion within me.

"My temples provide some of the safest employment for women across your country. Talase turned to her faith for this reason, ever the practical one. Now that you and soon your sister are of age, she wants the same security for you both. No one dares to hurt or otherwise cross a Nilarite woman, out of fear for the goddess they serve. Me." Her voice echoed to the heavens, and the air chilled in an instant.

In the wake of her casual use of power, I saw a ghostly outline out of the corner of my eye. An impossibly tall woman with the shadow of broad wings behind her. When I turned to look for myself, it was gone. When I saw my actual mother again, she'd die to know what I'd learned.

"But where my temple provides her safety, it would be your prison. Any sign or encouragement from me at all would've swayed you to your mother's side, meaning you would give up your beloved gryphons and a love for the outdoors to tend to others." Her silver gaze seemed to burn right through me as she read my somber expression and nod of agreement. "Sivana, I would not clip your wings. That is why you are not a Nilarite. It took you a while, but you know you are on the path that is best for you, which means you are here to meet a different god who has earned your service."

"Lord Orion," I murmured. His call has brought us all this way, yet even with the Mother herself explaining it to me, I found it nearly impossible. I'd insulted the God of Man by Linking with one of his blessed beasts as a woman. "Does this mean he is my patron?"

"Yes. He always has been," she said.

My world tipped on its axis. All this time, I'd been

begging for the attention of the wrong deity, but... "Isn't he angry with me?" I asked in a small voice.

I met her eyes again, glowing out at me like twin shards of moonstone. Her smile was warm, the kind of look I found hard won from my own mother. But even without her present for this conversation, I felt like I understood her so much better. She only wanted to secure my safety in an uncertain world, the same thing that led countless mothers and daughters to the light of Lady Nilara.

"I will let him answer that question for you," she replied. Yet I had a good feeling from her. Maybe it was the smile or the gentle radiance on my face, but reassurance was a cool balm over old, deeply rooted worries. She glanced to the sky. "Our time together draws to a close, it seems."

Already? But with her revelations, I had a hundred questions and wanted to bask in her gentle regard for a little bit longer like a flower turns toward the sun. Her fingertips skimmed up my cheeks, and she cradled my face in her hands, all her might and power focused upon me for one exhilarating moment.

"Never fear. I will be your protection. Fly to us at night, under the cover of the moon. You and Arimus will not suffer any more attacks," she murmured. "And in addition, I give you a task. Something that will give you the practice you need to overcome a later challenge."

With that, she pressed her lips to my hairline, and I woke up with a jolt of energy charging through me head to toe like a blast of lightning. A large shape jerked away from me, and I startled backward before realizing it was Ari, sitting beside me and radiating concern.

I touched my fingertips to my scalp where it tingled. Sparkles rained down from my cheeks and glistened on my skin, a pure white like dust from the moon.

"You've been asleep an entire day," Ari said.

"I'm sorry. I just...it was amazing," I replied mentally as I

got up and started packing up my bedroll. It was another warm evening, and the sky winked down at me from dozens of early stars.

He pushed a confused feeling over our Link.

"I met Lady Nilara herself." As I projected that thought, a laugh bubbled out of my mouth. I laughed with relief, throwing my arms open to the caress of the wild wind whipping past us. A weight was lifted from my shoulders, and only with it gone did I realize how heavy it truly was.

I wasn't a bad Nilarite. *I wasn't a failure.*

I told him everything as the moon rose, bigger and brighter than it should've been. He twittered in quiet awe as I described the sight and what we needed to do next. *"If we fly at night, we won't encounter any other gryphons,"* he said slowly. *"And maybe the eldrafn will be at rest too. With my blindness, I don't care if the sun is up or down."*

"Exactly. It'd make the journey safer... I can't believe we didn't think of it sooner."

He nuzzled up against my side affectionately. *"It's okay. Let's get in the air."*

"You're ready to go now?"

"Roshawk took me to see his flock and tried to talk me into staying. It was an easy day and...I'm ready to go," he said. Feathers swished as he shifted with some discomfort.

I felt the twinge of pain from his bruises and realized I didn't have the same problem. Lifting the hem of my shirt, a sparkle of moon dust covered immaculate skin, like I'd been healed the instant Lady Nilara touched me.

Before anything else, I let my hair out of the knotted tail I'd tied it into before my rest. Red hair fanned around me, made extra wavy from extended time in a braid. A flash of silver caught my eye, and I twisted my hair around, finding a stripe half a lock of hair wide bleached from the touch of the Mother's power.

"Gods above," I murmured. Literally. She'd really given

me a task. Women on the Mother's business bore stripes of silver in their hair as an outward sign of her protection. I knew I'd be mistaken at a glance for a Nilarite now, the very thing I'd just learned I *wasn't*.

"*You're right, let's go,*" I said, quickly braiding the evidence back from my face.

CHAPTER 8

HUNGER AND ICE

Under the cover of darkness, I turned Ari's beak toward the north, and we followed the call leading us ever onward. The nights blurred together as the land became colder and more inhospitable. It became a challenge to find shelter from the cutting current of icy wind, which whistled around us and brought stinging bits of snow along with it.

Ari and I talked through what he'd done while I was unconscious, as he'd learned more about the culture of his kind in those hours than his whole life as a tame gryphon. I caught a glimpse of it too as he described the smells and sensations of his time with Roshawk's flock.

"I learned he has a much larger flock than most wild gryphons," he told me. "All his doing. He's spent his life gathering up those who've lost loved ones to human poachers and building up the flock he started with my mother."

"Did they know you're not wild?" I asked.

"Of course. But I'm Roshawk's long-lost son, and that earned me some respect too," he said proudly. "Sivana, it was so nice. There were no expectations beyond hunting. I laid around telling stories and sharing news of loved ones."

I worried my bottom lip between my teeth. It did sound

like a dream for a military gryphon who'd only known academy life and the hardships of war afterward. Ari seemed to agree over our Link, already wistful to repeat the experience. *"I learned my father's a hero. In the early days of his flock, he killed an eldrafn singlehandedly."*

"That must be how he got his scar," I commented.

"Yes. It sounds quite large," he murmured. *"He's an exception to gryphon kind, a male flock leader, a skyfather. I'm glad I got to meet him."*

I thought of the big, scarred male and his stare, plus the blast of his hostility toward me. *"I'm glad too. Now you know where you come from,"* I said, deciding to be neutral. It wasn't like we'd meet him again.

One thing I did see more than once was Lady Nilara's task. From the first time Ari and I lay down together to rest through the day, we shared the same dream, and it came back at random times. Sometimes two rests in a row, sometimes a week between them. But in each, I closed my eyes just to feel the sensation of wind and moonlight on my face.

From my time in the temple alongside Mother, I learned all about the goddess's tasks. Half of the time, they were straightforward and physical, like delivering a message or arriving just in time for those Lady Nilara knew would be in need.

Unfortunately for me, I had the other kind of task, a mental trial. And true to my experience with the goddess, she did not reach out to explain what we had to do. She'd called this task *the practice I needed to overcome a later challenge.*

All I knew was that I would become aware of a dreamland where I was fully equipped in a gryphon knight's lightweight armor, with a kite shield strapped to one hand and a lance secured under my right arm.

Ari struggled to fly against rogue winds that tore at his feathers from all directions. Still blind in this dream, he called out with the throaty sound that signaled he was lost in the darkness. That just meant I witnessed our opponent alone, spotting movement in the sky ahead of us as a massive creature flapped wings made of sparking clouds.

Instructor Signe's verbal descriptions barely did the eldrafn justice. It loomed over us with feathers billowing from its storm-forged wings made entirely of misty ebon clouds. Its head was as large as a mansion, with almond-shaped slits where its eyes glared down at us. Lightning flashed from its open beak as it roared with the boom of thunder. Silvery bolts of lightning laced through its wings before several shot at us.

The first dream, we were hit immediately and woke to the sensation of falling. Ari writhed next to me, shrieking in denial and panic. "It's okay, it's okay." I quickly smothered him in affection. That's how we'd first realized we were sharing this awful dream.

Every night it came, it was the same dream and the same outcome. I could barely maneuver Ari without both hands on the reins, and the lightning struck us instantly each time in a web of bolts.

Ari subsided to silence after too many falls in our dreams. I reassured him multiple times that I was still inspecting the saddle and keeping it in good shape as the climate became more hostile. "We're going to be okay," I murmured as I groomed his pelt. I needed to do it nightly now to make sure he was as dry and warm as possible despite the constant fall of snow this far north.

He shook me off when I tried to massage the pads of his stiff back paws. *"The sooner we go, the better,"* he muttered.

Lady Nilara's protection came at a price, I realized, as I felt Ari dwell on the sensation of falling together to our certain doom. The scent of burning hair stuck with me, but it was the fall that bothered him. It reminded him of his last moments with sight, when a damaged saddle slid from his back, taking his last rider with it.

We ran out of food with no end in sight and nothing on

the icy slopes to hunt. I'd stretched out our meals as much as possible, but even the generous rations from the Commandant weren't enough to get us to our destination.

I regretted travel by night with the cold sinking deeper into my bones and empty belly every day. I could crunch on all the ice I wanted, but the distant memory of my last scrap of hard tack would prove more nutritious.

"This is where most gryphons fail," Ari said. After several nights of consuming just snow and ice, his wingbeats were heavier. We shared the same kind of dread. We'd survived for several weeks on rations and the occasional catch of fresh meat, but could we make it to the end of the path before fatigue and starvation finished us?

"We won't fail." I said this for myself more than him. I could feel how loose my flight leathers had gotten over the course of this journey. We'd flown for ages, it felt.

The sensation behind my belly button grew stronger every day, tugging more insistently. We had to be close. The elements constantly whipped into my face, searching for any bit of exposed flesh to bite.

A few sunrises later, we were preparing to settle for another rest when we found a small waterfall and nowhere to go but *up* with only taller mountains ahead. The air was thin here, and I struggled to stay conscious, with black spots threatening my vision along with a heavy dose of vertigo.

Ari huffed harder for breath, struggling against the wind and the elements as they did everything possible to drag him out of the sky. *"I want to keep going. We can't stop,"* he said.

Exhaustion pulsed between us. I was nearly frozen to the saddle, my bones aching from the thin, sheer air. *"The weather's looking bad,"* I admitted. Dark clouds had rolled in, covering the setting moon and dumping snow over us. I could barely see despite my flight goggles.

"If we stop, I don't know if I could take to the air again," he growled.

"Okay. This is the last push. We have to make it," I said. The only other option was falling out of the sky, because I doubted we'd find much shelter below us anyway.

A hint of panic drifted from Ari's side of the Link. What if he couldn't do it? What if we failed and froze this close to the gods' home?

"We've overcome worse odds," I reminded him. *"Remember last year? If we can survive a year at the Gryphon Rider Academy, we can get through a snowstorm."*

He released a throaty sound. *"I can't feel my wings,"* he whispered.

I could sense what a struggle it was to flap them, let alone navigate the cold air currents that numbed them further. *Gatekeeper take us.* Either we stop anyway and risk freezing or pray the end of this journey wasn't too much farther. I shut my eyes for a moment and clutched the reins with frozen fingers, begging anyone listening for help.

CHAPTER 9

RIVER OF ORIGIN

Above the wind's howl came the distinctive call of another gryphon. I opened my eyes to see a winged shape emerge from the gloom, his feathers gleaming even in low light. There was no mistaking this beast, especially when he was twice Ari's size, much larger than any gryphon should be. He slowed the beat of his wings, swooping in so he was flying just before and underneath Ari.

An unfamiliar presence tickled the back of my mind.

"This way." Glorium's voice was deep and sure, matching his stature. He spoke to me as clearly as Ari, and if my face wasn't frozen, I could've cried with relief as he guided us through the worst of the driving snow. We could've flown together for an hour, but with his help, Ari held out until the last moment.

We crashed together across a stretch of green grass, coming in for the kind of hard landing that bruised us both anew. Ari tipped to the side with a low chuff, resting my weight on the ground rather than his back as he panted and shivered, shaking chunks of ice off his pelt.

This place was exactly like Valtora described. The air was warm, quickly making my flight jacket and cold weather gear wet and sticky against my skin. My fingers were still stiff as I unlaced my legs from Ari's saddle and lay out on my back. A pomea fruit tree waved round, ripe green orbs above me, and my mouth watered to taste something fresh for the first time in countless days.

"Are you okay?" I asked Ari. My legs throbbed with various tender places, but I knew the impact had to be twice as bad for him.

The gryphon groaned. *"I'll live. Probably."*

I sat up slowly and crawled to his side, helping right him on his belly. A shadow fell over us as I inspected him for any sign of a deeper injury, and Glorium's presence brushed against mine again. *"I'll take care of him."* The massive gryphon waited, his feathers twinkling like iridescent stars as the sun broke through the cloud cover, but only on this plateau laced with the gods' magic.

"Thank you," I said, though I flanked Ari, helping him stand and lean on Glorium. He took him to the river rolling by placidly, bisecting the plateau with a ribbon of clear water.

"Drink in slow sips. It will restore you," Glorium coaxed.

I cupped my hands and drank a mouthful as well, feeling the water roll down my throat crisp and cool. While Ari tipped his beak back, I stood to get a better look at where we were. Mist rolled from a small waterfall that gleamed with multicolored specks of dancing magic. There was no way to see what was beyond that waterfall—so I figured that was the gods' home, just barely out of reach.

The whole plateau was about as big as Fortress Aerie's mess hall, designed to feed hundreds all at once. My gaze drifted to the grove of several ripe fruit trees, and that's when I saw him. A male figure reaching up and plucking a pomea fruit from its tree despite that being an impossible distance for an ordinary man to reach.

Glorium nudged my shoulder with his beak, nodding when I glanced to him. I swallowed thickly as I took that first step. There was little mistaking who I'd find here at the heart of the River of Origin, with his gryphon only yards away. But when Lord Orion turned to me, I froze.

He wore a familiar face with frown lines permanently etched around a thin, serious mouth. A solid brow set above narrow eyes, with a gold-plated pendant of Lord Orion resting over the breast of his riding leathers. Commander Davis scowled back at me like a phantom from the past.

"Good morning, Sivana," he said, but his voice wasn't quite the hateful sneer I remembered.

I knew I should kneel, even prostrate myself, but all I could do was blurt out, "W-why a-are you him?" Of all the men whose visage he could wear, Lord Orion chose the face of the instructor who'd tried to kill me.

The god glanced down at himself before holding out his hand to me. He offered me one of the big pomea fruit he'd plucked from the tree. "I did not choose this form. Unfortunately, this man is who you associate with me most. Come and sit. You have had a long journey. There's no need to lower yourself." His words echoed Lady Nilara's when I started attempting to kneel on stiff knees.

I eyed him uncertainly as I approached, like a wild, hungry animal offered a scrap of food. He rolled the pomea into my hand and sat at the base of the tree with one of his own, patting the grass next to him in invitation.

I laid my aching self in the grassy cradle of the tree's roots and eyed the God of Man over the fruit as I took a juicy bite and savored the crunch of dozens of tiny seeds between my teeth. While he had the face of my instructor, his eyes were full of golden power, crinkled around the edges with the kind of smile I'd never seen Commander Davis make.

Okay, I could do this. I could talk to him no matter what he looked like. "Lord Orion, you called Ari and me, and we're here," I said.

He dipped his head. "I see this. But do you know *why* you're here?"

I munched through another bite of the pomea for time as he waited. How often I'd turned this question over, thinking he would answer it when I got here. "Lady Nilara suggested that you are my patron," I said quietly.

"I am. But I could've told you that over a month ago when you set off," he said.

Gods above, had it really been that long?

"In a way, we didn't think you would believe it unless you met us face to face. My wife especially wanted to reassure you," he continued. "Your circumstances are special, Sivana. You've probably grown tired of hearing how remarkable it is that we now have a female gryphon rider."

I nodded slowly, then asked, "Are you angry with me for saving Ari's life? Truly?"

He sighed, a twinge of annoyance there. "No, dear. I don't care what gender riders my gryphons have. I gave you all the gift of Linking with my blessed beasts so more people could bond with one, not less."

My shoulders fell, relieved of yet another weight. It was incredible to be validated by the same god whose name was used to drag me through the mud. Could he write it down and sign it in such a way no one would question who it was from?

"But your people have strayed far from what I first intended, twisting around my gifts. I am the God of Man*kind*. My wife and I never intended to divide Altarians along gender lines." He shook his head sharply. "Yet only men ride gryphons, and only women turn to Nilara to channel her healing magic. It's time we intervened to set things back to rights. Which brings us back to you."

"Me," I echoed with an uncertain chuckle.

"You, the first woman in several ages who has successfully Linked to a gryphon despite so many precautions against it.

You have started a cascade of events and hold the power to guide them."

I definitely wasn't sure about that. It felt like I was still a pawn in the game of nobility, pushed between King Cortes and his sons to wherever they wanted me.

"I know your heart, Sivana Walker. From the moment of your birth, you glowed with potential. I almost made you a Tulari, but that would've only ruined the good you can do for my gryphons." He fixed me with a serious, assessing look. "You care deeply for my beasts in an age where they are quickly being driven to extinction."

A gasp escaped my lips. "What?" I murmured.

Lord Orion looked troubled as he spoke. "What Skylord Roshawk told you is true. His kind is being overhunted by the Altarian military. Humans have become too good at taking the beasts when they're at their most vulnerable. Gryphons separated from their mates and young, happening so often that many wild couples are choosing not to have children. At the rate we're going, the only gryphons will be ones born into captivity within a generation, and we know what dangerous lives they live."

"No. That's horrible," I said. To know Roshawk was right didn't sit well alongside the pomea in my belly.

"And that reaction is why you are here." The god's smile was like a ray of sunshine, warm and approving. He glanced up and clicked his tongue. Soon Glorium joined us, helping Ari walk and settle at my side. The other side of my Link didn't sit as heavily with exhaustion and pain.

"I swallowed one of the river stones. He helped me pick one out," Ari told me. He flopped his head and neck into my lap and yawned hugely.

"Do you feel stronger?" I asked.

He tilted his beak back and forth. *"Not really."*

"Lord Orion, is there anything you can do for Ari's sight?" I asked aloud hopefully. The god was distracted with

Glorium sitting at his side, petting and cooing praise over the massive beast. I hid a smile behind my hand. He seemed almost human in that moment.

Then his glowing eyes roved over me and watched as I stroked Ari's wing. "When you heard the legend of my gryphon, the first thing you thought of was his eyesight," he commented. "A possibility that you both could strengthen your Link to the point he could see through your eyes."

I didn't dare to breathe as Lord Orion considered. "To come all this way to advocate for your gryphon...yes, you are the right choice," he said.

"My lord?" I asked.

"It used to be that each of the gods selected a single mortal every generation to represent them to our people. The tradition needs some dusting off, I think. I pick you, Sivana Walker. You are Chosen." The words echoed with power and formality, setting over me like a warm shroud.

Yet internally, there was a screaming voice, carrying on about how I didn't deserve such an honor. Especially not representing the God of Man...kind. "My lord, surely—"

He held up a hand for silence, and I cut myself off.

"And in return, I offer you a token of magic." His fingertips glowed golden, forming a spell circle that hovered an inch above his touch. Rubbing a hand through Glorium's feathers, he withdrew three that'd been loose. "In return for your service as my Chosen, I present to you a tool. Arimus will grow to his peak strength with water from the River of Origin in his belly and a stone steeped in its depths in his gizzard. But your side of the Link can be stronger."

With a snap of his fingers, he was holding a physical item that combined his spell circle and the glimmering feathers. It was a religious pendant, much like the version Commander Davis wore. The feathers were plated with gold, joined together in a perfect circle, quill to tip, with real magical runes swirled on the inside.

He offered it to me. "This is one of a kind. It will give you the power to speak the language of gryphons and create your own flock of sorts. With patience and practice, you and Ari may just achieve the powerful Link you hope for," he said. When I reached for it, wanting what it could do more than anything, he drew it back.

"But first I need you to understand what it is to be Chosen," he continued. "The time is not right to announce it to the world, and I imagine you don't want that kind of attention anyway. But there will come a day you will advocate for my interests with your words. Your actions will shape my worship, and your deeds may yet save my blessed beasts. Do you feel like you are up to the task?"

I folded my fingers into my lap. A powerful token in exchange for a weighty responsibility. I imagined the crusaders of old, who'd maimed and burned heretics for a lot less than declaring themselves Chosen. With the god wearing Commander Davis's face, I thought about what reaction my old instructor would have if he heard the news.

He would try to kill me openly, I thought. At some point, Lord Orion had become the god of men, and I had already experienced the hostility from being a woman in that sphere.

"I'm not sure Altare is ready for this," I said honestly.

Ari nudged my hand for attention. *"I think you are the right person for the job,"* he said before projecting a memory into my mind.

Over a year ago, he'd been saddled and ready to ride, walking out of the First's stables alongside Alamid. His old rider had paused and looked over into a stall, silently cuing Ari to do the same. There in the stall was...me. My spill of frizzy hair blocked me from noticing them as I sat cross-legged in the hay across from a tiny gryphon hatchling.

"Okay, Ironfeather, I have some delicious meats for you." This past version of me lifted a plate by my side, covered in bits of different kinds of raw fish, plus cuts of chicken and pork. The little beast turned his beak up immediately. "C'mon, little one. If you don't eat, you won't get big. Then how's someone going to ride on your back?"

Aww, my picky boy, I thought as the memory ended with my past self noticing I had an audience and startling. I'd tried dozens of options until figuring out he liked cuts of beef best. Taste tests usually ended with the hatchling snuggled in my lap, reluctantly eating from my hand. Thankfully, Ironfeather had gotten less finicky about food as he got older.

"He wants you to advocate for gryphons, something you've done all your life. Say yes," Ari urged.

If I accepted, Ari might be able to see again. I could speak for wild gryphons like Roshawk, who hated humans and thought of us as parasites because of what we'd done. Then I imagined more female gryphon riders, no longer held back because the God of Mankind was silent.

Lord Orion waited by my side as I thought it through. "Nothing will ever change in Altare unless someone takes the first steps," I said finally. "I would like to accept the job as your Chosen as long as I have your guidance along the way." No more unanswered prayers or guesses. I needed to be more sure I was on the right path now that I'd met two of the gods and learned how off many common assumptions were.

He smiled and dipped his chin. "If you need it, you shall have it. Here, treat this with care." The pendant was warm when he put it into my palm. It was a big, bold statement piece, like most religious tokens, and links of magic appeared and threaded through the eyehole of the pendant, taking form as a delicate, silvery chain to wear around my neck.

"You need to hide it until the time is right. Do not talk about what occurred here today or who you are to me, else it will shatter, and you will lose its magic."

I held it a little tighter. "Of course, my lord."

"Until then, you will pose as a Nilarite." He gestured to

the silver streak in my hair. "You are under my wife's protection."

Ari churred unhappily. *"Falling in our dreams. Some protection that is."*

The god's gaze turned toward him. "I believe Nilara aimed to mimic a challenge in your future. When you're older, stronger, and wiser, you will not need her protection *or* the practice her task provides," he said, holding up a finger. "But until then, many outside forces seek to influence you both. My last advice is to be careful who you listen to."

I turned the pendant over in my hand, lips quirked in thought. Even though the middle of the piece was made of magic, it felt solid under my touch. "Yes, my lord," I said simply. Seemed the military part of me took over, the one that saluted and said "yes, sir" no matter what. I cleared my throat and put the necklace on, feeling a shock of static over my skin when I tucked it under my collar. Its long chain made it settle over my heart. "What is my first goal?"

"Oh, very simple. Pass through the second year of your academy training. In the meantime, I will be watching how you use my gift with interest. That will be difficult enough without me over your shoulder," he said. "You have about a week left of your break, though. It's time for you to go enjoy those days."

I thought of the long flight awaiting Ari and me and breathed a sigh. A week wouldn't even be enough; we would be late to the Academy. One of the drill sergeants would be assigned just to me, day and night, with an ever-expanding list full of demerits and duties.

"I believe a young man's been waiting for you," he said.

I blinked, and Lord Orion held the letter and map from Weslecker that'd been at the bottom of my saddlebags this whole time, rumpled and out of shape. I almost asked how he retrieved it so quickly, but he was a god. Surely some things are explained by magic.

"Before you go, though…" He reached over and rubbed Ari's head, scratching behind the gryphon's ears. He murred happily, the Link flooding with a shock of simple pleasure from the magic of Lord Orion's touch.

I gaped as a shimmer of magic settled into Ari's feathers, giving them the same sheen of other gryphons who'd completed the Path of Glorium. He was now as shiny as Night, or Roshawk, or even Valtora. The tawny brown of his feathers shaded with hints of copper. "Do you pet every gryphon who makes it here?" I asked on a sudden realization.

"How could I not? I love gryphons." His smile was warm on Ari, and it just about melted me. "Until we meet again, you two. You might want to close your eyes."

A massive spell circle was weaving around where Ari and I sat. I realized some serious magic was about to happen and clenched my eyes closed, glad I did as a bright flare turned my vision red.

CHAPTER 10

THE SUMMER ESTATE

W HEN THE LIGHT FADED, I carefully peeled my eyes open one at a time. There'd been a sensation of movement and a shift of warmth, the sun suddenly beating down on us with unrelenting summer afternoon heat. I was dressed for the wrong weather and sweating under my layers of leather and fur.

Gulls cawed and wheeled above us, and the ocean roared as its waves pounded the shore. We were still seated on grass, but my boot heels were sinking into a plot of sand where it met the beach. I scrubbed my eyes, but the view remained the same. Somehow, we'd been transplanted from the roof of the world to here.

"Are you complaining right now?" Ari asked, sprawling out to soak in the sun on his feathers and puffed-out fur. I watched him roll sand into his pelt and shook my head with an amused sigh. His hide had a new, shiny glint in direct light, a stunning copper sheen to his brown feathers. I knelt to pet his wing in appreciation.

"Only a bit," I said. I pulled off my riding jacket and gloves, packing them away before getting to my feet for a look around. The first thing I noticed was a sandy path artfully winding around patches of greenery like the one we'd

landed in. We'd trampled a plot of bright orange flowers, and Ari was sticking his beak into the bell of one, sniffing deeply and sneezing.

Further down the beach, a driftwood fence linked up with a white brick wall that marched uphill and joined to the side of a distant, three-story building. I thought of the invitation in Lord Orion's hand. He must've sent us to the summer estate Weslecker had invited me to.

What'd he say about this place again? His parents probably wouldn't be here, but he had invited "a few friends" as well as me. That'd been over a month ago. It was possible they were all gone by now. *"I'm going to look around,"* I told Ari, who'd turned to expose part of his belly to the hot sun.

He yawned lazily. *"Okay."*

I had the feeling he was about to drift off into a nap, well-deserved after such a long journey. We'd gotten used to sleeping through the first half of the day anyway, so I was stifling my own yawns as I hiked up the hill toward the estate.

I caught a strain of masculine laughter further down the line of the beach. Two young men stood in the surf, tossing a brightly colored ball back and forth. Pushing from the water between them were two winged forms, trying to catch it. The sun cast a glare off the water, making it hard to pick out who they were.

When I was closer, though, one of the gryphons whipped in my direction and went charging out of the water. He knocked me down in a sodden gray blur, standing on my chest with his beak parted on a happy string of birdsong. "Ironfeather!" I wheezed. His front paws felt like they were compressing my chest.

His joy flooded over me, and he dipped his head to nuzzle against my nose, careful of the sharp hook on his beak. He dripped on me for a moment, until Mireille shouldered him aside and gave me a chance to sit up and catch my breath.

With her feathers soaked through, she was nearly the same color gray as her brother.

She eyed me as if uncertain when I held my arms out to her. "Hi, baby," I coaxed. They were both yearlings now, and even wet, I could see Ironfeather developing the skinny hips and sloped belly of a fast-flying male, while Mireille was growing thick around the middle with extra muscle and fluff. This was also the age where many females started gaining nippy personalities, even with caretakers. Considering who her rider was, she'd probably come to accept more distance between us.

Mireille answered my doubts by pushing me over again and rubbing her beak and feathery neck against mine in affection. Her emotions twisted into a question, something like, *where have you been?*

Ironfeather turned and peeped happily, tearing off down the beach, chasing the brightly colored ball. I peered past Mireille's bulk to see both Weslecker and Prince Mateo coming toward us. It was a little surreal to see them both out of uniform, let alone shirtless and tanned from the sun.

The prince called his gryphon's name, and she stubbornly lifted her beak as she eased down to sit astride my lap. He crossed his arms above me, bronzed and disappointed when she refused to come to his side.

He breathed a sigh. "Why's Walker here?" he asked.

Weslecker was kneeling beside me at this point, helping me sit up and dusting off the back of my flight leathers. "He invited me," I said, turning to smile at the other young man.

He'd let his auburn hair grow long again, slicked back from his face and wet. While Mateo's darker complexion had tanned deeply over the summer, Weslecker was red around the corners.

"I thought you weren't going to come," he murmured.

If Lord Orion himself hadn't somehow transported me here, I wouldn't have. But all I said was, "Well, I made it."

His gaze traveled upward, fixing on the streak of silver in my hair. "What happened to you?" he asked, rocking back on his heels. "Is that…?"

"I was given a task by Lady Nilara," I confirmed.

The two of them exchanged a glance. While they had second looks at me, Mireille twittered impatiently and rested her neck in my palm. I took the hint, scratching her neck and ruffling her wet pelt.

Finally, Weslecker made a gesture of respect, drawing his fingertips in a crescent over the middle of his chest. I'd seen countless women make Lady Nilara's sign toward each other, but it was rare for a man…unless acknowledging a woman on one of the Mother's tasks.

Unfortunately, at that moment, I really noticed how close he was and how defined his chest had gotten after a year of PT at the Academy and a flush stole over my cheeks. Mateo was similarly strong. I'd thought about my fellow cadets as boys for so long that it was a shock to realize that wasn't accurate. Both of them were young men now, less than two years from being knighted by the king and risking their lives for Altare.

With some reluctance, the prince also made the gesture of Nilara at me. "Where's your gryphon?" he asked.

I pointed behind me. "Napping. We just got here. Do you think…maybe I could go refresh inside?" I asked Weslecker hopefully. With my flight leathers sticking to me from a combination of sweat and ocean water, I knew I'd be peeling them off me. It'd be an ordeal to clean them.

He broke into a beaming smile. "Let me give you the tour."

THE ESTATE, I learned, was the second one acquired by the Weslecker family. The Duchess Weslecker preferred the third one they'd bought a couple years ago, leaving their other two summer homes for her children. It was staffed with enough servants to see to the needs of a small group, but it'd still startled me to come out of my bath to find a stranger standing there waiting to dress me.

Thankfully, I'd hidden Lord Orion's pendant before undressing, so I snuck it back on after getting dressed. The estate had plenty of women's clothes to spare. The maid had laid out several options for me, and I picked a lady's fine, light green sundress. My battered leathers were nowhere to be seen, likely whisked away. Though I hadn't let her dress me, I had been grateful for her help in taming my hair and trimming it to a more manageable length.

Weslecker had met me at the door and offered his arm. "You look lovely," he said. The words and gesture were practiced and formal, but his smile was genuine. It smelled like he'd caught a quick wash and changed into a shirt and casual pants.

"Thank you," I said, feeling a touch of color rise to my cheeks again.

I saw most of the estate on his arm before we settled in a dining room with a platter of finger food set out for casual grazing. Prince Mateo sat close to it, leaning back in his chair and chatting casually with a girl who looked about Rissa's age. A burly man stood at the back of the room, his dark eyes immediately flashing to me. I recognized the dark armor he wore, with an embossed yellow gryphon rampant across the front. A royal bodyguard.

"Gods above," the girl practically squealed. My attention flashed back to her as she got to her feet and approached with her hands cupped close to her heart. "Are you really—"

As she got closer, I noticed the beauty mark on her lip and the familiar set to her jawline. Her skin was a shade lighter than Mateo's bronze, and she wore an ivory dress studded with tiny pearls, stiff attire with a high lace collar. Mother of pearl clips restrained her mass of black, pin-straight hair, which flowed behind her like a lady's cape.

"You're—" I blurted at the same time, pulling away from Weslecker to fumble into a curtsy.

The princess caught me in a bone-crushing hug first. My eyes widened over her shoulder at Mateo, who watched with his lips in their usual slant of disapproval. There was no mistaking her for anyone else than Princess Odalis, the youngest and most reclusive royal.

"I'm your biggest fan! I'm so glad you could come," Odalis gushed, releasing me to grab both of my hands. Her face split into a beaming smile, flashing bright teeth. Behind her, her brother scoffed and stuffed another bite of his sandwich into his mouth, and the royal bodyguard watched us like a piercing hawk. So he was here for her, then, because Mateo never had a bodyguard at the Academy.

She continued to chatter as she drew me to the food. "Acton said he'd invited you, but it sounded like you were too busy. And look at that streak in your hair. That's really cool! Did Mother Nilara give it to you for representing her at Gryphon Rider Academy?"

I heaped a plate with cute little sandwiches and bites of fruit and vegetables while she talked. When she stopped for a breath, I said, "It's nice to meet you too."

"Mateo brought me here for the summer. Isn't the estate lovely?" Smiling, she pulled me over to sit on her other side. Weslecker sat across from us with his own plate.

I tried to savor the food, but I was starving, and it tasted incredible. Other than a pomea fruit, I hadn't had anything fresh in so long. "Where's your gryphon?" she asked while I stuffed my face.

It took me a moment to swallow and answer her. "He's basking on the beach with Ironfeather and Mireille, last I heard," I said. As a matter of fact, I'd brought in his saddle and the nearly empty saddlebags that'd once been filled with provisions, but they'd probably disappeared to the same place as my riding leathers.

"Will you introduce me?" she asked. As I ate, I learned that she'd already tried befriending the twin yearlings. Ironfeather didn't mind her, but Mireille was truly growing snippy toward strangers. I assured her that Ari was a gentle beast but thought if she approached him with the same twitchy energy she exuded now, he'd get nervous too. Gryphons required a steady hand and tended to strike out if they sensed their caretakers' nerves or fear.

I polished off their finger foods plate, not a crumb left by the time my belly stopped rumbling. Prince Mateo turned a serious look toward me as I leaned back in my chair and breathed a sated sigh. "What's your task, Walker?" he asked, gesturing toward my hairline.

Glancing between them, I felt the air shift. Odalis turned curious eyes toward me, but the two young men wore more solemn expressions. "Well, as far as I can tell, the Mother wants me to slay an eldrafn," I said honestly.

Odalis recoiled in surprise. "That's so violent!"

I nodded in agreement. Ari and I had fallen a dozen times in our dreams already, charred by eldrafn lightning. There was no mistaking this was a far more brutal task than the Mother's usual. Training for combat was more in Anrathor's domain as the God of War, to the point where I wondered if he knew about the task too.

"Gatekeeper take us," Weslecker muttered.

Prince Mateo turned to him with a nod. "We have to keep my father from learning about this for as long as possible."

I glanced between them, frowning. "Why does it feel like I'm missing something?"

Weslecker opened his mouth and then closed it with a grim shake of his head. It was the prince who leaned past his sister and answered my question. "He's funded a newspaper to rival the *Kaiamear Gazette*."

It felt like ice gathered along my spine as he spoke. "Let me guess. The first thing it did was run a fake story about me," I grumbled.

"Not quite. The first edition ran late last week, and it was mostly a lecture on religious roles. I'll see if we have a copy lying around," he said.

I nodded, glancing away from him so he wouldn't see the suspicion gathering in my expression. The Prince Mateo I knew wasn't this helpful and civil. We'd been rivals since I'd arrived at the Academy, and anything he did ended up being for his benefit.

"Most people don't know *Voice of the People* is funded by the Crown," Weslecker added.

Despite myself, I snorted. "Did he really name it that?" What a touch of irony from someone as out of touch as the king seemed.

Mateo sighed. "Nothing about this is funny. You're breaking religious roles right now. A violent Nilarite. A woman gryphon rider. He's trying to stir public opinion against you. Know what I think? We need to get you a dye potion and cover up that streak."

"But she's supposed to be safe if she's on a task for the Mother," Odalis protested. I'd nearly forgotten she was there, sitting perfectly still and listening intently. "It's not that she's breaking anything. The gods themselves are!"

I gestured to her with both hands. "Exactly!"

Mateo pinched the bridge of his nose. "That's just not how things are done. If the gods wanted to change something, they wouldn't send just one person to challenge how we run the gryphon knight corps"—I bit my tongue with effort to tell him that he was wrong—"and my father's not going to let it rest."

The princess huffed, propping a fist on her hip. "Well, he

and I are going to have a conversation about this," she said. It'd be a little more intimidating if her voice didn't crack.

"Okay, you do that." Mateo drew a hand over his military-short hair, blowing out a frustrated breath. "And Walker, you'll take the dye potion?"

I bit my lip, cringing away from the idea of covering up the mark of protection the Mother had blessed me with personally. "It would be a huge insult to Lady Nilara."

"Surely she'd understand," he snapped. "You can uncover it when it's safer."

I flashed an exasperated face at his tone. "Look, I'll go to the temple and ask for her wisdom. There is a temple here, right?"

Weslecker nodded.

"I'll take you," Odalis said brightly.

"No," both young men said at the same time.

"I'll go alone, *and* I'll wear a hat. Happy?" I grumbled toward Mateo.

"Extremely," he replied.

For a moment, his expression was drawn in serious lines, concern in the gaze that met mine. But then I blinked, and he glared like he'd caught me staring. Or like he'd just remembered that we were on two different sides of a political line his father had drawn almost a year ago.

CHAPTER II

A NEW SUNSET

I ventured out of the servants' entrance as the sun was rising the next day, dressed in a maid's uniform. My hair was braided and stuffed under a wide-brimmed hat. Weslecker had raided his mother's stash of clothes and tossed aside a small hill of fashionable hats before finding this piece, which looked like it was spun from coarse threads but was soft and comfortable.

I hadn't had it in me to visit the temple yesterday, instead ending up lying in the sand next to Ari, soaking in the sun's warmth until I could feel my skin tingling with the promise of a burn. Ironfeather had let me use his flank as a pillow, while Mireille spread out next to us, eventually shading my face with her wing when I otherwise would've gone inside. Turned out, when Mireille was old enough to growl and glare at Mateo as he tried to keep her away from me, he started respecting our friendship.

As I navigated the streets of Port Lindell, I wondered about the puzzle that was the prince. He'd seemed genuinely concerned for me, though he had an interesting way of showing it. Because of him, I was awake this early, weighing asking the Mother to remove her protection until the Crown moved on from its dangerous fascination with me.

I passed through the market, a lively place with fresh fish and heaps of produce wheeled out for sale. I started regretting the disguise when every fishmonger and vendor thought I was here to buy for the Weslecker estate, voices raised for attention. Just like in Kaiamear, surrounded by shouting and calls for attention, I felt part of my brain shut down from so much noise directed at me.

"Make way!" A man's deep bellow cut through the sound. I looked up to see everyone else scrambling backward, clearing a wide path for a strange beast rushing down the cobblestones. Though I pressed back into the edge of a vendor's stall, I leaned forward to gape as it passed, carrying a male figure shrouded in a heavy gray cloak.

That was a real nightbloom, not just a diagram in a crumbling book. It was said the Gatekeeper formed each nightbloom as a custom gift for each of his Mercy, combining the spirit of a common beast with a seed of life to give it another chance as a supernatural steed to bring its master back and forth from the afterlife. I caught a glimpse of glowing white eyes and a feline-like lope under a thick carpet of grass supporting the Mercy's saddle. Vines ran down its legs, anchoring the shimmering outline of its spirit to the living world.

Giving myself a shake, I murmured a blessing and continued along my way, thankfully not following in the wake of the Mercy. I didn't want to be anywhere near an event urgent enough to summon a rushing agent of the God of Death.

I continued on to the port's modest version of Temple Row, stopping before the painted white façade of Nilara's temple and swallowing hard. She hadn't promised me anything, only given me the streak in my hair because of my mother's demands. There was no guarantee my questions would be met with anything but the usual silence.

Silver drapes shrouded the entrance, and the small room beyond already had several women consulting with the robed priestesses and healers. Giggling drifted out of a side door from the pack of kids waiting on their mothers. I swept further inside, seeking the inner shrine with its statue of Lady Nilara, just to find a woman polishing its face.

I stopped short, eyeing her perfect platinum bun and the way her white robes fit the curves of her figure. She hummed a little tune I'd heard thousands of times. "Mother?" I asked in disbelief.

She turned, and instead of the goddess's silver power, her eyes were leaf green and wide with surprise. "Sivana. Thank the gods," she murmured, tossing aside her towel and sweeping me into a hug.

"How are you here?" I tilted back to look at her, my mouth dropping when I spotted a lighter streak woven into her bun.

"The Mother said my services were needed at this temple. What are you doing, wearing all this?" Without hesitation, she snatched the hat off my head and gasped as my braid rolled free. She lifted the tail, bringing it as close to her face as she could with it still attached to me. "Look at you. You're…sunburned."

I opened my mouth to explain I'd met her goddess when she'd already pivoted to turning my chin up and peering at my cheeks. I felt myself flush under her inspection. "Mother, please."

She handed me back the hat. "We need to talk. There should be a consultation room open," she said briskly, leading me from the shrine to another side area, which held private rooms for the very sick or injured, plus others for private conversation. I was used to the temple in Kaiamear, where the consultation rooms weren't the size of broom closets, but when the door closed behind us, I still relaxed to have a room where we could speak more freely.

There were two cushioned chairs and a skylight, lending the little room enough diffused light for it to be comfortable. "So, she listened to me," Mother said, a hint of triumph to her tone. "You've met Lady Nilara at last. Whose form did she take with you?"

"I did, and she looked a lot like you," I said.

She nodded. "Ah, and she comes to me as my mother in her prime, Gatekeeper bless her soul."

I met her familiar gaze, and it felt as if a dam burst within me. "I'm sorry," I blurted out, earning an arch of her brow. "I-I'm sorry I didn't tell you where I was going or that it'd take so long. You…you were so proud of me after tea with the crown prince, and I knew you wouldn't have wanted me to go and—"

"You really think I would've stood in the way? You were called by a god," she interrupted, breathing a disbelieving laugh.

"At the time, all I knew was that it'd be dangerous," I said, stumbling over my thoughts. "And I heard you and Father arguing…"

Her lips moved, a crease appearing between her eyebrows. "Oh, yes. About you going back to that dreadful Academy." She reached over and rested her hand over mine. "You don't have to apologize. I was disappointed we didn't have more time together to practice speaking to the royals, but Mother Nilara filled in what your sister didn't know. She said you were on your way to meet your patron."

I watched a hint of disappointment flicker over her expression. So, she knew for sure that I wouldn't be a Nilarite. "Is that when you asked her for this?" I asked, pointing to the streak in my hair.

She laughed, shaking her head. "I've asked for that every day since you saved Kaiamear from a rogue rozash. Sometimes guilted, demanded, or cajoled, but the goddess moves in her own time. She's chosen to give you a task now for a reason I'm sure will come in time."

I bowed my head, overcome with a rush of shame. The very thing Mother had spent so much time campaigning for was what I'd come here to potentially have removed.

"What's wrong?" she asked.

Taking a deep breath, I told her everything Prince Mateo had shared yesterday, catching her nod of recognition when I mentioned the new newspaper, *Voice of the People*. She hummed, turning her gaze toward a square of sunlight slowly making its way down the wall after I was done, thinking quietly for several minutes.

"This situation…it's my nightmare," she said, holding up an elegant hand when I opened my mouth to reply. "Ah-ah. Just listen. Times are changing. Much as I disagree with how Prince Isaac is positioning himself politically, he's not *wrong*. Your generation is different. Smarter, savvier, and dissatisfied with how things are. Nothing proves that more than how Altarians are reacting to you. No, not you personally, but the idea of you.

"The king may dig in his heels and scream about tradition, but it's too late." She looked me in the eye and repeated herself more quietly. "It's too late. The gods are involved now, and in their infinite wisdom, they have embraced you and the change you represent. They will continue on even when the king is forced to retire.

"Yet I've asked myself, what could I have done differently to keep you from being the one caught in the middle of all this?" She sniffed, her eyes shimmering like gemstones. Nearly crying, I realized, tears pooling dangerously close to spilling over. "I've wished someone else's daughter was first. Selfishly, I admit. I'd rather you safe at home instead of venturing back to the Gryphon Rider Academy wearing the goddess's protection, which may just another target to your back. But…my wishes are only standing in your way. You're going back there before the week is out."

"I have to," I murmured. She stifled her dignified crying with pats of a handkerchief, and I felt my eyes sting in the wake of her speech.

She hiccupped a laugh. "You're so much like your father. You would move Altare itself for that gryphon, wouldn't you?"

I licked my lips, sharing a thought even though it was the height of immodesty. "In a way, I already have," I murmured.

She squeezed my shoulder. "That's right. My daughter, the great symbol of change, all for one gryphon. Well, I'm here to help in any way you need. Where do you plan on staying?"

We shared a smile, and I hoped this was the first page of a new chapter between us, because I needed her steady savvy just as much as my father's military experience.

"Weslecker gave me a bed in his summer estate," I answered.

Her smile turned playful at the corners, reminding me distinctly of Rissa. "Oh, did he?"

I rolled my eyes. "It's not like that."

"He is from a very nice family…"

"Prince Mateo and Princess Odalis are there too," I said, flustered.

She patted my shoulder. "Want to see if they have room for your dear old mother, too?"

I promised to ask and left the temple without a second glance backward. I was keeping the sign of Lady Nilara's protection. It might cause me trouble in the future, but it was truly a symbol of two women I called Mother, and I wouldn't dare disrespect either of them.

Having Mother at the same table as Prince Mateo was one of the most awkward experiences of my life. They were perfectly polite to each other, but there was a level of stiff formality that settled over my companions to have an adult taking meals with us, save for Odalis's silent bodyguard. The royals and Weslecker spoke around him like he wasn't there, while Mother was a presence that couldn't be ignored.

I retreated to my guest room to lie on the carpet with Ari, staring at the magic pendant I hung between two fingers tangled in the silvery chain. I held it for hours, like it'd give up its secrets that easily. As incredible as it was to hold a piece of magic made by Lord Orion himself, it hadn't come with instructions. All I remembered from the chat with the god was to be patient and to practice speaking the language of gryphons and make a powerful Link with Ari.

I wore it every day, secreted under my clothes, hoping its magic would leach into me. When I wasn't on the beach, playing with the gryphons or Odalis, swimming with Weslecker, or sunning with Ari, I was seated across from Mother, pretending to have tea and acting like a noble.

On the second day, she'd roped Weslecker to sit with us and pretend to be the king. He was frighteningly good at delivering veiled insults with a bland smile on his face. But of course, he was a *real* noble, trained for this kind of thing.

"Gods above, Sivana. You can't just tell the king he's wrong," he said halfway through the first hour. "Say something with your tone, not your words. *Finesse.*"

I grumbled uncharitably under my breath.

"No muttering, either," Mother added.

I knew it was necessary, but even while I embraced this daily training, it felt like they were ganging up on me. They talked my logic in circles with their words, flustering me to come up with witty responses and backhanded compliments without hesitation or a hint of a stutter. I agreed to things I didn't mean to or descended into a faltering mess more often than not.

"I'll keep working with her, Missus Walker," Weslecker promised when we called it quits on our last day here, to her nod of approval. I'd be taking the next day to fly Mother back to Kaiamear and a second one to return to the Academy with enough time to spare to spend the weekend preparing for the challenges ahead.

In the time she'd been here, the lighter streak in her hair had faded back to her natural platinum. Her task was complete…either by being there in the temple to talk me away from the edge of insulting Lady Nilara or by returning to the summer estate to drill me on how to navigate the political waters that threatened to drown me otherwise.

Whichever it was, I'd never been so relieved to jump into something I wasn't good at. And even more grateful when it was over and I had a bit of sunlight left to enjoy the beach. Ari rested outside in the warmth with Ironfeather, who stared at his feathers' new shine in fascination. At a distance, I noticed my gryphon's change in size best, as his limbs seemed longer with him stretched out next to the yearling.

"Wait!" Weslecker hustled over to join me halfway down the manicured path downhill to the waterline. "Mind if I join you?"

I shrugged. "I was just taking a walk."

"Perfect. There was something I wanted to show you," he said.

Following my lead, he kicked off his sandals, and we waded into the damp sand. I enjoyed how it squished between my toes and left a brief sign behind that I'd been here—before getting washed away under the surf. "What is it?" I asked since he didn't seem to be in any hurry to go somewhere else.

"You'll see it soon," he promised.

I took his word for it and stooped to retrieve a spiraling

shell halfway buried in the sand. Part of the beach was littered with them, with small, bug-like animals fighting each other to hide within them. "You might not want to do that," he warned as I held the opening up to my eye trying to spot if this one was occupied or not. A tiny pincer emerged, reaching for my lashes.

Laughing, I placed the shell back in the sand. "I just want an empty one as a keepsake."

"Well, kick the bugger out, then." He retrieved it and gave it a little shake, the bug within clinging to the shell's edge and foaming up at him.

"No, Acton. That's its home," I said.

He put it down, looking startled. "I think that's the first time you've said my name unprompted."

"I had to protect the crab-thing."

He rolled his eyes. "Uh-huh." But he helped me inspect the other shells until we found one without an occupant. I pocketed it and made to continue down the coastline when Weslecker caught my hand. He drew me back, pointing with his free hand. "Look. Have you seen a prettier sunset?"

The tide washed over our ankles as we watched the sun set below the line of the water, the world reduced to a contrast of orange and teal for several moments. I smiled to myself, thinking of a different night almost a year ago now, when Ari and I had watched what I'd thought of as his final sunset. It'd been beautiful too, like the elements had wanted to honor my gryphon in some small way.

"It is now," I said, glad to notice a new sunset while Ari was safe and content with a new life and rider.

Weslecker tugged on my hand, and I looked up at him— by the gods, he'd gotten *tall*—and then his lips were on mine. He muffled my sound of surprise but pulled away when I didn't kiss him back. "Oh." His mouth quirked with disappointment. "I had to try, at least."

I drew in a shaky breath. "N-no, it was j-just unexpected,"

I stammered. A rush of embarrassed heat flooded my face, mortified that I hadn't seen that coming. Now he thought I didn't like him back.

Rissa had tried to warn me. It was either a "we can never" or a "we can't right now," and I needed to pick. There was no more time to waver between the two or to pretend this wasn't happening.

"It's okay. You can't blame me for trying, right?" He laughed half-heartedly and scuffed his foot through the wet sand.

"Wait. I just…" I held his hand harder when he tried to pull away. "I like you. You're kind and patient, and if you pick up training me in talking like a noble, that's two things I'm awful at that you've tutored me on."

From the way his expression twisted, I could tell this was just making this worse. "I can't right now," I blurted. "I can't see *anyone* until we graduate from the Gryphon Rider Academy. It's a long time, I know, but if you're still interested then…"

He gave my hand a squeeze. "If things were different, you'd have kissed me back?"

I considered for several moments, but he waited until I began to nod. "Yes. I would've."

He flashed a sad smile. "Then I promise you that I can wait a little longer. I'd never endanger you, or Ari, or your place at the Academy."

I pulled him into a hug, too overwhelmed to speak. Under the warm halo of the setting sun, I memorized the faint smokiness of his cologne alongside the tang of salt and fresh air against my cheeks. When I thought of him, I'd remember this moment and his promise to be patient with my situation.

CHAPTER 12

HIERARCHY

Next thing I knew, it was Sunday, right before classes started again, and the Green felt empty with only the four second-year flights scrambling to line up. Several drill sergeants added their voices to the mix, creating an explosion of noise when Harrier Flight lined up in the wrong spot.

As was customary for the Gryphon Rider Academy, the trainers told us as little as possible and left us to figure it out. We lined up outside for an early evening group session with Weslecker, our newly crowned flight leader, trying to get us in the proper order.

I heard Sharde snicker somewhere in the back of our group, Kite Flight. We'd lost the quick and precise line-up we could've done in our sleep at the end of our first year, tripping over the fact that half the young men in the flight had grown over the summer. Biggs, in particular, had shot up like a weed, leaving me in the first spot in the front row as the shortest person in the flight.

Ari kept his beak raised beside me, his ears pinned back. He'd assumed the classic "at attention" pose for a gryphon, with his weight resting on his haunches, ready to move at any moment.

"I didn't miss all the shouting," he groused to me privately.

"Me neither."

Though it'd been nice to see all my flight-mates again, the reunion had been incredibly short lived between their trips to the barber to get their grooming within regulation and the sudden demand that all the second-year flights form up on the Green for an address from the Commandant.

Out of the corner of my eye, I could see him standing there waiting only a couple yards away with Night yawning beside him. He waited until the flights were properly lined up in order of our ranks last year. Kite Flight was first, and next to us stood Falcon Flight in second place, with Prince Mateo as the flight leader, followed by Osprey, and finally Harrier Flights.

"Good evening, cadets." The Commandant reached a deep-chested bellow similar to a drill sergeant, impossible to miss.

"Good evening, sir!" we shouted back.

"Welcome back for your second year at the Gryphon Rider Academy. It is the hardest year here, designed to pick apart every aspect of you and your gryphon to catalogue your strengths and weaknesses. You will be in the saddle as much as possible to make this possible. You learned your individual rank last year, but don't get complacent. It will change many times in the coming months," he announced.

I held in a sigh of relief. My rank felt like a spit in the face, number thirty-five of thirty-five. One step away from failing. For any other cadet, failing out meant repeating a year, like Sharde had done with his first year. But for me, failure meant Ari's execution. The king only allowed us to attend as long as we passed and proved we could overcome every challenge.

"Your personal ranks are also loosely tied to a new hierarchy within your year group, which echoes the real gryphon knight corps. Expect to be shuffled in and out of jobs regularly. Listen carefully." He called up Prince Mateo and

Weslecker, our first- and second-ranked cadets. They were announced as our cadet High Command, both Cadet-Generals.

"Shouldn't someone take control of the flight?" I asked Ari as a quiet murmur rose from the other cadets. The Commandant stepped back, the two Cadet-Generals at his side. He called two more cadets to stand between two flights, our newest Cadet-Marshalls, who commanded multiple flights and conveyed orders from High Command.

When we got to Cadet-Commanders, that was when several of us were tapped. Chatty Feyring was made our flight leader, and Biggs was assigned a first-year flight to mentor. I didn't get my hopes up that I'd get a job or promotion. I just had to hope I'd earned one eventually.

After we were properly lined up again, the Commandant nodded his approval and turned to an instructor who'd arrived. "Commander Rudrick will explain the next new layer of your training, elements and how they work," he said.

Rudrick dismissed us from our formal flights and had us gather into a semi-circle around him. He was a friendly face, a former member of the First who rode Snowpoint, the leery-eyed white gryphon standing next to him. "All right, cadets," he said, clapping his hands and rubbing them together. His gaze roved over us all, and I swear he lingered on me for an extra-long moment.

"Elements are a fixed part of a knighted gryphon rider's life. All combat flights are made of three-to-six elements of five fliers each. We've found that these small teams stack the odds best in our favor against rozash," he told us.

"However, there's no guarantee more than one or two of you will be assigned to the same flight after graduation, so your element teams at the Academy are temporary arrangements. This year, we will have Elements A through G, all led by a Cadet-Captain randomly assigned to lead the V-formation you will be trained to fly in as an element. Know what *that* means?"

Rudrick flashed his teeth in a wide smile. "The best Cadet-Captain in your flight will be the XO, which stands for executive officer. Their job is to take over from your flight leader should he or she become compromised."

Because he mentioned it, I had to assume being "compromised" would be part of our training.

"That's right," Ari put in, listening into my thoughts. *"The idea is for you to keep a cool head if your Commander dies in combat."*

"Are they going to run us through every possible scenario?" I asked.

"Of course. High Command is dead. What do your Cadet-Marshalls do? Your Cadet-Commander and XO die, who is next in command?" He tilted his head in my direction. *"That second one has an actual answer."*

I considered as Rudrick fielded a few questions. I caught him telling another cadet that this would be second nature eventually, even if it seemed like a lot up front. *"Aren't Knight-Captains ranked by their element? So if the Commander and XO both die at the same time, the second ranking Captain takes command,"* I ventured.

He nudged my side with his shoulder. *"That's right. I'm proud of you."*

It felt good to finally transpose some of the incessant competition and comparisons in the Academy to something that'd help once we graduated.

"Finally, you will now show proper respect to cadets ranked higher than you when you're in uniform," Rudrick said, interrupting my thoughts. "So, if, say, Cadet-Lieutenant Sharde walks by Cadet-General Cortes, Sharde will salute first and say…" He pointed to Sharde standing at the back of the group, and I caught the faint sound of a long-suffering sigh.

"Good evening, Cadet-General Cortes," the young man muttered.

Rudrick nodded in approval. "Or whatever time of day it is. This gets tricky when ranks have been shuffled around, so pay attention when someone is promoted, fired, or even 'compromised' during your field exercises, because that changes their cadet rank and job. Two cadets of the same rank do not need to salute each other. Also, remember, you are not required to memorize the ranks and jobs of the third years, no matter how much some of them want extra respect."

I thought to my least favorite third-year, Victor Callan, not doubting for a moment that he'd lord his rank over me the moment we met again. He'd been the Ace-to-be of his year group, rank number one. That probably meant he'd be a Cadet-General unless things were different for how the third-years were starting off.

With all that, he dismissed us for dinner and promised our first element assignments would be posted tomorrow. I walked back inside in the middle of my flight, listening in as Feyring chattered to Korvic. "Can you believe they put me in charge first?"

I could practically hear the eye roll in the other young man's tone. "No, not at all." Some things didn't change. Somehow, those two dissimilar personalities were still thick as thieves, even if it didn't sound like it. Korvic's sarcastic streak made most of his words hold a mean edge, but I knew him well enough to realize it wasn't personal. That's just how he was.

"And I'm getting my own flight of little cadets!" Biggs exclaimed. I still wasn't used to looking up at him.

"Will you call them Smalls? Since you're Biggs?" Sharde asked.

"That's a great idea!"

Sharde snapped his fingers and pointed. He drifted to my side as we entered the mess hall and got in line for food.

"Feels weird to be on this side of the line," he remarked. His baby blue gaze drifted toward me. "Hey, disappearing act. When are you going to tell us how this happened?"

He pointed at the white streak in my hair, and I felt the other guys shift their attention to it. It'd been the focal point for everyone I'd talked to so far, rather than them meeting my eyes. I cleared my throat awkwardly and said, "I kind of can't talk about it."

"Please." Now Sharde was the one to roll his eyes. "You know there's going to be gossip about your task. What is it, before Callan exaggerates it to something awful?"

"Let's not do this in the dinner line," suggested our shyest flight member, Credell. He was a broad young man from the southern farmlands, with all the physical strength and bearing of a gryphon rider. I imagined the recruiters took one look at him and selected him rather than listen to the mumble of his voice and the way his shoulders stooped to take a smaller posture when talking to someone shorter than him.

"I'll tell you all when we're back in our roost," I said in agreement.

The kitchen was serving a fish fry tonight along with hearty vegetables, a celebration meal sure to stuff all of us. We sat at our customary table, next to another with boys sitting with younglings, a first-year flight. It was amazing to see how young the cadets seemed, fresh-faced and fumbling as their newly Linked companions tumbled around or tried to steal some fried fish to supplement their diet.

"Can you believe that was us last year?" asked the last of our flight in attendance, Pereyra, who followed the line of my gaze. He wasn't quite asking me, because I'd arrived late with a fully grown gryphon, and the others made various noises of agreement and playful disbelief.

"Mmhmm." Sharde raised a brow and fed some of his fish to Puzzlebox, who was trying to sneak up on his plate. She butted her beak into his palm affectionately. It was hard to forget he was a year older than the other guys in my flight, seventeen like me.

He'd continued filling out his leathers over the summer, while Puzzlebox was about the same size as always, a shade between yearling and adult gryphon with fuzzy youngling fluff between her more developed feathers.

Weslecker joined us late, looking a little chagrined when we all made a point of referring to him as "Cadet-General Weslecker" at least a dozen times in otherwise casual conversation. He looked relieved when we moved back to our dorm together. We'd gotten a communal setup much like last year but moved down one level to signify our position as second-years.

Our last, honorary member was already in the area we shared, her feet propped up on a slightly less shabby cushion and her nose buried in a book. A plate of fried fish sat on a low table beside her, forgotten.

"If Cadet-General Weslecker would permit it, I'd like to hear about the task now," Sharde said. Ellie looked up from her book at the sound of his voice before hiding a shy smile behind its cover.

I sighed as we settled together in a circle, perched on thin armchairs, desks, or sprawled on the floor between our gryphons. There was still time before lights out, so we'd bed them down later.

Taking a deep breath, I told them about the eldrafn nightmare Ari and I were still tangled up in. It drew an extended silence from everyone but Weslecker, who already knew about it.

"And what did you feed Ari?" Sharde asked, pointing to lounging gryphon. "He looks bigger. Longer, maybe? And so shiny."

I bit down on a nervous laugh. I'd expected Ari's changes to get noticed, but maybe not so quickly. Sharde seemed extra keen too for a serious answer, and I thought of Puzzlebox's smaller stature. "My brother made an experimental oil for Ari's feathers, and it's a little too strong. He's not bigger, though. He's already an adult," I lied.

"Uh huh," Sharde said, looking unsatisfied.

"Anyway, I'd love to hear what you all did over your summer. Much more interesting than mine," I said, trying to laugh it off.

Feyring jumped on the bait and bragged about impressing the girls back home with tales of the Academy.

"Who has time for girls?" Pereyra said. He shared how he'd gone hiking for most of the break, getting lost with only his gryphon as a companion.

"Not far off what we did," Ari said.

"That sounds really nice," I commented aloud while rubbing down the fine feathers around Ari's brow. Something told me I'd miss the open sky and the freedom of travel in the months to come.

CHAPTER 13

STARTING FRESH

Actually, I started missing my break early the next morning, when I got a face full of grass after collapsing mid-pushup. "What did you do all summer, cadet? Sit around stuffing your face?" shouted Kite Flight's assigned drill sergeant as he watched me struggle.

Sergeant Kobarn was Ellie's father, stationed here after she'd earned an academic scholarship and hadn't had the money to pay the tuition at one of the universities that catered to noble clientele. I'd only seen the softer, kinder side of him when he was around her, and if it weren't for that, I'd think the athletic PT enthusiast only existed to make morning training miserable. His job was to whip my flight into shape, and chasing us around the Green was his idea of forceful motivation.

He ran me for several laps, and with my lungs threatening to burst afterward, it really sank in how little exercise I'd gotten recently. I felt eyes on me. Unlike yesterday, all cadets were present for morning PT and the distribution of schedules afterward. I steeled myself for my first glimpse of Callan, who stood a few yards away in line for his schedule with the other third-years.

He greeted me with the gesture for Lord Orion, ending it with a flick of his fingertips in my direction. He looked like he'd barely broken a sweat this morning, standing there grinning beside his stunning maroon gryphon, Sunset. I gritted my teeth and forced my attention forward.

Callan was the driving force behind most of the bullying I'd experienced here. I couldn't prove some of it, but I was sure he'd penned the first message and been the one to make calling me a heretic stick with some of the other cadets. He'd thoroughly trashed our former relationship by revealing he'd been using my ties to the First to get ahead.

Winning at any cost was Callan's personality. I could feel him inspecting my profile as the lines shuffled forward. He'd see Lady Nilara's mark of protection as another opportunity to prove that I didn't belong here.

"I don't see what good it is to keep her protection if it's just going to cause problems," Ari groused.

He hadn't seen what I had, even in passing while running laps around the Green. *"Some of the boys here acknowledged me properly. It could help me see who I can trust,"* I told him. My friends had made the gesture of respect immediately, while some of the nastier personalities in Falcon Flight had already turned away or refused to acknowledge it.

"Seems like a loose reason to me," he muttered. *"Doesn't feel like either of the gods helped us."*

"Sure they have," I said.

"Okay. How? We have nightmares and a magic piece of jewelry that hasn't done anything. And since I've grown enough for Sharde of all people to notice, I bet you I fly slower as well."

I frowned, saved from answering when it was my turn to get my schedule. A soldier dug out a folded sheet of paper and gestured for me to check the posting board behind him. "Your first element assignment," he said.

I went nearly shoulder to shoulder with the Harrier Flight boy ahead of me. My name wasn't all that hard to find, actually, listed in Element A along with Sharde, Weslecker, Prince Mateo, and…

"Gatekeeper take me," I muttered to Ari.

There was a method to this madness, combining the two top cadets with the two bottom ones and assigning someone from the middle of the pack to round out the element. But they'd picked an unpleasant boy from Falcon Flight, Hale Barlowe, a cadet who was practically Callan's shadow last year.

I walked Ari to the mess hall as I told him about our element. *"We've flown with three of the four, at least,"* he said.

"That's true. Maybe it won't be so bad." We went through the breakfast line and kept going rather than sitting with any of the other cadets. I was used to speed-eating something small on the way to the women's bath to have just enough time to make it to my first class without earning a demerit for being late.

Along the way, I read my schedule to Ari. *"What is Advanced Anatomy and Tactics?"* I asked. The unlikely duo of Rudrick and Lord Gadric, the resident master Tulari, was teaching it.

"Oh, that's a fun class. I won't ruin the surprise," he replied.

I sat through an entire session of History and War Strategies II to find out. I'd need to hustle this year, because the instructor, Commander Olivandry, never had all that much patience. Last year, I'd started the academic day with Lord Gadric, who'd look the other way if the drill sergeants didn't catch me running behind. Olivandry was not quite as generous.

My next two classes were flying-focused and hosted on the Green. When the Commandant said we'd be in the saddle more, he wasn't kidding. Advanced Anatomy and Tactics was a second-year class, but after that was Jousting for third-years, a class we'd earned a place in since Ari was already fully grown.

Rudrick was already on the Green to start class, which was composed of my whole year group. He was flanked on either side by a black and a white gryphon. The presence of Night meant the Commandant had lent her to this class just in case one of us fell or lost control mid-flight. She had a perfect track record of saving cadets thus far.

"Good morning, cadets," Rudrick said, getting a choral reply from us. "This is the only day most of you will be reporting to the Green for this class, unless you've already passed Flight Training or have shown enough aptitude already in flying rather than flailing through the air. Elements Alpha and Bravo, that's you. Everyone else, you get a taste of what's to come."

I exchanged a glance with Sharde, who stood with me toward the back of the group. "Guess we're special," he said.

The elderly Lord Gadric was crossing the Green as we waited, followed dutifully by Ellie, his assistant and apprentice. She carried two towering armfuls of scrolls, brushes, and what I assumed were spell reagents. On one of the Tulari's umber-skinned cheeks was the circular mark of magic, which for him was the deep sapphire color of a wizard.

"Gods. I think we're about to see real magic," I said under the hush of the murmuring crowd as we waited.

The elderly instructor stopped halfway to us. He took out a wand from a pouch tied to his belt and plucked a heavy-looking spell book from the pile Ellie had arranged at his feet. His lips moved, wand tracing glowing runes which hung one after the other like he was writing midair with magical ink. While he worked, Rudrick addressed us again, "You've all passed a basic anatomy class. In theory, you know the weaknesses of our greatest foes, the rozash. In this class, you will practice it."

Tingles rushed up my arms, and I gaped as the air above Lord Gadric and his spell started to shiver. He built a rozash for us from the inside out, starting with a serpentine ribcage and two serrated skulls fused at the neck. Then came the organs and sinew, the four canvas-like wings gaining definition with all the accuracy of a textbook. The illusion finished when it was clothed in sandstone-toned scales, coming alive as its two heads opened in a scream.

Actually, it was completely silent. I realized the shriek came from Puzzlebox, who ducked to hide behind Ari. Several of us startled away from the sudden noise, but most of my peers turned their attention back to the illusion.

Sharde knelt and hugged his gryphon around the neck. "It's okay, Box. It's not real. Just magic," he whispered. Ari churred and combed his beak through her trembling wing. Between their attentions, she stopped making soft, whining noises and took a hesitant peek at the sky.

I looked up too. I hadn't realized Rudrick had a lance waiting until he and Snowpoint flew past us and circled the monstrous rozash. Unlike most of the boys in this class with me, I'd seen a living rozash up close, but it'd been trying its best to kill Ari and me rather than hovering in place with its four wings churning the air rhythmically. It was about three times the size of a gryphon length-wise and thick enough around to ride.

We'd learned that Lithosians typically rode the two-headed variety into battle, as they were twice as smart and just as lightning-fast as rozash with one head and two wings, who were typically released to attack without the guidance of human riders.

Suddenly, the illusion lurched into motion, one set of jaws snapping at Snowpoint while the other expelled an abrasive cloud of sand. I smiled to myself as the gryphon rider avoided both attacks, engaging the rozash in an aerial dance that took them back and forth across the Green. The serpentine creature was faster than Snowpoint, but Rudrick was an experienced rider who made weaving around and outmaneuvering it look effortless.

"I could outfly any rozash," Ari said in response to my thoughts, almost spectating with me despite his blindness. *"They're just showing off."*

Well, it was working. Except for Sharde, who remained kneeling and soothing his gryphon, everyone's eyes were on the sky. We hadn't been taught much about actually fighting rozash yet, only that they were best engaged in teams of gryphon riders.

"One to be bait, four to break the wings," Ari supplied. He still prided himself on being excellent bait.

"He's going for the neck," I reported. Seeming to tire of the game, Rudrick rammed his lance into the fleshy juncture between its two heads. One seemed to die, flopping uselessly.

"Daring," Ari said. *"If you kill one head, the other goes berserk."*

"I don't think the illusion's going to do that." In fact, it faded away like he'd succeeded in killing it completely.

Snowpoint landed close by, and Rudrick hopped off her back, continuing class for the rest of the hour while Lord Gadric and Ellie returned to the fortress. In that time, I learned that the cadets attending Flight Training this year would be doing bookwork until their gryphons learned how to catch them if they fell out of the saddle. I remembered the struggle Ari and I had had with that last year and shuddered.

I remained in place as a bell signified a class change, watching most of the second-years file back inside. In their place came many familiar faces from my Flight Training class, third-years here to learn jousting. I waved to Valentic, the third-year who'd been my flight's leader last year. His gryphon, a speckled male named Birch, loped ahead of him to nuzzle Ari's neck. Some emotion passed between them before Birch circled around to flank Puzzlebox and comb his beak through her still-ruffled feathers.

Not every face was so welcome, however. Callan approached with one of his friends, smirking when our gazes met. "Hey, heretic," he said, crossing his arms as he stopped a few feet away. "Isn't jousting too violent for a Nilarite like you?"

I turned my head away with a "hmph" rather than acknowledge his baiting question.

"Seems like you're in the wrong place," he continued, not to be denied. "Maybe you should go live in a temple, where you belong."

"Shut up, Callan," Sharde said for me.

"Cadet-General Callan. I didn't see a salute from either of you, actually."

Rudrick shouted behind me, "If it isn't the Ace-to-be!" The instructor was beckoning to Callan.

If possible, he looked even more smug to be called up by his rank. "Remember your respects next time. Else you'll have a bad time during field training," he muttered before shouldering past Sharde and me to the front of the group and saluting smartly.

Rudrick waved him away and started class, explaining that Callan would be the first to come up and demonstrate. Callan had already taken this class last year, it turned out, but it was the kind the Academy had us repeat for extra mastery. While he talked, I turned to Sharde. "What's field training?" I asked in an undertone.

He sighed. "I'm not sure, actually. I just know it was why sometimes the second and third years would disappear further into the mountains for a day or two. I can pull an Ellie and deduce it has something to do with training in a field, though."

I rolled my eyes. *"Something like that,"* Ari agreed.

"What is it, really?"

"I think I'll leave you in suspense since you didn't ask me first."

"Ari..."

He clicked his beak at me with a rush of playful emotion. I rubbed the sensitive spot behind his ears as I watched Callan go through a few demonstrations for us. I was surprised to learn that we were starting with lance skills right away, everyone getting a chance to climb onto their gryphon with a practice lance.

Our task was to stay on the ground and attempt to spear a blemished fruit or aged vegetable resting on a stool. When it was my turn, I was surprised by the weight of the practice lance. I'd already seen that these were designed to shatter if they encountered any serious pressure—like a cadet's shield —but it would be a long time before we faced one of our peers.

Almost everyone who'd gone before me had missed the giant, wilting crown cabbage on their way by it. The lance wobbled unsteadily in my hold when Ari sped to a run. I lowered it, trying to stab the vegetable, and ended up plowing the wooden tip into the ground. With a *crack* it split in half, and Ari grunted at the sudden jolt that made me drop the lance completely.

"It's cheap, don't worry," Rudrick laughed, handing another to the next cadet after I collected the biggest shards of the broken lance.

Still, a few of the third-years jeered as I guided Ari back to our spot between Sharde and Valentic.

"You can't avoid violence here," Callan said as I passed him. "Just go home, Nilarite."

My cheeks stinging with embarrassment, I kept quiet and watched as a few of the most experienced third-years went last, each hitting the crown cabbages or little pieces of fruit without a problem. Well, now I knew how Callan would heckle me this year, even while I wore Lady Nilara's mark of protection. I secretly fumed, hoping she'd come smite him when Rudrick called him up last to show off by spearing multiple targets set up just for him.

Unfortunately, he remained free of godly wrath and returned inside while I shuffled off to my next class, Ground

Combat. It was just like last year, with a shirtless Commander Falirin expecting us to begin training with the long cavalry saber like we'd never had a break. I glanced around until I spotted Weslecker, breathing a sigh of relief when he smiled back at me. I had a chance at passing this class with him here to help.

My muscles were already aching by the time we sat for lunch. My whole flight sat at our usual table. "Hey, what's your last class?" Biggs asked. His schedule was already wrinkled beyond repair, and he rubbed it against the edge of the table while the rest of us dug out ours.

"Logistics," Weslecker said first.

Feyring recoiled from his schedule with a furrowed brow. "Linguistics?"

"Gryphon Taming," I said.

"Same." Sharde offered me a fist bump.

"So we're all kind of doing something different. Wonder what's going on with that," Weslecker commented.

"You mean you don't know, Cadet-General?" Korvic snipped.

"Contrary to what you might think and despite the title, I'm still a regular cadet," the young nobleman said with a heavy dose of his highbrow accent.

"Hey, instead of fighting, why don't we just sleep through the next class and find out for ourselves," Sharde drawled. "Who else has World Cultures next?"

About half of us did, myself included. I bounced in my seat, happy to see my favorite class. "I'm going to go get a good seat early," I said, leaving with Ari as soon as I finished my lunch.

World Cultures with Instructor Signe was our only glimpse of the life and culture of the warlike Rathi people who occupied the islands north of Altare. It was the only class taught by a woman, who was already seated on her stool when I came into the classroom and had a seat up front.

A maid cleaned up around the instructor, who kept her pride by pretending it wasn't happening. Signe had a few new wrinkles, her back tilted at an elderly slant, but her unusual lilac eyes were as sharp as ever. She had the icy skin tone and ivory white hair of a Rathi northerner and a twisted leg from a devastating injury that'd left her an outcast from her homeland.

In the back of the room, a scribe was already set up to record her next story. Over time, I'd pieced together that she was sharing things that otherwise wouldn't leave the Rathi Islands. And the stories were fanciful; heroes, monsters, personal legends, and sometimes even eldrafn featured in the tales she spun.

She didn't speak until the whole class filed in, most with less enthusiasm than my quick entrance. Sitting around listening to stories of a distant land wasn't all that interesting to some of the more action-minded young men who wanted nonstop talk of war and battle tactics, if they weren't picking up a weapon to train with.

Signe began in a hush. "This year, I am expected to teach you something new. Let us give thanks for another moment of time we are all together, breaking metaphorical bread and learning the tales and ways of my people."

Somewhere behind me, I picked up the sound of Sharde muffling a yawn.

"In the coming months, let us discuss war. I believe some of you will find use in that, yes?" She canted an eyebrow. "Up north, every day, warriors fight and die to defend their village and conquer a larger part of their island, perpetuating a cycle of violence that goes back centuries, all for the chance to live through the winter."

A few of us shuffled forward as she launched into her latest story. Today, she left off with her tale half-finished, dangling a tidbit to look forward to tomorrow.

CHAPTER 14

SPECIALTIES

Ari and I climbed to the top floor, where we were ushered to the back of the stables to join a small group of second-years. Five of us lined up to meet our instructor for Gryphon Taming, an average-looking gryphon rider wearing a set of thick, battered leathers that looked gouged by gryphon talons and maybe even a few bites.

"Hello, cadets," he said. I opened my mouth to reply "good afternoon, sir" in the same learned chorus as all our other instructors greeted us, but it seemed he didn't care if we greeted him. "I'm Captain Gemon, XO to the Commander of the Second Gryphon Flight and head tamer here. You've been selected to learn about the taming process, either because you have demonstrated a special bond with multiple gryphons or because you just have good reflexes."

I started to chuckle before I realized that wasn't a joke. Considering the state of Captain Gemon's armor and the fact that he was alive, good reflexes were a must for taming.

"The Academy offers second- and third-year students the opportunity to take a few different specialty classes. Since we have need of new, skilled tamers, this is a bigger group than usual," he said, tisking as he looked over us. "If you're a success, you'll be invited to join the Second, which is focused on the recruitment and training of cadets, the capture and taming of wild gryphons, and the continued welfare and aptitude testing of our trainees. Let's get started..."

Ari shifted uncomfortably next to me. *"I hope you can request a different class,"* he said. I picked up on his emotions and frowned. *"If you became a tamer, you'd end up being everything my father hates."*

My blood went cold. He was right. Roshawk had practically spat venom, talking about the humans who stole eggs and female gryphons from their nests when they were most vulnerable. I didn't want to be the one to break up wild families that way.

Captain Gemon introduced us to an adult gryphon temporarily named Rocky for the slate-colored stripes across his flank, using him to demonstrate different ways a wild beast might attack and in what situations it'd happen. I softened to the man while watching him speak softly to Rocky, making sure he didn't startle the wild-born beast too much.

"With patience and care, we will get Rocky Linked to a new cadet and off to train here at the Academy," he told us before dismissing class.

I started heading for the Commandant's office, seeing that we had a small window of time before dinner. "Hey, Sivana," Sharde said, catching up in a few long strides. "I need to get out of this class."

I turned a surprised look his way. "Uh, me too."

He stopped me in a corridor, a firm hand on my shoulder. "I'm sorry, but I need out a lot more than you," he said. There was a shadow in his gaze and a tremble in his fingers. "It's really important."

"What's wrong?" I murmured.

"Tell you later," he promised before going down toward

the Commandant's office ahead of me, with Puzzlebox rushing to keep up behind him.

With my brow still furrowed, I followed, just for us to find the door locked. "Maybe he'll be available after dinner," I said, startling when Sharde cursed and slammed his fist against the wood.

"I'm going to wait right here. You can too, if you want," he muttered, sitting propped against the wall across from the Commandant's office. Puzzlebox twittered softly and laid out in his lap.

Ari and I checked our Link at the same time, a moment similar to us exchanging a glance. *"I think we should stay with him,"* I said, to his agreement. I sat too and helped guide Ari to the ground so he could rest against me.

Several silent minutes passed. Sharde slowly lost the tension in his shoulders as he ruffled his gryphon's white belly fluff. He sighed heavily. "I know Captain Gemon already," he told me. "What he hasn't explained yet is that the Second Gryphon Flight screens every gryphon hatchling funneled to the Academy and puts down any that are deemed defective." His arm tightened defensively around Puzzlebox.

My gaze went from him to his sweetheart of a gryphon and back. Gods, just the implication of "defective" made me nervous. "You told me you Linked with her by accident?" I said, like a question.

"C'mon, you know me better than that," he scoffed. "But I didn't come here expecting to be a gryphon rider. I just wanted a job, and one of the soldiers admired my grit when I came to the front gate with a black eye, begging for a place to stay."

My brows raised, dozens of questions jumping to my tongue. "I was from the village. You know the one I've never earned a leisure day to visit? It is so remote that Fortress Aerie was literally the only other place I could go unless a courier from Final Flight had mercy and flew me away," he said.

"Oh, I didn't know," I said with quiet sympathy.

He waved that away. "That's just how I became a caretaker. They always need fresh faces to help with the gryphons and the dishes. Technically, I was an employee of the Second, even though my main job was taking care of the cadets' beasts."

I nodded in understanding. This, at least, was familiar, because I'd been an employee of the First when I was a caretaker in Kaiamear. We'd both been similarly insignificant pieces that kept the gryphon knight corps running.

"When the hatchlings arrive every year, it's an all-hands kind of event. Dozens of little gryphons and boys coming and going. It was pretty obvious Puzzlebox was different from the other hatchlings when she arrived. She was smaller and so clumsy and shy. Most of the candidates were too rough with her, so she'd hide. I watched the other gryphons find their riders quickly, but not her.

"It didn't take Captain Gemon long to suspect that she was 'defective' and started testing her. No one really wants to put down a baby gryphon, but let's face it, this is the military. If a gryphon doesn't show any aptitude to be a proper war beast one day, it's deemed a waste of resources."

"I know that all too well," I said bitterly, holding Ari all the tighter too. "Gryphons can't be owned as pets. They're property of the Crown alone, wild or tamed. What kind of tests can a baby gryphon even do?"

"They were very basic," he said with a sigh. "One of them was like the cup game fake magicians play. We'd take three cups and put a treat under one of them and swap it around, giving her points for how quickly and accurately she could identify the cup with the treat under it. Another was laying a blanket over her and counting how many seconds it took for her to crawl out from under it. There were five tests. She failed them all."

I inhaled sharply. "So, you Linked with her to save her?"

"I mean, yes, but that was after I tried a lot of other things. First, I worked with her to figure out why she was failing the tests. I took time to sit in her stall to try to 'socialize' her." He put up air quotes. "She tended to hide under her nest all the time after being handled by so many strangers, so I'd sit against the wall and try to solve the stupid puzzle one of the other caretakers had given me." He pulled out a worn puzzle box, the kind with each of its faces painted a different color. It was hopelessly jumbled up, but his gryphon perked up immediately when she saw it.

"She was scared of me too at first, but she really liked this." He twisted the box, making it click as it rotated. Puzzlebox squeaked and pawed at him, leaning forward until he placed it in her beak for her to chew on. "Eventually, she would come out to sit with me and watch me try to solve it. Her head would twitch a bit each time it clicked, and I had an idea. Her third round of testing was coming up, and if she failed again, that was it. So, I ran her through all five tests and taught her how to pass them. Like, I'd lay a blanket over her and then click the box, and she rushed to come out from under it. The day came, and she ended up passing four out of five with me and the puzzle box there.

"And I reasoned with Captain Gemon that the last one was unfair anyway. A Tulari would generate a lot of noise or a scary illusion, and any hatchling would be afraid of that." He frowned, likely thinking back to her reaction to the rozash illusion this morning like I was. She'd been the only gryphon afraid of it. "So, she passed. And after that, I Linked with her because she'd become my buddy. I couldn't imagine anyone else as her rider, even if it got me in a ton of trouble at the time. But…maybe you see now why I need to get out of that class. Gemon was already suspicious of me. I don't want him to get a good look at how Box has developed since then."

"You think he'd try to test her again?" I doubted Gemon had that kind of time on his hands, but Sharde knew him better than I did.

"It's possible. So, I'd rather not leave that option open." He looked up and scrambled to his feet. I followed suit automatically, the two of us greeting the Commandant together as he returned to his office with a stack of folders.

He let us in and sat behind his desk, arranging folders as Sharde and I asked to be moved out of the Gryphon Taming class. Night settled into her nest, prickling the hair on the back of my neck. The Commandant's office was set up with uncomfortable chairs that trapped a cadet between two equally deadly forces—a ranking officer in charge of discipline and his wild-born female gryphon listening in behind us.

The Commandant steepled his fingers. "I personally assigned both of you to the Gryphon Taming specialty," he said pointedly. "Being chosen as a tamer for the Second is a high honor that rarely goes to low-ranking cadets."

"With all due respect, sir, I would still like to be removed from the class," Sharde said.

While I'd reeled back at the Commandant's tone and the insinuation that this was more than I deserved as a cadet with a lower ranking, Sharde hadn't missed a moment and didn't flinch away from the glare leveled his way.

"I don't permit any cadet to come change around their schedule without a really good reason," the Commandant said. "It's been all of one day."

"But sir—" I began to say.

"The answer is no. The gryphon knight corps needs tamers more than ever. I would go so far as to say both of your placements in the class is nonnegotiable." The commanding officer's expression grew more severe.

I knew that was the end of the line for now. I tugged on Sharde's elbow, motioning with my head to the door. His jaw was clenched so hard, I feared his teeth would crack, and he turned back to the Commandant to demand, "Why is it nonnegotiable?"

"Careful, cadet. You're coming dangerously close to insubordination."

"Just help me understand. If I have to be there, tell me why," he pressed.

The Commandant brushed his bottom lip with a thumb. "There are thirty new cadets at the Academy this year," he said. "Every year, there are fewer gryphons. When I first took over this position, we would have fifty-some beasts needing riders. One year, we had a record: sixty-two."

I rested my palm over the symbol of Lord Orion hiding under my uniform. "They're not having babies," I said.

He considered, eyes darting between Sharde and me like he was thinking of how much to share with us. "We have reason to believe there are fewer wild gryphons than there used to be," he said with a sigh. "There is a need for compassionate young tamers who understand gryphon behavior to have a chance at gentling the most vicious of adult beasts. When I thought of which cadets would be able to rise to this challenge, you two came to mind first. I *know* you will succeed.

"Besides, this way, neither of you will see combat." I noticed his gaze on me and sat up straighter. "You will be an asset to the corps and out of the nation's gaze. That is why it's nonnegotiable. Now, you are both dismissed. Rest up. You've finished the easiest day of this year."

Sharde and I walked to the mess hall silently. He brushed his hand through Puzzlebox's feathers, his gaze far away, while I tingled with awareness. Gryphons were becoming extinct. Lord Orion had told me as much: *At the rate we're going, the only gryphons will be ones born into captivity within a generation, and we know what dangerous lives they live.*

I had the uncomfortable feeling that, as unpleasant as it was to consider a future where I contributed to the capturing and taming of wild beasts, this was too related to my conversation with Lord Orion. He'd known this was in my future, and he expected me to produce a solution to a problem decades in the making.

No pressure.

CHAPTER 15

ELEMENTARY

For a couple weeks, I got by on things I'd learned ahead of time. While the other second-years were learning how to play hoops, a fast-paced aerial sport, Ari and I scored a few easy wins. I may have lost some of my physical fitness, but after my summer adventure with Ari, I knew we were in sync over every flight exercise.

Except for one, of course, early in the day. It was impossible to practice flying in an element alone, so I had to learn the hard way. There were five positions to an element, with our captain at the front of the V-formation, flanked by two people on either side. Prince Mateo was immediately the captain of Element A, with Weslecker to his right and Barlowe to his left.

Ari and I flew behind Barlowe, who remained his same insufferable self even without Callan's leadership.

"He's banking early," I reported one morning as we circled the illusion of a stationary rozash in Advanced Anatomy and Tactics. Barlowe had his gryphon tilt her wings sharply. If I didn't notice it, Ari would read the shift in air currents and inevitably break formation.

We'd crashed into Barlowe twice already and ruined a

perfect V-formation countless times. But I didn't ask to switch around our placement. A soft warble from Puzzlebox reminded me why. With us tilting right, it put her closest to the rozash illusion. Even with her panicking midair, she had Weslecker and Ironfeather's steady presence to help her and Sharde stay in position.

"Mireille says we're trying this again," Ari told me. We didn't bother with shouting orders aloud, instead relying on the gryphons' subtle magic. Mireille conveyed orders from Prince Mateo, who was determined not to be embarrassed at the first monthly competition tomorrow. For second-years, there was an added layer of complexity. We were no longer competing for our flights, but instead our elements. That made way for seven placements rather than four.

We were a built-in hoops team and would be flying in V-formation for our first event, showing off our coordination… or lack thereof. By the time we landed at the end of class, I was simmering with frustration at Barlowe.

"If you want to win the competition tomorrow, you'll stop messing us up on purpose," I said to him, loud enough for the whole element to hear.

Prince Mateo's dark gaze flashed between us. "Don't blame him for your troubles, Walker."

Barlowe grinned when our captain's attention turned away. He was a wiry thing, all sinew with hair so fair I could see through it to his eggshell-like head. "I'm not doing anything. You're just imagining things," he said, shrugging. "Sucks to be rank thirty-five, huh? Guess you better go retire to a temple somewhere."

My hands balled into fists. Ari pushed his bulk between me and the other cadet before I could do something I would regret. *"We'll probably get reassigned to a new element after tomorrow,"* he said. *"Let it go."*

I turned on my heel and crossed the field to Ellie's side, helping her pack the various items Lord Gadric needed to summon his illusions. This was the only time I saw her unless it was the evening and she was deep in a textbook. "How goes the project?" I asked her, wanting a distraction.

She adjusted her glasses and broke into a wide grin. "We're still experimenting with wires, but I'll have results to show you soon," she said.

Much of Ellie's training, I'd learned, was based off the whims of Lord Gadric. She was going to be an engineer for the military one day, but until then, her mage mentor had her take on various projects to reverse-engineer magic-made items and build them back up again with her own two hands.

"Lord Gadric's been trying to create a magelight that doesn't use any magic his whole life," she'd told me at the start of this project. "He thinks we can do it this time."

The only thing I'd learned from watching her was that inventing was a difficult, demoralizing process. But I watched her get up and dust herself off again and again as each of her round, wire-filled glass balls refused to float or light up on command.

"We just need to be successful once," Ellie said with a smile. "We just need to get the internal power source to cooperate."

I gave her a friendly nudge. "I know you're going to get it. Imagine how many lives you'd change if you managed to make a magic-free magelight."

"Not only with inexpensive light, but saved magic for all the craftsmen Tulari." Her honey-toned eyes twinkled with possibility. "Think of what *they* could make if they didn't have to waste their gifts on magelights."

While I was nodding in agreement, Puzzlebox slunk over and sat on her haunches behind Ellie. "You did a good job today, Box," I said, reaching out to stroke the gryphon's wing.

Leaning around Ellie, Puzzlebox met my gaze, sadness rolling off her in a thick wave. Static shivered over my arms, leaving goosebumps behind, as something between us clicked into place, like Sharde sliding a panel on her favorite toy. She didn't just let me take a glimpse at her emotional state; she spoke to me as clearly as Ari.

"This isn't fun anymore." Puzzlebox sounded like a little girl, scared and teary. I went down on one knee, holding my arms out to her and feeling her take comfort as she slid into my hold. She hid her face in my chest.

"It's going to be okay. I know the illusions are scary, but they're not real," I whispered to her, stroking down her neck.

Her eyes flicked closed. *"Scary thing gone?"*

"Yes, we're done for the day."

In the pause that followed, I had a realization. "Do you understand what I'm saying?" I asked aloud.

She tilted her head at an inquisitive angle to match my tone but didn't reply. I took a deep breath and focused on her as if we had a Link and could communicate as freely as I did with Ari. *"We're done for the day,"* I repeated.

Puzzlebox twittered with relief. *"Noah says we have to do this every day,"* she said petulantly. Gods above. She *was* a little girl on the inside. What was it Sharde had said about her, when he introduced us? *She's my big baby.* I remembered it being a strange way of talking about a gryphon.

It was about time for a class change, and Ellie was about to pick up her things and go. She was watching me and Puzzlebox, wringing her hands.

"Well, it's just like a game," I told the gryphon, feeling her perk up. *"The monsters aren't real. We're pretending they are so we can learn what to do if we meet a real one."*

Puzzlebox sat back on her haunches, head cocked at a birdlike angle. Her beak parted a bit with happiness when Sharde came to join us, my connection with her fading to nothing but that static feeling even as she bunted his thigh.

"Someone's ready for jousting." He ruffled her feathers, earning a playful squeak from her.

Ellie opened her mouth and then closed it again, shaking

her head. "See you guys later," she said, flashing a shy smile Sharde's way as we both waved in farewell.

As I went about the rest of my day, I shared what happened with Ari, sure it was a breakthrough with the magic pendant. He projected some steep disbelief. *"You've talked to my mother in the past,"* he pointed out.

"Not like this, though! My connection with Puzzlebox was a lot clearer." I paused for a moment, trying to probe the Link for a better idea of his emotional state. *"That's okay, right? I wanted to try talking to her again, see if it's possible."*

"If you want," he said. Amazingly, I sensed nothing negative from his side of the Link. He truly didn't mind. Last year, I'd learned the hard way that he didn't appreciate me giving attention to other gryphons. We'd both come a long way since then.

Sensing the direction of my thoughts, he added, *"Puzzlebox is a friend. Of course you can talk to her, as long as you talk to me more."*

"I will," I promised.

"Good," he said. *"We're kind of stuck with each other."*

We formed up bright and early for our first monthly competition, spreading out into our elements. Across the Green, a drill sergeant was loudly explaining how the monthly competition worked to the first years, who would be seeing it for the first time.

Prince Mateo paced in front of Element A, lined up and waiting. The formation flying competition was first thing for us. "I want to see Element Alpha's flag in the wind for the next month. You're all either Kite Flight or Falcon Flight, used to being first," he was saying.

Beside me, Barlowe snickered. "Yes, sir. *We* are," he said, indicating only the prince and himself. Prince Mateo was still one of our Cadet-Generals, so we'd gotten used to deferring to him.

Our first major field training assignment was next week, where theoretically, all our ranking cadets would be put through their paces in a military exercise meant to mimic a real-life situation. The third-year I'd asked had been sparse on the details of what exactly we might face.

"That means putting aside petty differences," the prince continued, his gaze flashing to his flight-mate. "If you have someone behind you, fly well and make them look good too."

"I always do," Barlowe said.

I sneered. "Liar."

"It's not my fault your beast is blind."

"No, but I swear to the gods, you better not make us crash again," I said in an undertone.

"Or else what?" he asked just as quietly.

I hesitated to truly threaten him and missed my chance when we were called up to fly first as Element A. The task was simple: perform three aerial maneuvers as an element. The team that was most in-sync won. Night would monitor the sky and, through the Commandant, tell our captain what he wanted to see next.

Of course, since Elements A and B were learning these techniques in class already, we'd be given the harder maneuvers, while the other elements would be allowed to fly lower to the ground and just do their best.

We took to the sky, Prince Mateo out first, flanked by Barlowe and Weslecker, and then Sharde and me forming the end of our V-formation. "*Sharp right,*" Ari reported. Mireille turned in a hard bank, and the rest of us followed suit. No problem. We could do this.

The second maneuver was a dive, a harder one to get right as a group. Mireille and Barlowe's gryphon were slower than Ari or Ironfeather, who had the advantage in body shape.

Puzzlebox just tended to fall, and at the end of today's dive, she struggled to pull up while the rest of the team outpaced her.

The last thing we needed to do as a team was a switch-back, the hardest move Rudrick had taught us so far. There were two ways to turn around, and the switchback was the vital one for high-stakes combat, with each of us turning on a different pattern of wingbeats to turn around rapidly.

Up front, Mireille had the sharpest change in direction, whipping around fast. While Ari executed the turn, his wing clipped Barlowe's gryphon. We spun with too much momen-tum, flipping vertically rather than horizontally several times before Ari regained control. I tasted bile, sure I was about to be sick.

Barlowe and his gryphon had spun the opposite way, while the rest of our element continued flying. We hurried to catch up, but the damage was done. There was no way that was a first-place performance, and it was obvious Prince Mateo was thinking that too when we wheeled around to land and he pierced me with a disgusted glare.

"Great going, Walker," he muttered.

Barlowe heaped on within a heartbeat. "Don't mess up hoops for us too."

"Maybe if you knew how to turn, that wouldn't have happened," I snapped.

"Your gryphon clipped mine!" Barlowe protested.

Sergeant Kobarn shouldered between us. "Yap yap yap," he said, flapping his fingers. "Walk it off before one of you does something stupid."

I breathed an aggrieved huff and paced onto the Green to watch the other elements perform. As Element B showed off with nearly perfect coordination, I replayed that moment in my head. I was fairly sure Barlowe had drifted closer to us and turned at an incorrect angle so our gryphons would clip each other. It'd happened within a split second.

But it still stung that Prince Mateo had immediately decided I was the one who'd messed up. Even if Barlowe hadn't intended to throw me off, he was still equally liable for messing up the maneuver. Ari fumed next to me, just as upset even if he hadn't seen the details.

That was the mindset we went into the next event with. We played hoops in our elements, and usually, Ari loved this game, but we were both too focused on coming back from the embarrassment of clipping Barlowe's gryphon. We had something to prove now with most of the Academy watching.

Hoops was played with two differently sized balls, and there were different rules for each when it came to scoring. A good hoops player could watch both balls and the third target as well, a neutral gryphon circling above us with a large brass ring clasped in their beak. Today, it was Snowpoint, and I watched her like a hawk. The brass ring was worth several extra points if it was successfully caught and flown through one of the hoops, but if it hit the ground, it couldn't be picked back up.

Ari and I were determined. We were going to score as much as possible before getting that brass ring. We'd secure the win for our element singlehanded.

We were doing great when Snowpoint dropped the ring. *"Dive!"* I exclaimed, even as another cadet from Element B did the same.

Ari and I arrowed past them, committing to a speedy fall with Ari elongating his body and folding his wings tight to his body. Wind ripped at my face, pulling and distorting the skin uncomfortably. I leaned in the saddle, holding my hand out for the ring. It was maybe a foot out of reach.

Tingles rushed over my skin. Ari burst out a screech of surprise and adjusted so I could snatch the ring. As soon as it was in my hold, I pulled up on the reins. His wings burst out, and we sailed upward.

But first, Ari scrapped his talons across the grass. He loved doing that after a successful dive.

I was simultaneously pumping the brass ring in the air and releasing a gryphon screech of joy as we flew straight through one of the hoops. I jerked away from the feeling, blinking rapidly. For a moment, it'd been like the first time Ari and I had flown together, sharing emotions and feelings so closely over a new Link that we'd practically been the same person.

I'd felt Ari purposefully waiting until the last second to complete the dive and guide himself through the hoop without my help.

I looked down at him in astonishment, and he echoed it back. *"That's right. I saw through your eyes,"* he said.

"It worked!" I touched my fingertips to my heart, where the symbol of Lord Orion rested, warm against my skin. When he landed, I dismounted and flung my arms around his neck, hiding my tears in his feathery neck.

It's really worked. All the hardship we'd gone through to reach the gods had been worth it for my brave gryphon to have another chance at sight. He keened with me, both of us crying with sheer delight.

I couldn't imagine what it looked like, for the two of us to break down into a tearful embrace over what looked to everyone else like a routine hoops victory. But for once, I didn't care.

CHAPTER 16

SECOND RIDER

I WAS SO THRILLED that I didn't even care Element B's flag was raised at the end of the day as the second-year victors of the monthly competition. It was a simple flag, a yellow "B" on a white background.

I was smiling when our ranks were posted and I saw my name at the bottom, still thirty-five of thirty-five. We kept our same elements in anticipation of our first Field Training day. It didn't matter.

Ari had seen through my eyes! We didn't quite know *how* it'd happened, except it'd felt like we'd gotten so in sync he'd naturally shared my senses. If we could figure out how to repeat that moment, it would be a huge breakthrough.

I rode that high until lights-out, when I closed my eyes and entered the same nightmare of Ari and me facing an eldrafn with a wingspan that filled the horizon. Our Link soured with the fear and dread of dying yet again in our dreams. The now-familiar tingling rushed over my skin, erupting around the magical token resting against my chest.

Ari jerked back and slowed, projecting a feeling of dizziness as the first lightning bolts arced toward us. I leaned left to drag him out of the way, expecting the attack.

"I never realized how awful human eyesight is," he commented.

"You didn't complain earlier!" I leaned the other way, panicking when a web of electricity threatened to close around us.

"We were playing hoops. I've caught the ring and flown through a hoop countless times."

As he talked, he started weaving around in the air, dodging the eldrafn's lightning bolts by pure luck. We survived for several minutes, a new record, while I clutched the combat lance and kite shield, looking for some kind of way to harm this creature of electricity and wind before it killed us.

"Look left," Ari demanded. *"No, more left!"* I jerked, spotting the attack a split second too late. The dream shattered, and I soon woke.

I moved to leap out of bed. *Wait, it's Saturday.* My weight thumped back on the mattress, and I smiled to myself. My element hadn't won the competition, but we hadn't been last, either, which meant I had a full weekend to myself.

I reached out over my Link, trying to get Ari's attention. When he was bedded down in the stables a few levels above me, our connection was noticeably thinner. Still, I received a sensation back like Ari snipping his beak at me. *"No,"* he said, picking up on the direction of my thoughts.

"C'mon, don't be lazy," I cajoled.

With some hearty grumbling on his part, I had him groomed and saddled within the hour. The sun was just beginning to peek over the raised horizon of the mountains. *"You know, most cadets sleep in on the weekend,"* Ari said, resting on his haunches next to me while we waited in front of the single open grate for more warm sunshine.

"Most cadets don't have..." I drifted off when a familiar man's voice drifted by us. Ari raised his beak, hearing Captain Gemon too.

The head tamer was deep in conversation with two senior caretakers as they headed deeper in the stables.

"They're talking about Puzzlebox," Ari confirmed for me. While I thought I'd heard a hint of her name, his sensitive hearing must've picked up on everything. He nudged me encouragingly when I wondered if we could pick up on more of the conversation from his stall.

I led him back to the stall and pretended to be oiling his flight feathers, while he tilted his head up and closed his lids over his fake eyes in concentration. *"Gemon is venting,"* Ari reported. *"He watched Puzzlebox fly yesterday and knows she's not suitable for military service."*

I shook my head in disbelief. Sharde had been right about Gemon. *"I suppose it was only a matter of time,"* I mumbled. Puzzlebox's struggles in the air were becoming too severe to ignore. Sharde had outpaced her growth, I thought, becoming too big and heavy for her to carry.

"The Commandant is dragging his heels on approving another round of testing for her. He's frustrated," Ari said. *"It sounds like all three of them agree that Sharde should be performing better than he is, too. He was a quick study as a caretaker and shouldn't be such a hopeless case as a cadet."*

"Gods above. This is bad," I said. I sat back in the hay, dragging a hand down my face. *"Ari...you've been through all this before. Tell me the truth."*

My gryphon clicked his beak uncomfortably as I took a moment to think of how to verbalize the question I didn't want to speak into existence. It felt like I was about to say the Gatekeeper's true name and invite death into the Academy.

"Would they really execute her if she failed their tests now?" he said for me gently. *"Maybe. I've met a couple gryphons like her when I was here with...with Alamid. They had failed to find riders, so one day, they just disappeared."*

"But Puzzlebox has a rider," I said, clinging to a shred of hope.

"The cadet that purposefully fails at everything." He tilted his head thoughtfully. *"To get attention on him, not her. I think he's going to need new tricks if he wants to graduate. Do you want to help?"*

I was nearly affronted he had to ask. *"Of course!"*

"Good, because they're talking about excluding Sharde from the testing process when the Commandant approves it. But they might try to bring in other cadets to watch how to test gryphons."

"We have to be there," I said.

"We have to be there," he echoed in agreement. *"And…I have another idea."*

I felt his hesitance. Whatever the idea was, it was hard for him to stomach, but I felt his protective emotions for Puzzlebox fight off his trepidation. *"You talked to her the other day,"* he said quietly. *"I felt it. For a few minutes, you were Linked to her."*

My nostrils flared in astonishment. Linking to two gryphons was impossible.

"If you could Link with her again, maybe she'd tolerate you as a rider. You could take her flying instead of me. I can pretty much guarantee you weigh less than Sharde."

I saw where this was going. If I could just give her experience pulling off the maneuvers she struggled to do with Sharde on her back, perhaps it would help her. But this was also one of Ari's fears…that I'd find another gryphon and abandon him. He shook himself as I remembered the moment the Commandant had reprimanded me for paying more attention to other gryphons rather than him.

"No, it's different. I'm giving you permission," he said, nudging me with his beak. *"It's never been done before, and it might not work, but I see how you can help Puzzlebox, and I think you should do it."*

"Okay," I murmured. But first, I hugged him tightly around the neck. *"Remember that I love you. You're my best friend."*

He shifted, nearly embarrassed. *"You don't have to get all mushy on me."* I supposed males were males, human or otherwise.

I kissed him on the beak and left him to rouse Puzzlebox, resting in a stall on the other side of the stables. "Good morning, Box," I cooed, letting myself in as she peered at me blearily. "Want to play a game?"

Oh, now she was awake for that. She twittered and looked around in excitement. Maybe she didn't fully understand human speech, but "play" and "game" had an immediate reaction. I sat across from her, looking into her liquid dark eyes, but she was too excited to sit still, instead getting up and winding around me.

After giving her a thorough rub, she finally settled in my lap and met my gaze long enough for me to feel a stirring of emotion. Last time, her emotions were heightened, and I think that affected how quickly we created a temporary Link. *"What's the game?"* she was asking.

"We can't play without Sharde," I told her, and she tilted her head with a bit of confusion. *"Without Noah."*

"Oh! He's awake," she reported. *"And confused."*

"Can you tell him to come see us?"

"Okay!"

It didn't take him long to arrive. Maybe, like Ari, he felt something strange along his Link along with whatever Puzzlebox had told him. "We need to talk," I said.

Sharde was still rubbing the sleep from his eyes. "You know, no one likes to hear those words. Ever."

"Feel like going for an early morning ride?" I suggested.

Though suspicious, Sharde saddled up Puzzlebox and followed me into the sky. We were allowed to leave on the weekends, but it was frowned upon unless we'd won some sort of reward. Usually, the gryphons alone would spread their wings and fly to the northeast, which was the direction I chose.

There was a patch of land that I learned was used for Field Training, which was far enough away from the fortress that I hadn't known about it as a first-year. It was large enough to have upward of sixty cadets at a time doing…whatever Field Training was about. We'd find out soon.

I landed in the middle of a clearing, where we could talk without interruptions. Puzzlebox wrestled with Ari behind us as I told Sharde everything I'd heard today. He paled the more I spoke, fear twisting his expression.

"Without me," he said. "They want to test her without me there."

"Yes. But…I have an idea." This was the hard part, though, because I couldn't tell him I was using one-of-a-kind magic from a god. "I was thinking, maybe she needs some strength training to bear your weight in the air. Maybe if Puzzlebox starts taking turns and dives better, they won't want to test her at all."

His lips quirked. "Yeah?"

"What if I took her into the sky?"

"That's impossible, Sivana. Gryphons only have one rider," he said with a scoff.

I flashed a sheepish smile. "It's worth a try? She can always refuse to fly if she doesn't want to." Without telling him about the magic I wore, I needed him to give it a try here. My temporary Link with Puzzlebox was broken again, but in a strange way, I was aware of her behind me, rolling around with Ari, who I sensed in full definition.

"You know, I've never considered what'd actually happen if we tried to ride each other's gryphons," he admitted. He called over his gryphon by making kissy noises, rubbing her fluffy wings affectionately after she came running. "Try it, I guess, but I won't feel bad if she bucks you off."

I stood, waiting until she was distracted and gazing up at Sharde with adoration. That was when I grabbed her saddle horn and swung myself into the narrow-set saddle over her shoulders. She immediately flattened like a cat, head craned all the way around to stare at me with wide eyes.

"See, I told you," Sharde said.

What he didn't realize, though, was she and I made a new connection in that moment, clearer than ever. *"What are you doing?"* she squeaked in my mind.

"I was thinking we could go flying together, if that's okay." I was tempted to frame it as a game, but I recognized not everything could be one. Puzzlebox would see right through me if I tried to use that as the reasoning for everything.

She turned back to Sharde, who nodded and patted her neck reassuringly. He laughed in disbelief. "I think this is happening," he said.

Puzzlebox backed away from him and pranced up to Ari, a bouncy ride for me. Strangely, their emotional exchange wasn't a one-way feeling anymore. Ari assured her he was okay with her taking me flying, and she was practically vibrating with excitement, thinking it'd be fun.

She lurched her way into the air, huffing from the effort. As we ascended slowly, I sensed the strain on her shoulders and wing joints, all soreness that hadn't faded yet. We circled up and up at a pace she could sustain. *"Okay, Box, time for you to show off,"* I suggested with a smile.

She perked up. *"Okay!"*

We practiced every maneuver she should've already mastered with Sharde. Diving, banking, turning. So used to my gryphon's precise motions, I felt a little seasick on her back. Her flying was curved where it should be sharp, slow and wobbly especially at the bottom of dives. I hadn't realized how big a difference there was between her and my own beast.

However, no matter the maneuver or how sore she was, the only thing she felt in flight was pure joy. I laughed and grinned even as I noted where she could improve. When we landed and I climbed out of her saddle, she dashed straight for Ari and nuzzled up against his neck.

"Glad you had fun," he murmured, pawing at her until she settled and let him groom her wing feathers.

Sharde stood in the middle of the field, flight goggles on. "Well, what do you think?" he asked. "She seemed to enjoy that."

"I think I can work with her, as long as you're okay with it." I watched his expression, sure I could see some uncertainty there. "Just until Gemon stops trying to test her."

He sighed, rubbing a hand over his military-short hair. "You're not acquainted with Gemon if you think he's going to back down. You know what, though? If he's looking for my tricks, he'll miss yours. Even if we fly out here every weekend, nobody at the Academy would suspect Puzzlebox has a second rider."

We agreed, however, that someone would accuse us of fraternization first. He planned to invite a few of our flightmates and Ellie out next weekend. In the meantime, he explored the field for the rest of the day while I tried to train Puzzlebox. Maybe it'd give us a leg up for our first Field Training day.

CHAPTER 17

TRAINING IN A FIELD

A few days later, we assembled to one side of the training field a short flight away from the fortress. The third-years lined up on the other side, and I stood at attention with the rest of my flight, minus a few people. Weslecker was deep in conversation with Prince Mateo and the Commandant, learning what our objective was and finally acting as our Cadet-Generals.

Sergeant Kobarn had finally explained what we were doing, simulating real combat. The third-years were the Altarians today, which meant the second-years were Lithosians. Most of the instructors expected us to get utterly annihilated by the more experienced cadets, but not Sarge. He'd taken Kite Flight aside and shown us a crudely drawn map of the training field and the best places to hide our "king and queen," who were Ironfeather and Mireille for the first game.

"Make me proud," he'd said loudly, clapping Feyring on the shoulder hard enough to stagger our current flight leader.

Feyring stood at attention in front of us now, quivering with nerves. There were a few rules, but the most important one was to follow orders. He'd be the one to communicate orders to us and make sure we followed them properly.

"I think the best we could hope for is to give the enemy some resistance," Ari suggested as the minutes ticked by. We were waiting for our High Command to come to a decision on our strategy. *"We would need some serious dumb luck to outfly the third years."*

"That's what I'm worried about," I said. Many of my peers weren't cleared to do much than hover yet, so they would be easy pickings in the first part of the battle. We'd carry thin pieces of wood and "tag" each other with pokes of them. Anyone tagged would be considered dead and sit out the second half, when the survivors would fight each other with practice swords until one side "killed" the other side's royalty.

A game could take all day, I'd learned. Well, it would once we knew what we were doing. The drill sergeants were apparently betting that we'd be playing three games today before the sun went down.

Eventually, Feyring was called up to learn the strategy; then he had us huddle to discuss it. "We're hiding our royalty at the very edge of the field boundaries to the northeast. Surviving cadets will all be going on the offensive. We expect they'll be doing the same, so they won't have many cadets hanging back to defend their royalty."

"Gods, we're going to lose, aren't we?" Sharde laughed. *"That's* their great plan?"

"Well, once we do this a few times, we'll have a better idea of what strategies will work," Biggs suggested.

Sharde shrugged. "I'm just saying, we're supposed to be coordinating as flights."

I watched Korvic's expression turn sarcastic. "Guess you'll just have to take charge next time," he said.

"I don't think they're ready for *my* battle strategies."

Korvic rolled his eyes. "Okay, Sharde. We'll see if they ever give you command."

"You're going to regret saying that one day," I said.

Off in the woods, the instructors blew a horn. It was our signal to get in the air. We scrambled onto our gryphons and separated into our elements. Lucky for Element A, every cadet flew this round, which meant we were a full five strong. *"Mireille says we are to avoid engagement. We want as few cadets tagged as possible,"* Ari reported.

"Roger that." I leaned us into a hard left bank as we avoided the rush of a third-year element. Immediately, the air filled with gryphon shrieks and competitive cadets.

"That shouldn't count!" shouted a Harrier Flight member nearby.

A different element of third-years were screaming their heads off as they chased us around. *"Can you see from my eyes?"* I asked Ari.

"No. I think you're too excited."

That would make sense. My heart threatened to burst from a combination of exhilaration and fear as more than one weapon came swinging our way. We weren't even using practice lances, and I saw why now, as an enthusiastic third year cracked his stick in half while whacking Barlowe across the back.

I snickered. Couldn't have happened to a nicer young man.

I tried to calm myself for Ari's sake. I'd come to realize that he and I were rarely as in sync as we needed to be to reach the point where we were sharing senses and that was on me. Even now, I felt the steady drumming of his heart as he responded to how I turned and tugged on the reins, focused and excited in a subdued way to be in the air with me. His emotions today were a steady stream, and mine the sailed fish that kept leaping out of the water.

While I focused inward, a streak of red and maroon flashed in the corner of my eye. I turned with dread to see Callan pushing Sunset hard to catch up with us, but there was no stick in his hand.

The blunt tip of it bounced off my shoulder with bruising force a moment later. "Ow," I muttered. That must've been a perfect javelin throw to hit so hard.

"Hah! You're dead, Walker," he shouted, cupping his hands over a victorious grin.

I glared his way and pulled on Ari's reins, slowing him and wheeling carefully past a few low fliers to land in the middle of the open field area, where the "dead" were gathered. Three more third-years poked me on the way down, uncaring that I was already out.

"Long time no see," Korvic greeted dryly when we landed, and I loosened the riding harness to dismount.

I curbed my scowl, glaring at the grass like it'd personally wronged me. "I got distracted," I said.

"S'okay, you're in good company." He hooked his thumb behind him, where most of our peers stood around in various states of disgruntlement.

Sarge was here too, shaking his head in disappointment beside two of the other drill sergeants. They were supposed to be in the woods, making sure cadets stuck to the rules, but by their lack of urgency, I knew they'd already written off this game.

"You ever see them laugh before?" I asked, gesturing toward the three relaxed men. Sarge had a deep belly laugh that he unleashed while another sergeant recalled a victorious moment when last year's graduated Ace, Karos Seaworth, knocked three of his opponents on their rears after executing a surprise attack from one of the trees.

Korvic smirked. "No way. Drills, being real people?" he said with a hefty dose of sarcasm.

Credell came over to join us as the horn sounded again, and the surviving cadets swerved into the woods. "How long do you think this will take?" he murmured.

We had about ten cadets "alive," while they had double the number. There was a five-minute pause here, where survivors could huddle and amend their strategy, while the royalty got into place too. Gryphons from both sides mingled and groomed each other, the more experienced ones settling in to wait.

"Not too long," I said hopefully. Especially when one of the drill sergeants decided they didn't like all this standing around and had us start PT. Running laps rather than hiding out in the forest with a training sword *definitely* felt like punishment.

It couldn't have taken more than an hour before we were called to line up in our flights. We'd lost, of course. Commander Rudrick went down our chain of command and fired everyone before calling up the young men who'd take their places. I leaned forward slightly, eager to hear my name as one of the promoted, but of course it wasn't called.

"Five minutes. We just have to avoid being hit for that long," I said to Ari as we waited for our new High Command to strategize.

Ari flashed a feeling of resignation. *"Callan is going to come for us again. I assume it's his personal mission to get us out every round."*

He was probably right. We took to the air again, but this time, I was ready for the adrenaline rush that hit the moment ten enemy gryphons swarmed our element. Somehow, I had to keep myself calm enough to match Ari, who was astoundingly unruffled, if I wanted his help navigating the sky. *"It's because all I have to do is follow orders. I can't see the odds we face,"* he joked.

"No kidding," I sighed. It was a lost cause, though, because I realized I was too jumpy to match emotional states with Ari, and trying any harder would get me smacked by a practice weapon. I watched my element get picked off instead. Sharde was an easy out with Puzzlebox chirping happily to the two gryphons passing by her as their riders tagged hers.

Mireille squawked in frustration when Prince Mateo was

targeted next. I ducked under a thrown stick and broke formation by dipping Ari lower in the air when I saw Weslecker was tagged too. Barlowe was on his own... I wanted to play in the next round on the ground.

"Do you have eyes on Callan?" Ari asked.

The sky around us was full of chaos, whooping and screeching cadets chasing each other. There was a sense of coordination to our opponents, but I noticed a single figure turn and spot me, breaking away from his element as well. Callan hefted his stick with a grin, holding it out like a lance as he and Sunset raced to meet us. *"Yes, coming right for us. Hold steady."*

At the last moment, I had Ari lean out of the way and held my own weapon out. Callan broke it in half on his way by. "Got you!" I exclaimed, laughing. It'd worked! He scowled as I pointed toward the ground with the broken tip of my stick.

With him out and only half a weapon, I led Ari through a few sky sprints. His beak parted with joy to really spread his wings and zoom through the air, and for a few precious moments, I shared the same exhilaration. My skin prickled with awareness.

"Oh, now you're calm," Ari teased. He clicked his beak closed and had me lean forward, eyes pointed in the directions he flew and turned.

"I'm faster, aren't I?" he asked.

"I think so."

"Maybe the gods' blessing is worth something after all." It seemed that he'd become more streamlined and longer from the river stone in his gizzard, rather than bulking out like a female gryphon would. This realization pleased Ari immensely.

Too soon, the horns called us to the ground, and our connection broke. Ari landed with a heavy stumble. *"It's incredible we can do that,"* I said, stroking his wing. That felt like an understatement. I just wished it lasted longer or was easier to achieve when we needed it most.

He bunted my side enthusiastically, staggering me. *"I agree. But go, you'll have to hide out in the woods now,"* he said. With a yawn, he lay out in the grass and turned his beak toward the sun's warmth.

I left him with some reluctance to huddle with our new High Command, who were two unfamiliar Harrier Flight boys, plus the twelve others who'd survived the latest round in the sky. Their strategy was fairly straightforward. Half of us would be going on the offensive, while the other half would hang back and distract the third-years. They put five of our defenders to the south while placing our royalty deep in the woods to the north with me as the "scout" meant to shout if the decoy didn't work.

We gathered up our wooden cavalry swords and headed off. It sounded a little like I'd be in the middle of the woods alone until we lost, not trusted to fight anyone off, but I tried not to be offended as I traipsed through the underbrush until I spotted Mireille and Ironfeather's gray feathers where they sat on a mossy outcropping together.

A friendly twitter called to me as I explored around them, finding a good path to patrol. I could see most of the second-years PTing at the end of my patrol and stopped to watch for sight of Callan jogging with a big grin on my face.

When he did run by, he must've sensed my attention, because his dark gaze cut to mine. His lips curled back immediately, like the sight of me disgusted him. *What a sore loser,* I thought, turning back to the woods and settling into my patrol.

I couldn't hear any practice swords clacking from here, just the rustling of leaves from a gentle breeze and the soft twitters from one of the two gryphons. Boredom rolled over me as time passed and nothing changed.

Like static, a tiny voice said in the back of my mind, *"So bored."* I almost confused it for one of my own thoughts, especially when it seemed to reply, *"Shush."*

My belly grumbled, and I checked the sky, wondering when we'd call it quits for the day. Did Flight Training games continue into the evening if we managed to stall for long enough?

"Walker!" I was deep in the forest, at the end of my patrol path, when I turned to see Callan striding through the underbrush with a practice sword in his grasp. He pointed its tip at me, taking a ready stance.

"You're not part of this game. I got you out, remember?" I said.

A fact he didn't seem to care about as he lunged in a quick strike aimed toward my face. I leaned back and lifted my sword, trying for one of the safer jabs from the Gryphon's Extra Talon style since he already had me on the defensive. He evaded without a problem.

"I want you to answer a question for me, Walker," he said. He smacked the flat of his blade against my ribs, hitting as hard as possible. I gritted my teeth, counting on another bruise come tomorrow morning.

"What is it?" I wheezed out. I held my weapon up, catching the blunted blade of his when he tried to hit me again. The wooden swords met with force and a distinct *clack*. He wasn't pulling his strikes, and he proved his strength as he bore down on me and forced my sword away. My muscles strained to resist, so I disengaged first.

He pointed his weapon toward my head. "I want to know if it's real," he said. I caught his next strike again, my bones jarring on impact. "Will she come to your defense? I wonder."

Callan attacked unpredictably, gaining strikes as I failed to guard against him. He was supposed to stop by now, with me "dead" within regular dueling rules.

"Ari, I need help," I projected to my gryphon, realizing the danger of being deep in the woods with Callan.

"Stop. I surrender!" I shouted, hoping someone would hear me. But I'd be a fool to think that'd give him any pause. Instead, he tripped me, and my head rang as the flat of his blade met my skull.

Lights danced through my half-lidded eyes. Dimly, I recognized my body jostling as Callan kicked my side, the pain distant but sharp at the same time. Ghostly doubles danced around him as he pulled his arm back.

"*Sivana?*" Ari's voice sounded hazy, panic thick in his tone. "*Where are you? What's happening?*"

"*Do you hear fighting?*" whispered that voice, the one that sounded like my thoughts.

"*Kind of. Sounds like we're about to be discovered again,*" it seemed to answer itself.

I wheezed, realizing I must be hearing the voices of gryphons. I reached out mentally as Callan's wooden blade walloped the side of my head. Metal flowed over my tongue, and I lost focus.

"*Did you feel that?*"

Maybe the other gryphons hadn't slipped from my awareness, though. I slumped with relief a minute later when one of the beasts screeched and Callan released a startled curse. With effort, I peeled up my eyelids to see him on the ground with Mireille's beak inches from his face, a menacing growl rumbling from her throat.

Ironfeather filled my vision a moment later, his silvery gaze filled with concern. "*Oh no, you're hurt,*" the voice said. A little high pitched and boyish, but it was him, hovering over me anxiously.

"*Go get Arimus.*" The order came from his sister, who sounded remarkably similar to him, but now I heard a sweet, whistling quality to her voice.

Her growling grew more urgent as Ironfeather dashed off. Callan squirmed, trying to buck her off him. He raised his hand to strike her, but she caught his forearm in her sharp beak. Crimson streaked down his skin. "Get off," he snapped. "No one cares that you're the prince's bird. I'll have you put down for attacking me!"

She understood him well enough, starting to balk in alarm at the threat. Callan cuffed her hard and took the opportunity to squirm out from underneath her and take off running. She watched him go, standing guard over me until Ironfeather reappeared, leading Ari and Sergeant Kobarn straight to me.

Ari sat down at my side, sorrow filling his side of the Link. *"I'm sorry I wasn't here to stop this."*

"It's not your fault." I winced, feeling a spear of pain between my brows at how hard it was to focus and talk to him mentally.

Sarge made the sign of Nilara across his chest. "Gods have mercy on the boy who did this to you," he murmured. "After *I'm* done with him."

CHAPTER 18

THE ENEMY YOU KNOW

This wasn't the first time I woke up nose-to-beak with Ironfeather, sluggish from the aftereffects of healing magic. He leaned over my bedside, his gray eyes full of concern I could reach out and feel.

I was aware of Ari stretched out along the line of my body, his head tucked in the nook between my head and shoulders. He was fast asleep. Across my legs rested Puzzlebox, radiating anxious energy. When Ironfeather realized I was waking up, he crowed and danced on his front talons, drawing Puzzlebox to perk up.

"Hi, yes, I'm awake," I croaked while wishing I wasn't. The dim light of the setting sun was nearly too much for my sight, like the stabbing of tiny daggers into my eyeballs.

Ironfeather shifted closer and nuzzled my cheek. His young voice entered my head. *Are you okay?*

"I will be," I said.

You've been asleep for an entire day! They just let us in.

Wow, that was a long time for some bumps and bruises. Callan may have hit me harder than I thought, or maybe the military healers had been busy. The last thing I remembered was being discovered by Sarge.

"Thank you for helping me." I reached out with my eyes still shut, stroking his feathery neck. If it weren't for him and Mireille, I don't think Callan would've stopped. There was a difference between anger at losing and what he'd done.

"Um. There's something you should know," he said timidly.

I tried to take a deeper breath and felt the tightening of bandages around my middle. A cold sweat moistened my palms. Had the healers found my token from Lord Orion? I fumbled to feel my way down my neck, catching my thumb on a warm band of metal leading below the undershirt I wore. The necklace shifted with a familiar weight on the end. Phew, it seemed okay.

"Don't be mad," Ironfeather hedged.

"What is it?"

He nudged my cheek until I cracked my eyes open to meet his gaze. Our connection strengthened enough that he projected a memory to me.

I recognized the viewpoint immediately. Ironfeather had been sitting next to his sister in what looked like one of the dorms. Callan and Prince Mateo squared off a few feet away, but the older cadet had his hands held behind his back by Weslecker. "Let's get one thing straight," the prince was saying. "You threaten my gryphon again, and I will make sure you're off my father's payroll forever."

Despite being outnumbered, Callan was smirking. "She attacked a gryphon rider. You know what the punishment is for that."

A deep, aggressive rumble rose from Mireille. In this memory, Ironfeather glanced toward her before taking her cue and growling in a higher pitch.

"I mean, listen to them. Gryphons have to be put down if they realize they can kill riders, and your yearlings are already so willful," Callan said, inclining his head in their direction.

I knew that wasn't quite how it worked. The military

valued gryphon lives but took notice of the beasts that attacked humans. Harming a caretaker seriously or injuring a rider at all was grounds for sending a gryphon to rehabilitation for their aggressive streak. Usually, that was the end of it, and I'd seen it since Valtora had endured rehabilitation several times with no change in behavior. Valuable beasts were never put down unless they killed or seriously maimed a human.

It seemed like Weslecker and Mateo were unaware of this, both of them going pale at Callan's threat. "She just realized what kind of scum you are," Weslecker said tightly.

Mateo shot him a warning look. "Our silence," he said to Callan, "in exchange for yours. You won't talk about Mireille's aggression, and we won't ruin your alibi."

Weslecker clenched his teeth as he shot the prince a disbelieving look.

"You've got yourself a deal," Callan said.

They released him and stepped aside so he could go. With Callan's hand on the knob, Mateo called his name. "Find a different way," he ordered.

With a nod, the third-year left the room, and Weslecker rounded on his friend immediately. "What was that! He should be expelled for what he pulled," he spat.

Mateo clicked his tongue and gestured, getting Mireille to return to his side. Ironfeather padded over to Weslecker, bunting his hip and earning a distracted scratch behind the ears. "My gryphon nearly bit his arm off. If we're going to take Callan down, I'm not letting him drag Mireille with him. There will be another opportunity..."

I jerked back to awareness of my own aching head. Ironfeather ducked his head in shame. *"Sorry..."*

I breathed as heavy a sigh as the bandages would allow. *"Where is Mireille right now?"*

"Her rider wants her to stay away from you," he murmured. *"I hate it! Why can't he just let her choose for herself?"*

Despite everything, a smile played at my lips. He talked exactly as I expected, and our connection was strong. Even though he was a year old and of size to take a rider into the air, he was still my picky little boy.

"It's okay, baby. Prince Mateo is just scared right now." I gestured for him to come up on the bed, and he did, straining the wooden frame until it creaked loudly in protest at the weight of one person and three gryphons. Still, he snuggled tightly to my side for comfort. *"I'm scared, too."*

"So am I." He slow blinked up at me. *"You keep getting hurt. So many of the humans here are mean to you for no reason."*

I looped my arm around him to give him a squeeze, putting on a brave face. *"But I have good friends too, like you. What you just showed me helped a lot."*

It'd take me a while to come to terms with some of it, though. Like how Mateo had implied that the king was paying Callan. It didn't take much for me to leap to the conclusion that he was earning money by making my life at the Academy about as pleasant as a sprint through the three hells.

Maybe he'd earn extra now because he'd hurt me so badly.

"Acton didn't know until yesterday," Ironfeather told me, his eyes rounding owlishly. It was almost like he was reading my thoughts like Ari always did. *"He's so mad at Mateo and Callan right now."*

"Good," I muttered.

But I couldn't help but linger on the brief exchange between Weslecker and Mateo at the end of his shared memory. *If we're going to take Callan down...*

Was the prince secretly plotting to help me? I didn't know how I felt about that.

Puzzlebox took that moment to climb off the bed and round to the side where Ari still snoozed. She twittered happily and pointed her beak toward the bedside table. *"Someone brought you a present!"* she squeaked.

I craned my neck, spotting a sealed jar with a tiny green ribbon tied around it. Ari jostled awake when I reached for it, grumbling quietly. He probed our Link, and I sensed his relief when he realized I was okay. I was just happy he didn't seem to be blaming himself like the last time I'd ended up in the infirmary.

"Next time, I'm following you into the woods," he said in answer to that thought.

"No complaints here," I said.

I sat up slowly and read the note tied to the ribbon, snorting in surprise. When Ari seemed curious, I read it to him. *"'Because you need a thicker skull. Signed, a friend.' Whoever it is wrote out that it's a potion for muscle and bone strength and included dosage. There are four measures in here."*

He hummed. *"The anonymous friend again."*

I switched my mental attention to Puzzlebox, who watched with her head cocked as I inspected the jar. *"Hey, Box. Did you see who brought this?"*

She pulsed the mental equivalent of a shrug. *"What is it?"* she asked.

I unsealed the potion and took a glimpse inside. Lime-green liquid glowed within. *"Magic,"* I answered and then looked at her with sudden realization. She tilted her head the other way. *"I want you to have it."*

PuzzLEBOX WAS EXCITED for the present all through the night. I was well enough to get out of bed and lead all three gryphons back to our flight's roost the next morning and mixed the potion into a bowl of water for her to drink. Her elation turned to disgust at its taste. *"It's good for you. Drink up,"* I encouraged, hoping it would work for her.

The Commandant called me to his office not long after to talk about the new "incident." Even though neither Weslecker nor Prince Mateo would report what their gryphons saw, I still told the truth, knowing I was risking more retaliation from Callan after his alibi was put to the test.

I came out in time for lunch and my last two classes for the day. The Commandant had given me the last three copies of both the *Kaiamear Gazette* and the *Voice of the People.* He'd handed them off with an angry scowl, but something told me that his ire wasn't aimed at me.

I ate and read while nursing a lingering headache. The healer I'd talked to had said I'd be getting bouts of headaches for a few weeks and maybe some shortness of breath as well.

Surprisingly, four of the six newspaper editions had no mention of me. I supposed the Commandant kept a copy of them to show that the coverage of my life was starting to wane. *Thank the gods.*

The latest edition of *Kaiamear Gazette* ran a piece on the bottom half of the front page titled "LADY GRYPHON RIDER'S MOTHER SPEAKS OUT," and I held it at arm's length for a few moments.

The gigantic letters didn't rearrange themselves by the time I reread the headline. I skimmed the article, more shocked than embarrassed to see that my mother had really sat down to an interview with Miles Glimmerwick. The details were too accurate. It was a tasteful article chronicling my early life and instant connection with Valtora, ending with Mother calling for more female gryphon riders to be accepted to the Gryphon Rider Academy, as I couldn't be the only woman out there that loved and connected with the beasts.

At some point during my reading, Weslecker joined the others at the table with me. I ignored the way he tried to catch my eye, not sure I was ready to talk to him about what'd happened during Field Training.

"News from the outside world," I said, passing around the other newspapers as I picked up the last one and felt my stomach sink.

Voice of the People had published a religious rebuttal addressed to my mother. My eyes picked out one word, big and bold in print: **HERETIC**.

The king, through his paper, made a case for why there shouldn't be any more female gryphon riders. It explained Lord Orion's teachings in detail for anyone who picked up this copy of the newspaper.

Thing is, I *knew* something about this article was bent off course, because I'd spoken to the god. Frustration made my head feel like it was splitting in half, and I nearly tore the fragile paper when my hands formed two fists.

"Sivana?" Weslecker asked quietly after me as I folded the pages jerkily, creasing them all wrong, and stomped toward my next class early.

He followed me, of course. Weirdly enough, I was aware of him through Ironfeather's presence by his side, half a flight of stairs behind me. "Cadet-Lieutenant Walker!" he called for the sake of a few other cadets heading to class too.

"Yes…" I turned and furrowed my brow, trying to remember his new rank after all the mass firings during Field Training. "Cadet-Lieutenant Weslecker?"

He smiled faintly. "I saw this." He flapped the poorly folded newspaper as he climbed the rest of the way up the staircase and stood across from me just out of the flow of foot traffic. "Um. Ironfeather told me he…somehow told you…"

I scowled. This was exactly the problem. I could tell him his gryphon had talked to me like we were Linked, but I couldn't give away what I knew about Lord Orion. It was like I had the key to the lock of all my problems, but my hands were tied behind my back.

"He shared a memory, yes," I sighed. "It was pretty, uh, vague. Something about a deal."

Weslecker's expression tightened. "Yeah. Look, I learned something important." His voice dropped to an urgent whisper. "Callan's being paid by the king to hurt you, maybe even *kill* you. If he didn't have blackmail against Mateo, we'd get him expelled. But you're not safe."

He took my hand between both of his as I nodded grimly and resisted the urge to tell him I knew all this already. "We're going to do the buddy system from here on out, okay? If you have to go off on your own, especially in Field Training, promise me you'll have either me or someone else you trust around."

"That's a good idea. I promise," I murmured.

As other cadets flowed past us, he looked down and realized he was still holding my hand. We pulled away from each other, and he patted my shoulder awkwardly. "Mateo and I are coming up with a plan. We've had enough of him."

My lips pressed to a line, and I found it hard to meet his gaze. "Weslecker." I lowered my voice to a whisper. "Do you really think that, if somehow Callan went away tomorrow, the king wouldn't just pay someone else?"

"Well, um…"

"The enemy you know and all that. We need to get to class. But read that if you want to," I said, gesturing to the newspaper he'd tossed aside.

He stooped to pick it up and balled it tightly until it was squished in his fist. "I know you, and I know you're not a heretic. Nor do you deserve to have a Callan in your life."

CHAPTER 19

OPERATION BOX

I LEFT World Cultures with my eyelids drooping. Instructor Signe had talked about Rathi mythology and led us through the poetic sagas that formed it, but today, I just couldn't seem to focus. This was going to be a rough week; I could already tell.

Ari and I took the stairs up to the stables, past where Rudrick was teaching the first-years about basic gryphon care. My gryphon stopped short and cocked his head at about the same time I realized there was a raised voice ahead of us. *"Oh no,"* he murmured.

I turned a corner to go deeper in the stables, toward my Gryphon Taming class. The shouting was Sharde carrying on behind the closed door of one of the wild gryphon stalls, which were built with higher walls for more privacy.

"Be careful, Cadet Sharde. This is insubordination," came Captain Gemon's strict response.

"Oh, well, Gatekeeper take me!" Sharde shouted. "I won't sign that!"

I lined up with the other cadets in this class, the four of us wide-eyed. I assumed Gemon had drawn my friend aside for some privacy, but their raised voices ruined it.

"I know why you're refusing, and it will only prove this is necessary," Gemon said.

My blood ran cold. There was only one thing they could be talking about: our instructor had finally gotten the Commandant's approval to test Puzzlebox's aptitude as a war beast.

Sharde's response dropped to a whisper, inaudible from here, and Gemon responded in kind. Not long after, the two men emerged from the stall, with my friend stiff-backed and red in the face. Instead of joining us, he seized Puzzlebox's saddle horn and dragged her away.

"Good afternoon, cadets," Gemon said like nothing happened. We mumbled greetings back, and I watched Sharde leave, catching a bit of Puzzlebox's distress when she looked over her shoulder.

I faced forward with my hands balling to fists at my sides. *"I caught a bit of what Gemon said. I'd be angry, too,"* Ari commented.

"Well, what'd he say?"

"That Sharde will still have a place as a tamer in the Second without a gryphon."

My head throbbed as I ground my teeth. Clearly Gemon knew he was pushing for Puzzlebox's execution.

It reminded me of what my father's chain of command had said when Ari was branded a failure to thrive following his rider's death. They'd called him a "defective beast." He'd been a "waste of resources." A year ago, we'd proven them wrong, but that alone hadn't fixed the way the military viewed their gryphons.

The system I was now a part of was overdue for something even more extreme than the first female rider. It needed to change. Was I the only one who saw that?

The military killed perfectly fine gryphons who otherwise couldn't fight. It was a cynical view, like they weren't worth the resources, no matter how loved and cherished they were.

I was so angry that my eyes filled with tears. I didn't hear more than a few words from Gemon as I trembled there, impotent. Ari echoed the same feeling, and suddenly, my skin filled with static tingles.

"Oh." Ari looked around. *"Your sight is blurrier than usual."*

I blinked rapidly and swiped subtly at my lower eyelids. He watched Gemon through me as I started focusing on the here and now. "…Will help me conduct a round of five tests on her. This is a rare and tragic moment in a tamer's life, when a defective beast has to be appropriately identified and removed before it takes up three years' worth of training and resources.

"It's even rarer to see a beast's development not meet expectations, but it does happen," Gemon said.

Instead of having us try to groom and attend to the partially tamed gryphons today, Gemon taught us the ins and outs of the five tests Puzzlebox needed to pass. With Ari watching everything through my eyes, the two of us memorized everything she'd be faced with.

"Puzzlebox, sit," Sharde said, gesturing downward. The white gryphon did as commanded.

"She recognized your gesture. The tamers have to stand with their hands behind their backs," I said, standing between him and Ellie in our flight's common room.

Ellie clasped her fidgeting hands and said, "Puzzlebox, stand up." Puzzlebox got to her feet. "See, she understands us just fine!"

Then the gryphon came over to Ellie and nudged her to sit on one of the cushions behind her. She snuggled into her lap with a happy twitter.

Sharde drew his hand down his face. "I had time to

prepare her when she was a hatchling," he murmured. "How are we going to do this in only a few days?"

Gemon had told the rest of the class the testing would be this Friday. I was running the test we were trying to practice here, having Puzzlebox respond to commands spoken aloud. As it turned out, understanding human speech was a measure of gryphon intelligence.

I'd taken for granted that gryphons like Valtora and most of the First always seemed to understand me when I was a caretaker. However... "I think we should focus on a different test," I said. "Gemon's going to get a Tulari to make illusions to test her reaction to frightening images and loud noises."

"That was the one test she failed." He frowned, gazing down at his hands as if they had some answers for him. "How do we practice that? She's always been afraid of both of those things."

I looked down at Puzzlebox, who had rotated to show her belly, happily taking scratches from Ellie. Every time Lord Gadric summoned a rozash illusion for Advanced Anatomy and Tactics, she screamed in fear. Not only did she need to pass these tests, I thought, she also needed to perform in class before it became obvious to everyone that she was not a combat gryphon.

"I should've never started trying," Sharde muttered. "Things were so much easier when I was a failure first-year. No one looked too hard at Puzzlebox when *I* was the one in trouble."

Ellie cleared her throat. "I have an idea," she said.

She didn't tell us what the idea was until after dinner, since Sharde was on punishment duty indefinitely for insubordination. For him, that meant he was stuck preparing and serving the evening meal. Bags were developing under his eyes when we called a flight meeting, but he stood up and told everyone the same story he'd told me about his early days with Puzzlebox.

Feyring held up a hand after I helped Sharde explain the five tests Puzzlebox needed to pass this Friday. "Wait, let me get something straight. Her life is on the line?" he asked.

Most of us glanced over at the gryphon, who was play tussling with Echo, Biggs's gryphon, while we talked. Much like her rider, Echo had gotten a growth spurt and was nearly the same size as Puzzlebox already.

"That's right. And that's part of why I've tried taking Puzzlebox out to fly on the weekends," I said since everyone was in on that too. "She doesn't look or act like a military gryphon, so we called you all together with a plan to help her fake it for now."

Sharde sighed heavily. "I've told you all this to ask for your help. Will you save Puzzlebox with me?"

"Absolutely," Weslecker said.

Murmurs of agreement came from around the room. Even Korvic, for once, had nothing sarcastic to say.

Ellie stood, which was my cue to sit. I put myself between Ari and Ironfeather, who leaned against my sides companionably. "It is possible for a craftsman Tulari to enchant an object with an illusion so that when it's used—worn, usually—it transforms the person wearing it in some way. Lord Gadric has a ton of random enchanted items lying around.

"I propose that we borrow a few to get Puzzlebox used to illusions. They won't be as scary to her if she sees them more often and thinks the people she loves are just playing a game with her."

"When you say borrow..." Credell said quietly.

"He doesn't let me take old magic out of his workshop, so it would be borrowing without permission," she hedged. "I'd need help getting them, too."

Feyring crossed his arms with a skeptical look. "And then we're going to scare Puzzlebox until she's not scared anymore?" he asked.

"Until she can tell the difference between an illusion and

real life. Unfortunately, she also needs to get used to loud noises." Ellie frowned to herself. "I suspect she gets over-stimulated."

There was a pause as everyone thought this through. Pereyra was the one to speak up. His hand was buried in his gryphon's feathers, and he looked the most upset about Puzzlebox's upcoming testing out of the rest of my flight-mates. "What behavior are they looking for? Why is that relevant to her being here?" he demanded.

Ellie wrung her hands. "I imagine battlefields are quite loud," she pointed out.

"You all haven't seen Puzzlebox during this particular test. She's scared of any illusions and shuts down when there's a loud of noise. Just...hunches in and panics until it's over." Sharde pulled in his shoulders and ducked his head, trembling in place. "Gemon will make a case for her not being a capable war beast if she can't handle it."

"I hate everything about this," Pereyra said, slamming a fist into his thigh. "Just because she can't pass a stupid test or two shouldn't mean that she has to die. Why can't they let you go off to Final Flight like you're always talking about, Sharde?"

Sharde shook his head with a scowl. "They don't need any more men to deliver the mail when I could be a knight or a tamer. You all know our gryphons aren't pets. They're property of the military, which means they can't be flawed." My hold around Ari tightened reflexively.

"When do we get started?" Pereyra asked.

"Tonight," Ellie answered. "I need three volunteers to sneak into Lord Gadric's workroom with me."

She turned to Sharde and shook her head when he insisted on going. She took his hand and murmured, "You look like you're going to fall over. Let us take care of it. I need three *stealthy* people."

I watched Sharde nod instead of arguing with her. He was

putting a lot of trust in Ellie. In all of us, actually, but she was the kingpin of the plan. If she couldn't secure any illusions, that was the end of it already. She picked Pereyra, Biggs, and me for the first step—getting into the workroom and finding suitably scary illusions we could borrow.

"We've got about an hour before lights out," Ellie said. "Operation Box is a go."

Despite himself, Sharde grinned for a few moments. "You're really naming it that?"

"Getting in's the easy part, trust me," Ellie said as she led us down to Lord Gadric's classroom. At his age, he didn't burn the midnight oil like he used to, so no one was inside as she led us to the back and unlocked the workroom. She was often the only person working late in this space.

It was a squat, circular room set under the staircase leading down to this floor. A single magelight lent clean, white light to the space, and we could hear the muffled thump of the occasional person above us. To the left was an alchemy table with an assorted set of clear glassware. A silvery mixture sat at the bottom of a giant stoppered flask, but otherwise, the tools were clean and awaiting use.

"I see what you mean," I whispered, aware that someone on the stairs may be able to hear our voices in here. Lord Gadric was apparently not much better than Ellie at keeping a space clean and free of clutter. The right side of the room was full of boxes and bins full of tools and reagents for both magic and alchemy.

"Some of this stuff has been around since before Lord Gadric. Most should be labeled, at least," Ellie said. She slid the first box off the top of a tower of dented cardboard.

"Operation Box, all right," Biggs said, following suit. "I

didn't believe he just had illusions lying around, but there's gotta be a few in all this junk."

"Aren't there rules for storing magic?" I asked. It didn't seem like it was getting followed here.

Ellie shrugged. "Lord Gadric would sense if anything was unstable or dangerous. He's gone looking through all this before for one enchanted item."

We worked and whispered, passing boxes back after a quick rummage. The ones closest to us appeared to be all reagents, things like herbs, spare wands, and tiny crystals that gleamed from the inside. "So, looks like we won't find anything before lights out," Pereyra said. "Did you have a plan for how to get back to our dorm too, Ellie?"

"Well, we can't get caught carrying enchanted items we stole," she said.

"Uh huh," he muttered.

"Good thing I've been working late recently. I've figured out the sergeant assigned to our floor tends to take a nap after midnight."

Biggs snorted in surprise. "Really?"

"You've been out that late?" I asked, my brows rising. I usually passed out as soon as it was lights out, so she really could sneak in at any time after that, and I wouldn't know the difference.

She bobbed her head. "Yeah. My project is close to a break-through, I think. I've been trying to capture different light-creating compounds in glass. One of these days, it will work. Imagine a world where we don't have to rely on torches and lanterns at night."

"Unless you're rich and already have magelights," Biggs murmured.

"In this scenario, everyone will have these kind of mage-lights," she said.

Pereyra cleared his throat. "That's great and all, but let's try to focus," he sighed.

The horn that heralded lights out echoed down to us, and on habit, we hushed up for a while. "How are the Smalls, Biggs?" I asked in a whisper, just to break the monotony.

His teeth flashed against his sienna-toned skin. "Great!" He managed to be quiet and enthusiastic at the same time. "They came in third in the first monthly competition, but I have high hopes for them."

I smiled, glad to see he had somewhere to channel that competitive spirit. "That's a good start."

"I let them know all the good Kite Flight secrets. You know, so they can swoop in and win at the end."

Pereyra looked up from the box he sorted through, raising a brow. "We have secrets now?" he asked.

"Yeah, we do." If we were outside, I know Biggs would've whooped those words rather than whisper them. "Always help a friend in need." He gestured to what we were doing. "And listen to Walker." Then he flourished both his hands in my direction.

The other young man nodded along. "Wise words, great teacher. Very useful to a flight with no Walker. I see why they made you a Cadet-Commander."

Biggs punched his shoulder. "Okay, Korvic."

"I'm not *that*—"

"Guys," Ellie hissed. The door behind us, which led into the classroom, creaked open.

CHAPTER 20

THE IMPOSSIBLE TEST

STANDING in the threshold in his pajamas was Lord Gadric himself, wand upheld in front of him with a sizzling spark on the tip to light his way. He squinted at us. Biggs smiled hugely while hiding a box behind his back, while Pereyra and I froze.

Ellie stepped forward. "Um, hello," she said tentatively.

The usually kindly old mage shot a strict look her way. "Young lady, what's going on? Why have you brought all these cadets here? The wards on this room went crazy since they're only attuned to you and me."

My heart sank. There went our chances to find illusions to use on Puzzlebox. We shuffled out of the workroom at a defeated pace and sat at the desks the instructor indicated. He stood there with his arms crossed as Ellie launched into what we were doing at double-time, her words tripping over each other in her rush to speak them.

Lord Gadric raised his wrinkled palms. "Slow down. You're looking for...illusions." His brow furrowed as he glanced toward the worse mess we'd left his workroom in. "Some of the magic in there hasn't been disturbed for centuries. I don't think you understand how dangerous your plan was."

"We were only going to borrow them for a few days," she protested.

"Sir, the life of a gryphon is on the line," I said.

He considered us for a few moments before pulling a chair behind another desk and sitting as well. "I know," he said with a sigh. "Who do you think was called to produce the illusions for Puzzlebox's upcoming test?"

My jaw hung for a moment, and I shut it with a snap. Of course they'd get him to do it. He was the go-to Tulari for most things, as most able-bodied mages were on the front lines.

"My attempts to explain her neurodevelopmental condition were used as proof that she needs to be tested again. The whole affair is in bad taste, in my opinion." He rubbed his eyes with a "hmph" and looked up, startled. I wasn't the only one staring at him.

"Her what?" Pereyra asked.

"Her brain development," Lord Gadric said. "It is quite the advanced topic, and I'm afraid none of the military brass here are willing to listen to me instead of jumping to a conclusion. Were I younger and still hungry to prove myself in academia, Puzzlebox would be an excellent candidate for study."

"Can we save her that way?" I asked quietly. I could see the nightmare of bureaucracy already if the military had to face a leading university for the rights to study her.

"Oh, no no, dear. An academic would want to run her through some very stressful tests before dissecting her brain," he said. I felt myself pale immediately, and Biggs made a sound of dismayed disgust. "Students, please. Most of our medical advancements came first from opening up corpses and identifying what killed them and *how*."

"That's not making it any better." Biggs sounded like he was about to go vomit, and I wasn't faring much better.

Ellie raised her hand, and the instructor tipped his hand toward her like this was a real class. "Can you help us with the illusion portion of the testing? Maybe make them less frightening for Puzzlebox?"

Lord Gadric stroked his jaw in thought. It was a good idea, I thought, if we could stack the deck in her favor. He eventually shook his head. "I'll be asked to redo any illusion deemed too weak. My biggest concern here is that the ink is already dry on the decision you wish to change. If I have noticed this gryphon is unique compared to her peers, so have the brass, trust me."

I studied my interlaced fingers, stricken by a queasy sensation. We had to save Puzzlebox. There had to be a way to get her to pass every test.

"Perhaps I shouldn't be sharing this, but I am privy to the fact that the round of testing on Friday will not select whether Puzzlebox lives or dies. Only the Commandant's judgment decides," he told us. "As a Knight-Marshall, it is his hard decision to make. But you may want to keep it in mind as you prepare Puzzlebox for her impossible test."

He lifted his wand and drew a simple rune in the air. There was a muffled crash from the workroom, drawing a wince from Ellie, before a single box floated out and came to rest on my desk. I wondered what dangerous magic items had taken a tumble and if we needed to worry about that.

"You may borrow these," he said. "But as punishment for breaking into my workroom, you will have evening duty for a week, organizing it for me. You can start next Monday after the testing."

"Yes, sir," I said, echoed by my friends. It was a small price to pay while also about to be way too much work even for one week's worth of evenings. "But...what do you mean, impossible?" I asked in a small voice.

He smiled sadly. "Unless you can somehow explain it in a

way she understands, I doubt she will ever realize an illusion isn't reality."

I nodded and took a peek in the box, spotting small things like headbands and gloves within, even a pair of socks. The box was labeled "FRAGILE: MAGIC" with no indication what each item did. *Huh, we really do have enchanted items just lying around in that workroom.*

"Thank you for your help, sir," I said. Somehow, him saying it was impossible woke that part in me that wanted to prove him—and everyone else—wrong.

PUZZLEBOX CRIED in dismay the next evening when I called her from Sharde's room and, instead of me, there was a snow pine in the common room. The illusion wasn't *scary*, but I could sense her unhappiness at the trick. There were dozens of different little illusions in the box Lord Gadric had lent us, mostly innocent like this one.

"It's me, Box. I'm the tree," I told her.

She whined and nosed at the spiky leaves on one branch. It was an odd experience, because I could see the illusion overlaying me, except it was transparent. I could move if I wanted to, but the illusion would tear and show my legs underneath, as snow pines didn't have feet.

"How did you turn into a tree?" Puzzlebox asked innocently.

Behind me, Ari groaned. *"It's not real, Puzzlebox! She's wearing an illusion."*

The other gryphon huffed, her feathers puffing out. *"This game isn't fun! Why is everyone playing it today?"*

"It's not a..." I drifted off as she lifted her beak and flounced off. Lips twisting, I took off the little silver ring holding the snow pine illusion and shook off the sense of disorientation at having two skinny arms rather than several branches full of silvery needles.

I sat with Ari, scrubbing at my face. *"Instead of identifying that what she's seeing isn't real, she believes it every time,"* I said to him. *"Any other gryphon would question how a tree appeared in the middle of our common room."*

Lord Gadric had called this. He'd known she would struggle telling an illusion from the real thing, just like he'd somehow figured out how she differed from her gryphon peers.

"That's the impossible part, like he said," Ari said. I'd shared the whole late-night conversation with him, so now he turned it over with me. *"If only I had my sight... She needs to hear how to tell an illusion from reality from a gryphon."*

"Can you tell when I'm wearing an illusion?" I asked him curiously.

"Not at all. They're all visual. You smelled like yourself, even as a tree."

I hummed and kept it in mind for a full day, thinking through the problem again and again. My flight-mates kept wearing random illusions to test Puzzlebox, but she still failed each time. This wasn't how we were going to teach her. She had to sit down and *understand* how to intuit whether something was real or not.

Wednesday was mail day, and I had a few letters to read after dinner. Ellie had come back up early, sitting across from me wearing an illusion of a living fish with rainbow scales. She swam around a few feet up in the air.

"I have to say, this is my favorite illusion so far," I told her.

"It's really hard to control!" she said. The fish's bulbous lips flapped with her words, and I giggled at the sight before returning my gaze to the first letter I'd opened, from my parents.

They'd stuffed in the most recent edition of the *Kaiamear*

Gazette, and I barely glanced at it, too distracted to read their advice. I put it aside and opened the next envelope, which had my name written on it in elegant script. My eyes just about popped out of their sockets when I caught the signature at the end of a rather lengthy letter.

"What is it?" Ellie asked. Her fish illusion swam over to peer over my shoulder.

"It's from Princess Odalis," I said. I figured the royal was too busy to converse with the likes of me, but the letter read like any ordinary, bored girl writing to a friend. She had little to say and asked that I write back and tell her what was going on during my training.

Actually...on second glance, I realized that there were little lines underneath certain letters. I pulled out my note-book for class and copied over each one until I reached the end and read back the message, adding punctuation to make it make sense. "I tried talking to Father. He won't listen to reason when it comes to you. And I suspect CP's plan for you."

CP? I showed it to Ellie. "She wrote me a secret message," I said. I thought it was clever, considering she had to have orderlies reading her correspondence coming in and out.

"The crown prince?" Ellie guessed.

"Sounds fitting," I murmured.

"What does she mean, his plan for you?"

"Looks like I'd better ask." I went ahead and tucked the letter away for now. Our flight-mates were trickling in, and I caught Weslecker and Ironfeather, calling them over. While Weslecker was distracted poking Ellie's illusion, I reached out and connected to his gryphon with only a moment's diffi-culty. It was becoming easier, like the token under my uniform was letting me solidify a Link with him.

"*Can you tell that's an illusion?*" I asked, pointing to Ellie's fishy self.

He snorted. *"Yeah!"*

"How can you tell?"

He sat a little straighter, like he was proud to teach me. *"It smells like Ellie instead of fish! Besides, fish drown outside of water, else we'd have tasty snacks flying around with us."*

I scratched his cheeks proudly. *"Good job. I need your help."*

Ironfeather agreed to what I asked him to do and waited as I called Puzzlebox out. I showed her fish Ellie while Weslecker stood to the side. She twittered curiously, opening her beak and approaching to nibble at the illusion's tail.

"No, Puzzlebox, that's not a real fish," Ironfeather said, nudging her off course.

While I was still connected to him, I felt some strain on my mind as she replied. The words washed away before I could hear them, but she looked just as affronted as ever to be tricked by yet another illusion.

"Don't get mad." He nuzzled her and murred until she started to relax. *"Let me show you how I know…"*

"Sivana, what's happening?" Ellie asked, holding very still as both gryphons circled her. Ironfeather pointed with his beak, I noticed, a little gryphon quirk that had the wicked-sharp tip inches from her magicked-invisible skin under the illusion.

"I think he's helping," I said, proud to hear the young gryphon patiently explain to Puzzlebox that fish couldn't just jump out of rivers or oceans and start swimming around in the air.

When he was done, there was a pause as she leaned forward, her head bobbing as she sniffed. *"Oooooooooooooh,"* I heard her say.

"I think you can take the illusion off," I said. The moment Ellie did, Puzzlebox tapped her front paws in delight and brushed against the girl in a clear request for attention.

IRONFEATHER FOLLOWED PUZZLEBOX, helping her when she hesitated around illusions. She picked up the idea a lot better with his help, but that was only half the challenge.

She protested when she tasted the second dose of the potion for muscle and bone strength. The first dose hadn't created a noticeable difference in her stature or muscle tone, but I was hoping by the time she had all four, she would gain more bulk and fly better with Sharde on her back.

"Where does Puzzlebox love to be groomed the most?" I asked Sharde. It was Thursday evening, and he was drooping with dark shadows under his eyelids. He held on to his gryphon even as it grew late, looking like he had no intentions of returning her to the stables.

Puzzlebox hadn't screamed when Lord Gadric summoned the day's rozash during Advanced Anatomy, but she had hunched down when he made it screech a battle cry. Ellie had tried manufacturing earplugs for her, but we'd been afraid the wax would fall into her ears and get stuck.

Fact was, the gryphon spooked with every loud noise and hunkered down if it went on for too long. It'd felt cruel to practice when the reaction was always the same. She wasn't allowed to have another gryphon around to comfort her during the real test, so I was down to my last idea.

"Her belly," he answered with a resigned sigh. "It calms her down, usually."

I pulled a grooming kit out of my pack. We didn't usually have these, but I'd borrowed it from the stables and selected a wide-tooth comb. I nudged Ari to lie on his side, and he grumbled as I started combing his soft belly fur. *"She might love this, but I don't,"* he complained.

"Close your eyes. Just focus on how it feels."

He snipped his beak at me, and I realized my mistake.

"*Sorry, turn of phrase,*" I added. "*Can you send Puzzlebox what you're feeling?*"

"*I suppose.*"

"Ari and I are going to be there tomorrow, and I wonder if we can keep her calmer if she relaxes from the feeling of grooming," I explained aloud to Sharde.

"It's not a bad idea," he murmured.

We had Credell come out of his room and bang on a pot with a wooden spoon. Puzzlebox flinched immediately, ducking her head with her ears pinned back.

"Well, it was an idea," Sharde said, watching that reaction with a troubled frown.

Ari nudged me with his beak. "*I want to try something else.*" I called Credell off, feeling Ari focus his attention on Puzzlebox. She recovered from her hunch, perking up, even. "*I'm sending her a happy memory. Try now.*"

Credell started hitting the pot again, but this time, Puzzlebox flinched less. "That's it!" I exclaimed.

"What?" Both of my flight-mates asked, out of the loop.

"Ari distracted her with a happy memory. Maybe if we do this during the test... Credell, one more time," I said. This time, I focused on trying to send Puzzlebox a memory too, of a sunny, lazy day last year with her prancing around on the Green, carefree and covered in dried grass.

"*I remember that day!*" she exclaimed.

Meanwhile, Credell hit the pot. It worked! She was too much into that memory, too distracted to retreat into herself.

"*I miss when we could do that,*" I said to her.

"*Me too. Maybe we play there this weekend?*" she asked.

Someone slammed on our front door. "Quit making so much noise!" shouted one of our neighbors from Falcon Flight. So excited with the idea of taking a weekend off, Puzzlebox didn't even jump.

PUZZLEBOX'S real tests came along during Gryphon Taming the next day. Sharde was excused from the stables, accompanied on either side by a burly drill sergeant. Though nervous, she turned to her mental connection with me for comfort in his absence. *"It's okay, Box. We're just going to play a few games you should find familiar,"* I told her, hoping our lesser Link meant she couldn't sense how tense I was.

The Commandant stood off to the side, along with Lord Gadric, a few caretakers, and two uniformed tamers of the Second. Ari pressed to my side to remind me of his steady presence. *"She's going to be fine because of us,"* he said.

"I hope you're right," I murmured.

The first few tests were no problem. The blanket test was a joke with a gryphon of her size, as she just shook it off with a confused chirrup. I helped her through the next one so she picked the right treat under the set of cups after they started rotating. When it came my turn to come forward and test her, I put my hands behind my back and gave her commands both out loud and in her mind, where she understood better.

"Why so bossy today?" she squeaked. *"Can you make Noah come back?"*

"Very soon, I promise," I said, stepping back with a nod. It was time for the noise test, which would be made with a pair of horns and a set of drums. Swallowing nervously, I started showing her my favorite memory I had of her.

Ellie had taken me aside last year to make sure I had a break, and while we painted our nails, Puzzlebox had come into the room looking for attention and ended up presenting her talons for us to paint too.

"We should do that again," she said. The horns started blaring, inexpert honks made by the two tamers. She pushed her ears back, but so did every other gryphon, a few of them

making squawks of protest further outside of this corner of the stables.

"I totally agree. How about this weekend?" I suggested.

"After we play in the field?" she asked, her beak parting happily.

Someone else banged on the drum too. The noise was awful, and she started to notice it, I think, hunching in on herself. *"What do you want to play?"* I asked her. *"I can bring a ball. Or maybe your favorite toy?"*

She didn't reply, and my heart sank as the noise continued for a minute more before subsiding at last. Captain Gemon seemed to smile and nod to himself, and in that moment, I don't think I hated a man more.

"Finally, the illusion test," he announced, motioning Lord Gadric forward.

"Right, Box? You want your favorite toy?" I coaxed, putting my hand in my pocket, hoping she'd shake it off and look at me. No one wanted to miss the magic of the illusion being built, even if it was smaller than usual to fit in the stables. But for a moment, she did turn to me, and when she did, I slipped her battered, old puzzle box out of my pocket.

Delight sparkled from her, and I smiled to myself when she turned back to the illusion and didn't even acknowledge it. I felt attention on me and glanced to the side; the Commandant also wasn't looking at the magic taking place. He was staring directly at me and the toy in my hand, a stern expression on his face.

I flushed cold like I'd been dunked into ice water. I hid the puzzle box back in my pocket and watched as he stepped to the side to deliberate with Gemon. *"The Commandant caught me,"* I explained to Ari, balling my hands into fists to hide their trembling.

We echoed the same fear, and that moment of unity had him looking through my eyes when Puzzlebox walked up to us for attention. She twittered quietly, a question mark projecting from her as she looked between us. It seemed she was just starting to realize how tense the air was around her.

"See to it that she's returned to her rider. I will make a final decision over the weekend," the Commandant announced. His boots thumped as he approached us, and he gestured for me to follow him. "Come along."

I kissed Puzzlebox's beak and turned to trail behind him as he silently left the stables and started down the stairs. We went all the way down to his office, and only then did his expression change, relaxing from a strict military bearing.

"Cadet Walker," he said.

"Yes, sir."

"She passed."

I went limp with relief. Gods above, when she'd shut down during the noise test, I'd thought that was it. Gemon's smug look would be branded in my memory forever.

"So did your flight."

My brow drew in. "Sir?"

A slight smile touched his lips. "I've known of Puzzlebox's slow growth and unique struggles for two years. Captain Gemon believes he achieved something today with testing her, but he hasn't been around to see the great lengths Cadet Sharde has gone through for her. I see such promise in that young man. When he stops pretending, he will be an outstanding leader."

I frowned, not sure if Sharde would get behind that idea. He'd self-sabotaged for over two years, after all.

"Do you believe Gadric didn't tell me about your late-night break in?" he asked.

"Uh...n-no, sir. I-I didn't think he would," I stammered.

He clapped me on the shoulder. "Well, I watched your flight rally to protect one of your own. Your leadership, in particular, reminds me of your father."

I fought a losing battle with smiling, feeling like that was the highest of praise from him. "Thank you, sir."

The Commandant nodded. "Oh, and Cadet Walker, if you could refrain from spreading around the fact that I've already made a decision. Gemon has to believe I actually considered his side."

"Yes, sir. One more thing…does this mean I'm not going to be rank thirty-five of thirty-five anymore?" I asked hopefully.

"Don't get your hopes up," he replied.

CHAPTER 21

NOMINATED

RANKS WERE POSTED that next Monday, and the only thing that tipped me off to a change was Sharde pumping his fist. "Yes! First loser," he exclaimed.

We'd spent the weekend playing with Puzzlebox just like we'd promised and celebrating, even though Korvic had complained about us putting so much effort into something we hadn't needed to panic about in retrospect. Still, we'd scored a victory, and as I found my name at rank thirty-four of thirty-five, just above Sharde's, my spirits lifted further.

"It's just one place," Ari pointed out as I whistled on my way to class.

The Commandant acknowledged us. It's not just a change in rank. I think it's the start of something, I said.

Ari remained dubious until we got to our Jousting class. "Why are you smiling, Walker?" Callan asked scornfully, hitching a thumb toward Sharde. "Celebrating being better than that loser?"

I just smiled wider at him, watching him recoil slightly with new determination in my chest. I didn't reply to him, but I did turn my attention inward to Ari. *Now that we know Puzzlebox is going to be okay, I want to focus on us getting better.*

"Okay. At what, exactly?"

"Dueling, for one thing." I hadn't put up enough of a fight when Callan thought he had me cornered and alone. *"And jousting, for another. We're going to qualify for the Cadet Games this year."*

He snorted his disbelief. *"Us?"*

"Every year, they let a handful of second-years compete. Why not us? Especially if you and I can perfect balancing out our emotions so you can practice seeing through my apparently awful vision."

"It's pretty blurry, to be fair," he said.

"I'm rolling my eyes at you."

"I know. I sensed it."

"So, what do you say?" I asked.

"I suppose you want to do extra training again," he said with a thread of reluctance. *"But if it means I get to see more often, even with your human eyes, I'll do it."*

I bent down to hug him around the neck. *"Great!"*

Today, we were still learning how to take a hit, which meant hunkering down behind our shields on gryphon back while another cadet, on foot, rammed us with their lance. We'd gotten our kite shields at the end of year ceremony last year, freshly painted and lacquered. Mine was already dented, the paint flecking off in places.

It'd been so pretty when it was new, but someone had painted the closed gryphon eye of my personal symbol silver instead of the requested yellow. I hadn't heard the end of it since Callan noticed and assumed it was silver because I had a Nilarite-white stripe through my hair.

"Go home, Nilarite," I heard dozens of times a day. It got old.

Callan, of course, was going first today to show how it was done, holding his battered shield up as a second-year ran at him with a practice lance. I watched in dismay as the younger man lost control of the length of wood and ended up slamming it into Sunset's chest instead, drawing a pained screech from her.

Wooden shards exploded everywhere. I cringed from how much that had to hurt, especially if a giant splinter ended up under her skin. Rudrick rushed forward and checked the wound after Callan dismounted. "Looks serious. Go take her to the healers," he said.

"She's going to be okay, sir," Callan answered.

"That was an order, cadet."

With a salute, Callan ushered his gryphon away. I breathed a guilty sigh of relief to have at least one class free from him.

THAT WEEK PASSED LIKE A BLUR, with evening duty every night alongside Pereyra and Biggs to rearrange and organize Lord Gadric's workroom. We'd told Ellie we had it under control, so she worked on her project at the alchemy table while the Tulari himself sat by with a book, wand resting in his lap just in case he needed to save us from any spell we accidentally set off.

There were moments where I had time with Ellie before lights out and she showed me her work. "Craftsmen Tulari are able to infuse magical runes into items to make them work. For something like the small illusions we were using, they take a simple day's work to do. But science can't create anything like it," she explained.

She had a diagram of the rune array Tulari had to create to imbue a ball of glass and powder with the magic it needed to float and create light. It was highly complicated to my untrained eye.

"So, how are you going to make a magelight with no magic?" I asked.

"We're trying to focus on making it create light, because when you break down what a magelight can do…it's got a lot more going on than just light. It floats, responds to commands from either clapping or snapping your fingers, and knows the bounds of the room it's activated in." She sighed heavily. "Lord Gadric thinks the most vital thing we can do is make a successful prototype that gives off light. Even if it doesn't float or dim on command, just having something that glows can be revolutionary."

"I agree," I murmured. "Put it in a cube rather than a sphere so it doesn't roll away while someone works."

She scribbled my idea down with a few bobs of her head. That was about all the help I could offer, but I hoped she figured it out and got rich selling the idea across Altare.

I didn't start training extra until after the workroom was nicely organized, and usually, it was with Weslecker. Either we dueled and I tried to get stronger, or we met each other on the Green and went through jousting exercises on the ground.

When he learned I was training myself extra in the evenings, I had a surprise tutor in the form of Sarge, who would interrupt me mid-duel with Weslecker and force us to toss our practice weapons aside. He drilled me extra hard on hand-to-hand combat, and over time, I noticed no other cadet got this treatment from him.

I ended up writing Odalis back, and it was harder than it looked to properly encode a secret response. "What is the CP's plan?" I asked within a fairly boring letter about academy life.

It was such a busy time that I didn't realize the next monthly competition and Field Training day were coming up. I just looked up one day and realized it was mid-October and I could sense a gryphon in pain as I left Gryphon Taming for the day. I had Ari wait for me and turned to look for the beast that feeling was coming from.

I stopped in front of Sunset's stall. The gryphon rested on

her side, one wing extended out flat. She seemed to ignore me as I unlocked the stall door and stepped inside, watching her carefully for any sign of aggression. "Hi, Sunset. Is there something wrong?" I asked, taking a knee a few feet from her head.

She snapped her beak, a sign that that was close enough.

"If you'll look me in the eye, we might be able to talk," I whispered.

Slowly, she lifted her head and looked at me directly. Her eyes were a rich buttercup yellow, a vibrant hue to match her stunning and rare maroon and red plumage. A temporary Link slammed into place, as forceful as her words. *"You should leave before Victor finds out you're here."*

"Gatekeeper take him. You're hurt?" I asked.

She growled, an uneasy sound. *"I strained my wing today. It hurts. He's worried I won't be able to fly during the competition tomorrow if I have to see the healers, and we'll lose the first-place rank."*

"It'll only get worse if you push yourself," I said, shocked he'd just left her here to stretch it by herself. I got to my feet and crept closer, exaggerating my motions so she knew exactly what I was about to do.

She let me feel the muscles and tendons along her extended wing, hissing when I found where it hurt. I worked my knuckles in just the right place to help her release some of that tension.

"Why are you helping me?" she asked, watching me work. *"Don't you know Victor's planning on ruining Field Training for you again?"*

If she wasn't able to fly this weekend, I *would* have a better time, but I just shook my head. *"I don't care about that. I don't hold you responsible for his actions."*

"Thank you," she murmured. After about five minutes of tending to her, she clicked her beak for attention. *"Go. Now."*

Our connection broke as she yawned and closed her eyes,

her wing still extended but held less rigidly. I hurried out of her stall and was just collecting Ari when Callan approached his gryphon's stall with a saddle over his shoulder. He must've sensed the judgment in my stare, because he turned to sneer back at me.

On my way out, I snagged a caretaker and let him know that Sunset needed a trip to the healers.

ARI and I dreamed we faced an eldrafn two nights in a row, connecting instantly for him to see through my eyes and heading into the storm of lightning and tricky winds. *"If only we knew what we were doing,"* he groused when awake, as both times, we'd been taken down by a swift bolt of lightning.

"Did you learn how to face an eldrafn the last time you were here?" I asked him.

We were forming up for Field Training after another unsuccessful showing at the monthly competition. Element C had won, and just to mess with us, the trainers had scrambled us into new elements to fly in today. I was in Element D alongside Biggs and three less familiar cadets. As far as I could tell, though, Callan wasn't here.

I assumed the healers had grounded Sunset to give her time to heal her wing. Thank the gods Ari and I could experience a Field Training day without him around to make it extra unpleasant.

"Yes. You learn to fight eldrafn in your third year," Ari said. *"Before you ask, I remember it being disappointingly brief. The strategy is to attack it as a group because it can only focus on a few targets at a time. The riders who don't get electrocuted enter the eye of the storm at the center of the eldrafn and pierce its heart with javelins."*

"There's no strategy for facing one alone?" I asked with a frown.

"It's impossible. If we're going to keep having this dream over and over, we're going to die...over and over."

"Lady Nilara must believe we'll find a way."

He huffed a sigh. *"Keep telling yourself that."*

I perked up my ears as our Cadet-Commander, today Credell, called us from parade rest to attention. "We are to meet in our elements and pick captains." When he shouted, it sounded like his voice was straining. "The strategy for this round is full aggression. You are to take out as many of the enemy combatants in the air as you can."

"Yes, sir," we chorused.

He dismissed us, and I sought out my new element. "Let's cut to the chase, gentlemen," Biggs said, putting a hand on my shoulder. "This is Cadet Walker, our ticket to victory. I nominate her our Cadet-Captain."

"Hold on a second," complained the single Harrier Flight cadet in our element. "Isn't she the worst-ranked person here?"

"No, that's Sharde," Biggs said, hooking a thumb over his shoulder. "C'mon, Element Delta. Give it a chance."

"What's the worst that could happen?" I asked with some humor, not expecting to get any agreement past that.

The other three cadets glanced between each other, and with a few indifferent shrugs, I ended up a Cadet-Captain for the first time. I waited for the feeling of great importance that came with a sudden promotion, but it didn't happen. It just felt like I had four young men waiting for me to tell them what to do now.

"I believe you mean to say, it's my time to shine," Ari said.

"Is it?"

"As long as I can see. Until that happens, we're doing arrow-head formation."

I said out loud, "We're going to start with arrowhead

formation." It was a simple method of attack we'd all learned by now, with us as tightly tucked together as possible. Flying straight ahead like that was fairly straightforward, but only really coordinated elements could pull off almost any other maneuver without spreading back out or clipping each other.

Ari patiently fed me the rest of our strategy. "We're only going to do right turns. No dives. Even though our leadership wants us to be aggressive, once the air clears some, we only engage in combat in a small area around our flight path rather than chase down stragglers. Questions?"

"Sounds like a solid plan to me," Biggs said, flashing two thumbs up.

"Oh, and no panicking. We don't want to break formation," I added since I'd seen way too much of that already in the limited element flying we did for the competition days and during Advanced Anatomy when the rozash illusion tended to scatter frightened cadets with its lunging and roaring.

Before we knew it, the horn that signaled the start of the first round blew. We had to survive for five minutes in the air without getting hit by one of the lengths of wood the third-years were carrying, while also trying to do the same to as many of them as possible. *"Our odds are better this time, at least,"* I said to Ari, and not just because Callan wasn't here. I was calmer this time, knowing what I was getting into as a cloud of third-years sped toward us, whooping and screeching like animals.

I felt Ari was holding back from top speed to keep from pulling ahead of the others in our formation. Our vision connected, and he turned us about fifteen degrees to the right, cutting between two enemy elements. *"Don't look back,"* he ordered when I started to crane my head around.

Right. I tapped his flank, seeing that we were nearing the outer bounds of the "battlefield," and we wheeled around for another pass. "That's right! We're coming for you!" Biggs shouted, pumping his weapon in the air as we headed straight for an intact enemy element.

Their captain spotted us, and the five gryphon riders went in a bunch of random directions. *"That's a starburst. Don't chase,"* Ari ordered. I got the feeling he was transferring this information down to the other gryphons in our element, but the Harrier Flight cadet peeled off anyway to try to tag the nearest enemy to him.

Despite Ari's earlier order, I glanced back to see the end of the starburst maneuver, when all five cadets converged on my teammate and smacked him soundly for his mistake.

"That was stupid," Ari said.

Echo screeched off our right shoulder. It almost sounded like she agreed with his statement.

We only lost one more teammate, leaving Element D the most intact one coming for a landing for the second round. I took a moment to be proud when I saw the tatters of our forces huddling up to strategize.

"This is all you, actually. You did a great job leading us," I said to Ari. He already knew the advanced strategies and could recognize and react to them.

He preened and lifted his beak. *"I know."*

Weslecker looked up from the huddle and smiled, gesturing for me to join in next to him. "I'm your wingman this time," he murmured.

I opened my mouth to tell him I didn't need a wingman with Callan stuck back at the fortress while Sunset's wing healed, but then I closed it. It would be nice not to wait in the middle of the forest alone and maybe even spend some time talking rather than practicing for class.

Ari's emotions lit with amusement. I looked down to see him and Ironfeather pressed together, and the younger gryphon beamed a feeling of approval my way. With a little flush, I refocused on the strategy meeting and realized I'd missed it. I jogged past the tree line, following Weslecker until he crouched behind a broad tree and disguised his wooden training sword under a scattering of leaves.

I did the same and hid behind a slightly slimmer tree sprouted a few feet from his. "Hi," I murmured.

"Hey."

"Did they really put their best swordsman on defense?" I asked.

Weslecker shrugged. "Mateo's leading the charge this time. It'll be all right. I'd rather be back here with you."

I didn't really know what to say to that without putting my foot in my mouth. "Yeah, thanks," I finally said. It felt pretty inadequate.

He scratched the back of his head, looking out into the woods. "So, we're just out here until someone comes along."

"That's right."

"At least we don't have to do extra PT huh?"

We both chuckled. Gods above, where did this awkwardness come from? I talked to him all the time...but never quite alone like this.

"Are you glad you're here?" I asked, turning back to him.

His brow took on a little notch from the abrupt change in subject. "Like, playing defense?"

"No, I mean, at the Academy, as a gryphon rider," I said. If I closed my eyes, his prim accent still befitted a spot across from the crown prince for a meeting over tea, designed to manipulate in the way of nobles.

He lifted his shoulders in a carefree way, reminding me of the way Sharde always responded to criticism. "Sure. Training is not fun, but I'm one of the privileged few that get to know what it's like to Link with a gryphon. Or is this about being in Kite Flight? I have to say, everyone did grow on me."

We both seemed to loosen up, laughing together quietly as we waited for any third-years to cross our path. It took hours, but eventually, a pack of six young men came through. We were more a minor block on their path, but Weslecker took two with him, and I finished off a third he'd "wounded."

Our side lost shortly after. But the instructors rearranged our command structure before we could play another match. Commander Rudrick came to the assembled Kite Flight and pointed to the ground in front of us. "Cadet Walker, take command!"

Next to me, Ari left the impression of a smug smile on his side of the Link. *"Perfect,"* he said.

Under my stoic expression, I was grinning. *Finally, a chance to prove myself.*

THE NEXT RANK UPDATE, I was number twenty-five of thirty-five and retained my title of Cadet-Commander of Kite Flight until the trainers got tired of the command structure we had. I learned two things for the month I wore the bold stripes of a commander while in uniform.

Number one: if another cadet remembered my rank was above theirs, I, too, was a "sir."

Number two: Cadet-Commanders actually had extra responsibilities. At every Pass in Review, I marched my flight around the Green. I reported to my Cadet-Marshall on Kite Flight's activities and passed down orders from those that outranked me. Somehow, Prince Mateo had ended up at the top of our chain of command again, and he was tired of losing to the third-years, so the answer to that was, of course, more PT.

I didn't care about winning a match during Field Training. The third-years had a whole year of experience on us, plus more mature gryphons and…Callan.

Third-year rank number *two*, Callan. From the look I got when reporting to Jousting class that Monday after he was forced to sit out Field Training, he knew I was at least a bit responsible for his drop in rank. I'd smiled back, as serene as I could be to the face of my true enemy, and made the gesture of Mother Nilara in response to the flick of his fingertips.

"He's going down," I said to Ari. It was time to combine his experience with my stubbornness and finally deal Callan the defeat he deserved. That thought got me through grueling hours of training on his back, taking hits with my shield with such force that, despite the mandatory padding, my left arm was covered in ugly bruises and sometimes too sore to lift.

Weslecker wasn't the only one training extra with me anymore. Prince Mateo came to the Green one evening, already outfitted with extra padding and carrying a bundle of practice lances over his shoulder. "Heard someone's trying to get better than me," he'd said gruffly in my direction.

"Hard to do that when I'm already there," I boasted, glad to see that twinkle of outrage in his dark eyes. He didn't pull any strikes, and that was what I really wanted, even with the pain that followed. Neither did Barlowe and the other Falcon Flight cadets who slowly started joining us. Soon, over half our year group was practicing jousting, though none so determinedly as Weslecker, Mateo, and myself.

Callan wouldn't take it easy on me if I qualified for the Cadet Games. But that was the true challenge. I had two rounds of Field Training to get through before the event in December. "We only invite qualified second-years to joust in the Cadet Games," Rudrick had said when I asked after class.

"How do I qualify?" I asked, watching the other cadets drift off to their next class.

He must've seen some of that motivated fire in my eyes, because he didn't brush off the question. "Well, Cadet Walker, I just learned about the process myself. You have to be in the top half of your class with good grades and a mature gryphon. We don't send up second-years just to be fodder for the third-years to show off. This is their debut for the Commanders looking for squires. Do you remember how you ended up one of ten cadets who started in Elements Alpha and Beta?"

I nodded. At the time, they'd identified those who'd already taken advanced flying classes.

"That means only those ten have a true chance at qualifying." He clapped me on the shoulder. "Get to rank seventeen or so, and I'll recommend you for the Games. Good luck."

Rank seventeen. We could do that.

Maybe.

In the meantime, I watched a war of words between the *Kaiamear Gazette* and the *Voice of the People* when I finally found time to read my mail. The next edition had an article telling off the *Voice* for presuming to know the gods' will, and I realized halfway through that the writing style was different than what I expected from Miles Glimmerwick.

I'd flipped the paper back to the front and held the byline close to my face. No matter how I stared, the "Talase Walker" printed under the bold headline didn't change.

The *Voice* responded by trying to smear my mother's good name.

Mother wrote an article a few days later detailing her unfailing service to Mother Nilara, with an exclusive interview with the High Priestess from the Kaiamear Temple quoted for agreement.

The *Voice* seemed to ignore it and reported a historical piece detailing how the last Crusade started after an uprising in southern Altare when a coalition of farmers refused to pay tithe to the temples since "the gods have no need for coin or grain, so it all ends up in the pockets of fat priests." It seemed to pose a question, asking if history would repeat itself.

"Hey, guys, Walker's mommy writes for the newspaper now," Barlowe announced one morning, slapping a fresh copy of the *Kaiamear Gazette* in the midst of his Falcon Flight friends.

I got up and snatched it, desperate to know her response. "Oh, she's good," I said, skimming her reply.

The main headline read: "VOICE OF THE PEOPLE WANTS MORE WAR"

"Why does anyone purchase the sensational garbage published by the so-called *Voice of the People*? Any learned person knows the Crusades were a thin excuse for the Churches to murder and extort. The gods were watching, and without their favor, the historical First Church of Orion crumbled under the assault of an earthquake even the Tulari couldn't stop. Natural disasters ruined villages across Altare. Does the *Voice* really want to repeat *that*?"

The paper was ripped from my hold. "Hey," I protested.

Barlowe grinned and waved the crumpled paper. "What, embarrassed?"

Quite the opposite, in fact. I'd just written home to tell Mother how proud I was for her to push back against the Crown-owned *Voice*, and clearly, she was the right person to discredit what it had to say.

"I know my mother's articles are too advanced for you," I replied coolly. "Maybe if you applied yourself, you could understand them."

A few of the young men listening to this exchange hooted and pounded on the tables.

"What's gotten into you, Walker? You used to be nice." He faked a sniff.

"That's ma'am to you all. Cadet-Commander Walker." I hitched my thumb toward my chest.

He hid a smile by wetting his lips. "Yes, sir," he said.

I supposed that was the opening to my own word war. I didn't really know what'd "gotten into me" except for a distinct sense of being tired of my status as a verbal punching bag. I punched back now. When any young man made the sign of Lord Orion at me and flicked their fingertips rudely, I either pointed to the streak of white in my hair or made the sign of Mother Nilara back.

Some of them actually backed down, but not Callan. He'd attacked me in the woods and gotten away with it. On some level, he was the only one who knew the Mother's protection was a façade, a thin veneer to disguise me as a Nilarite until Lord Orion was ready for me to act as his Chosen.

He wasn't my only problem, though. Odalis finally wrote back, and her secret message made my blood run cold. I'd asked her what Crown Prince Isaac's plan was, and she wrote, "Civil war in your name. Watch the news. Talk at Yule?" I replied a yes to that, needing to know what was going on.

I was watching, all right. Every time the *Kaiamear Gazette* and the *Voice of the People* published responses to each other, I imagined the type of people who were reading.

Would someone like Commander Davis, wherever he'd gone, read both sides or just the *Voice*? I imagined he consumed only that newspaper fervently. There were more of him out there, people like the king too, who didn't want change.

But was there an equal and opposite amount of Altarians agreeing with the more established newspaper, the *Kaiamear Gazette*? The crown prince had hired my mother, a bulldog of a writer, to savage his competition. She was doing it for me, I thought, but she was serving the agenda too.

There was little I could do from the Academy, though. I wrote Mother with my speculations, and her response was, essentially, not to worry yet.

Time slipped through my fingers again. I'd climbed to rank twenty-two by December when the Commandant paid a visit to my Jousting class.

"Great news, everyone," Rudrick said, rubbing his hands together. "We will be assembling the jousting bracket in the next week. Second-years, do your best to show that you are ready for the visiting Commanders to watch you joust, and you may be invited to compete.

"Third-years, as a reminder, this will be your last chance to earn one of the more coveted squire-ships being offered. Your second semester will be spent learning the tips and tricks from the experienced knights of your assigned flight. Someone in the know has whispered that the First, Third, and Sixth are looking for top talent."

Excited murmurs rose from the more experienced cadets. Next to me, Sharde was already shrugging and tuning out, absently petting his gryphon instead.

"Watch out. One of those spots is mine." I picked out Callan's boast from the general chatter. He'd rebounded to being number one again, Ace-to-be of the third-years. I hoped Father wouldn't be forced to take him as a squire because of that.

"All right!" Rudrick clapped his hands, a habit he'd picked up since becoming an instructor. "Let's get our gear on and get into the air."

Slowly, we'd worked up to jousting in the air, which required a different set of gear that was quite cumbersome. We jousted wearing an actual breastplate of plate mail, too heavy to take into regular combat but necessary to keep a cadet safe during the ceremonial sport. As I understood it, jousts between actual knights were exceptionally rare due to how dangerous it was to conduct outside of the Academy environment.

However, how else would we show our prowess in the air to prospective Commanders without hitting each other? I donned the smallest breastplate they had, made for a short man. It had a base built in that provided a resting place to balance the practice lance and prevent it from sliding around due to wind resistance. The moment I first jousted with this, I'd never missed another target, hitting each of my jousting opponents square in the shield.

No one had missed my shield, either. Duels were decided by the results after impact. Whichever gryphon was knocked more off balance was determined the loser, and I knew defeat in this, just like in everything else.

The soldiers set up a tilt for us, just a rope lifted high and pulled taut by the poles we used to create aerial mazes. With the poles attached to a heavy cart, the tilt only swayed subtly in the wind.

Everyone got to duel at least once a day, and today, Ari and I were blessed to get called up early. I loved participating in the actual event, and so did my gryphon, the two of us connecting with the familiarity born from grueling hours of practice. We approached the left side of the tilt while our third-year opponent took the right, and we flew in a loop at a leisurely speed.

I lifted my lance straight up to rest on the base of my armor as Ari and I passed the other cadet, who did likewise. We nodded to each other, the equivalent of a salute, an acknowledgment of respect and mutual readiness, because the moment we were past each other, Ari leaned forward and scooped air under his wings to finish the loop as fast as possible.

We were lighter than any other jouster, but faster too. The only part that mattered in the joust was the end: the impact. Who could hit harder and stagger their opponent?

Ari took an aggressive turn around the end of the tilt, and I turned into his momentum to lower my lance back into position. I'd lost my practice lances dozens of times practicing this maneuver, but thankfully, I didn't fumble today under the Commandant's watchful eye.

Across the tilt, the other cadet was just finishing the loop and lowering his lance. We accelerated toward each other, lances crushing against shields in explosions of wooden shards. *Bang!* Ari jolted with the impact, spinning away from the tilt no matter how firm his down strokes were. We came to a spot several yards from the tilt while the third-year and his gryphon were already recovered and circling down for a landing.

"*Not our best,*" Ari sighed.

Our hearts pumped to the same rapid pulse of adrenaline. I wanted to go again, despite the throb in my arm promising yet another bruise.

"*It's over too fast,*" I said as we landed as well. "*I wish we practiced with three rounds.*" A real joust had three, where the best two out of three rounds decided the winner.

I dismounted and got back in line. Sharde gestured for me to go in front of him. "Don't plan on going?" I asked as he ushered in Prince Mateo behind me.

Puzzlebox made an unhappy chirp at the idea. "Maybe once," he replied while also smiling and gesturing the next cadet to go ahead.

The line moved quickly. We practiced without the full pomp and ceremony. Some cadets could circle several times during the actual Games, taunting each other, until they finally lowered their lances and finished it. I wondered if the Commanders hated watching that kind of showboating from riders who hadn't been knighted yet.

"C'mon," I murmured, leaning to see how far away another match was for Ari and me.

"You're impatient today, Walker," the prince commented.

"I need the Commandant to see I can joust," I said.

The line stopped, and I turned to him. Mireille looked over at me with big, soulful, silvery eyes but didn't come closer even though she turned a hopeful expression toward Mateo. He, in turn, was inspecting me with his brow drawn. "Why is it so important?" he asked.

I sighed through my nose and leaned in. "You know how you thought I was trying to get better than you?" I whispered.

"Not actually my thought process, but go on."

I resisted an eye roll. Barely. "I want to embarrass Callan at the upcoming Games," I murmured.

His eyebrows rose to his hairline. "*That's* why you've been practicing so much?"

"Yes."

"No offense, but what makes you think you'd do anything but lose against this year's Ace-to-be?"

The same question Ari asked me all the time. But I did have an answer. "I've watched him show off every day. He thinks he's so ahead of us that he makes the same mistake every time he goes into a joust," I whispered.

"He was nearly first place at the last Cadet Games when he wasn't even up for a squire-ship," he pointed out.

"Doesn't matter," I said.

"What, exactly, is this mistake?" he pressed.

I fought a smile just like I crushed the urge to brag about being so intensely focused on Callan's jousting style that I realized he leaned a little too far into his opponent's lance. Some lean was good to brace for impact, but he set Sunset off balance. She was an outstanding gryphon, big and solid, so it never mattered all that much.

But a lightweight, aggressive woman who practiced holding her lance at just the right angle might be able to knock Sunset into the tilt, immediately disqualifying them for a round. If it happened once, *just once*, in front of all those Commanders, it'd be the kiss of death for his dreams as an Ace.

"That'll just have to be my secret, Cadet-General Cortes, sir," I said, with a salute for good measure.

He waved me away. "All right, whatever."

We ended up facing each other at the tilt. At the last minute, he pulled on his reins, slowing Mireille's momentum. Ari and I won the duel.

"You threw that," I said while we watched the last jousts of the day.

The prince smirked, but he didn't deny it.

CHAPTER 23

LONG OVERDUE

The instructors posted the last rank update and the bracket for the Cadet Games at what felt like the last possible second.

"They want to keep you in suspense," Ari had teased.

Well, it worked. I was toward the back of a stampede when new sheets of paper were nailed in beside the second-year grade postings. As I made my way to the front, someone clapped me on the shoulder, and I looked up in surprise at Mateo. "Good job, Walker," he said.

There was my name at number sixteen, barely in the threshold to qualify. "Thanks," I murmured back to the prince, who was still sitting at number one, the Ace-to-be. Everyone else's ranks changed with the whims of the instructors, it felt, except for his.

"In the very unlikely chance we were to meet at the tilt, I won't take it easy on you." He pointed out where he was in the second-to-last joust of the first round, up against Weslecker.

"They really like pitting you two against each other," I commented. It didn't take me long to find my name, facing off against Callan in the last joust.

I stepped to the side to let the next cadet take a look at the bracket, and to my surprise, Mateo followed me. "A possible challenger for Ace-to-be." He shrugged and drew me aside for a more private conversation. "I don't think you should joust tomorrow. Not against Callan, at least."

I scoffed. "I'm not going to back down now. This match against him is long overdue."

"Look." He drew a hand down his face. "I overheard Callan asking to have a match against you."

I spoke without thinking. "Did the king pay him to do something?"

Mateo's mouth dropped open, his finger upraised. For a moment, he was frozen that way before he shook it off and started putting up a more neutral expression. "I already know," I said, figuring he was retreating behind a mask of ignorance. "Actually…answer me something. Are *you* involved in that too?"

He'd been attached to Callan's side last year. When they thought me cornered in a closet, he'd been just as willing as Callan and his friends to beat me up then and there. With that memory in mind, it wasn't much of a surprise that the third-year would escalate to cornering me in the forest.

But the prince… He'd clearly disapproved of what had happened on our first Field Training day. He wanted to run Callan off and was apparently plotting with Weslecker on how best to do it, but I only knew that through Ironfeather. To me, he was a closed book, a cold façade and scowl slamming into place. "What are you trying to imply, Walker?" he growled. "That I'm involved in some plot to kill you?"

"*Are* you?" I asked, leaning in with a glower of my own. "How can I trust what you have to say when it's your father trying to get me hurt…or worse."

He grimaced. "I suppose you can't. This was a mistake…" He met my gaze, and for the first time, I realized how close we'd gotten in one angry moment. Mateo flinched away with a hasty step back. "Never mind. Do whatever you want."

I watched him stalk off and took a few deep breaths to calm myself. Ari clicked his beak next to me for attention. *"So, are we jousting, or not?"* he asked.

"We are," I said. Rather than answer me, the prince had left the conversation in a hurry. On some level, I knew he was involved in his father's plots… He had to be.

MY OWN FATHER arrived late that evening, one of several commanders. Ari and I waited in the stables, which inevitably led to me tending to the exhausted gryphons who'd made the flight here from several places across Altare.

When Valtora touched down, I sensed it and thought it might've been Ironfeather or Puzzlebox, as she set off the same pleasant tingly feeling with her presence. I came out to see her growling at the caretaker trying to take her reins from Father. She spotted me and jerked out of his hold, arrowing straight for me.

"Watch out!" the caretaker shouted.

I held my arms out, and she nuzzled my face and neck with a low murr. "Hello, skymother," I murmured.

"I've missed you," she said directly to my mind.

Whoa. I'd never connected faster with another person's gryphon.

"We've always been a little bit connected." Her mental voice was exactly as I imagined it, a deep rumble of strength that belied her softer, more feminine edges. *"Your mental presence is much stronger now. This is the blessing of the shining man?"*

"Who?"

"The male at the end of the Path of Glorium." She projected a bit of frustration. *"I've forgotten his appearance, except for his shine."*

Father saved me from answering, pulling me from his

gryphon's affection for a brief hug. "Hey, kiddo. Thought I'd get to surprise you again this year," he said.

"I was hoping you'd get here a little earlier." I beamed up at him. "I'm going to be jousting tomorrow!" Last year, I'd gotten to picnic with him and watch the Cadet Games. This time, I'd be restricted to the sidelines with my shield and jousting breastplate, ready to go at a moment's notice.

We were ushered into the stables to make room for the next arrival. Valtora and Ari leaned together, with her guiding him behind us. "You qualified!" He squeezed my shoulder. "I'm so proud. You must've worked hard to earn it."

"I didn't exaggerate in my letters," I said.

As soon as the four of us were in Valtora's guest stall, I lowered my voice and told him about the strategy I'd been building to embarrass Callan in the joust. His smile turned slyer, and he gave me a few pointers. "Send him into the tilt tomorrow, and he'll kiss Ace-to-be goodbye," he murmured.

I let the giddiness at my plan carry me through that night, still smiling through Pass in Review even though Father didn't get to see me marching my flight as Cadet-Commander since I'd since been demoted. When I joined the forty or so cadets jousting today, the Green was full of lounging first-years, with the Commanders and a few more guests sprinkled amongst them.

The tilt was raised in the middle of the Green, with the jousters assembled in a big cluster to one side of it. The third-years would be showing their prowess with more games and competitions after the jousting tournament to present their skills one last time to earn the best squire-ship.

I waited for my turn at the tilt between Weslecker and our former Cadet-Commander, Valentic, whom I'd barely seen this year. Both Valentic and Birch, his speckled gryphon, had gained newfound confidence going into the Cadet Games. "I've been practicing to get into the top five," he said. "I'm hoping there's a big upset at the tilt today so I can get a squire-ship with the First or Third."

"Well, I don't want to brag or anything," I said, drawing my shoulders back. "But I'm facing Callan first, and I've been practicing quite a bit as well."

I also regretted not putting in a good word for him with my father when I had the chance. Hopefully, Valentic would stand out on his own merits and get picked up by one of the more prestigious flights.

We wished each other good luck, and conversation turned to the matches. I put my flight goggles on and tilted my head far back. Last year, I hadn't paid much attention to the jousting, but I was a lot more focused on how it worked with three rounds.

A basic joust was six trips around the tilt. The salute was also a moment to acknowledge whether your opponent was ready to lower their lance and charge on the next rotation. Other cadets used that moment to taunt and withhold their salute, so they circled each other exchanging barbs instead. Those matches lasted upward of twenty minutes, quite obnoxiously.

There was some chivalry as well. One second-year accidentally got tangled in the carrier bag, which held his second and third lance, so his opponent kept circling slowly until he fixed it and lifted his next lance into place. It was the height of disrespect to lower a lance to someone unprepared, and incredibly dangerous too. Even the strike of a practice lance, designed to shatter on impact, could hit with enough force to unseat a rider.

Night's familiar shadow swooped around us, prepared to catch anyone should an accident happen. We were five jousts in when someone tapped me on the shoulder. It was a maid, offering me a flower. "Um, thanks?" I said.

She left with a shrug, so I checked the bit of paper tied

around the stem. *A token for good luck. –A friend.* I shared what it was with Ari mentally when he seemed curious.

"Huh." Weslecker read the note with me. "That's a sun lily."

It was quite pretty, too, with delicate yellow petals and a flaming red center complete with orange stamens. "What's wrong?" I asked, noticing the uncertain tilt to his expression.

"Well, for one, knights give tokens to pretty women rather than receiving them," he said, sounding a little put out. I ducked my head, trying to hide the hint of warmth that rose on my cheeks. "And for another…well…maybe it's nothing."

"What?" I murmured, twirling the flower by its stem.

"There's a language of flowers that many nobles use. Each one means something when given as a gift or put into an arrangement for display," he explained. "I don't remember much of it, but sun lilies…I think they're a warning of danger. Unassuming outside but bright red on the inside. If you receive one as a gift, the giver is trying to tell you something."

We looked down at the flower like it'd catch fire at any moment. I glanced up, feeling eyes on me. It was Callan, who eyed the flower with a smirk. "Secret admirer, heretic?" he called.

My fingers balled reflexively, crushing the bottom half of the lily. "I don't see you getting any tokens," I replied, lifting my chin. "Jealous?"

He shook his head. "Don't be delusional."

"It's okay, you can admit it. You want a flower too," I said. A few of the young men around us started to laugh.

"Sivana…" Ari nudged our Link with a feeling of uncertainty. *"Both the princeling and your mysterious 'friend' have tried to warn you of danger."*

"We've worked for months to earn a spot at this joust." I tossed the ruined sun lily behind me, eyeing the profile of the bronze-skinned young man waiting several yards away with a few of his Falcon Flight buddies.

"I know, I was there. But surely you can put this stubborn streak aside to acknowledge Callan is being paid to endanger you?" he pressed.

"What could he possibly do? He's going to be focused on keeping his place as Ace-to-be. Most every flight's commander is here, taking notes on his performance. He would be stupid *to risk endangering all that."* I simmered in frustration, my hands two fists at my sides. *"I know Callan. He would never damage his reputation and future. He is focused only on the victory."*

Ari warbled quietly. *"But what if hurting you is the victory today?"* he murmured.

"But it's not. This is the one day I can say with certainty that he will be too focused on himself."

"I hope you're right," he said.

I knew I was. For once, I was willing to ignore those trying to hold me back to give Callan the knock off his pedestal that he deserved. The jousters were thinning out around us, only winners returning to the waiting area after their matches.

Valentic went up and won his match. Soon, I was watching Prince Mateo and Weslecker circle on the tilt, sharing a more detailed blow-by-blow with Ari while he stretched his wings in preparation for our match next.

"They are…nearly identical," I admitted. Ironfeather was developing the same kind of swiftness Ari had in the air, but Mireille was solid and steady.

Either of their riders could be the Ace-to-be. They'd reached the pinnacle of our year group, setting the goal posts for the rest of us.

"If the twins weren't on the same level, I'd be shocked," Ari commented. *"Mireille will win, though."*

A soldier barked my name, getting Ari and me lined up and ready to go next as the current joust neared its end. I tied myself into his saddle and secured the lengthy canvas bag containing my two spare lances to Ari's hips, where it'd hang down like a saddlebag on his left side.

"You were right," I said as cheers echoed across the Green. Mateo took the victory, breaking the tie with a win in the third round.

"Females have a better jousting build." He had a nervous edge, like he spoke to distract himself. I rubbed down his neck and flank in soothing circles despite my heart fluttering like a hummingbird's within my chest. Across from us, Callan and Sunset were just taking to the sky, so I nudged Ari into motion as well.

We connected instantly, our feelings blending together into one. We were both nervous, but anticipation had me gripping my lance tighter as we ascended to the top of the tilt. The rope boundary was as high as it could go, swaying this far up no matter how well-grounded the poles were. The spectators below were featureless shapes, and Night a bird-like blur as she circled far below.

It was just Callan and me up here. "Let's see what you've got, Walker," he shouted as our gryphons aligned on their proper sides of the tilt. We saluted each other with lances straight up and a nod, and I didn't waste breath trying to reply. I imagined catching me winded was part of his strategy.

Ari rounded the end of the tilt, and I lowered my lance, leaning into his tight turn and burst of speed. Callan leaned out a hair too far, like he always did, but Sunset powered forward too quickly for me to hit his shield just right. *Bam!* Our lances disintegrated, and Ari slid sideways with a pained grunt.

The shield vibrated on my arm from the forceful impact. Maybe I'd been a little too confident—Callan was clearly quite strong, to compliment his gryphon's innate advantage.

He didn't make a move to draw his next lance on our next lap around the tilt, so I didn't pull mine either. "Really, I shouldn't have expected more from a girl with a defective beast," he called.

"Your last chance to hit me before you leave, and you waste time boasting," I shouted back.

"It should be illegal to salute a heretic." But this time, he reached down and pulled out his second lance, so I did as well. We went one more pass around before saluting, lances up.

I gritted my teeth and focused as Ari surged forward. The lance tip didn't want to point downward, the very air fighting back as I aimed for the bottom third of Callan's shield. No wonder he risked a little extra lean, but this time, I hit his kite shield where it began to taper and caught a flash of shock on his face before Sunset dipped into a roll over the tilt.

Ari and I skidded to the side again, but Callan was on the wrong side of the tilt when his gryphon recovered. I imagined a shared inhalation from the watching crowd below, even though my ears were numb and full of the whistling of cold air. A victorious smile curved my lips anyway.

We were even, the great third-year Ace-to-be and I. Another round like that, and he'd never be number one again. I guided Ari back to the tilt, and he sped up until we were on the opposite side of Callan again. As I expected, he hadn't drawn his last lance yet. "How's it feel to lose?" I called.

"I will never lose to the likes of you," he spat.

"Really? Because you're about to!"

His teeth flashed. "Impossible." We drew our last lances and took a rotation to balance them upright. I blew out a tense breath to center myself. This was it, the moment I showed the watching commanders just where Callan deserved to be for his squire-ship.

Ari pulsed with determination. I felt him draw on all his strength after Callan and I finally indicated that we were ready. He elongated his body, tucking in to reach maximum acceleration. My lance pointed straight and true at the battered red field of Callan's shield. *Crack!*

Splinters of wood exploded around us. Sunset batted her

wings in hard strokes as she reared back. But Ari, his momentum bent strangely. It was over so quick I only saw the bloodied tip of a weapon *through* his wing, spraying crimson droplets over my goggles. Callan's teeth flashed in a vicious smile as Ari flapped, and the damaged wing flexed backward with a brittle series of snaps.

Ari *screamed*. His agony hit me on a delay as we fell into an uncontrolled sideways spin, pinwheeling toward the Green with nearly the same speed as we'd hit Callan.

Oh, gods. We were going to die.

Night's shadow flashed by us, I think. Her talons were a blur as we rocketed past.

Darkness closed in as my eyes rolled back.

The fragmented hilt of my last lance blew from my hand, its tan wood smearing with the green of the approaching grass.

"I'm sorry. I should've listened," I whispered to Ari.

He couldn't reply. His pain filled the Link, crippling in intensity.

They say your life flashes before your eyes when you know the end is coming.

All I saw was that stupid sun lily, signed by a friend.

And then the wind stopped whipping past my cheeks, my body bobbing into the momentum of a spin that didn't happen. I struggled past the screeching tone in my head to force my eyelids to lift. The sweet abyss was right there, welcoming me, but just out of reach when Ari and I were laid on a bed of green.

Ari's body rolled, and he made a low sound in reply to the chirp of another gryphon. Something nudged me next, pushing me onto my side. *"Stay awake,"* a female voice ordered.

Standing over us was Valtora, her golden feathers glorious with the haloing of the sun. She turned her head toward the sky, her wings mantled out and feathers brushing in all directions. Bracing her barrel chest, she inhaled. My Link with her vibrated with her fury, mounting higher and higher, until she released it in a roar that could shake the very clouds.

"Skymother, no," I whispered. As the blood rushed from my head, I recognized her intent.

Her pupils were mere pinpricks. *"He's the one who's been threatening you,"* she stated. She didn't wait for me to confirm. *"No more human mercy. It has never worked. I will kill him myself!"*

CHAPTER 24

LEARN TO LISTEN

The world blurred between my fingers as I reached for her. "Valtora, y-you…you can't," I labored to speak. Ari's pain was sinking into my body. My shoulder hurt with a phantom wound, like I had a wing under me and it, too, was irreparably shattered.

Valtora leapt into the sky, powerful wings carrying her away. "Gods, no." I was too weak to even get myself out of my riding harness, let alone stop her in a full rage.

Dozens of hands were on me the moment Valtora was gone, helping cut me free of Ari's saddle and holding back my hair as I heaved and vomited until my mouth ran bitter with bile. I felt better with an empty stomach.

When I lifted my head, I realized the sudden cut of relief was from a healer Tulari's magic. Green runes glowed above her wand as she held it toward Ari's head, vapor-like magic spilling from the tip and lulling him into unconsciousness. A team of medics and soldiers surrounded us, though the latter were shouting and running.

I tottered to unsteady feet. "P-please, t-tak-ke care of him," I said. My tongue didn't want to speak, and my body didn't really want to move, but I forced myself into a stumbling jog at the back of the group of soldiers. A cloud of red and maroon feathers was still floating down from the sky, and several gryphons filled the air with screeching.

Sunset flapped her wings uselessly under Valtora, who had her pinned. The golden gryphon's beak was stained with blood already, held open as she strained and snapped against three men who tried to pull her away by her reins.

"Nathaniel, tell them to let me go," she spat when my father reached the scene. *"He hurt your daughter. He attacked my son. He deserves to die!"*

Father held her neck, peering into her furious, slitted eyes. I was forced to stop several yards from them when a soldier turned and realized I was in the mix of people converging on the scene. "You need medical attention, miss," he said, blocking my way.

"No!" Valtora was screaming. *"No more chains of command! No more appeals! Human justice is* weak. *The fact he still breathes is testament!"*

I screamed her name past the man in my way. "You can't kill a rider," I cried. Tears slipped down to pool at the bottom of my goggles. It was too late, I thought. She'd already lost control and drawn blood.

Valtora's fierce gaze alighted on me for a moment before her eyes glazed over. A second Tulari approached her from behind, his face pale with fear as he held his wand out toward her. She collapsed, unconscious.

I slumped down to the ground as well, staring ahead in a daze. I didn't resist when someone nudged me to lie out on a stretcher, a crush of strangers coordinating around me like white noise while I was hustled off the Green.

The female Tulari appeared at my side, already weaving new runes with her wand's glowing tip. "My gryphon? Will he be okay?" I whispered.

"Hush now," she said, sending me into unwelcome darkness with a swish of her wand.

I woke to a bouquet of sun lilies at my bedside and no gryphons. It was unnervingly quiet in the infirmary without them and even more eerie to wake up like I'd just had a good night's rest rather than slog back to consciousness after receiving magical healing.

I glared at the flowers, more than tempted to dash them on the ground. If only I'd listened to the warning of the first one, or to Prince Mateo, rather than trusting my own faulty beliefs. I noticed there was a string around one of the stems and reached into the vase to pull out what was hiding where all the flowers converged.

The note was just above the water line keeping the lilies alive, tied around a magestone the size of my fist with a big, emerald-green rune etched on it. My whole hand vibrated holding it. I checked the message first.

Learn to listen. This is for your gryphon. Happy early Yule. –A friend

"Yeah, whatever," I muttered. I balled up the message and got dressed in the change of clothes left at the foot of the bed, tucking the magestone away in a spare pocket.

I went around the infirmary, looking for a nurse. One of them would be able to lead me to Ari. The other side of my Link was blank, just a void. He was still unconscious somewhere and, judging by the lack of staff around, being tended to by the healers.

Father jumped to his feet the moment I stepped out of the infirmary and found him rather than a staff member. "Thank the gods," he said, pulling me into a tight hug. "It looked so bad. For a minute, I thought you were going to die."

"I'm fine," I murmured. "Where's Ari? And Valtora?"

He sighed into my hair. "Your mother was right. We should've never let you come back to this place." He released me and led me toward the stairs. We headed up to the stables together, and he filled me in on what I'd missed.

Callan was resting in another part of the infirmary, sleeping off a round of healing magic. A Tulari had made sure his shattered collarbone, courtesy of Valtora, would mend. However, they'd given him the same treatment as I'd had last year with my broken arm, so he had a long recovery ahead of him.

Good. And when Father shared that he wasn't allowed at my bedside, on the small chance he'd finish what his gryphon had started, I wasn't surprised. The Commandant had issued an emergency restriction order to keep both Callan and me safe. We couldn't be in the same room or within a certain distance of each other without supervision. Father was under the order as well.

He wouldn't tell me about the gryphons, though. I saw for myself that the stables were mostly empty. Ari was in his usual stall, resting off his own healing with his tongue lolling from his beak. He lay prone on his belly, right wing limp and the left stretched out and splinted heavily.

"Sivana...I don't know how to tell you this," Father said, hesitating. We stood there watching his chest rise and fall. I knew I shouldn't go in and disrupt his sleep, not when it would bring him back to a world of pain.

On some level, I already knew what Father was going to say. "The healing magic didn't take, did it?" I murmured.

"Very little."

"I...see." My fingers flexed on the stall door as my eyes filled with tears.

"In the day you were unconscious, the healers have performed several surgeries to help align what they couldn't do with magic. He will have to heal naturally."

There was no news worse than this. The magestone hummed in my pocket, taunting. Magic lost its effectiveness with too much exposure to it, but it was a foreign concept to someone who'd only broken a couple bones in her lifetime. Ari, though… Ari had had much of his face reconstructed in the past, plus a decade of bruises and breaks from life as a combat gryphon. He'd taken too much healing magic, and there was no coming back from that.

Father put an arm around my shoulder, squeezing me to his side. "We have to have faith that it'll be all right," he said, shaking me from my reverie. "He can still heal and get back up from this. It will just take time."

"And what if his wing heals wrong?" I asked in a small voice.

"He's going to have all the care he needs here. It's going to be okay."

I inspected the stall and realized something was missing. Though Father wanted to comfort me, there was another thing I worried wouldn't end up all right. "Where's Valtora?"

His expression drew into a grim line, but he led me into the back of the stables, where we kept our wild gryphons. This time, he opened the stall door for me, and I froze in the threshold, my mouth dropping open. Valtora lifted her head with a low murr, clicking her beak in greeting. Chains looped around her middle, securing her wings to her back, and her back paws were encircled by heavy manacles with chains connected to the wall.

I turned a horrified look toward him. "You allowed this?" I demanded.

"He had no choice," Valtora answered. *"Come help me. There's an itch I can't reach."*

I went over and knelt down, working with her to find an itchy spot on her belly, hidden between two loops of chain. Father sat by his gryphon's head, but she turned away from him. "There are going to be two trials soon. You have to understand…Valtora wounded a gryphon rider with intent to kill him. It's being treated like a serious offense, even under the circumstances."

"She was defending her child," I argued.

"I know. But she also has a history of aggression." My stomach dropped like a stone, hands freezing in her belly fur. She had attended rehabilitation several times to blunt her talons, and now that'd be used against her.

"I'm not saying I agree with it, kiddo. I'm just telling you the facts," he sighed. "The Commandant has tapped one of his men to investigate what happened yesterday, and he's moving quite quickly, given the circumstances. He's going to come by and interview you since you're awake. Are you on good terms with Commander Falirin?"

I thought of the usually shirtless combat instructor and shrugged. "Decent, I would say."

"Good enough. It would've been Rudrick, but he had to refuse, considering how long he was in the First. So, Falirin will come speak with you and, if he has the evidence he needs, present a recommendation for court-martialing Callan. He has Callan's weapon in his possession, so the chances are very high it'll happen.

"But after Callan appears in court, I will next, representing Valtora. There is a chance..." He took a sharp breath and bowed his head.

Valtora huffed. *"I may die for the crime of defending my family,"* she said. Her tail thumped, agitated. *"I should have gone for the throat while I had the chance."*

"I'm so glad I'm the only one who understands her sometimes. She's still bloodthirsty," Father murmured, and I bit my tongue, secretly agreeing with her.

A growl rumbled from her. *"We have bathed in the blood of our enemies, yet this one Altarian boy evades his fair comeuppance."*

He ran his fingers down her neck, which she pointedly ignored. "There will be justice. You'll see the weapon, Sivana. We will be able to prove this was premeditated, because his lance was metal—a standard combat lance, in fact—covered in a layer of wood to disguise it," he said.

"How could he have possibly snuck that in?" There were soldiers and near-invisible helpers swarming events like the Cadet Games, making sure everything was running smoothly.

Father shook his head. "He had help." He heaved a long sigh. "We need to go home. If and when Callan is court-martialed, it will be in Kaiamear. A couple of men from Final Flight are still here, waiting to take us back to the city once you speak with Falirin."

"But…what about Ari?" I asked.

He patted my shoulder. "He can't be moved right now. It'll be hard, but you'll have to spend some time apart from him."

COMMANDER FALIRIN and I spoke for over an hour. He was all business, asking me about my relationship with Callan dating back to when I was a caretaker enamored with a smooth-talking cadet and his beautiful maroon gryphon.

"Just so you are aware, Marshall Jamison will expedite this process so that we may have a day in court before Yule," he told me, referencing the Commandant's actual name. "You will be required to provide testimony under truth serum."

I wetted my lips, trying to fight a hopeful wave within. "Will Cadet Callan also have to take a truth serum?"

He kept a military-strict expression. "Refusing a truth serum is as good as an admission of guilt, Cadet Walker."

With that, he dismissed me. I packed the last of my things and went to check on Ari one last time. His eyelids were shut, but I had the barest sense of groggy emotion coming from him. I let myself into his stall and stroked his neck and back until he stirred.

Father stood close by, giving me time to say goodbye. I think I spent hours there talking to my gryphon and making sure he understood why I had to go to Kaiamear without him. If Callan really had snuck a real weapon into the jousting tournament and it was in Falirin's hands, I had no doubt I would have to speak up for myself very soon.

"Goodbye for now. I love you." I hugged him around the neck, burying my face in his fur. He smelled like herbs rather than his usual feathery musk.

He made a low murr and rested against me. *"I love you too,"* he murmured.

CHAPTER 25

SEASONS TREASONS

I barely mustered a smile, greeting Mother, Rissa, and my little brother, Nate, upon arriving at home. A distinct half of me was shorn away, the steady and mature part that always seemed to know what to do. I kept catching myself reaching out for my Link to find it present but too distant to touch.

I went through the holiday motions for a day, stringing cranberries for Mother with grim, silent focus.

"They're delicious this year," Nate said, stuffing a few cranberries in his mouth. He did a miserable job of hiding his cringe at the wave of bitter juice that washed over his tongue. I tried to smile while Rissa forced a laugh and ate one too.

It was the opposite of old times. They were willingly eating the berries while I pierced them with a sewing needle, adding them to a line one at a time.

Rissa's little dignified nose wrinkled as she swallowed. "Wow, so good."

They chattered around me while I focused on keeping my fingers moving. Rissa was excelling at the first tests at Lady Nilara's temple to become an acolyte, and for a moment, her gaze alit on me with guilt. She spoke of the same round of tests I'd failed because the goddess wouldn't speak with me.

"Congrats," I murmured. I couldn't say I was happy for her, because I didn't think I was capable of that anymore. Not with both Ari and Valtora's futures uncertain due to my stupid mistake.

"How about you, Nate? Learn any magic?" she asked.

"A bunch of theory!" he replied cheerfully. "You should see my textbooks. They're even larger than last year."

"Do you actually read all those pages?"

"Yup! One at a time, you know."

"Yeah, I know that's how books work."

He flashed his goofy smile, complete with a little dimple to one side. "Really? Have you read one recently?"

I knew they meant well, but it was a relief when Mother came in from her shift at the temple and called me to our dining room table. "How are you?" she asked in a quiet voice. I just shrugged. "Well, as good as expected, then. I promised you I'd explain why I'm writing for the *Kaiamear Gazette*."

I thought back, *way* back. I'd suggested what Odalis had sent me in code, that civil war was on the horizon due to the crown prince. She'd wanted to talk to me in person; to explain without code, I imagined.

"Your father and I are working with Prince Isaac," she said. If I wasn't sitting down, my knees would've turned to jelly at her statement.

"Y-you what?" I stammered.

"The king does not intend to step down anytime soon, unless...persuaded." She laced her elegant hands on the table, completely at ease.

I could hardly believe it. "You support civil war?"

"If that's what it will take to retire King Cortes," she said. "But I am one of Isaac's consultants in turning public opinion so this business can end without bloodshed. I took on your debt to him, sweetheart, so he won't be calling on you anymore. You don't owe him a thing."

I nodded slowly. No wonder she didn't want to write this

down on paper. To have a hint of the crown prince's plans was one thing, but to actively participate was quite another. "You're talking about treason right now."

"Yes. I could be caught, that's true. But I have nothing to gain for loyalty and everything to lose." A frown marred her composure, and she reached over to grasp my hand. "Sivana, there have been at least three attempts on your life because of the king's influence. His agent has hurt your gryphon and may be the reason your father loses his lifelong career. I—no, *we*—owe the king nothing. I will gladly bow to a new king who embraces change and holds *you* in high regard."

I held on to her hand like an anchor, shocked so much had changed in my absence. "You don't have to do this for me." She was risking her life to put her name on articles challenging the *Voice of the People* and the king's will.

"I will do it all again in a heartbeat to protect you," she said fiercely. "Your father has served that man for years, and even he has agreed this is the best course of action."

I pictured Father's unshakable loyalty fracturing under pressure. First from the callous way the king blew off Alamid's death, to the news that he'd hired Callan to harm me at the Academy.

"He hasn't had to do anything yet. But the possibility is there," Mother told me. As Commander of the First, Father turning against the king could leave him without a way out of a hostile situation. Treason from him would either end in a bloody death for the king or with my father on the hangman's noose.

She gave me time to think and turn over her words until I realized she was right. It would be best to support the royal who didn't want me killed. "What do you need me to do?" I asked.

"Fight like you're trying to escape the three hells. Your father has learned that Callan's court-martial is in three days," she said. "Which means...Valtora's trial is in four." The

Commandant had definitely succeeded in expediting both trials.

I nodded. I could fight. After what he'd done, Callan should never enter the Academy again, and Valtora should fly free.

I PACED like a caged beast after receiving my official summons for both upcoming trials. I'd sent a letter to Odalis, telling her I was back in Kaiamear and wanted to meet with her, but she didn't send a reply right away. It was the height of rudeness to do anything but wait for her to invite me to a meeting, Mother said.

With nothing else to do, I visited the gryphon stalls to spend time with the First's beasts. They filled part of the hole in my chest where Ari's presence should be. The more time I spent away from him, the worse it felt. All the while, I knew this was just a taste of what Ari had experienced when he lost Alamid.

A few gryphons came and went, but when I heard a familiar voice, I crept to the edge of the First's stables to be sure I wasn't imagining things. An elder rider was untethering his gryphon from Sunset before coming over to help Callan from his saddle.

My lip curled. He'd seen better days. Bandages lassoed him from the neck down, and one of his arms was in a sling. Of course, the moment his feet were on the ground, his gaze flashed over to where I was standing. We exchanged glares and gestures, my hand making the crescent moon of Lady Nilara on habit now since he always took an opportunity to flick his fingertips at me.

Caretakers moved to take Sunset, and he accepted their help...walking away from me and into the palace. That wasn't how this usually went. I shrugged to myself and went back to meeting the newest addition to the First, Breeze, a surprisingly sweet, dun-feathered female who liked belly rubs almost as much as Puzzlebox.

Maybe it helped that I could speak to her, because she seemed to respect Valtora quite a bit. We missed the golden gryphon together until Breeze decided she wanted a nap. That's when I decided to return to my room and nearly tripped over Callan in the stairwell.

"Finally," he muttered. He wasn't even all that stealthy, his bandages standing out from the shadows of his chosen waiting spot.

"I have nothing to say to you," I said coolly. "Get out of my way before I push you down the stairs."

He flashed his teeth in a grin. How had I ever thought that expression was handsome? He eyed me like a cat might as it toyed with its prey. "I just wanted to say, you put up a better fight than I expected, but it's over. I've won."

"Of course, Victor." I snipped out his first name. "Always focused on the win. We'll see when you have your day in court."

His eyes crinkled at the corners, somehow amused at the looming threat of his entire career on the line. "The king will pardon me, of course," he said, wincing when he tried to shrug. "Don't get your hopes up. I will have the best representation influence can create and water for a truth serum. The judge will be sympathetic to my cause. And even if I should lose, that royal pardon is in my future."

My teeth set on edge. In all this time, the possibility of a royal pardon hadn't come up. How deliberate and slimy would the king want to seem in this situation? "Whereas you." He forced a laugh. "You're ruined. Your gryphon isn't likely to fly again, *and* your father's beast is going to be put down. I'd say I did my job very well."

I found it difficult to breathe, my hands balling into fists.

"How much?" I gritted. "To sell out your dignity, how much was it?"

"A private benefactor offered me something generous indeed to get rid of you. Doubled my rate, in fact," he said, then tilted his head stiffly and tapped his cheek. "Go ahead, Walker. Free shot."

I shifted my weight, ready to take his offer, when I realized how he'd manipulated me. His back was to the stairwell, and he was sure to fall down it if I struck him. How he'd cry in his court-martial about *me* attacking *him* when he was at his most vulnerable. "Gatekeeper take you. Move!" I practically roared, shoving him to the side to slip down the stairwell.

Two flights down, I turned and made eye contact briefly with a cloaked man dressed more properly for blending into the shadows. He had a forgettable face, but still, he wore arrogance in the slant of his lips. My skin prickled with goosebumps, so I hurried back to my room, thinking there were worse things than a little boredom.

Besides, I had a letter to compose. I wrote to the crown prince, asking to meet.

Unlike Odalis, Prince Isaac sent for me within a couple hours. Now that he and Mother were allies, I assumed it was safe to talk to him alone. I needed to talk to him right away, considering the court-martial was tomorrow.

"It is nice to see you again," Isaac said, stirring a pinch of sugar into a cup of tea as we settled into his solar, this time with the windows shut against the winter chill outside. "Though I understand misfortune has struck your family recently."

"Yes, there was another attempt on my life," I said.

He tisked quietly. "Say it's not so. I presume this is why you wanted to meet with me."

Just like the last time I spoke with him alone, something about his smile was a little unnerving. A touch too knowing, perhaps, like he was aware of exactly what I needed that only he could provide.

Still, I shared with him word-for-word what Callan had said in the stairwell. "Ah, stacking the odds in his favor. That will not do," Isaac said when I was finished. "I can help, but there will be a price."

"What do you have in mind?" I asked.

Mother's advice echoed in the back of my head. *Accept no open-ended bargain, no matter what.*

He took a long sip of tea and popped an entire little teacake in his mouth. I fidgeted with my fingers below the line of the table, feeling the tension in me increasing with each quiet moment.

"Your mother has been very helpful of late. A much more impassioned writer than Glimmerwick," he said. Smoothly dodging around my question, I noticed. "I suppose hunger is born when you have a child to defend with only flimsy words and thin paper. It's been an honor to work with her."

"I'll have to tell her you said so." I realized my urgency wasn't going to make this a quick meeting and started nibbling on one of the sweets from the pile heaped between us.

"It really is a blessing to meet someone whose ideology aligns with your own. I get hope for the future every time it happens, especially when that person is from the generation before yours and mine," he said, sitting back with his cup of tea. "Not everyone is so intransigent in their beliefs as my father. That is why it's necessary he leave the crown to someone more willing to embrace the times. Don't you agree, Sivana?"

I nodded, knowing he was referring to himself.

"My plans have come across an unfortunate roadblock. I have plans for a rally, you see, to bring together my friends across all of Kaiamear and beyond." He smiled into his tea, like he was anticipating a huge party. "It was going to be during this time. Alas, I have realized it would be too premature."

"Not enough support?" I asked.

He waved his sausage-like fingers. "Nothing so dour. But this does circle around to you and your…dilemma. When the time is right, I would like you to be there, representing my interests. Stand by my side and let my friends see your face so they know that you're one of us. Promise you'll do this, and I'll have my people ensure the trial tomorrow is a fair one. What do you say?"

"I think…" I steeled my expression to exude control rather than show the burst of hope his offer gave me. Mother's training did me in good stead. "…your interests align with mine."

Crown Prince Isaac smiled in his unnerving way and finished his cup of tea. "Ah. Excellent."

CHAPTER 26

VICTORY'S PRICE

I ATTENDED Callan's court-martial in my formal cadet uniform, one of a dozen cadets seated in the crowd. I sat between my father and Ellie, who had returned to the capital with Sarge to attend the trial as well. Until now, I hadn't realized that a few of my friends had been in the city to testify against Callan.

The military court was part of an installation on the outskirts of Kaiamear, connected to a correctional barracks for those convicted of breaking serious military codes. Callan stood to one side before the bench, making sure to scan the crowd until he flashed me one last smirk. He was bracketed by his defense attorney on one side and none other than Prince Mateo on the other side, a symbol of the king's hand in the proceedings.

I sweated through the formal beginning of the trial, which was led by a grizzled judge. Callan's attorney first confirmed that he didn't want a panel, so he would be tried by the judge alone.

"I consent to the truth serum," he said next. A soldier stood by with a tray of shot glasses, each filled with a sip of liquid. My fingers bit into my palm as Callan received one.

From here, the clear serum looked identical to water. He tipped it back and swallowed.

I trembled with nerves as I watched Callan grip the glass tighter, looking down at it. His back was to me, so I had no idea if he was having a reaction or if it was just for show. If the crown prince had come through for me, Callan had just downed an unexpected shot of the truth rather than what he was expecting.

The prosecutor was a small, balding man with an unexpectedly deep, commanding tone. His opening statement had several of us nodding in the audience, painting Callan as a bully who'd fixated on me from the moment I'd arrived at the Gryphon Rider Academy and a young man willing to do anything to get ahead in a highly competitive atmosphere.

"A significant number of high-ranked gryphon knights were present when Mr. Callan ended his duel with Ms. Walker by using this weapon." The prosecutor gestured, and a pair of soldiers brought out a long glass box containing the metal lance, complete with a dried bloodstain. The wooden surface had split over half of it, revealing steel beneath a thin wooden casing.

I gasped to see it again. In the heat of the moment, its wooden disguise had fooled me, but in retrospect, it was clearly a doppelganger of the fragile practice lances we were supposed to use. The prosecutor pointed out how its counterweight had been sawed off to better hide it until the right moment.

"Your Honor, I believe you will agree with me that possession of such a weapon is inexcusable," finished the prosecutor before letting the defense have their say.

"This'll be good," Father muttered.

It was brief, at least, causing Sarge to snark over Ellie and me to my father, "They have no defense."

The defense painted Callan as a motivated cadet who excelled at the Gryphon Rider Academy. "Mr. Callan was set up with the weapon you see before you, Your Honor. He needed no such weapon to defeat Ms. Walker in a joust. In fact, the unexpected weight of it caused him to lose control of it and produce the unfortunate accident that injured Ms. Walker's gryphon."

The attorney turned to Prince Mateo. "We have a representative from the Crown as well."

Mateo stepped forward, clearing his throat. What he had to say could end this trial before it began if he implied that the Crown was on Callan's side and wanted to see him declared innocent.

I honestly didn't know what he'd do. He'd tried to warn me about Callan earlier, but he hadn't *denied* that he was involved in his father's scheme to pay someone to hurt me. The moment it took him to speak felt like an eternity.

"The Crown has an interest in seeing justice this day for a shocking event that interrupted an Academy tradition that dates back to the early years of the gryphon knight corps," he announced.

Huh. That was about as neutral as he could get, neither supporting nor condemning Callan.

With that said, the judge called Callan up for questioning. I was about as tight as a drawn bow as the prosecutor asked his first question. "Let us test the truth serum, shall we? Do you see that weapon, Mr. Callan?" he pointed to the lance in its glass box now resting across his desk lengthwise.

"Yes, sir. I see it," Callan answered.

"You held that weapon and broke the wing of Arimus, Ms. Walker's gryphon, with it."

Callan's face twitched, like it was caught between trying to make three expressions at once. "That...that's not a question, sir."

"You broke Arimus's wing with it, yes or no?" the prosecutor asked, not missing a beat.

"...Yes, sir," Callan answered reluctantly.

I leaned forward as the last question rolled off the prosecutor's tongue. An honest answer here would prove that he'd really drunk truth serum. "Did you intentionally sneak a real weapon into your joust with Ms. Walker, or was it an accident?"

He resisted answering the question, his mouth turning like the words tasted sour. A whole courtroom's worth of eyes pierced Callan, and sweat started to dampen the bandages around his neck, sticking to the apple of his throat as it bobbed. "I...I snuck it in intentionally," he said.

I gaped, turning to share that expression with Ellie. She seized my hand, the two of us having a victorious little moment in the midst of the awful circumstances that'd brought us here.

Callan's attorney had a sagging back by the time the prosecutor was done having Callan prove his own guilt with the truth. He tried to get a more sympathetic side out of his client during the cross-examination. Clearly, my bias was showing, as he sounded guilty even as he talked about his position as Ace-to-be and the hard work and dedication it'd taken to reach that point.

While he talked, I felt eyes on me. It was Prince Mateo, arms crossed, waiting to catch my attention. He looked bored, but when our gazes met, he winked.

For the first time since leaving the fortress without Ari, I smiled.

THE COURT-MARTIAL LASTED ALL DAY. I was the second person questioned after I downed a shot of truth serum. The little sip of clear liquid was *strong*, sending eddies of fog through my mind. I felt a little like my goofy brother, my head stuck in a lax tilt and a relaxed smile on my face as I answered every question honestly.

I was invincible for as long as that potion circled through my veins. The truth was the best thing I'd ever uttered. Unlike Callan, I didn't mind a moment of it, so I didn't resist the euphoria of uttering the truth to every question.

It was during my time with the prosecutor that Callan's habit of calling me a heretic came up. I demonstrated his version of the sign of Lord Orion, complete with the finger flick. "Discriminating against you on religious grounds is a serious offense," the prosecutor said with a sly glance toward the judge.

Other than moving the proceedings along, the judge was a stoic figure who mostly grunted when addressed directly. He seemed like he hated every single one of us. He eyed his glass of water like he wanted something much stronger as several witnesses came forward afterward.

Both Ellie and Sarge were called, but so were a number of Callan's buddies willing to speak well of his leadership and skills as a gryphon rider. Mateo refused to come forward for questioning. "The Crown does not wish to influence the court-martial," he said. He also remained quiet during closing arguments, other than confirming that the Crown would accept any decision the judge made.

The same information came forward over and over, painting both Callan and me in detailed strokes by the time the judge left to make a decision.

I waited outside, chatting quietly with Ellie as we both tried to work off the lingering fog of the truth serum. Our fathers chatted like old friends, and I heard a trip to a pub was in their future. Sarge offered to buy, considering Father had another trial to attend tomorrow to fight for his gryphon.

The sun was starting to set, and I sighed to see the darkening sky over the cityscape. It reminded me too much of the day I'd thought was Ari's last. I wondered how he was doing and if his wing was healing well. His absence felt like the worst kind of heartache, thrumming pain in my chest.

"We might have to wait until tomorrow," Ellie said, following the direction of my gaze. "This was a really long day."

I opened my mouth to agree with her when one of the soldiers told us that court was reconvening. Almost no one had left, so we packed the room again. The judge stood at his podium, his voice booming over us. "I have come to a decision regarding this case." He gestured for one of the soldiers to read off the verdict.

"Cadet Victor Callan is hereby guilty of breaking the following codes," the soldier announced, announcing the proper articles.

One count of assaulting a fellow cadet.

One count of injuring a combat gryphon.

And finally, a charge for attempted murder. Callan's head bowed with defeat, at last exposed for who he truly was in front of everyone.

"You will never be a knight," the judge said to him in a glacial tone. "My verdict will be passed to Marshall Jamison in the morning, and he will decide your sentence." He gestured for Callan to be taken away in cuffs, ending the trial.

I didn't cheer; it wasn't appropriate in the same room as the dour judge. I kept it bottled up until Ellie and I returned to my family's apartments and I had Rissa trapped in an enthusiastic hug.

"The judge said he'll never be a knight," I crowed. "Today's the day Victor Callan finally *lost!*"

⁂

I GOT DRESSED in my best again for the next day in court, just for an unexpected visitor to arrive at our door before Father and I could leave.

It was the Commandant himself, looking as severe as ever in his immaculate uniform. "A few minutes of your time, if you please," he said, inviting Father and me on a walk.

"The walls have ears around here, though I imagine they've already heard the news," he said, hands behind his back. We were going on a very specific path I'd taken hundreds of times, the one that led most directly to the gryphon stables. "I was informed of Victor Callan's guilt to every expected charge yesterday evening. I was prepared to have him Link-stripped, in an effort to save him from the execution block for holding a Link to one of the finest young gryphons we have."

"Link-stripped?" I echoed quietly, looking up at my father.

"It's a once-in-a-generation move, Cadet Walker," the Commandant answered for him. "Very rarely, a gryphon can break an established Link with Tulari assistance, but the Link has to already be damaged. The rider has to be abusive or neglectful, and *that* is nearly impossible when we share every heartbeat with our beasts."

I blinked rapidly. I hadn't known it was possible to break a Link at all…or that a rider could potentially be so awful to a gryphon they were bonded to.

"There won't be a trial today for your gryphon, Commander Walker," he continued. "I already canceled it before hearing the news, due to Valtora's aggression being aimed at someone who was no longer a gryphon rider. You may go retrieve her from Fortress Aerie at any time. The corps will pay for your expenses." He gave Father a key, presumably for her shackles.

Father breathed a heavy sigh of relief. "Thank you, sir."

We started climbing toward the Gryphon Yard. Even from here, I could hear the distinctive wailing of a mourning gryphon. "You said there's news, sir?" I asked.

"Early this morning, Victor Callan hung himself with a bedsheet." We soon emerged into the light of day on that shocking statement. The keening grief of a single broken-hearted gryphon was echoed by the sympathetic cries of nearby beasts.

Callan was *dead*?

"He tied a bedsheet with a broken collarbone?" Father asked, raising a skeptical brow.

The Commandant's lips pressed together. "We are waiting on news from an investigation, but I can confirm to you, he's dead."

I reeled back in shock. Despite everything, I hadn't wanted him to die, just lose publicly after everything he'd done to me. I could hardly believe that he was just…gone. No more rivalry. No more looking over my shoulder just in case he found me alone again.

The Commandant turned to me. "Sunset will be returning to Fortress Aerie with you, cadet. I have personally assigned her to you, as you are the only individual on recent record to rehabilitate a gryphon with a broken Link."

I accepted this immediately. Sure, I'd only saved Ari by personally Linking with him and helped him slog through the pits and valleys of loss by walking by his side through them, but… "I'll do everything I can to save her, sir," I promised.

He fixed me with his most piercing stare. "See to it that you do," he said. "Three hells, get her Linked to a woman if you have to. We can't lose another gryphon."

CHAPTER 27

UNBEARABLE

Sunset had been too worked up to approach. She needed some time, too immersed in grief and pain to do anything but attack the nearest person. I went back to my room and changed into more comfortable clothes, sitting in a daze for a while.

Callan's death was being called a suicide among the other riders, the news getting diluted from person to person. Few, it seemed, knew about his collarbone injury, just the reputation that'd followed him out of yesterday's trial. Someone so motivated by success that his court-martial was the pinnacle of defeat. Through that lens, it was logical he'd take his own life.

I didn't believe it. If anything, Callan would've still been hopeful for a royal pardon last night, not ready to give up. Even under truth serum, he'd managed to avoid mentioning the king during his testimony. There was probably a pardon on the king's desk right now, the ink not yet dry.

An invitation arrived for me while I rested. Odalis, at last, had sent for me for a lunch date. My mood lifted quickly. Despite not knowing the princess well, I was looking forward to seeing her again. She'd asked me to meet her in a room in the same wing as Prince Isaac's solar.

It was rather small for royal standards when I arrived and took a look around. As a corner room, it had a massive double-paned window, with a view overlooking the city out into the distance. The decorations had a feminine edge, cluttered along the walls like Odalis had run out of space.

The princess herself smiled broadly and came forward to take my hands in hers. "Hello again, Sivana! It's so nice to see you," she said cheerfully. Her slender frame was trapped in a tight navy-blue gown with a satin sheen, stiff with lace around the high collar and sleeves. The impressive mass of her raven-dark hair was braided into a complicated coronet looped around her head a few times, and the rest was left in a waterfall down her back.

"Good afternoon, Princess Odalis. I hope you're well," I said formally.

"Hey, we're all friends here, right? No titles needed." Smiling, she gestured for me to sit at the square table in the center of the room, and that's when I realized Mateo was here too, standing against a wall in place of her bodyguard.

She wiggled a plate of finger foods at him to coax him to sit with us. I felt an awkward little twist in my belly when he and I made eye contact. I'd thought I'd just be eating lunch with Odalis, not the young man whose motivations still confused me.

"Are we all friends here?" I asked him quietly.

He shrugged as he selected a little sandwich with its crust removed. "I feel like I've been your friend for a while. I just endured my father's rage for over an hour for you, Walker. So you tell me if that meets the definition."

"For me," I echoed.

"He didn't think I did enough to help Callan yesterday. I don't think he realizes I dropped the first tray of truth serum when I discovered it was water."

"You did what?" I asked in shock.

"Yeah, all of it was water. So, you're welcome."

I gaped at him for a few moments. The crown prince had promised to check the serum for me and make sure it wasn't water. It sounded like he hadn't come through with his side of the bargain after all. "Thank you," I said, feeling a little numb. If Mateo hadn't been there, things could've ended much differently.

"To be fair, all Father knows is you just kind of stood there," Odalis commented. My brow furrowed; she hadn't even been in the courthouse. "You hear things around here."

"My sister fancies herself something of a spymaster," Mateo told me.

She smacked her lips in offense. "How many times have I helped prep you for your meetings? The nerve."

"Well, you are getting better at it," he conceded.

I nibbled on the fancy food she had set out for us and listened to them with a quirk of my lips. They sounded like they were close. Good for Odalis, who was said to rarely leave the palace. I saw evidence of that all around me. She'd turned this room into a nest of sorts, evidence of years collected on the walls and piled around the bookshelves and comfy seating to one corner.

"So, that brings us to the topic of today's meeting. Treason," Odalis declared. I nearly choked on a mouthful of water.

I cupped my face and coughed, assisted by Mateo pounding on my back.

"Sorry, sorry," she said. "I get excited. I've been spying on Isaac, you see, trying to figure out what he's planning. He's got a lot going on."

"Have you told Father anything you're about to share?" Mateo asked.

She shook her head. "It's not like he really listens to me, or like I have every piece of the puzzle. He already knows Isaac is plotting, but he's not taking it seriously."

I nibbled on my lip, thinking of my parents and everything I'd overheard between Mother and Isaac himself. "Shouldn't he?"

Odalis gestured to me with both hands. "Yes! But he gets all huffy and stubborn." She puffed her chest off and attempted to deepen her voice to mimic the king. "Isaac's not ready for the throne yet. Why would he want it early? He's not even married! Altare needs stability, not reckless change."

"Sounds like him," Mateo commented.

She deflated and returned to her normal, more stately tone. "Meanwhile, I hear Isaac meeting with dozens of people every day. He's been complaining about a setback lately, but he's been shifting around his assets into just the right place, waiting for just the right time to make his move."

"Do you think…it might actually happen?" I asked in a hush. "He might force the king to step down?"

"I don't think my father would ever step down unless he's actively dying," Mateo said dryly.

Odalis nodded in agreement. "Isaac's planning something. I don't know if it will be full-blown civil war or how many people he truly has on his side, but I'm trying to find out. He promises change and upholds 'symbols' of it. You come up a lot—he uses your name to convince folks onto his side." She gestured toward me with a gloved hand.

I feared as much. He'd talked to me about change as well, and how I was a great symbol of what Altare could be. "How have you heard all this? Do you listen at his door or something?" I asked.

"A good spy never reveals her secrets," she said, lifting her nose primly.

"Yes," Mateo answered, gesturing toward the wall. "No one uses the room between this one and Isaac's solar. She sneaks in and listens."

She gave him a petulant look. "It's so much better when

it's a *secret*. Anyway, I've been paying better attention during language lessons. He's been talking to several people in Rathi lately."

His brows raised. "Now that's actually interesting. About what, exactly?" He tilted a hand toward her after she exaggerated a shrug. "This is the kind of thing you have to work on if you really want to be a spy, else you're just gossiping."

"I guess you don't get to hear my juiciest piece of *gossip*, then," she huffed.

"Is it about Walker? Is that why she's here?"

"No, I just think she should know her name is getting used so much by Isaac." She flashed me a shy smile.

"I appreciate it," I murmured.

She scooted in her chair and leaned over to whisper in my ear behind her hand. "I'll tell you what it is, though."

"I can still hear you," Mateo said.

"Isaac has a new favorite word. It used to be *change*," she whispered, ignoring him. "Now he keeps saying his cause needs…a *martyr*."

She sat back, seeming satisfied that she'd told someone that tidbit of information. I thought that was curious and concerning in the same breath. "Someone to die for his war," Mateo said after a longer pause. "I think you should try to get through to Father again. Make him stop obsessing over Walker and focus on the real danger to his rule."

"Wouldn't that be great?" she sighed.

He met my eye. "For the record, I've never agreed with him. He forced me to go along with his plans at the Academy, and with his spies all watching me, I couldn't be seen helping you directly. I thought Callan went too far several times, but if I'd known he'd try to kill you in broad daylight, I would've intervened on your behalf past a couple warnings."

His sister looked between us, her hands clasped close to her chest. Her amber-tinted eyes glimmered, like she was in on some secret…

"Wait," I said.

A *couple* of warnings? He'd taken me aside to deliver just the one, unless…

It was a jump of logic from what he'd said, but in the moment, it made perfect sense. "*You're* the anonymous friend who keeps giving me things." I watched his expression as the statement hung in the air until it became awkward. Maybe I was completely wrong and he wasn't trying to hint at something…

He sighed, turning his face toward the window. He seemed almost embarrassed, actually, a hint of color darkening his bronze cheeks. "Yeah, that was me. I felt bad, okay? Being a cadet is hard enough without a king paying someone to make you miserable."

I gaped, while Odalis bounced once in her chair in delight. "The pie last year was my idea. Did you like it?" she asked, referencing a cranberry-orange pie delivered still warm to my flight right after Yule.

"I…yes! It was delicious. But…all along?" My tone softened. "You've been trying to help me since the net incident."

"Don't get all mushy on me, Walker. I knew we'd be rivals if you had half a chance to be a cadet. Your gryphon is too good," he muttered, still not looking my way. "You can thank me by never mentioning this to anyone else."

"All right, Mateo."

Now he turned back to me. It was the first time I'd used his first name without the title aloud. "We *are* all friends here," I confirmed. "Even if it's just a secret."

Slowly, he nodded. "Just don't ignore my warnings next time."

"Yes, sir," I said playfully. "As long as you let me spend time with Mireille."

He tisked. "Not like I can keep her away from you." We shared a laugh, and our talk turned to more pleasant topics.

I bid my goodbyes with them soon after. Odalis caught me

in another bone-crushing hug when I admitted I was likely flying out of Kaiamear at the first possible opportunity. Father needed to unchain Valtora, and I needed to return to Ari's side.

It was strange to leave before the holiday. I'd barely seen my family, but at the same time, I couldn't stay much longer.

"Maybe they'll let me visit your school sometime. We don't see each other enough," Nate said before handing over a box about the size of my hand. "I made you this for Yule. It's a little, um, special, though."

I narrowed my eyes. "It's not going to explode, is it?"

"No! Probably not, at least," he said, gesturing for me to open the gift.

Inside was a glass implement. I turned it over, not making out what it was for on first glance. It reminded me of a wine glass, with a thin stem full of sky-blue liquid. Instead of a cup for wine, it had a ball of glass three inches in diameter, hinged in the middle to open and close slowly.

"It's a really small replicator," Nate explained, pointing to the hinged ball. "You put something in there and give it a shake. Here…"

He pulled off part of a branch on Mother's decorated snow pine, putting it inside the object. He held down the top of the ball to keep it sealed and shook the device up and down. The cup-shaped piece of glass at the bottom vibrated before the piece of snow pine shot out from it forcefully.

"It's only supposed to give you one copy, but sometimes… oh, yup." Several more pieces of the same snow pine plopped to the ground. "Like I said, it's special. Sometimes you get a lot more than what you bargained for." He handed it to me delicately, and I noticed the piece of snow pine was still inside the glass ball.

"Did it just make copies of this branch with magic?" I asked, inspecting the odd device anew.

"Yeah! Don't try it with food, though. The copies are usually rotten," he advised. "Everything it replicates will be a weaker version of the original. Like, watch." He picked up one of the copies of the branch and snapped it in half like a brittle twig. It disintegrated into ash a moment later. "And it doesn't work on things that have any magic, so don't try it! It'll break eventually, but I figured it was fun to have while it lasts."

"Thanks, Nate. This looks like it could be really useful," I said, snagging him for a hug.

"You're welcome. I hope it lasts a while." He scuffed his foot. "I'm so close to a breakthrough on crafting simple enchanted items. I might be a crafter Tulari if I really practice."

Crafter mages were rare and blessed with extra magic than most Tulari. That's about all I knew. The scarcity of crafters drove up the prices of magic-made goods like mage-lights, potions, and magestones.

I really hoped Nate was a crafter, but I was also aware that nothing he'd given me quite worked like it should. "Keep at it," I said after a pause. "You never know what you can push yourself to if you don't try."

He nodded in agreement. "I learned that from you."

Feeling warm from that conversation, I said my goodbyes with Mother and Rissa too. It was hard to leave them but unbearable to be without Ari, so a sacrifice that needed to be made. The same two men from Final Flight flew Father and me back to Fortress Aerie, and this time, I had a nice, albeit mostly one-sided conversation with the elderly gryphon who carried her rider and me. She reminded me distinctly of my late grandmother, who'd been just happy to talk and talk if given the chance.

Towed between the two older gryphons was Sunset, flying reluctantly with a haze of dark emotions hanging over her from her broken Link. She was my responsibility from here on out, cleared for travel and rehabilitation since she'd stopped snapping at caretakers and entered a state where she exhibited every sign of deep depression.

It wasn't unusual to have a few cadets and staff spending their Yule in the fortress, so we had a modest greeting between two caretakers as the sun set behind us. Father went straight to where Valtora was being held, while I untied Sunset and smoothed down the maroon feathers lining her neck. "C'mon, girl, let's get you bedded down somewhere comfortable," I cooed.

Her eyes were slitted, and she started to balk as I took hold of her reins and tugged her toward the stables. I didn't need to talk to her to understand she didn't want to go back to her old stall, which might smell of Callan still. "It's okay, Sunset, we're not going there," I told her gently.

There was only one set of stalls I knew she could move to long term, the ones in the back for the semi-tame beasts. I put her at the end, where her stall was surrounded on two sides by the solid rock of the mountain. She stood by and let me fluff the hay into a nice bed for her and remove her saddle and reins.

Her brightly colored wings curled in like a shield after she sank into the hay. A low growl echoed from her beak as I fussed around her. "Okay, I hear you. I'll get you something to eat and leave you be," I promised.

But first, my Link was prickling uncomfortably in the back of my head. Ari was awake and wondering why I wasn't by his side. I went straight to his stall, relieved to see he was better than I'd left him. His left wing was splinted out, but he was sitting up, his emotional state clear of the slow drugged sensation of healing magic.

"I couldn't take it. I had to see you," I told him, sinking down to rub his beak. He bunted my chest as I drew his head and shoulders into a hug.

"I'm glad you're here," he murmured. For a few long moments, we swayed together before I shared everything he'd missed. The trial, Callan's suspicious death, Valtora's release, and Mateo's identity as my anonymous "friend."

He scoffed. *"Of course it was him. I knew it all along."*

"Sure." I mussed the feathers over his good wing playfully. *"Let me go see if Valtora wants to come visit you."*

The answer was an easy yes, as his mother was coming around the corner and heading straight for me when I opened the stall door. I stood aside and watched her exchange nuzzles with Ari and settle to groom him. Her own pelt was a mess, feathers sticking out in random places, some clearly broken. I could still see the waves in her fur where the chains had dug into her skin.

"She's still angry at me," Father said, stopping by my side to watch the reunion as well. "She wants you to help clean her up tonight instead of me."

"I can do that, no problem."

I ended up taking my dinner back up to the stable, sitting between my two favorite gryphons before tackling the huge job of making Valtora presentable again. She obviously hadn't let anyone near her in the last week. At some point, I put the brushes and combs aside for a moment to rest and ended up dozing off, surrounded by their comforting presences.

Maybe that's why I was the one who woke up first to what felt like someone grinding their fingertip into my temple. My eyes snapped open, but nothing was there, just an angry presence trying to get my mental attention.

I reached out, making contact with what turned out to be a male gryphon. He was both unfamiliar and yet instantly recognizable by his growling tone dripping with disdain. *"Link thief!"*

Ari's father had the same kind of presence as Valtora. Powerful, *loud*, rattling my skull.

"Good morning, Roshawk. What do you—"

"I want to speak to my mate," he demanded.

CHAPTER 28

PAINT IT BROWN

I nudged Valtora awake, and she released a groggy murr, only cracking open one golden eye. "Roshawk wants to talk to you," I told her.

"Oh. He's been in range of the fortress for about a day," she muttered, shaking out her feathers and yawning hugely. I opened the stall door for her, and she slunk out, glancing over her shoulder. "Now I can meet him with dignity. Would you like to come too?"

"You haven't seen him in so long," I murmured.

She pulsed the equivalent of a shrug. "You've been in my life for much longer than he was. Let him see me for what I am now. Perhaps I can give you pointers along the way to improve your riding skills."

Roshawk's presence was gone, so I figured she was talking to him as I went to retrieve Father's saddle from further back in the stable. I was motivated by the idea of riding Valtora, arguably the most valuable combat beast still flying as the mount of the First's Commander.

There was no one else around. What was the harm in taking Valtora on a joyride?

She surged from the stables the moment I secured myself

to her back, screeching with joy as her wings caught the wind. She was solid and strong, steering herself toward our destination.

"*Ari told me Roshawk threatened you after you all met by accident,*" she said.

"*Well, yes. He hates humans and…he really misses you.*"

"*I hoped you wouldn't meet at all,*" she admitted. "*As much as I also hate humans, he has always been more fervent that your kind is no good.*"

Maybe he had a point. I thought of her in chains for defending Ari.

"*And you. I thought I'd lost two children, and it was just…so painful,*" she murmured, filling our connection with warm, motherly affection.

"*I love you too,*" I said, rubbing down her stout, feathery neck.

She blinked back at me over her shoulder for a few moments before starting to wheel into a descent. On the rocky cliff face below us stood the proud figure of Roshawk. He snarled when we landed and I dismounted. When he started to lunge at me, Valtora shouldered in the way, growling back.

"*You weren't supposed to bring the Link thief with you.*" I didn't think I was connected with Roshawk, yet I heard him like he was shouting from the outside a Link.

Valtora, though… I felt her protective anger and the complicated rush of emotion that washed over her from being so close to her long-lost mate. "*I wanted her here. What has happened to you, my love?*" She began to pace around him, and he stood for her perusal. The lightning scar across his side was crimson in direct sunlight, dimming the handsome gleam of his chocolate-toned feathers.

"*I defended our flock. For years, I have carried the aches of my fight with a sky terror. Its last act was to scar me before I tore its heart in two,*" he said with a measure of pride.

For a moment, they came together, rubbing flanks and

murring with affection. Standing at a safe distance, I smiled to myself. What a beautiful moment for a mated pair that'd been separated for so long.

"*And what have you accomplished in this time?*" he asked a little pointedly. It was his turn to inspect Valtora, and more than once, his beak plucked the straps of her reins and saddle. "*You wear these traps like a beast of burden. Your fur is so soft…not a scar mars you.*"

"*I have a purpose with the humans and my rider. I'm a leader, one of the strongest gryphons they have,*" she said, turning her beak up.

"*Purpose?*" he echoed. "*What greater purpose could there be than to defend your flock?*"

"*I've defended countless humans instead, fighting to win wars. Every day is full of hard work.*" She was eyeing him now, a wary twinge to her emotions. Her tail lashed. "*Tell me of your accomplishments. Sunning yourself until your pelt grows hot? I know what life in a flock is like, Roshawk. You have it much easier than I.*"

His pelt brushed out, wings beginning to mantle. "*Several days ago, I felt you. Your rage. Your passion. And the sharpest sense of pain from our son. What happened?*"

"*A human broke his wing,*" she answered.

He rumbled, turning to glare at me accusingly. "*And you killed him?*" he asked.

"*He is dead.*"

"*But did you kill him?*"

"*I tried.*"

"*As I feared. The humans have made you weak,*" he growled. "*The Valtora I knew would have no mercy for any harm to our son.*"

"*She would've killed him had there not been intervention. But he is dead still,*" I ventured, nearly regretting it the moment his presence brushed against mine like a hot, angry sun.

"*If I wanted your opinion, I'd ask for it,*" he snapped.

Valtora shouldered him, and he staggered. "*You limp now,*"

she commented. He snipped his beak at her, and she got further into his space. With both of them puffed out, it was obvious she was still bigger than him. *"Sheath your claws, or we leave, and I never speak to you again."*

He bowed his head first and let her push him onto his side, her talons on his neck. *"Humans are worth one thing. Sivana, come here,"* she said.

I approached, keeping an eye on Roshawk. His hostility was restrained, and Valtora held him down when he twitched at my nearness.

"Do you see this female? She is as good as my daughter. We are a mated pair, which means she is yours as well. She saved our son's life."

"I know," he mumbled. *"Arimus told me."*

"Most humans are good to us, despite how we often end up in their care unwillingly," she said more gently. *"My fur is soft because Sivana tends to it. You don't need to let her touch you today, but she has clever little hands. Perhaps she can ease your scars."*

"There are ointments and oils to improve the flexibility of scars," I ventured. I was close enough to see how thickly his flank was spiderwebbed in the patterns of a lightning strike. It would be a ton of work to rehabilitate him to the point that he had full mobility again, if it were even possible.

"I will never allow you to touch me, Link thief." Valtora growled meaningfully. *"I mean, human."*

"Okay. Totally fine," I murmured, backing away. He pulled out from under Valtora, shaking himself in a huff.

"Was that why you brought her?" he asked Valtora.

"No." She turned to blink at me. *"I thought I might need a reminder that I cannot fly away with you. I have duties and a life that have come about in your absence. I loved you, Roshawk, but I have a couple of humans and Ari to take care of now. You cannot come with me, and I cannot go with you."*

He started to turn away, flaring his wings to prepare for takeoff. *"I see I was mistaken to call for this meeting."*

"Quite the opposite. I'm glad you did."

He tilted his head, birdlike in his confusion.

"Ari and Sivana will be here for some time, still. Perhaps you can visit them like this, get to know them like family should. It is the best our situation can offer," she said.

Roshawk folded his wings again with a soft huff. He didn't answer her out loud, but he did press his beak into her neck, inhaling her scent. She did the same back, and I glanced away to give them privacy. The next thing I knew was the sound of wings catching the wind with a strong *whump.*

Valtora and I watched him fly away until he was a speck on the horizon. She wrapped one of her wings tight around me, silently yearning to follow him. *"Let's go back, before Nathaniel wakes up,"* she murmured.

THE REST of the break flew by as soon as Father and Valtora soared away. I was a glorified caretaker for those couple weeks, my attention split between Ari and Sunset.

My gryphon required extra time, and not just to maintain his grooming. The Tulari healer who'd stayed at the fortress to tend to him had me adjust his legs and wing every day as he worked his magic. The spells he worked kept Ari's muscles from atrophying as much as he sat there with his wing splayed out. Even with his resistance to healing magic, this seemed to be working. Boredom was his closest companion, something even I couldn't fully chase away.

Sunset spent her days sprawled out, haloed by negativity at all times. She refused to meet my eyes or talk to me at all, hanging limp when I spent time tending to her.

I moved more slowly as my break lost most of its meaning. I slept during the day and paced during the night, worrying what would happen if Ari's wing wasn't healing properly. After everything we'd been through, he couldn't be brought down by an injury like this.

But there was little I could do to help. Even though it was next to useless, I still used the healing magestone on Ari's injury, tucking it under his broken wing, where its resonance would help him the most.

"Fate, and the gods, will decide for sure," I said to myself.

Ari lifted his head in my direction and clicked his beak thoughtfully. *"Bring her here,"* he said.

"Hmm?"

"Sunset. I want to see her…well, you know what I mean."

I thought of her misery, worried the emotions flowing from her broken Link would draw him back to the dark place he'd lived in after losing Alamid.

"Trust me," he murmured.

It was easier to take care of them when they were together, at least. Once I moved her to his stall, she didn't want to leave. She tucked herself under his good wing, making herself small.

She was there when the healer began to test Ari's wing and allowed him to fold it back against himself at last. Her keen, canary-yellow eyes watched as the healer and I positioned and stretched it, making sure there were no sharp pains.

"He's healing quickly. He should be able to fly in a few days when your training begins again," the Tulari told me at last. "Just take it easy for a while, okay?"

We were about to start the Trial by Fire, the most strenuous time for a cadet. I bit my lip, and he must've taken it for hesitance. "I mean it, young lady. I'll inform the Commandant as well. Light exercise only."

"Yes, sir," I said. He wrote down a list of things Ari could and could not do in the air until his wing was fully mended, and it was daunting. We'd have to avoid diving, with no sharp turns or steep ascents either.

What if we were forced into a maneuver that would damage his wing anew? He'd need another month to recover, maybe, time we didn't have anymore.

I sat with my back against the stall's wall when the healer left, eyeing his scratchy handwriting until the words blurred. Worse, what would happen if Ari was injured again? Healing magic didn't work for him.

What if we went into battle in a year, or two years, or five and he was more severely hurt? Would he bleed out, unable to receive battlefield triage?

Ari cut into my thoughts. *"Sivana, stop it. You're making Sunset anxious."*

He was steady on the other side of our Link. It was the maroon gryphon who curled further into his side, trembling. "Sorry," I mumbled.

"You're more connected than you seem," Ari said. *"Maybe not Linked, but the longer you two sit together, the more she reflects you and you reflect her. Why don't you go see if any of our flight-mates are back? Maybe...have some fun?"*

He actually nipped me the next day when I tried to linger, insisting that I needed to see my friends. One by one, they arrived back at the fortress. The topic on everyone's tongue was Callan, but no one knew anything new. The investigation into his death was ongoing.

Sharde was amongst the last to arrive and sprawled in an armchair as he caught the tail of another conversation about Callan. "Good riddance, I say. Maybe we'll have a normal semester without him acting like such an arse," he said.

"We shouldn't speak poorly of the dead," Credell murmured.

"But it was *Callan*. Surely the Gatekeeper understands," Feyring burst out.

Puzzlebox padded over to get neck scratches from Ellie, greeting her with a bunt to the chest, before going over to where I lay on the floor with Ironfeather and plopping her weight over my chest. "Oof, Box," I wheezed. She wasn't much heavier than the last time she'd done this, though. I thought perhaps she'd reached her maximum weight and size, stuck somewhere between a yearling and an adult.

"Sivvy!" she squeaked along with a smatter of sweet birdsong.

Aww. I put my arms around her as she rested her head on my chest, slowly blinking up at me.

"Guys, you wouldn't believe what I found for sale," Sharde said, pulling out a small, articulated doll from his pack. Bright red yarn made its hair, and it held a sword at an odd angle until he adjusted it. It wore a tiny version of a cadet uniform.

Weslecker laughed. "Is that…?"

"It is! It's a Sivana doll!"

I flushed, feeling like I could sink into the floor. A doll of me, how mortifying. "Where did you get that thing?" I asked.

He grinned, affecting a lazy shrug. "You know, just for sale. I also got…" He dug into his pack again, withdrawing a box. "Doll clothes, too!"

"That's amazing. She can be our mascot," Ellie suggested.

"No, wait. Let me see that." Weslecker held his hands out, catching the doll when Sharde tossed it. The look he flashed me was practically wicked. "I think this could fit in your replicator."

"Oh, great idea," Ellie said.

"I mean, if you *really* want one," I hedged. Since Puzzlebox was lying on me, I let Ellie go retrieve it from our room and watched as she and Weslecker stuffed the doll into the glass tool my brother had given me. Weslecker had known what it was immediately. He'd been given one as a toy when he was younger, so he seemed confident as he gave the rod a shake and withdrew a near-perfect copy of the first doll and fumbled as two more fell out of the replicator with a fizzing sound.

"Well, this is perfect," he said before making more copies of the original doll and passing them around to all our flight-mates. I inspected my copy, realizing that if I hadn't known it was me, I wouldn't be able to guess. It had little blue button eyes and brown paint flecked on its wooden face for freckles.

Sharde revealed that the toy shop had wooden gryphon toys too, but the one he'd bought was too big and rigid to fit into the replicator. It was plain, blocky wood, a gift for a kid to paint their own gryphon. I'd probably have fifteen or more of them in my room back home if I was a little younger.

"You should paint it brown," Biggs said. He'd joined us upon being presented with a copy of the Sivana doll and was hard at work using my replicator to make copies of the mini clothes Sharde had brought.

"No, gray," Weslecker said.

Sharde scoffed. "I'm going to paint it Puzzlebox colors. White with a couple spots."

"Tawny brown's not a bad color," I pitched in.

After we all tried to make a case for our gryphon's color, he held a hand up. "Tell you what, let's have a competition. When's the last time we had a good prank?"

The last one I could think of was last year, when a set of my brother's faulty magelights nearly got us in serious trouble.

"Forever ago, right? Let's all think of a prank. We'll do the best one, and the person who thinks of it gets the gryphon painted whatever they want," he said.

"You're so on!" Biggs announced. "Get ready to paint it brown."

I glanced his way, and we nodded to each other. Our

gryphons were similar enough that a brown gryphon toy could be either Echo or Ari. Logically, we could partner up with a little compromise on shading.

"Okay, I give you guys two weeks to think of something great." Sharde held the original Sivana doll high, its tiny sword pointed to the sky. "May the best prankster win!"

CHAPTER 29

TRIAL BY FIRE

The first day of class began in the bleary hours of the morning with the shouting of drill sergeants. A few pounded rhythmically on a set of pots and pans up and down the hall. Not just one, but three drills were in our common area, rousing us and performing room inspections while we stood at attention outside.

"What's going on?" Ellie asked, squinting up at me without her glasses. She muffled a big yawn while I replied out of the corner of my mouth.

"The Trial by Fire."

With the third-years off on their squire-ships, a whole group of drill sergeants were reassigned to double down on the second-years. I'd watched the exhaustion of Callan, Valentic, and the rest during this time last year as they worked and practiced well into the evening most days.

Now it was our turn, and it sounded like the drills were having a party outside, causing the kind of commotion that could wake the whole fortress.

"Oh, right. Good luck," she murmured.

Sergeant Kobarn let her go back into our room and close the door before calling for us to line up in our common area.

He and the other two drills surrounded us with noise, and I cringed away despite knowing what they were doing: discipline training. When the common Altarian pictured time at the Gryphon Rider Academy, or any other prestigious military institution, this was probably the first thing they imagined.

The sergeants ordered us to do basic things. Button up a PT jacket, take it off, quickly now, put it back on. Push it off your left shoulder. No, cadet, your *left* shoulder. Look left, look down. Turn around. It was like my fingers had stopped working for these simple tasks at first, accompanied by the chaos of drills shouting different instructions at my flight-mates. The idea wasn't to think, just to follow orders *right away*.

Gods, I was tired already, and the day had just started. We were ushered up to the stables to retrieve our gryphons, allowed to glide down to the Green—if our beasts would agree to it, considering it was still full dark outside. Ari pulsed with sleepy amusement, waking from the commotion before I even reached his stall with a saddle and his specialized reins. *"I remember hating this,"* he told me as he knelt for the saddle. *"Alamid and I had to take the stairs with everyone else when I refused to fly this early."*

"You don't have to fly if you don't want to," I said. He was flexing his wing, testing its range on his own. Sunset watched us from the shadows, hunkered down in the heat of the nest Ari was leaving.

"Don't be silly. We're taking the easy way down." He nudged me toward his back once he was saddled up and ready to go.

"If you don't feel ready to fly, it's completely okay."

"Get on my back," he ordered.

I slung myself into the saddle and cinched down. *"I just don't want you to get hurt."* All the while, he paced out of the stall. A cold wind buffeted us as he guided himself toward the open shutters looking out over the Green, stopping only to inhale fresh, clean air. I felt his relish as he opened his wings slowly, letting the breeze roll over feathers that had gone unused since our last ill-fated joust.

I held my breath as he leapt skyward and unfurled his wings to their full span. We started descending in a smooth glide and…it was fine. I caught no sense of discomfort from him. Instead, he screeched to the sky, free to fly once more.

"See? Nothing to worry about," he said. I helped him land, and we were amongst the first to line up for PT.

Sergeant Kobarn stopped next to me as other second-years filled out the flights. "Cadet Walker!" he barked.

"Yes, Sarge!" I replied, shouting too.

"Your gryphon has a medical waiver! He is permitted to sit out any PT too strenuous on his wing."

I replied to the affirmative, and he went off to go loudly correct Pereyra when he and his gryphon arrived and nearly crashed from him mistiming the landing. Ari pulsed a feeling like his eyes rolling. *"I'm going to be okay."*

I kept an eye on him anyway, as best I could when this PT session was extra vigorous. He didn't challenge any other gryphon to sprint like he used to, instead relying on his seeing-eye gryphon, Ironfeather, to guide him in laps around the Green.

He had a bounce to his step as we grabbed a quick breakfast, and he even plunged first into the bathing pool when we went to clean off before class. Feminine squeals rose from the other women as his bulk sent up a big splash. "Welcome back, Ari," chirped one of the maids, even helping me shampoo his fur after he had a good frolic in the water.

His good mood rolled into mine at last, chasing away the gray specters of fear that lingered and probed at my mind. I didn't question what would happen the next time he got hurt, only knowing the joy in his heart to have his mobility back.

"We're going to do great things this semester. I know it," he promised.

I was smiling when I got to my Advanced Anatomy class and already found the illusion of a rozash circling overhead. A cluster of drill sergeants ushered us into our new elements and stood watching to give critiques on our formation flying afterward. This time, we were assigned to Element E, and I insisted that our Cadet-Captain had to be Biggs to give him and Echo a chance to shine in the group named after his gryphon.

The group of sergeants stayed with the second-years through Jousting and Ground Combat, their approach softening to firm critiques. It was like having four to six teachers in each class rather than one. There was always someone willing to give more one-on-one attention and attempt to stamp out mistakes in form and precision.

I thought to myself, *Maybe this semester won't be so bad after all.*

And then I arrived in Gryphon Taming at the end of the day. "Hello, cadets," Captain Gemon said, briskly dodging the scripted greeting like he usually did. "I have excellent news for you."

"Oh, great," Sharde muttered next to me. There was still bad blood between him and Gemon. My friend had only come down from full insubordination through the Commandant's intervention and to stop endless punishment duties.

"We have caught your project for this semester. This year is all about the taming portion of what we do in the Second, but you've never seen a feral gryphon fresh from the wild... until today." Gemon smiled with relish. "Come with me."

He led us to the stall next to the one where Valtora was chained. I could hear metal sliding, links clinking together. "Behind this door is our newest catch, Blue. We brought him in last night," he told us. "I will be taking you through every stage of the taming process with him. Be careful, he is fully grown, in the adult age range. This is most challenging for us."

I swallowed as he let us get a peek in the stall. The gryphon released a roar and lunged, just to stop cold with little slack on the chains. He was more bound than Valtora had been, chained with his wings pinned to his back, manacles around his back legs, and one heavy loop around his neck.

Still, froth leaked from his beak, and he projected unpleasant images into our heads, like him gutting fish and swallowing their innards or severing their heads with one neat snip of his beak.

Gemon was still speaking, but my mind was hundreds of miles away, remembering the gryphon who'd taken Ari and me out of the sky by tangling his white talons in Ari's saddle. He looked silvery in the shadows of the stall, but I knew his feathers gleamed with blue tones in the sunlight, where he belonged.

Blue was from Roshawk's flock, and his eyes were focused on me, narrowing accusingly. *"Link thief!"* he screamed. *"You're the one who stole Roshawk's son!"*

I reeled back, murmuring, "I can't do this."

I couldn't be the one to help tame a gryphon so close to Roshawk. I'd be the despicable human, the Link thief they cursed, to break the pride of an unwilling adult beast.

A hand landed on my shoulder, and I startled hard. "Get used to a few mean images, Walker," Gemon said. "You and Blue are going to be best friends by the end of this semester."

THAT EVENING, I had a rare moment of peace with Ellie. She lay back on her bed and thought with her eyes closed while I paced the length of our room. "What makes this gryphon different from any other they could bring in and order you to tame?" she asked.

"I...I know him!" I'd already told her about meeting Roshawk and some of the male gryphons from his flock this summer.

"But how does that really make him different?" she pressed.

I heaved a sigh. "I guess it feels more personal. Like I'm spitting into Roshawk's eye."

Not like the male gryphon had done anything but express disdain at my very existence.

"It's not your fault they brought him in, though," she said. "You're just doing your job."

"Like Captain Gemon was doing when he pushed to test Puzzlebox again?" I asked.

"Yes, actually." She peered sideways at me and shrugged when she saw my expression. "That's what doing a job is about. If it were fun, it wouldn't be a job."

I shook my head, thinking this conversation hadn't really helped. "Lord Gadric and I are testing out different ways to contain light. It feels like I've failed hundreds of times to make a magic-less magelight, and that's not fun either. Check out our latest prototype." She dug into her pack and withdrew a ball no bigger than a coin, which she tossed to me.

It bounced from my fingertips and ricocheted off the ceiling. I giggled in surprise, smiling despite myself. When I finally caught the thing, I held it close to my eye to see a little glowing circlet suspended within what looked like dark gray jelly. "Hey, it's not bad. It glows," I said.

"And it doesn't use magic," she said proudly.

"Really? No magic at all?" I squished it, and it shot out from between my fingers, bouncing around our room.

"None! But it's very dim, so it's another failure. I think we're getting close, though."

I caught it midair before it could go flying above my head. A grin stretched across my face. "I have an idea."

She squinted at me. "That's usually my line."

"Want to partner up with Biggs and me for Sharde's prank competition?" I asked.

She agreed once she heard me out about what I wanted to do with the toy gryphon. Instead of painting it brown, I'd decided to advocate for a different gryphon who might enjoy the gesture more. Ellie, Biggs, and I pitched the idea by the end of the week, after a few ideas from our flight-mates.

"I'm on board with all of these, honestly," Sharde said. "*But* I think Sivana's team wins. I know exactly who to prank, too."

"One of the classrooms?" I suggested.

An impish smile crossed his face, and he shook his head. "No. Better."

CHAPTER 30

BOUNCE BACK

We took our time. Every evening, one of us was using the replicator, creating copies of the original bouncy ball. These copies were even more slippery and just as elastic, but the weak filament of light within them was too dim to be seen.

We filled a box at a time. Ellie drew complicated diagrams based off our guesses to the dimensions of our target's room, and we learned we needed hundreds of bouncy balls as a starting point, a daunting task even if my replicator made up to five copies every time it was used.

Meanwhile, the Trial by Fire was going about as well as I expected. I got used to the extra attention from drill sergeants and even fell into the routine of getting dragged outside after class to practice formation flying rather than eat dinner.

Our ranks stabilized, much to my relief. I remained a lowly Cadet-Lieutenant at rank sixteen of thirty-five, with the promise of having that completely turned on its head by our next Field Training day.

The only thing that wasn't going my way, I'd say, was Gryphon Taming. Blue realized I was the only one tending to him that understood him fully.

"I will gut you while you're still alive and screaming," was his favorite threat.

Three of us had to hold him down to groom him despite his thrashing. I dreaded these days, as I'd already demonstrated that I had the experience and reflexes not to *actually* get gutted if he attempted to lunge at me. *"I'll wear your skull for a crown,"* Blue said while snapping his beak at me. *"And decorate my nest with your bones!"*

"That's enough," Ari interjected, growling from where he sat in the corner of the stall.

"Wait until Roshawk hears you allowed this, traitor!" Blue hissed.

"You will still speak to my rider with respect."

"She is not worth respect, as a Link thief!" Emboldened, Blue made this grooming session as unpleasant as possible with his creative descriptions, despite Ari's presence.

I slumped into Ari's stall afterward to repeat the process with silent Sunset, who seemed to only get the dregs of me after a full day of classes and exposure to Blue's hostility. Still, she didn't resist grooming, and her broken Link was no longer leaking the heaviest emotions. She'd gotten a full month here without being disturbed or threatened, whereas Ari had faced the threat of execution several times by this milestone.

After she was clean and fed, she shifted to rest her head and shoulders in my lap with a sigh. Her eyes were firmly closed, but I felt her presence brush mine, leaving behind a lingering sense of gratitude.

"You're welcome," I murmured. We were still making progress, even if she didn't want to talk. I had the feeling she leaned more on Ari than me, sharing her heartbreak with another who understood it best. She refused to move to a stall by herself, and Ari seemed to like her company just fine.

Before I knew it, it was Field Training day. I'd wondered how this would go without third-years, and none swooped in at the last minute to fill out the other side of the clearing. Instead, we were split in half. Kite and Falcon Flights on one side, Harrier and Osprey Flights on the other.

Commander Rudrick called my flight to group up with him. "All right, kites. Time to see what you all learned last semester. You will be assembling your own command structure for this first round," he said before referencing a sheet he'd folded under his arm. "Starting with Cadet-General Sharde."

Feyring released a surprised spit. Most of us turned to stare at Sharde.

"You heard me, cadets. Come forward, *Cadet-General* Sharde," Rudrick said.

The tall blond separated from our flight, his face nearly split in half with a smug smile. "Yes, sir," he said.

"Pick your Cadet-Marshall," Rudrick instructed.

Sharde pointed straight at me. "Cadet-Marshall Walker, sir."

The instructor gestured me forward, and I stood next to Sharde, shocked. This was the highest I'd ever ranked in our military games. "Pick your Cadet-Commander," Rudrick told me.

Multiple hopeful looks turned my way, and I hesitated, not finding this a knee-jerk decision. In the end, I picked our quietest member, Credell.

Rudrick was acting as the Paragon for our side, while the other side reported to the Commandant. Sharde and Falcon Flight's chosen Cadet-General, Barlowe, peeled off to meet with Rudrick to discuss strategy.

I looked over to see who my fellow Cadet-Marshall was

for the upcoming exercise and met Prince Mateo's dark gaze. He gestured me over in the space between our flights. "It's easy, Walker. We're just communicating orders from High Command and making sure they're followed," he said.

"Yup, I've noticed—"

He quickly made a shushing gesture. "My father does not have anyone who's taken Callan's role," he murmured close to my ear.

"Really?" I whispered. I'd noticed a general lack of hostility now that he was gone, but then again, all of the third-years were absent. My year group now ruled the roost, so to speak.

"Callan was grooming Barlowe for the job, but he declined it." He held up a hand as my gaze shot to the young man now arguing with Sharde over something out of earshot. "I'm only naming him because he said he respected you too much to take over harassing you. He's not a bad person. But I imagine how it ended for the last guy had a small influence on him saying no."

"So that's it, then? No more antagonist," I said with a hush of hope.

He started to smile when a taloned paw closed around his arm and pushed him away. Mireille stepped into the spot where he was standing, bunting my chest affectionately. I scratched into her neck and held her with a laugh at her sudden appearance. "I thought it's safe enough that you and she could spend time together," he said, petting her wing. He seemed reluctant, still, to share her.

I was trying to make a temporary Link to say hello to Mireille when we had to separate and talk to our respective Cadet-Generals. Sharde was wearing his most mischievous smile as he whispered the plan in my ear. I flashed him a shocked look.

"Barlowe didn't agree to that, did he?" I asked.

"*Pfft*. Of course not."

I passed the word along, doing my best not to laugh when Credell gave me the same look I'd given Sharde. "That's the plan," I insisted.

"Hmm. Yes, ma'am," he replied in his slow drawl.

My flight flew in reduced elements of four riders each. The other flights had nine people apiece, a number I was unexpectedly jealous of when Falcon Flight split into three even groups of three fliers.

The first round had adjusted rules as well. Instead of one hit counting as a kill, we had to strike an enemy three times to send them out of the sky. Somehow, it didn't devolve to chaos immediately. Most elements managed to stay together for multiple minutes. It just felt nice to fly with the people I was most comfortable with rather than a full element of semi-familiar cadets from other flights.

To my delight, Ari and I "survived" along with Sharde, Feyring, Credell, and Biggs. We picked up our practice swords and circled up.

"Flight, it's been an honor," Sharde said, pretending to swipe a tear off his cheek. "You are the finest young men—and woman—I've ever worked with. If we die this afternoon, we die with glory!"

Out of his back pocket, he pulled out his Sivana doll and held it to the sky. "Kite Flight! Whoosh!"

We echoed the call, and I started to laugh. "To glory," I giggled, not able to take him or his plan seriously anymore.

When the horn blew to start the second round, we didn't hide in the forest, instead standing at the tree line in full view of the enemy. Barlowe had wanted a distraction so he and his team of surviving Falcon Flight members could sneak past enemy lines undetected, but he'd left the method of distraction up to Sharde's imagination.

And Sharde, of course, had chosen to have us break into a popular kid's dance, the solis slide, clapping a beat and saying the lyrics. "Slide to the left, wiggle to the right. You an' me, we'll dance all night."

It didn't take long for us to get noticed, a group charging at us with swords raised. "Dance with us!" Biggs called.

"Evasive maneuvers!" Sharde called, clapping at twice the speed.

I sort of kept doing the solis slide but switched up the wiggling and the sliding part so it wasn't quite as easy to predict. The other cadets kind of just…stared for a few seconds before glancing to the group being led through PT. On cue, Weslecker, Pereyra, and Korvic started dancing and got the shouting attention of half a dozen sergeants.

They eventually attacked us, and we all were eliminated by standard dueling rules but kept dancing. Sharde was pretty sure they'd join us. One did, the others rushing off to the woods in search of our royalty. This round, we had two queens in Puzzlebox and Mireille.

"Darn it, it almost worked," Sharde said after a cheer rose from behind us. "It *was* pretty distracting."

We lined up again for a second try, and Rudrick wasted no time in patting Sharde on the shoulder and saying, "You're fired. Walker! Get up here."

He made an impatient gesture when I glanced around, like a second Walker would materialize and take the Cadet-General spot he expected me to come fill.

"*Finally,*" Ari said. We huddled up with Prince Mateo and Mireille, also recently promoted back to the job he'd had for half of last semester already.

"Well, cadets? What's our strategy?" Rudrick prompted.

"They're going to expect a distraction, so we need a new strategy for round two," I said.

"*I have some ideas,*" Ari said.

I bit my lip as I glanced down at him. As much as I wanted to win, I didn't want to rely on him too much and not be able to strategize for myself.

"Well, that's fine," he said in answer to my thoughts.

"You should teach me what you know," I suggested.

"Everyone's used to me playing it safe and holding most of our people back on defense," Mateo was saying. "If we really want to do something unexpected, we should blitz them with everyone."

I nibbled on my bottom lip in thought. "If that fails, then we've lost everyone. Why don't we hold one person back? There is one thing they won't expect..." I thought back to a conversation I'd overheard about last year's Ace picking an ambush spot from a tree and suggested it.

Mateo started to smile. "I'll stay behind and try it. Are we still going by the rule that unseen attacks are an instant out?" he asked Rudrick, who nodded.

It ended up being a smart borrow, as my side won the second and final game that day after Mateo successfully ambushed and took out two people while we quickly pushed a win on the other side of the field.

Our ranks reset over the rest of the weekend, and I found my name at twelve of thirty-five, holding the Cadet-General title. It wasn't good enough for Ari, who made me review military strategy in my limited free time and drilled me randomly during the day. For once, I was the one needing a bunch of extra practice.

"TODAY IS THE DAY," Ellie said one evening as the rest of us lay around after a grueling session of inclement weather training. She'd dragged out box after box full of copies of her bouncy ball, the last few filled by her personally.

"Is today the day?" groaned Biggs from where he lay face down in his gryphon's fluffy wing.

"It's the day we have almost three thousand copies of my

prototype." She adjusted her glasses with a little nervous laugh before lifting my replicator out of her pocket in two uneven pieces. "And, uh, that's all we're getting."

I glanced from the broken toy to the boxes we'd filled. "Shame it broke, but it did a darn good job," I said.

"It's not too late to change the target, though," Credell murmured.

Sharde rubbed his eyes and stretched from where he was resting next to Puzzlebox. "There's no way he's going to know it's us. Seriously, Credell, don't look at me like that. When's the last time anyone's had the stones to prank the Commandant?"

We glanced around and shared shrugs. "Completely harmless, too. We just have to pick the time to put them in his office," Ellie said.

"That's the harder part. He's always working," I pointed out.

Sharde shook his head at me. "This isn't a late-night kind of thing."

His plan was simple enough. Ellie observed the Commandant's schedule for us for an entire week. It was pretty obvious that a gryphon rider as experienced as him would have a strict timetable for most things, but midday, he was either holed up in his office with a stack of paperwork or randomly checking in on classes to make sure everything was running smoothly.

We couldn't keep using her as our lookout if we didn't want to be suspicious, though, so the next time we noticed the Commandant and Night heading down the stairs, Ellie and I hustled to her workroom to retrieve the full boxes. They were sealed, though the last one was overflowing with one corner lifted and showing the gray, jelly-like spheres wiggling within.

We carried them through the quiet classroom and down a

level, nearing the Commandant's office, when a deep boom called out, "Ellie!"

She jumped and froze, the overfull box wobbling on top of the three she was already carrying. We both turned to see Sarge coming over, hands out. "You look like you need help," he said in the gentle way he talked to his daughter.

"N-no, no help needed," she stammered.

He plucked the top one off the stack she held anyway. "Huh, light as a feather. What…"

I held my breath, realizing he'd taken a peek inside. His gaze went right over Ellie to settle on me. "What are these, cadet?" he demanded.

"Bouncy balls, Sarge," I answered.

"Why do you need—" He counted with a finger. "—eight boxes full of bouncy balls?"

I was pretty much frozen, but Ellie responded in a perky tone, "We don't!"

His lips twitched toward a smile. "So, I don't know about this?"

"Nope!"

"Guess I'd better not see what you actually do with them." Shaking his head, he placed the extra box on top of my stack and left us.

I leaned past my burden. "Did he just…?" I whispered.

Her expression reminded me of Sharde's in full mischief. "Secret weapon, remember?"

CHAPTER 31

HIS PROTECTION

I can't say if the Commandant was annoyed by our prank or not. Those of us who knew it was happening were also the ones making sure to be nowhere near his office when he walked in again.

Two thousand eight hundred and fifty-four bouncy balls ended up being about knee high. Ellie grumbled about proper measurements as we dumped the contents of our boxes quickly and cleaned up the spill of them that escaped when we did.

I waited all day for her father to rat us out. If not Ellie, then the rest of my flight. Nothing happened.

Maybe at PT, then. I breathed a sigh of relief, though, when it was its usual grueling self, but nothing out of the ordinary.

Until the Commandant called me to his office in the middle of class that day. *This is it,* I thought, in a cold sweat the entire way there.

The gryphon toy was in my bag now, painted in shades of maroon and red by Ellie, who'd found the only paint in the whole fortress to make it happen. It would be worth whatever the Commandant had in store for Sunset to have it.

I knocked timidly and came in after the Commandant's call to enter. The room was mostly clear of bouncy balls, except for piles in the corners and around Night's nest. She lay on a throne of them.

"Good afternoon, Cadet Walker," the Commandant said, gesturing for me to sit.

"Good afternoon, sir."

He eyed me sternly, and I gulped a swallow. He knew I'd pranked him. Perhaps Night identified my smell, or it was Sarge. But judging by our surroundings, it was mostly taken care of, and I would be taking the punishment for it alone.

He let me sit tensely for several moments before saying, "I would like another report on Sunset's progress."

For a prolonged moment, I blinked at him owlishly. He didn't want to talk about the several hundred bouncy balls still in the room with us?

"Y-Yes, sir. She is doing quite well, I believe she's going to make it," I replied. "She spends a lot of time with Ari, and it seems they've bonded over their shared experience. It seems like the best thing for her is knowing another gryphon who lost a rider."

"Excellent." He glanced down and scribbled something on one of the many forms spread out over his desk. "I will send for a few promising young men to start the re-Linking process."

I opened my mouth to suggest that she not might be ready for that, but it had been quite some time since she lost Callan. She'd been given the luxury of leniency, the time, space, and support a gryphon needed to have a chance to recover from the trauma of a broken Link.

Either I could be bitter that Ari hadn't received the same treatment, or I could embrace the fact that she was, in fact, ready to get up and move on *because* of the trauma and unfair treatment he'd survived.

"That would be great. I can't wait to see her breaking in a new rider," I said.

He asked me a few more questions before dismissing me back to class. I steeled my nerve, thinking of what I'd do if I didn't already know about the prank. "Sir, what's with all these?" I asked, gesturing to one corner.

"Some enrichment for Night, cadet. I told you that you're dismissed," he said.

Enrichment? I glanced at his gryphon, who was chewing on one of the bouncy balls. It popped into a wisp of colored air, as it was one of the weaker, later copies we'd made. A soft, whistle tone came from her, a laugh.

I stepped out of the office and re-imagined the moment a ton of bouncy balls came rolling from the threshold when the Commandant first opened the door. Beside his annoyance at the prank was Night, pouncing on the toys and frolicking into the room like a gryphon half her age. I smothered a giggle as I walked back to class.

The day went by quickly. Before Gryphon Taming, I stopped by Ari's stall. Sunset lifted her head and trilled to him as he came in behind me. He responded with a quiet murr.

"Hey, Sunset. I have something for you," I said, kneeling by her head. She tilted her neck in clear request for scratches.

It was odd to hear silence back when I talked to a gryphon I was close to. I'd gotten so used to the extra magic Lord Orion's token gave me.

Sitting up, she watched me pull out the painted toy gryphon. "We did our best to make it look like you." I flapped its little wooden wings, holding it out for her to take.

She clasped it gently in her beak and laid it before her, nudging it this way and that with her talons. "Our time together is almost done," I said, hoping she liked it. "There are going to be new boys here soon, hoping to meet you."

In reply, she settled back into her nest of hay and tucked

the toy gryphon into her side. Her canary-yellow eyes stared at the far wall, her body turned away. Pensiveness rose from her.

"Why don't you talk it through with her? Maybe that will help," I suggested to Ari.

"Sure. You're late to class anyway," he said.

Gods, so I was. I left them, finding my Gryphon Taming class already in session and Blue held down by the neck as the other cadets cleaned him.

"That's two demerits for being tardy," Gemon said, barely turning to acknowledge me as he watched this grooming session.

"I was taking care of Sunset, sir."

"The model cadet doesn't get distracted on the way to class," he said curtly.

I simmered with annoyance. Of all my instructors, Gemon was the one who should understand the value of a tamed gryphon's life the most.

"As I was telling your classmates, we've begun efforts to make Blue more docile," he said. "He is on reduced feed."

I felt a queasy roll in my stomach, even though we'd covered this in depth earlier this year. It was easier to think about in the abstract rather than know it was happening to a living, breathing creature.

There were only a few ways to have leverage over a wild gryphon, especially an unmated adult male. The most effective method was to take away their food source. If food only came from a friendly human hand, the beast would eventually stop trying to bite that hand, in theory.

"We've weaned him down to about twenty percent right now. We're going to zero tomorrow," Gemon said. "Give it a couple days, and you'll see how quickly he turns around."

He ordered me to go help, and as I did, I realized the wild gryphon was barely putting up a fight within his chains. I imagined how much worse it would be with only water in his belly.

This is wrong, I thought. What right did we have to starve this gryphon until he submitted?

A plan started cycling through my mind.

GEMON and the other gryphon tamers went to dinner each night at the same time, laughing and joking at the far end of the mess hall. I observed them for a couple nights and found no deviation, so on the third, I went up with Sunset as my excuse.

The caretakers were in charge of seeing to the beasts in the evening if they weren't down in the mess hall with their riders. One had an overflowing bucket of fish filets on ice, and I stole two as I snuck by him.

The tamer's stables were dead quiet. I assumed these gryphons were fed last, if they were at least partially tamed. By the time they arrived, I hoped my stolen meal for Blue would be long gone.

He cracked one icy eye as I approached cautiously and placed the filets within the slack of his chains. Splayed out on his side, he didn't bother hopping to his paws and trying to lunge at me.

Instead, his voice whispered in my head. *"Trying to get something from me, Link thief?"*

"You deserve something to eat," I said.

He didn't move, just watched me through slitted lids. *"You've waited a few days. Sure this isn't you seeing how quickly I turn around?"*

I was confused until I realized he was referencing Gemon. Something the man had said to me, actually. *"That's not why—"*

"No? Then why are you so eager to learn how to tame one of my kind? I've watched you eat up everything else your teacher has said. You expect me to believe you're doing this out of the kindness of your heart?"

I turned away from his mocking, catching the sound of stall doors creaking nearby. *"You'd better eat that fast,"* I warned.

"I don't want your bribe."

"It's not a bribe."

"Or your pity," he snapped.

"I'm just trying to help you, you dense ball of feathers! Eat the fish," I practically ordered, pointing at the filets.

"Don't expect me to thank you for this," he muttered. Little did he know, I'd already heard that from a different, but equally proud wild beast.

"I'll come back to feed you every night I can. There's only one thing I want in return, and it's not gratitude," I said after he snapped up each filet in two swallows.

"What is it?" he grumbled.

"Tell me your name."

"Apparently it's Blue now."

"No, your real name," I insisted.

He laid his head down and sighed through his beak. *"My mother named me after the great rivers that flow fierce and deep far into the mountains where I was hatched. My name is the essence of freezing water and the eternal roar of waterfalls."*

Somehow, I realized my magic was translating him literally as he showed me images of cold mountainsides and flowing rivers. The essence of this narrowed to a single name: *Reyos.*

"Thank you, Reyos. Your name...and this food, they can be our secret," I promised.

I couldn't sneak Reyos food every day, but at least it was less suspicious due to his flagging energy levels. He grudgingly accepted our touch now, and Gemon gave the go-ahead to remove the chain around his neck.

"If I continue acting tame, will the rest be removed?" Reyos asked me in a rare moment of civility as I rubbed ointment into the raw wound encircling his neck. He must've felt every lunge and snap, as even our best attempts to tend to him hadn't prevented his injury.

"Well, yes. You're only tied up in the first place because you might kill someone otherwise," I said.

"And to prevent me from leaving."

"That too."

He turned his pale eyes my way, inspecting keenly. *"Why is it that you are the only human who talks to me in my language?"*

I pressed my fingertips to the token hiding under my shirt. *"Magic. Our brains don't work like yours... We talk in words, not images and emotions."*

"Imagine what life would be like if we could all communicate."

I did imagine. His comment stuck with me for days more, because I realized that was a true problem. Gryphons couldn't speak for themselves because most humans couldn't begin to understand how the beasts project meaning through their minds. They needed an advocate.

They needed...me. It was Lord Orion's plan all along, I thought. In giving me the token and time to use it, the god had ensured that I'd naturally go past helping Ari with it, straight into forming stronger relationships with every gryphon around me.

One such beast stopped me on my way back to Kite Flight's dorm one evening, sliding her bulk in my way and bunting my chest affectionately. Mireille didn't realize her strength and size anymore; I released a hard "oof" and stumbled backward.

"Sivvy!" she exclaimed.

"Isn't that Puzzlebox's thing?" Ari asked in amusement.

"Well, it's my thing too, now," she said. She lifted her head and perked her ears for scratches, which I gave while looking over her shoulder. Like always, where she was, Prince Mateo wasn't far behind, watching me carefully.

"Hi, baby. You can call me what you want," I laughed.

Mateo stepped forward to pet his gryphon's wing. "Hey, Walker. Just the person we were wanting to see. We need to talk," he said, gesturing behind him with a tilt of his head.

I followed him nervously to Falcon Flight's dorm, wondering what the king was planning this time. Like last year, his flight had magelights and nicer furniture, most of which was full of lounging young men.

On instinct, I froze when they turned to look at me coming in flanked by Ari and Mireille. The looks they flashed me weren't exactly friendly, yet no one made the sign of Orion or flicked their fingertips. It felt like the same reaction I'd get from walking into any other rival flight's dorm.

One by one, they turned back to what they were doing. My confusion must've been written on my face, as Mateo leaned in to murmur, "They know you're under my protection."

I chose to sit on the floor, resting my weight back on Ari's side while Mireille lay over my lap and stretched herself out to touch her rider too when he sat next to me. "Protection? That's news to me," I said.

He sketched a dismissive shrug. "Let's just say I got tired of pretending we're in fundamental school rather than a military academy."

"Like you went to fundamental school."

"I did, actually. It was one of my mother's last wishes, that her children receive the same education we ask the rest of the populace to send their kids to," he said. Rather than meet my eye, he bent to the task of plucking bits of fluff from between his gryphon's feathers. "I had tutors, of course, and father pulled me from public classes when I was about ten. But I *did* go. And I turned out all right, don't you think?"

I snorted. "Do you really want me to answer that question?"

He raised a brow. "Tell it to me honestly, Walker."

His flight-mates laughed a few feet away to something Barlowe had said, distracted with their own conversation. I hoped none of them noticed how Mateo looked at me. With his guard down and a smile teasing the corner of his mouth rather than his usual scowl, he was, well…

I felt myself getting warm under his gentler regard. *No. No no no. You can't have thoughts like that about anyone here, let alone him! Especially while 'under his protection,'* I told myself. "Then I think you turned out decently."

"Just decent?"

"People are going to be paying you exaggerated compliments your whole life. I thought you wanted honesty," I teased.

He scoffed. "Decent, then. I aspire to something better than that, and I know you do too. That's why I needed to talk to you, actually, from one Cadet-General to the other. I have a bit of insider information on how the rest of the year will go."

"Oh?" I leaned in, eager for any leg up.

The rate at which ranks and elements were changed around was slowing dramatically. It felt like the Commandant was pretty sure where we all fell, but I knew Ari and I at least deserved to climb to a single-digit rank before the end of the year between his experience and my newfound emergence from under Callan's cruel thumb.

"We"—he indicated himself and me—"will be assigning our elements from here on out, starting during the next Field Training day. Since I've heard it early, I wanted to talk it through with less pressure on us."

"That's a great idea. Maybe we can think of some strategies for the second round as well," I suggested.

"Just don't tell him everything we know," Ari cut in. *"You never know when we'll be going against him instead."*

"Okay," I said, though I hoped Kite and Falcon Flights stayed allied for a while yet.

I stayed there long enough that one of his flight-mates offered me snacks and one of the comfiest chairs they had. All we did was discuss strategy and shuffle around our flight-mates in theory to make elements where everyone got along and flew with similar skill levels, but it was fun.

Mateo was witty when given the chance, offering a sharp outsider's perspective of my flight-mates that had me snorting with laughter more than once. He seemed to relax as the common room cleared out. I wondered if his flight didn't hang out in the evening like mine tended to, or if they were just giving us privacy.

"I think we have a solid plan," I said, feeling like it was probably time I bedded Ari down for the night and went back to my dorm in anticipation of lights out.

He nodded in agreement. "We should do this more. I think we make a good team."

Something nice about me, straight from him? That really was a first.

"I agree, now that I know we're on the same team," I said, and I wasn't just referring to the Field Training days ahead of us.

"Side," he corrected. We stepped into the hall together, trailing our gryphons. "It's always been sides. There's my father's and my brother's, but I refuse to belong to either."

I wet my lips in consideration. "Then I'm glad I'm on your side."

CHAPTER 32
CLIMB THE HEAVENS

Instructor Signe missed a few weeks of class, leaving me with more time to help show Sunset to potential new cadets. Each boy was rejected, with the gryphon turning her beak up at the idea of meeting a single one.

No one was happy. Not the embarrassed noble boys, whose families had the connections to fly them to Fortress Aerie, nor the Commandant, who had to take the written abuse of said families when it was obvious Sunset was completely disinterested in finding a new rider.

"Will you tell me why?" I asked one afternoon, soothing the maroon gryphon by brushing her belly fur. Another boy waited to meet her outside her stall, while she lay limply in the hay with no intention of greeting him. She'd been moved to a space of her own and immediately regressed without Ari's steady presence.

I'd asked her this same question dozens of times now. She didn't want to make small talk or connect to me, that much was obvious by now, but maybe she'd respond eventually, even if it was just to ask for more time.

Her head came up sharply, and she glared at me, but we

did connect. My mind was full of a rush of noise that wavered before solidifying into a scream.

"Sunset! Sunset, get help! Tell someone—" Pitch perfect, Callan's voice scrabbled at the inside of my mind. The hair on my arms stood straight up. *"He's going to kill me!"*

"Are these his last moments?" I asked. The memory was warped, like it was louder than it should be rather than the mere whisper of a rider separated from his gryphon by a few miles.

"Yes," she whispered. *"He begged for help I couldn't give him."*

I sighed and tossed the brush aside, sitting in the hay while tapping my lips in thought. In a single instant, she'd confirmed the kind of information that could solidify a case that Callan was murdered. I was the last person who'd be informed if the investigation into his death was already completed, and it was *Callan*. But...

He and his family deserved the dignity of the truth.

"I know what he's done," she said, her tone echoing my thoughts. *"But he was still my rider, and I failed him. I would rather follow him into the afterlife than accept responsibility for another rider."*

"But Sunset—"

"That is my reasoning, and I won't change it." She drifted away from our connection, and I scrambled to hold on to it.

"Wait, wait. I'll send the kid waiting to see you away if that's what you want, but I need more information," I said.

"For what reason?" she asked warily.

"I can tell someone more important than me who was responsible."

Her eyes remained narrowed on me. *"I'll consider it."*

Sunset kept considering through my next run as Cadet-General alongside Mateo. Our side won two of two games, and I watched my rank climb to number nine of thirty-five. We remained in charge due to our successful performance, which meant I could look forward to another long evening chatting with Mateo.

I couldn't deny the way my heart fluttered at the thought. I longed to see him relaxed, as a friend rather than a rival. *Just a crush,* I told myself, too busy to really analyze how I felt otherwise.

I watched Sunset turn her head away from candidate after candidate to be her new rider. I knew even the Commandant's generous patience was being tested by her stubbornness.

On the other hand, Reyos and I were making progress. He was a smarter gryphon than I gave him credit for, clearly listening in on every conversation around him. He knew acting like he didn't despise human touch was the reason he was getting fed again and eventually unchained from the wall.

I still visited him in the evening, bringing extra treats and sitting out of striking range. I coached him on what to do, as I was willing to look the other way the moment the chains went sliding off his wings and he darted out of the stables and to freedom. In return, he showed me his home and flock, led by Skylord Roshawk. *"It means he has claimed one of the best territories out in the wild,"* he said when explaining the title. *"He is the most powerful male in our whole society, with a flock that rivals those of the great matriarchs."*

It was only because of him that I learned that *skylord* was a made-up title to counter *matriarch*, the skymothers who had defended their flocks into venerated age, keeping them safe from humans and fed well on prime stretches of territory. When I asked why not "patriarch," Reyos had told me it was because Roshawk wasn't considered venerated. He was a phenomenon as a male leader of his flock, but the matriarchs didn't think he was their equal yet.

Nothing was more valuable to the wild beasts than territory, family, and ferocity. *"Humans threaten all these things,"* he told me. *"They invade our territories, steal us from our families, and expect us to enjoy being* pet *like a common* animal.*"*

I stifled a laugh in response to his sheer outrage at the thought. *"You are a beautiful gryphon. It shouldn't be surprising that we want to touch you."*

He tilted his beak up proudly. *"I know I am."*

I snorted. Should've expected him to have an ego. *"Unfortunately, you have to pretend to like humans if you want your wings freed,"* I said. His annoyance flared up immediately. *"It's standard to wait for an adult gryphon to Link before we let their wings free. But frequent signs of affection for your caretakers could also be taken as a sign that it's safe."*

"I hate this."

"Of course. And no one expects you to suddenly start acting like you love us," I said. *"I'll bring it up to Gemon when you feel comfortable to start pretending."*

"Stand up," he grumbled.

I did so, watching warily as he followed suit and paced toward me. I was the only one who realized he was still fully wild and more likely to take my arm off than…

He lowered his head and bunted my middle with just the right amount of force. Out of habit, I scratched behind his ears, which pinned back immediately from displeasure. He wrenched himself backward with a soft growl.

"That wasn't bad, I guess," he muttered.

I chuckled. *"We'll work on it."*

WORD GOT AROUND that Instructor Signe was back. I was the first person in her classroom after lunch, sitting in the back when she waved me away from her and hacked a rattling series of coughs into her fist.

I'd had Mother Nilara's eldrafn dream again last night, the first one in a long while. After waking up to another death from a strike of lightning, I'd thought of Signe, hoping it was a sign that my Rathi instructor would be back on her feet today. She didn't look great. The icy tones of her skin were sallow, and it sounded like she struggled to catch her breath.

Though I was concerned, I didn't ask if she was up to the task of telling us another part of the sagas of her homeland. That Rathi pride would come out in full force, I thought. "I have a question, instructor," I said. "Is it possible for a gryphon rider to fight an eldrafn on their own?"

I was running out of ideas for how to defeat the thunderbird that haunted my dreams. It really felt like the Mother had given me an impossible task.

Signe's lips bunched together. "Of course it's possible, but the eldrafn would win," she huffed. "Only winds harsher than the eldrafn's or a strike to its heart can slay one, but it can deter a single gryphon rider without trouble."

Ari immediately grumbled in my head, still in a bad mood that the dream had come back to haunt us.

"What about…just a gryphon?" I asked. Roshawk wore his lightning scars with pride; he'd successfully killed one somehow.

Signe's laughter transitioned to another flurry of painful-sounding coughs. "Oh dear. I guess they haven't taught you that eldrafn eat gryphons if they ever hunger for flesh instead of static."

I opened my mouth for another question, but my classmates were starting to file in. She sat up straight and proud, eyeing the scribe sternly as he arrived after everyone else and set up in the desk next to me to record everything she said.

"Good day, students. It has come to my attention that there is a single saga I've never shared, which is a true shame, considering that it's my favorite," she said. Her breath rasped as she gathered her breath to begin.

"From the Thunder Saga, an epic about fair Idunn, who climbed the heavens herself to earn her throne next to her husband, the eternal warrior Anrathor." As she spoke, her storytelling presence smoothed out the rougher edges that sickness lent her voice.

"Idunn was the heir of a long line of women who tended the apple groves of Ungr Island. Food, as you know, is currency to the Rathi, as our lands yield little of it. By necessity, Idunn became a warrior to defend the groves from those who would slay her family for control of Ungr's fertile soil.

"Unfortunately for her, a few villages combined forces and attacked in the dead of night, killing her fellow warriors in their beds. Soaked in blood, she crawled away from the carnage and cursed her weakness. She was a coward, one who ran from a fight rather than staying to defend what was hers. The invaders discovered her and took her as a thrall—a slave.

"For years, she tended to the apples by day and fought in the thrall pits at night for her captor's amusement. A spark was lit in her the night she'd lost her family. She never wanted to run from another fight, so she threw her all into each match, roaring like the thunder itself as she emerged victorious night after night."

Signe went on to describe her captors as superstitious Rathi, who viewed her fury as unnatural and aberrant. They were sure the gods would punish them for putting a leash on a woman like her. When an eldrafn swooped over Ungr Island one day and uprooted two apple trees for consumption, it was seen as that punishment, especially when it created the kind of distraction that allowed Idunn to escape.

"She was emboldened by the favor of the gods. In Rathi

culture, we do not revere your soft Goddess of Life. The only goddess of Idunn's time was Hel, the two-faced Goddess of Death, and to her, Idunn prayed. Hel's influence was fading on the world, but she encouraged Idunn to undertake a journey to scale the distant mountains and beseech the pantheon of gods for assistance in retaking Ungr Island."

I twitched at the mention of Hel. A rare nod to a Rathi goddess who'd perished when her people stopped believing in her in favor of the hooded Gatekeeper, the much kinder god of the two, as he never trapped a soul within its body to enslave it as an undead, unlike Hel, who preferred her people in that state.

Signe described the journey east briefly, encompassing months of traveling by raft or on foot, until Idunn devised a plan to fly there. She'd scaled up high and taken an eldrafn by surprise by pouncing on its back, a stunt that horrified me. Instead of getting electrocuted instantly, the eldrafn had accepted her as a rider and taken her to the home of the gods.

"It's a story," Ari commented. *"None of this really happened, so it can be ridiculous."*

I shushed him in my head, too wrapped up to consider that this saga could be a tall tale. "My people don't truly know what happened next," Signe was saying. "We fill in the gaps with many ideas. The most popular of which is that Lord Anrathor promised to give her the vengeance she sought if she could defeat him in a duel. Did she win?"

She shrugged stiffly. "Considering she sits at his side as his bride and blesses my people with the ability to tame eldrafn, the epitome of harsh nature, I would say she won no matter the outcome. Ungr Island stands to this day, and so do Idunn's precious apple trees, but they are laced with electricity to punish anyone who would dare steal them. Only the goddess's chosen may consume the apples now."

As usual, the end of the story coincided with Signe gruffly telling us to leave and pointing to the door. I went to the stables with a big smile. Even if none of that was true, I still loved the idea of an ordinary woman becoming a goddess with enough determination and wits. Ari picked up on my thoughts, and I felt him comparing Idunn from the story to me. *"Only difference is we were stopped right before we went to the home of the gods,"* he mused.

"Think that might be something important?" I asked.

"Pfft. No. What would they make you anyway, Goddess of Stubbornness?"

"It's got a ring to it," I teased. He released a whistle-like laugh.

Gryphon Taming was fairly uneventful. Reyos obliged us in accepting meat from us while we wore protective gear resembling oven mitts, though he recognized the way the other tamers were afraid of him and had a soft laugh of his own.

"If I've learned anything from this experience, it is that humans aren't as scary as we give them credit for," he commented to me. *"Your kind must use tricks and misery to control me, because you could not do it honestly otherwise."*

"There is some…desperation. We are at war, and any gryphon who will help us fight could make the difference between victory and defeat," I admitted.

I passed the rest of the class time explaining our war against Lithos while Gemon delivered a lecture I didn't listen to. *"Lithos is primarily desert land, but the border between our nations is a stretch of fertile land constantly nourished by water from a river delta. They attacked us first, trying to chase off Altarian farmers, and they just won't back down. We call that part of the country 'rozash alley' because the Lithosians are constantly trying to ruin crops with rains of acid and fire. The flights assigned to the southern border have to constantly fend them off, or Altarians will starve."*

"A territory dispute, then. I understand that," he replied. *"But…what is a rozash?"*

Ari answered for me, showing him image after image of the winged serpents. Reyos made a sound of disgust at some of the memories of the carnage left in the wake of creatures able to weaponize breath made of pressurized acid, fire, or sand.

"I am glad to know why I was captured, even if I have no intention of helping. I still have a life waiting for me in my flock," Reyos said.

I nodded in understanding. *"Of course. You're my friend now, and I don't intend to force you into giving up your old life."*

He didn't reply to that, letting our temporary Link lapse to silence, but I thought I caught a hint of thoughtfulness in the medley of his emotions before they were gone.

Once class was over, Ari and I checked on Sunset, who was sitting primly in her stall. She looked up and connected with me immediately. *"I have come to a decision regarding your offer,"* she said. *"I...suspect I may know who killed my rider."*

I stifled a gasp and led Ari into her stall. She pressed up against his side as soon as he sat next to her, pushing her beak into his neck for a few long moments. He returned the gesture as she began to speak haltingly.

"You've cared for me when you didn't have to... I realize now, my old rider...he was not quite right. While I should have been there for him, I know I should have also pushed back against his earlier behavior. Maybe he would be alive right now..."

"You can't be blamed for his actions. He was still his own person," I said, trying to soothe her. She tensed the moment I touched her wing, so I pulled away and watched Ari groom down her neck and the line of her back instead.

"If Arimus told you something you were doing was wrong, you would listen, yes?" Gods above, she sounded ashamed.

"Yes, of course," I answered.

Her chest rose and fell rapidly, a soft keening emerging from her beak. Gryphons couldn't cry with tears, but she cried nonetheless. *"I never told Victor no. I wanted to be the best too and wore the Ace-to-be title with just as much pride as he did. But the things we had to do to get there...I'm sorry. I'm sorry he tried to kill you and that you have to see me every day and remember him."*

"Shh, it's okay," Ari murmured, nuzzling against her wing.

She leaned into him, and in that moment, I saw it. At least, I recognized what I was seeing. He'd looped his talons over her side, holding her protectively, and she took his comfort and support. The look in her eyes...the flow of emotion between them.

Good gods. *They* might be forming a new Link together, the kind that would make Valtora a grandmother.

"Really? The first thing you think of is chicks?" Ari asked privately.

"Noooo." Darn, he'd absolutely caught me imagining them in happier times, pressed together just like this while a pair of little red hatchlings frolicked nearby. *"I'm happy for you! I didn't realize, you...with her..."*

"It is very new. Who knows, when she gets another rider, she might completely forget about me."

I scoffed. *"She's not going to forget you!"* I didn't add my doubts about her finding a new rider, but he sensed the direction of my thoughts.

"If she doesn't, at least I know somewhere else she can go," he murmured.

"To the wild?" If anything, she could go with Reyos, free of the responsibilities and heartache of being a tame gryphon.

It would be a huge blow to the gryphon knight corps, as they were both outstanding beasts, but it might be the best thing for the beasts. *"I'll suggest it if Reyos actually gets a chance to escape,"* he said.

Sunset stirred and turned to me again. She wore her regret as a halo of emotion around her. *"Please, tell me what you know,"* I asked.

With another heaving breath, she pushed a memory into

my mind. She was standing next to Callan in the middle of the training field in the black of night. I felt her discomfort, as she'd been forced to fly him here and knew if she wanted to return to her warm, safe nest, she'd have to take him back.

"I received your letter," Callan said in his usual, arrogant way. There was someone else standing there, hooded and hidden in the embrace of darkness.

"And your response?" This other person's voice was a slow drawl.

"I require more information about this mysterious bene-factor. The sum of money offered is adequate, but to try to kill someone in the method detailed is very risky," Callan said.

"Adequate," repeated the hooded man. "It is three times what you make in an entire month of service to the king."

"And how do you know—"

"I know a great many things about you, Victor. This money could pay for your mother's treatments. It could help send your sister to university. You'll do it because you *need* the payment, not because you care about who knows you already work for the king," he said. Callan eased back a step, fists balling at his sides. "My benefactor requires a martyr, and you need this money. So, what is your response?"

"*Victor...*" Sunset murmured uneasily. She may not have stopped him, but she had her misgivings from the start.

"I...I'll do it," he said.

The hooded man withdrew an envelope practically filled to bursting from a pocket in his cloak. In the process, Sunset had caught a glimpse of his face, and I pulled back from the memory as I reeled backward physically.

"*I believe this man killed my rider,*" Sunset said.

Maybe so, but I remembered him. The man with a forget-table face, listening to Callan try to lure me into pushing him down a staircase. He'd been wearing the same hood, even.

"*The word he used,* martyr. *I've only heard it in one other place,*" I said.

He keeps saying his cause needs a martyr.

Very few had the resources to learn about Callan's identity as the king's man, and even fewer could pay him what must've been a heavenly sum. Crown Prince Isaac, though, had the money and the kind of cause that "needed" a martyr.

And that martyr was supposed to be me.

Chapter 33

MARTYRS AND GODS

"Slow down. You spoke with Sunset?" Prince Mateo asked. He and Mireille sat together in the Falcon Flight common room while I paced.

I'd let Ari stay and comfort Sunset while I went charging out of the stables to find Mateo right away. "Yes! And the man she showed me works for your brother."

He exchanged a glance with his gryphon. "And your only proof is that he was there when Callan threatened you before the court-martial," he said slowly.

"And that he said his benefactor needed a *martyr*! Who else has used that word that you know of?" I exclaimed.

He held his head like I was giving him the worst ache of his life. "My sister, who is also not a credible source of information. Why would Isaac try to have you killed? You're practically the mascot for his campaign for change."

I pointed at him. "That's why!"

"Do you know how crazy you sound right now, Walker? You have no proof, and this is a serious allegation against someone who's helped you a lot." His look was one of disappointment, which sobered me up just like a slap in the face.

"Fine. I'll write a letter to Odalis and ask if she knows who the hooded man is. And if he works for your brother..." I made a sweeping gesture with both hands.

"You do that, Walker," he said dismissively.

I WROTE to her and waited an agonizing two weeks to hear back. I knew I was on to something, but Mateo was right about one thing: I had no real proof. Sunset couldn't appear in court and tell her story; only I could do that.

That stopped me from writing home and sharing my suspicions. Mother worked for the crown prince now, and so did Father, in a less direct fashion. And the truth was, the best proof I had was already dead.

News of canceled classes circled the Academy as I waited hopefully for a Wednesday mail drop to bring me news from Odalis. Every cadet, soldier, and member of the support staff were called to the Green for a speech from the Commandant.

I came out of my room in a fresh formal uniform, as we were instructed to wear our best. Some of my flight-mates had their dolls of me out and were giving them tiny uniforms as well. "Guys, why?" I asked, baffled.

They all laughed. "Gotta look sharp," Weslecker said.

"What do you think the assembly is going to be about?" Sharde asked. He was often the least serious one here, but he wasn't smiling or messing with dolls today. "There hasn't been one called in the time I've been here."

"Really? Usually, you're our expert on this kind of thing," I said.

"I think something very bad has happened," he murmured.

"For the record, it didn't happen when I was here the first time, either," Ari pitched in.

I stressed as we waited for the last of my flight-mates and

Ellie to finish preparing so we could go to the Green together. What could possibly be so bad that we all had to appear in our best for news straight from the Commandant?

Once we arrived and stood at attention as a flight, I saw the instructors were all lined up behind the Commandant on stage. He held a magic device for magnifying his voice, like we were attending a graduation, but his expression was more severe than usual and the planes of his face more gray than white.

"Good afternoon, everyone," he began. A chorus of nearly two hundred voices echoed the greeting back. "It is with a heavy heart that I must share news of recent events and the contents of a royal edict signed and flown to us straight from the capital.

"Word of a massacre on the western coast has reached us through the diligent reports of civilian survivors. Approximately six days ago, an eldrafn and its rider swooped out of the sky and created a weather event that led to the destruction of the Altarian flagship and three more of our military vessels, while scattering several damaged ships further out at sea. Among the bodies we've recovered was Prince Valentino Cortes, may the gods rest his soul."

He paused as gasps sounded all around. Prince Valentino was the only royal I hadn't met, as he served as an admiral and lived at sea. He was Mateo's brother, though. My friend must be devastated.

The Commandant opened a letter, sending the sound of crinkling paper magnified by his device. "A coalition of Rathi villages have taken responsibility for the attack. By royal edict, King Alonso Cortes has declared war against this coalition and instated a draft to support our efforts on two fronts.

"This also means that most second-year students at this institution will be selected to accelerate their training and begin their squire-ship within a month to bolster our numbers on the northern front. Do not be alarmed. It is our job to ensure you are prepared for war no matter when you face its horrors. I truly believe that all our second-year students are strong candidates for selection."

"Yeah, sure," Sharde muttered.

My heart thudded wildly in my chest. I knew, deep down, that Ari and I would be selected. He was too experienced, and our rank was in the single digits now. The Commandant's desire that we never see combat would be overruled by this new disaster.

"Please take the rest of the day off. We will be reworking schedules and contacting selected cadets as soon as possible," the Commandant said, dismissing us from there.

I raced ahead of the group as soon as I scanned Falcon Flight and realized Mateo wasn't among the rest of us. As one of the first people to the staircase, I charged up it with Ari to reach his flight's dorm and let myself in. Feeling uncomfortable when I didn't see him in the common room, I called, "Prince Mateo?"

"In here," came a muffled response.

His was the first room, and he had it to himself. A single magelight illuminated a bed piled with fine linens, weighed down by the prince himself and the gryphon who lay over his lap, crying with him. He sniffed and scuffed his face quickly, trying to hide the evidence of it. "What do you want?" he mumbled.

"I'm sorry about your brother. I thought you might want, um…" Now I felt really dumb. Why would he want comfort from me? He had a whole flight of friends shuffling in.

"I'll be out in a minute. I need to talk to Walker," he said with more authority when a few faces peered through the open door behind me. They closed it, and Mireille got up. Mateo patted the spot where she'd been, and I sat next to him, hands in my lap.

He sniffed again and rubbed bloodshot eyes. "He was my

favorite big brother. I can't believe he's gone," he said quietly. "I am…willing to discuss Isaac now."

"What does he have to do with anything?" I murmured.

"Well, we got the same information from my sister. Who has been looking for a martyr? The same person who's been meeting with Rathi people in his parlor and conducting the meetings in their language." He gestured toward the small desk set up in his room, and I went to pick up the newspaper he pointed at.

It was a copy of the *Kaiamear Gazette*. The headline screamed at me: SECOND WAR THREATENS TO BANK-RUPT OUR GREAT NATION. Written by my mother.

"Gods," I sighed. She stripped down the king in her article for starting another war we couldn't afford, claiming the Altarian navy was too far north and was attacked for threatening some of the coastal Rathi tribes. It was fully treasonous, no punches pulled. She'd thrown her lot in with the crown prince, which had to mean he was acting on his plans as we spoke.

"People will already be protesting the draft," he said. "I can't believe…no, I can. Isaac has always been ambitious. But he's gone too far. Our country will collapse if he gets the civil war he's pushing for now."

"What do we do?" I murmured.

He sat up a little straighter. "Pray my father steps down from the throne. You should go, before my flight wonders what we're doing in here."

"Yeah." I bent down and gave him a hug. I meant to keep it light, but he crushed me to his chest with a heavy sigh.

Once he released me, I headed back up to my dorm to find two letters addressed to me waiting in the common area. Everyone else was pouring over their part of the mail drop or already back in their rooms. I slit open the letter from Odalis first, recognizing her script on the envelope.

She'd written another lengthy letter, with a message

disguised within. I scanned it three times to be sure and wrote out her response.

The hooded man sounds like one of CP's men. All I know is that he's a spy of some sort. Father pays him, but CP pays him double.

That was probably the best I could hope for. She didn't even seem to know his name. I opened the second letter and withdrew a small slip of paper, my eyes bugging out when I noticed who'd signed it.

Miss Walker,

It is time you paid me back in full. I require the pleasure of your company this upcoming Friday. Come to my solar by the time the bells ring for six in the evening.

Crown Prince Isaac Cortes

Gatekeeper take him. I wasn't allowed to leave the Academy during the week, not unless something awful happened, like a death in my family. Unless I was flying into the wilderness, it was frowned upon for me to leave during the weekend as well.

Being barred from leaving wasn't a possibility, I decided. Considering it was Wednesday, I would need to fly to Kaiamear tomorrow for a chance to talk to my family about what I'd discovered. Some things might be worth breaking the rules for after all.

Even if I would have more demerits than Sharde when I returned.

I HAD Ari saddled and ready to go after PT and breakfast, when Prince Mateo stopped at my gryphon's stall. "Got your message," he said, waving the bit of paper I'd slipped him when he lapped me during our daily run.

"The crown prince summoned me to Kaiamear. I was

wondering if you wanted to come as well," I replied in a low voice.

"Summoned you," he repeated.

"It's a long story. I'll tell you as we fly there, if you want to come."

"Wait. I'll get us cleared to leave." He disappeared for about thirty minutes, long enough for me to doubt he was coming back.

He walked by casually as I was considering leaving, saying, "I got us permission and picked up a stray along the way."

A familiar voice scoffed behind him before Weslecker passed by with a saddle flung over his shoulder. "Heard you have some trouble with a royal. I'd like to help," he said.

"You're welcome to come," I said, feeling myself flush when he winked.

"Should I be picturing your chicks now?" Ari teased.

The flush turned into tomato red mortification. *"What? No!"*

He whistled a laugh. *"Gotcha."*

"You're my captive audience on the flight to Kaiamear. Better watch out..."

"Please, you're going to be busy."

He was right, actually. We flew in an arrow formation with Mireille up front, and my time was spent sharing with her and Ironfeather what I knew. They relayed it to their riders and gave me their questions in return.

I came clean about what I knew, save for the fact that my family was working for the crown prince. Mateo knew most of it already, but Weslecker was shocked to hear that the hooded man was connected to Isaac rather than the king.

"So, he paid someone we already knew was working for the king. We naturally assumed Callan attacked you during the jousting tournament because of the king, not because someone new had paid him more," Ironfeather said for Weslecker. *"That's really clever."*

"Then killed him, might I remind you. We have no evidence that leads back to Isaac," Mireille said for her rider too.

"I'm most concerned for Sivana here. Isaac needs her in Kaiamear for a reason."

"He has his martyr." Somehow, I could feel Mateo's bitterness through his gryphon's voice. *"Now he needs someone to whip up the common folk."*

"She can't do it. She'd be hanged for treason."

"My father wants to kill her too, you know."

"So did the crown prince. We have no promises he won't try again."

My head started to seriously hurt. I knew I had a decision to make here that may affect the trajectory of our nation, but it felt like picking between a meal of rotten cabbage or blackened meat.

"You guys go on ahead to the palace. I have a stop to make," I told them as Kaiamear approached, silhouetted by the setting sun. We'd flown all day, and I still didn't know what to do or who to side with. With that in mind, I steered Ari to touch down on the front steps of a familiar temple.

A few people scattered out of the way of my gryphon's wake. Some fingers pointed in my direction, and I heard my name. Instead of getting surrounded, though, I guided my tired gryphon up the steps and turned to nod toward the weathered face of the clergyman greeting visitors at the door.

"Ah, the lady gryphon rider. Welcome back," he said.

I paused and looked again. He'd been sweeping leaves the last time I'd been here, and his name was on the tip of my tongue…

He put a hand on his chest. "It's Duncan. My my. I had to talk you into going inside when you were here last. Now you've barely spared me a glance in your haste to enter." He made the sign of Lord Orion and gestured grandly. "Please, be welcome."

"Thank you," I said and swept inside. Now that he

mentioned it, I did remember his kindness when I was led here. I took Ari to the inner shrine and lingered until a pair of elderly men shuffled away from the statue at its center.

I approached the golden visage of Lord Orion and made his sign respectfully before resting my hand over the token hidden under my leathers. "My lord, I have not abused your promise to lend me your guidance. I didn't call out to you earlier, but I am now. I...I need your wisdom."

I watched the statue, ready to see it pop to life to answer my request. Several moments passed before Duncan's voice answered, "So you shall have it."

In the corner of my eye, it wasn't actually Duncan, but someone far taller, wearing gilt robes of state, not the dull version of a clergyman. "You've taken a different form, my lord," I said.

"You have changed your associations to a kinder face. I approve," he replied. "What is on your mind?"

"Do you know what's happening right now?" I asked.

He smiled, his expression taking a distant quality. "I know of many things that occur in tandem, in this very moment. Though I suspect your question has something to do with a few recent revelations you've had about a member of your royal family."

"He tried to have me killed in December," I said.

"He did." The god's voice was completely neutral.

"While he also convinced my family to work for him *and* caused me to owe him a favor for an event he'd set in motion in the first place." As I spoke, he nodded like I was restating old news. "He wants me to do something major for him tomorrow."

"Helping turn a rather large crowd of Altarian citizens into a riot, in fact."

"To attack the palace?" I asked.

"No. The palace is heavily protected by men with proper weapons. He wishes for civil unrest, to create a situation that needs to be put down by the king's men. He wants animosity in the hearts of the people," he told me.

"Leading to civil war," I murmured.

"It may come to that if King Alonso does not step down from his throne. An outcome I thought you wanted." He gave me a meaningful look. "Right?"

I bit my lip. There was the rub; I *did* want this to happen, but I wasn't so sure anymore. The two men were no longer black and white in my mind, not as clear cut as one to support and the other to oppose. "I no longer know if the crown prince is the man I want sitting on the throne tomorrow. His ambitions have caused his brother to die and my country to go to war on a second front."

"So, why have you called me?" he asked.

I turned toward him fully, still a little off guard by his copy of Duncan with eyes of shining gold. "I wanted to know who to support, my lord. Who do you want on the throne? What is your will?"

"Who do *I* want on Altare's throne?" he mused aloud, stroking his jaw. "What if I told you that was the wrong question? Who do *you* want on Altare's throne?"

"I..." That was an impossible question. Both men had tried to kill me. "I don't know."

"You do. In your heart, you've already decided. You know the ruler Altare needs." He leaned in, his voice ringing with godly might, each word shaking me to my bones. "Who. Do. You. Choose?"

Either choice was risky. I knew I couldn't trust Crown Prince Isaac anymore after all he'd done, but he had his claws in my parents. On the other hand, the king had opposed me from the start, wanting to execute Ari if I so much as twitched wrong. Yet he seemed like a more straightforward opponent, who behaved by a set of rules that didn't include killing his kin or desiring a martyr to further his goals.

One I felt I could prove myself to. An older man set in his

beliefs, sure, but the alternative was his power-hungry son, who risked bringing Altare to ruin just to sit in a bigger chair a couple decades ahead of schedule.

"I believe King Alonso should keep his throne," I admitted.

Lord Orion accepted my answer with a solemn nod. "Good. Now go make it happen."

CHAPTER 34

STUBBORN OLD MAN

Despite the late hour, I met with Odalis in her room a couple doors down from the crown prince's solar. She was expecting me. "Mateo is waiting for an audience with our father right now, and Acton is resting," she said.

It seemed she'd snuck away from her royal rooms, as her serious-faced bodyguard wasn't here. We sat at her table with a dim magelight providing minimum illumination.

"We need your help. Have they told you what we suspect?" I asked.

Her head dipped in a regal nod. "I told them I'd share what I know with you, but…" She drew herself up, putting on an air of poise despite the wrinkled linen pajamas she wore. "If I am to help you, I need a favor granted in return."

Something about her demand wavered with uncertainty. I wondered if she'd ever bargained her knowledge for a favor before or what it could possibly be when I'd do a lot for her simply as a friend.

"That depends on what it is," I answered. As Mother had drilled into me, I didn't want to owe anyone an open-ended favor.

She twisted her lips, weighing what she said carefully. "I

need you to fly me somewhere when you next leave Kaiamear. It's not too far."

"Okay, reasonable. I agree to this," I said.

"Great. So, my Rathi isn't amazing, but I believe he's been smuggling weapons, armor, and battle plans to his allies up north. Meanwhile, my father has turned deaf ears to me trying to tell him anything." She drooped, her extra-long hair sagging in front of her face. "Which means we're at war now. Again.

"And you already know that tomorrow, Isaac wants his first riot down in the trading district before most of the men are drafted. He wants the population in full rebellion before a proper fighting force can be sent north so he can approach Father with a list of demands to get the unrest to stop and the Rathi to go away."

I had chills. "Does he really think it would be that easy?" I asked. If I had the king's power, I would have Isaac killed on the spot and make Mateo the crown prince.

"He'd sneak into Father's bedchamber or something. Not approach him on the throne, with a full retinue of guards around, and demand it. Preferably when rioters attack the palace, too," she said with a little smack of her lips. "Look...I don't know everything. But I think I know why this is happening."

"Because your brother is an impatient, power-hungry murderer?" I suggested.

"Um, no. Well, yes. He is now. But...my family is cursed," she whispered. My brows drew in as she hunched, weeping into her hands. "And it's my fault. *I'm* the curse," she mumbled.

I stood and circled around the table to rub her back. "I really doubt that," I said gently.

She took a ragged breath. Turning damp eyes my way, she took me in, and I think I passed some measure of her scrutiny. She snapped her fingers, and the magelight brightened, so when she unbuttoned the collar of her pajamas and drew down the fabric, I clearly saw the mark hidden right under the hollow of her throat.

Two scythes, barely an inch long each, with their handles crossing in an X. The one pointing left was solid black, with a wickedly curved blade, while the one facing right was entwined with a delicate pattern of red roses and vibrant leaves. Life and death. A mark too intricate for a human hand to replicate as a tattoo.

My mouth dropped open. "Y-you're a Mercy," I stammered.

A tear tracked down her cheek as she hid the mark under the buttoned collar. "No," she murmured. "I'm nothing. Father refused to surrender me to the Church of Mercy when I was born and hid that I've been touched by death since Mother died bearing me."

I dropped my weight back into a chair, holding my head. No wonder she spoke of curses. The Gatekeeper didn't claim many into his service, and it was considered a bad omen to deny death its due. His Mercy didn't have titles or family names. They most certainly were not princesses.

I didn't have words. I'd thought she was being dramatic, but her being parted from her patron god since birth was a dire situation.

"That's why I need you to take me away," she said. "Father won't let me go, but I know I need to. I have to release my family from the Gatekeeper's wrath."

Holding up a hand, I took this conversation back a step. "Let's clear up one thing; it's not your fault your father didn't send you to the Church of Mercy. You were a baby. You can't blame yourself for that."

Judging by her expression, she could and still would.

"Sivana, my family started a second *war*. There are going to be countless souls sent to the Gatekeeper early," she mumbled.

I was drawing breath to reply when Mateo rushed in. He nearly slammed the door behind him, catching it at the last moment and latching it before hissing out, *"That stubborn old man!"*

"He didn't listen to you either?" she sighed.

"Oh, he increased the number of peacekeepers that will be out on the streets tomorrow, but apparently, riots aren't out of the question when a draft first goes into effect." He slumped into a chair between us. "But Isaac? The man's too busy to do any wrong. He's been making overtures to the Lithosian royal family, trying to marry one of the princesses."

"I think that's not true," Odalis put in.

He shook his head. "True or not, we have no proof of *what* he's been doing, and until that moment, Father won't listen."

"Until it's too late," I put in. The moment the crown prince demanded the throne and revealed just how much leverage he had.

He turned toward me and tilted his head in consideration. "You're on the chopping block right now, potentially. Isaac wants you at his rally, which means word will get back to Father that you were there and potentially the one to set off the violence."

"Well, then I can't do it," I said.

"You said you want to help my father, despite what he's done. I have a…risky plan. Your mother writes for the *Kaiamear Gazette*, right? And she's a trusted Nilarite in the local temple?"

"Yeah." I eyed him suspiciously from the moment he mentioned my mother. Something told me the risk he mentioned would be one I'd have to take, though. And as he explained, I knew I was right.

To say I surprised my family by unlocking the door to our apartments in the dead of night would be a huge understatement. In various states of dishevelment, they sat with me and listened as I shared why I was there between jaw-cracking yawns.

We settled at the family dining room table, with Rissa and me facing our parents. It wasn't my idea to include my little sister in this discussion, but Mother thought she was ready to hear something so important to the future of our nation.

I was worried they'd poke holes in my case against the crown prince and point out I had assertions with little proof. But Mother puckered her lips into a rosebud as I spoke and, at the end, said, "That slimy weasel."

"Time for our escape plan?" Father asked tightly. I glanced at Rissa in alarm, recognizing the opening tone of Father's fiery rage. "I *knew* we couldn't trust him."

She glanced pointedly across the table at us. "Not an argument for right now," she said. "Sivana, if we had all summer to train you in noble ways, you'd know that you never agree to a tight situation without having a way to back out of it and maybe light the path behind you on fire as you go."

I blinked slowly in surprise. "You were expecting foul play." She'd believed everything I had to say without reservation, even.

"Of course I was. Working with the crown prince was to benefit you, but I knew at some point he would try to make me get my hands dirty for him. And you've already realized he's trying to do the same to you tomorrow. We can pivot from here."

She nodded primly. "You've learned a secret the crown prince actively tried to bury. If he'd successfully had you killed and a king's man to pin the murder on, he would've had allies for life in your father and me. Our grief would've solidified into furthering his cause. And we aren't the only ones that would be affected that way.

"Since you lived, he has had to resort to an even more extreme measure. So, I agree with Prince Mateo's idea. The population has to know." She began to smile slyly, the kind of expression that was frightful coming from her.

"The *Kaiamear Gazette* won't run its presses with a story the crown prince doesn't approve of," Father said.

"I will figure something out. And you will speak with the king," she said.

He shot her a disbelieving look. "You believe I can get an audience with him."

"In a matter of the king's protection, the First has priority over all else," she said. "And if there will be a riot in the streets tomorrow night, that's your chance. You'll tell him you'll take him out of the city as you are duty-bound to do, but along the way, you'll let him know it was your daughter alone that gave you the prior knowledge because his son is manipulating her."

I nodded slowly. "You want to frame me as some kind of hero," I said.

"More than just a hero of the hour. Someone brave enough to assist the Crown despite everything it's done to hurt you." She turned to Father again. "I expect you to inform him that you know of his involvement in these things."

He ran a hand over his short-cropped hair. "I can only do this if he believes his life is in danger. Terror makes an equal of all men."

"Time to exaggerate a little. This is the one chance we'll have to make him realize he's wrong about Sivana," she commented.

"I will turn in my resignation, then," Father said with a scowl. "Nothing will shake him more than knowing one of his defenders can no longer protect him because he has actively endangered my daughter."

Mother nodded in approval while my jaw dropped. "It's about time," she agreed.

"But Father...you worked so hard for that job..." I protested.

"I can't do it anymore. I'll let them send me back to war and earn a promotion to Knight-Marshall some other way," he said firmly.

I could see there wasn't anything I could say to get him to change his mind. "And about the rest of Mateo's plan?" I asked, stifling another yawn. It was getting hard to keep my eyes open.

"I believe it is sound, as long as you have Ari there for a quick exit." She put her hand over mine. "Let's practice what you're going to say tomorrow. Get some rest."

WESLECKER SPENT the day helping me practice while Mateo disappeared to navigate the complicated politics behind the scenes. I promised both young men that I'd see them back at the Academy after this was all over.

I was knocking on the door to Prince Isaac's solar before I felt I was ready. However, I could have months to prepare for this moment and still feel inadequate.

"Come in," the crown prince voice called. He sat at the head of the table with a couple other men, who eyed me top to bottom as I took a seat at the prince's left hand when he pointed. I came in my formal uniform, as they would expect, with Ari at my side.

"Miss Walker, these are my associates, Raphael and Auric. You will be working together this evening," Isaac said. "And of course, Sivana Walker and her gryphon need no introduction!"

We exchanged pleasantries briefly. This was no meeting over tea and cake, but an already decided event I was expected to go along with. I noticed the three men seemed to look through me until it came time to talk about what the crown prince really wanted.

"Like I've said before, a gathering of my friends from across Altare will be in the city square this evening, waiting to hear from you all, but Miss Walker in particular. You will be representing my interests. Raphael here knows the pain of sending sons to war," Isaac said.

"Three of my boys. And two more will be drafted soon." Raphael had a head of salt-and-pepper hair. The wrinkles on his face and skin tone reminded me of aged parchment, creased by time and experience. His deep, even voice was a comfort to listen to—I imagined that was why he was chosen to be a part of this event.

Auric was another older man who owned a grocery that'd serviced Kaiamear for generations. It sounded like Isaac expected him to be recognized and listened to by a crowd of common folk.

"Then there's you, Miss Walker." The crown prince turned his attention my way. "The people will be angry after listening to what these two men have to say. All you need to do is suggest that you know a better way and that I can be the change the people need to see. Here, I've had some remarks prepared for you…"

He slid a piece of parchment across the table. "Deliver your lines with appropriate enthusiasm and stand back. Fly away with your gryphon if you have to. I don't want you to be hurt by what happens afterward," he said.

I made a show of reading some of the prepared remarks, unsurprised by how incendiary they were. He didn't want me to protest the war so much as blame the king and his policies for it. "What do you expect to happen afterward?" I asked as if I didn't already know.

Isaac smiled, but his eyes didn't crease. "Why, a few things will get broken if it goes as planned. Do what you must to ensure you and your gryphon escape unharmed.

Now, you all should be leaving. The show starts as soon as you arrive."

While the crown prince remained seated, his two associates stood and motioned that I should follow them. We bowed, and they flanked me. I realized they were my escorts just in case I tried to escape. They would also report back what I really said at the rally.

We walked in tense silence as night fell above us. It was more than an hour's walk from the palace to the city square. I noticed several uniformed peacekeepers walking the streets, so the king had kept his word about increasing their presence.

"You have this. You're ready," Ari murmured.

"There will be time for you to read over your lines," Raphael said to me. We were standing before the fountain of King Altare and his gryphon, and passersby were beginning to gather behind us. Two magelights bobbed to full brilliance from a box a stranger opened nearby, while a second man gave Raphael a voice-amplification device.

I turned and watched several people call to each other, drawing up a crowd that grew rapidly. To my dismay, several peacekeepers were laying down their weapons and joining the assembly rather than dispersing it. I took a shaky breath and read through what I was supposed to say, biting my lip to keep from chuckling nervously.

I'd practiced saying exactly the opposite. And as I snuck glances at the crowd over the edge of the page, I noticed splashes of white and silver from Mother's friends at the temple weaving themselves through the group just as, I assumed, Isaac's people were doing.

Last night, Father had mentioned typical crowd control included having several people planted strategically to whip a frenzy into everyone else. Cooling off an angry crowd would be nearly impossible by the time they gave me the voice amplifier, but I would try.

"People of Kaiamear!" Auric took it first, standing on a

pair of wooden boxes with the magelights focused on him so everyone could see him clearly. He greeted the crowd like they were old friends, rattling window panes with call and response that I think was designed to get more people out of their houses to come see what was going on.

"We can do this," I murmured to Ari, mostly to tell myself that as the noise level had me cringing. I realized I had that in common with Puzzlebox, as I felt part of my mind shutter as people raised their voices.

The king was in serious trouble, as either his peacekeepers weren't going to shut this down, or they simply couldn't with the number of citizens forming a ring around the fountain. I hoped Father was evacuating him from the city as planned.

Ari brushed against my side for comfort. "The king's policies will bring you empty bellies and cold beds," Auric was saying. "And no man knows that better than my friend, Raphael."

He stepped down, letting the other man take his place under the magelights. "The war the king has decreed us into is insanity. Because of him, more parents will lose their sons, our blood, sweat, and treasure spilled over a border crisis caused by the Crown's ruinous policies!"

The crowd roared. I didn't even know what policies he was referring to—but it didn't matter. The folks listening hated whatever they were.

"I have already said goodbye for the final time to three of my sons due to the *first* war the king has failed to end," he shouted. "How much is too much? How much are we willing to sacrifice for one man's failures?"

"It sounds like they're going to riot before you even speak," Ari commented. He'd pinned his ears back, and I felt his disorientation as we were surrounded by a wall of angry voices as Raphael stoked the crowd.

Right before I could go deaf, Raphael said, "We have a special guest to tell you what she feels about all this. Say hello to Sivana Walker and her gryphon, Arimus!" He turned and offered me the voice amplifier as cheers and screams of my name echoed around us.

I took the handle of the device and stepped up onto the boxes. The magelights focused on me next, not just illumination, but enough heat to make sweat bead on my forehead and the back of my neck. *"Put your talons up on the box..."* I guided Ari next to me so his head and shoulders were also lit up.

"Hi, everyone," I said. My voice echoed from the device and magnified my nervous throat clear. What felt like hundreds of sets of eyes were focused right on me. Expectant. Furious. Demanding. "It's true what you've heard. We're at war with a coalition of Rathi now because King Cortes is responding to an attack from an eldrafn and its rider that resulted in Prince Valentino's death."

The energy level around me dimmed a bit. I wasn't nearly as loud as the two men before me. Torchlight in front of me revealed the Nilarite women turning to whisper to those around them.

"It's important for us to defend what we own. A-Any attack must be met with the same level of force in return," I said, cringing as I heard my stutter magnified. "While we can condemn the king for it, we must remember that he is a father mourning a son and the leader of a great nation that cannot condone a black eye without a response. Imagine what would happen if the king ignored the previous attack and Rathi guided their eldrafn to attack our borders indiscriminately. Would we protest if *that* led to war?"

Several responses were shouted back at me. Somehow, I heard Raphael behind me, demanding, "What is she *saying*?"

"Lady Nilara teaches us that we must accept the necessity of violence only when it is required. We must put away the anger in our hearts and prepare for the only war that matters —that in the north!" I shouted.

Any moment, someone would come rip the amplifier out of my hand, but until that moment, I squeezed in every word I could. "Prepare your husbands, your sons, your fathers, and your uncles! We will end this new war with haste, victorious!" Hands seized my arms with bruising force. "For Altare!"

"For Altare!" echoed from the crowd. Female voices, Mother's friends.

I made the sign of Mother Nilara as Raphael wrestled the amplifier away from me. Ari loosed a vicious growl, lunging at him with an exaggerated snap of his beak. I stumbled back as I was released, the two men more afraid of Ari than what I had to say.

"Stupid girl," Auric hissed. "All you had to do was read from the page."

Meanwhile, the crowd was starting to take up a new chant. "For Altare!" Men, women, and children alike, echoing the encouragement of the women my family had planted in the crowd.

I lunged for Raphael and shouted into the device he held. "Rally's over! Go home!"

He cuffed me hard, and I staggered away, catching myself on Ari's side. I looped my leg over his saddle, and he took off with haste, flapping his wings hard to gain altitude from a cold takeoff. My heart raced like a rabbit's as we cleared rooftops and I got my feet securely into the stirrups.

"I hope the king sees this for what it is," Ari said. He angled his wings toward the palace, seeing through my eyes automatically now.

"Me, too," I murmured. I hoped he listened to Father, even though it didn't seem like King Alonso listened to anyone.

I knew in my gut that the crown prince would be coming for my family in response to what I'd just done, but Mother already had a plan to keep everyone safe. She and Rissa would be seeking asylum in Nilara's temple, while Father was handing in his resignation as Commander of the First to prove a point to our stubborn king. My brother would remain at school, where he was safest.

Our apartment in the palace was forfeit. Most of my belongings were at the Gryphon Rider Academy anyway, where Ari and I would return as soon as we completed one last task here in the city.

We circled in for a landing in the middle of the grassy Gryphon Yard. It was silent here, and my ears rang as we waited.

Odalis didn't keep us waiting long, though. She emerged from the shadows wearing a heavy traveling cloak with the hood drawn. I helped her place her bags within Ari's saddle-bags, which bulged from the sheer number of things she was bringing.

"You're sure about this?" I whispered.

"Take me away. Please. It's all I ask."

I nodded, helping her into the saddle and mounting Ari behind her. It was a quiet flight, blessed by the light of a full moon, which helped me find the gothic towers of the Church of Mercy erected in the center of a massive graveyard. It was along the way to the Gryphon Rider Academy, a landmark I used to navigate.

It was an honor to be buried in the hallowed ground tended to by the Gatekeeper's Mercy. Ari touched down, and as my feet landed in the dirt, I thought of the thousands that had been laid to rest around us. Kings and heroes, but also the elderly and downtrodden who'd made a final pilgrimage here.

When Odalis was accepted, she would be among the Mercy who would greet these pilgrims and fulfill their final wishes. She'd don the gray shroud and become one of the chosen few that all Altarians feared and respected. But first, she hugged me fiercely. "Thank you. I'm sure we'll meet again," she murmured.

"I hope so," I said. "I'll miss you, junior spymaster."

She sniffled, her face hidden in my shoulder. "Do you think the Gatekeeper will need a pair of listening ears instead of a Mercy?"

"I guess you'll have to ask him," I murmured. She trembled against me. Perhaps it was nerves, or fear, but this had to be overwhelming. Odalis was on the cusp of giving up everything to walk through the doors to the church and show off the mark under her throat. No more high collars or the pampered life of a princess.

She released me with a sigh. "Good luck with everything. If I'm allowed to send out letters, I'll write to you and Father both and make sure he knows I want him to give you a chance."

I thought about how overwhelmed her father would be come daybreak tomorrow. A potential riot, Father's resignation, and Odalis's disappearance would all tumble on his shoulders. I may be on the king's side now, but I had caused him a huge headache too. Hopefully he never learned I was the one who finally delivered his daughter to the Church of Mercy.

"Remember to ask the Gatekeeper to give me more time, too. I need it to outrun the rest of your family," I said.

CHAPTER 35

AFTERMATH

Academy life embraced me from the moment I returned to my dorm and found a letter signed by the Commandant on my pillow. Ari and I were selected for accelerated training and would be reporting to the northern front to fulfill a squire-ship as soon as possible. The Crown promised compensation equivalent to the pay of a Knight-Lieutenant and a promotion when we could be spared from the war effort to be officially knighted.

"This is going to be hell," Ari remarked after I read the letter to him.

We barely recovered from our round trip before training began again at a blistering pace. I told Prince Mateo and Weslecker how the rally went over the course of an abbreviated dinner we were expected to eat quickly before reporting to a new, mandatory evening class for all second-years.

While the Commandant had suggested that not everyone would be receiving accelerated training, the reality was that all second-years were pulled into extra classes. Every drill sergeant at the Academy shared the responsibility of helping us through any deficiencies, and there was almost no yelling. We shared a new, solemn mood. This wasn't a game anymore.

The things they tried to cram into our heads could be the difference between life and death.

"There was a small riot after you left Kaiamear," Mateo told me. "My father was evacuated as we planned. He seemed shaken by your father's resignation as well."

I swallowed past a sudden drop in my belly. It was what we planned, but… "He served the king well. I hope he's reassigned to an honorable post," I said.

"I imagine we'll see him on the Storm Front, but I don't think a decision has been made yet," the prince said, naming what we were beginning to call the northern front. He wet his lips and looked me in the eyes. "Would you happen to know what happened to my sister? Because with his world falling apart, the thing my father cares about most is whether Odalis is safe."

"Hopefully she sends news to him soon," I replied, feeling sweat bead along my back as his stare grew in intensity.

"I think you know something, Walker."

"It's not my secret to tell," I said as levelly as I could.

He groaned into his palm. "You took her away, didn't you? She shared her secret with you?"

"Yes," I admitted.

Weslecker glanced between us and shook his head. "Is this really what we should be focused on right now?"

"No, we have training to do," Mateo answered. He got up from the table first and wouldn't acknowledge me for the rest of the evening.

I was feeling pretty low when I reported to Gryphon Taming, now a class that only met on Fridays since all of us were going to war. "We are showing rider candidates to Blue. You all have passed the class," Captain Gemon said by way of introduction. "He keeps asking for you to groom him, Cadet Walker."

"Me?" I echoed in surprise.

"I believe you have quite the promising future in the Second one day," he said, flashing a rare smile.

"Thank you, sir," I said while being privately glad I wouldn't be asked to tame any gryphons against their will anytime soon. The other cadets were dismissed, while I went to Reyos's stable to check on him.

He stood when I entered. *"Hello again,"* he said.

"They took the chains off."

His fur was still a little mussed, but any broken feathers were already smoothed out of his wings. *"They did. I took your advice and acted like I liked them,"* he grumbled. *"Now they think I want to carry a human boy on my back."*

Reyos let me approach with a grooming kit and get to work on the soft fur under his wings. *"Have you heard that we are entering a second war?"*

"I've gotten the impression."

"We really need you, if you're willing to fight."

He turned his head, fixing me with one leery eye. That was a no, then.

"I have a flock to return to. Human disputes mean nothing to me. But…I have stayed here and waited for you."

I blinked in surprise as he turned fully and nuzzled my neck, even lowering his head for a gentle bunt. This time, he didn't pull away when I scratched behind his ears. *"I wanted to thank you for helping me and for being a friend here while I've been all alone,"* he said.

"Of course. But your wings…will you be able to fly?" I don't think anyone had let him out of those chains for months.

"I will be fine. And if not, I've called my flock to come help. Skylord Roshawk has arrived personally to escort me and…there is another gryphon you wanted me to take into the wild, right?"

"If she's okay with it. I should go ask—"

"No need, as long as it's Sunset. She and I have had a few nice conversations, and she's saying her goodbyes to Arimus now," he said, huffing out a sigh. *"I will miss you. And…I'm sorry."*

"For what?" I was asking. The next thing I knew, he'd thrown his whole weight at me, sending me flying across his stall. My skull knocked against the wall, and my sight blurred with pained tears and over-bright stars. I heard more than saw him break down the solid wood door to the stall. Human shouts followed in his wake.

"Cadet Walker!" Another exclamation was close by, followed by rough hands helping me hold up my head. It was Gemon, who checked my wound before calling behind him, "Forget about the gryphon! Get me a medic!"

WE HAD an early mail drop while I was sleeping off my newest concussion, as I woke up to Prince Mateo sitting at my bedside with a letter addressed to me.

"It's from Odalis. She sent one to me too, telling me I'm required to forgive you and that she forced you to do as she asked," he said after making sure I was awake and aware.

"Well, am I forgiven?" I mumbled.

"Really hard to be angry at you when you're on medical recovery *again*," he replied, pointing out the weight behind me was a worried Mireille, who'd apparently bullied Ari off the bed to give her a turn cuddling to my back. I could sense him nearby, grumbling about it.

"Reyos attacked me," I said to him privately, matching his grousing tone.

"Sunset is gone. They both escaped while Gemon made a big deal about you getting hurt," Ari sighed.

I shut my eyes with a low groan. It felt like the wild gryphon had taken advantage of me…but wow, he'd thought of one of the only ways to get a head start on anyone chasing him down. I hoped he and Sunset made it back to Roshawk's flock.

"I'm sorry she's gone. I know you two were bonding," I said.

He sent me the mental equivalent of a shrug, but it didn't hide the twinge of hurt he felt. *"It was the best decision for her."*

Mateo told me aloud the same thing that Ari did, how Reyos and Sunset had escaped to the wild. I realized, due to the way it'd happened, no one would level a moment of blame at me. Reyos's attack was completely unexpected, and there was no sign that the two gryphons had planned this past going together. Maybe we'd *all* gotten what we needed in this exchange…even if I'd be nursing a killer headache for days.

"I just wanted to let you know…if my father does not appreciate what you did for him the other day…" Mateo scuffed his foot, glancing anywhere but at me before clearing his throat. "I still support you. There's always been my father's side and Isaac's side, but you can still be on my side."

I smiled to myself. "Thanks, Mateo. I think that's where I want to be," I murmured.

He helped me out of bed, and for the next week, I couldn't go through training without either him or Weslecker close by. None of my family sent mail during this demanding time, nor did the crown prince. The latter made me quite nervous. There was no telling what Isaac was planning in his silence, but it couldn't be good.

"Graduation" was coming up in a few days already. The trainers forced us through some of the hardest maneuvers and every scenario they could think of with an eldrafn. Lord Gadric alone was not enough to summon an illusion of one of the gigantic thunderbirds, so it was theory only.

Ari warned that theory alone wouldn't help us much. *"Have you fought one before?"* I asked while bedding him down for the evening.

"Only in my dreams," he muttered.

And not successfully, at that. But the purpose of Mother

Nilara's task was becoming clearer at least, when I knew we would be fighting Rathi and presumably their eldrafn soon.

"Never too late to learn new things," I said, giving him a kiss on the beak good night.

"See you tomorrow."

I exited his stall and raised a hand in greeting as a few of my fellow second-years passed by with their gryphons, including a rather exhausted-looking Weslecker and Ironfeather. Sneaking my hands into the pockets of my uniform, I whistled a lonely tune as I headed for the exit to the stables.

A firm arm hooked around my throat, pulling me into the shadows. I felt the cold edge of a blade at the side of my neck. "Don't move," a man whispered into my ear. I went rigid with fear, freezing up in his hold. "My benefactor is quite displeased with you, Sivana."

I knew in that instant who this stranger was and what he was here for. Months of self-defense training with Sarge kicked in, and I grabbed his forearm and wrist with both hands, wrenching up my shoulder and pulling the knife away at the same time to give me room to escape his headlock.

I pushed on his arm to try forcing the point of the knife into his side. He dropped it, and I kicked it away. The leather over his knuckles creaked. *"Help! I need help,"* I shouted mentally to Ari and any other gryphon who could hear me.

The hooded man punched me, and I tasted blood as my head whipped to the side. I balled up my hands and punched for his throat. He jerked out of the way, bringing up both fists and squaring up.

Darn it. If I survived this, Sarge was going to be so disappointed in me.

I knocked aside his next strike with my forearm, feeling the force of it bruise my skin. Just like every other male opponent I'd had to fight, he was bigger and stronger than I was. He used his presence to get me backing up a step and then another.

But I'd trained in this scenario, knowing that most men would underestimate me *because* of their natural advantage. I took another, exaggerated step backward and spun into a side kick. His muscle made it feel like I was striking a wall, but unlike one, he gave and staggered.

I got into his guard and thrust my palm up into his chin with all my strength. He fell backward, sliding down the wall into an unconscious heap. My brows rose. No matter how much Sarge said that'd knock someone out, I hadn't believed it until now.

A gryphon rushed between us, striking the hooded man's side and knocking him onto his back. Ironfeather sat on him, beak lifted proudly. *"I saved you!"* he exclaimed.

I gave his neck a scratch and laughed. *"Thanks. What would I do without you?"*

Weslecker turned a corner and spotted us a few moments later. "Grab some rope," I said. It was impossible to keep this secret, with other second-years spotting Ironfeather squashing this man. I grabbed Barlowe by the collar and ordered him to go get Mateo, while others peeled off to alert the instructors, I was sure.

By the time Mateo showed up, I got help from Weslecker and a few of the men from my flight to haul the hooded man's bulk into an empty stall. He lay there on his side, wrists and ankles tied.

"What's going on?" the prince asked, looking between the tied-up man and me standing over him, grinning.

"Hey," I said. "Want to meet your brother's man when he wakes up?"

He opened and closed his mouth a few times before scrubbing his eyes. "Walker...what..." He looked over his shoulder, where several of our peers were crowded around to listen at this point. "Are you crazy?" he hissed.

"No. But I am tired of hiding what's going on." I said.

We knew the Commandant had arrived when he started

shouting. "As you were! Back to your dorms!" He scowled in disapproval at the two young men who remained, the prince and Weslecker. "Did I hear correctly that this man attacked you, Cadet Walker?"

"Yes, sir."

"Okay, thank you. You three can go back to your dorms as well."

"But…"

His military-strict expression brooked no argument. He drew me to the side and lowered his voice. "But nothing. This was another attempt on your life in a place that should be impenetrable. Gods above, maybe you're going to be safer in a combat flight than living here after all."

"Sir, this man's involved with the crown prince. I suspect this was because I didn't help him start a riot in Kaiamear earlier," I said.

The Commandant held up his hand. "Let me investigate. You're far too involved in politics for a cadet when you should be preparing for what's ahead. It's my job to take care of him from here and find out how he broke into *my* fortress. You need to go rest, because soon you will graduate and head for the Storm Front."

· · ·

Sivana and Ari's adventure continues in Gryphon Rider Academy 3: Storm Front!

Interested in more? Join my newsletter as one way to get access to a bonus scene from this book! Sign up on my website.

• • •

STAY up to date with Gryphon Rider Academy and the Altare world by joining my Facebook group: People of Altare! In this community, we'll talk about fantasy book releases, share fun posts, and have the occasional giveaway.

PLEASE REMEMBER TO REVIEW! Reviews help other readers find stories they may love. Consider leaving a review for Gryphon Rider Academy 2: Chosen on Amazon and other websites.

ALSO IN THE ALTARE WORLD

ROYAL SPY INSTITUTE

Join an unlikely crew of five misfits and a mouse as they strive to become one of Altare's newest elite spy teams. Heists and adventures await!

The Gilded Wolves meets Six of Crows in this YA fantasy series in which a former thief uses her skills to become a spy. If you like clever heroines, strong friendships, and found family, then you'll love Royal Spy Institute!

- See Royal Spy Institute on Amazon -

About the Author

Elise Hennessy is an author of young adult fantasy full of adventure and found family. She holds a master's degree in journalism and enjoys crafting unique stories. When Elise is not busy writing, she's trying to reduce her prodigious TBR list. She lives in Texas with her family and is owned by two cats.

Find out more about her books at: www.elisehennessy.com

www.ingramcontent.com/pod-product-compliance
Lightning Source LLC
Chambersburg PA
CBHW021231190726
48289CB00005B/1266